Praise for ACTS OF GOD WHILE ON VACATION

"... a rollicking page-turner. Even though the tone is disarmingly flip and fast-paced, the deeply human themes at the heart of it give the book terrific resonance and generosity of spirit. This is Hawaii's best fiction book of 2011 and establishes the author as a Pacific Kingsley Amis."

— *Honolulu Star-Advertiser*

"The author's lighthearted tone makes the deep ideas a pleasure, while the inclusion of a diversity of spiritual belief systems makes this openminded novel as entertaining as it is enlightening."

— *Publishers Weekly*

"Some of this book is laugh-out-loud funny, while also ringing true ... Behold human nature, it seems to say, aren't we a funny lot—but maybe we laugh in order not to cry. Tillotson's book is very much worth reading."

— *Honolulu Weekly*

"A shamanically-skewed romp of brilliant insight and slapstick comedy."

— *Hawaii Public Radio* – *"The Conversation"*

"It's a comic novel with serious edges. Even more remarkable: It's one of the few fictions set in Hawaii that gets all the details right. Tillotson nailed it with this one."

— *Honolulu Magazine*

"*Acts of God While on Vacation* begins like a high-speed cab ride on a route you would have never taken on your own. The twists and turns amid unfamiliar but fascinating scenery keep you off balance until the driver's mastery becomes apparent and you know you are in reliable hands."

" . . . blends a sophisticated cocktail of humor, suspense, and compassion."

"Richard Tillotson skillfully manages to blend menace and hilarity in a page turner."

"The writing style is rich and satisfying, with characters who are well-drawn and life-like, each in his or her own detailed setting."

"The characters Tillotson has created—a Waikiki hotel manager, a hapless researcher stranded in the wilds of Borneo, a London party girl, and a desperate paparazzo—all come across as authentic people with authentic problems, which makes the meta-fictional elements of the story all the more engaging, especially since the meta-fiction promises to get metaphysical."

" . . . an eager eye for the telling detail and behavior, for situation and for a sense of place."

"A beautifully written piece of literary fiction."

ACTS OF GOD WHILE ON VACATION

ACTS OF GOD
WHILE ON VACATION

Richard Tillotson

ARLINGTON AVENUE BOOKS

Arlington Avenue Books
Honolulu, Hawaii
www.ArlingtonAvenueBooks.com

ISBN-10: 1460979494
ISBN-13: 978-1460979495

LCCN: 2011903981

Printed in the United States of America.

Cover photograph by David Murphey
Author photograph by David Takagi
Cover design by Tiffani Scalzo

For my family

CHAPTER ONE

"You will die in September."

"What?" Gordon Coburn stared down at his future as foretold by a fortune cookie from his previous night's dinner. "You will die in September," the prediction read. "What kind of fortune is this?" he asked aloud. "Is this some kind of joke?"

Ten miles offshore, a rogue wave furrowed the broad, blue expanse of ocean outside his office, imitating on a hemispheric scale the wrinkle of irritation that creased his normally smooth and happy brow. Unannounced, unseen even by Gordon who enjoyed a superb view, the wave surged towards him and his two thousand aloha-shirted and flower-bedecked guests, many of whom were bobbling about in the surf of Waikiki below like confetti in the glass of a tipsy drinker.

Gordon was oblivious to that vast, watery progress outside. Alone in the teak-paneled, plush carpeted, glass-walled splendor of his office, he held the tiny ribbon of words from his fortune cookie taut between the thumb and forefinger of each hand. The wrinkle of irritation in his forehead deepened into a frown of concern. How did this bizarre, ridiculous prediction get into his fortune cookie? He was General Manager of the Earl Court Waikiki Resort, and he was only thirty-two! He looked up and stared out through tinted slabs of glass directly at the rogue wave rolling towards him.

Rogue waves are not uncommon. Taking the Pacific as a whole, they must be occurring all the time. Generally not large enough to cause a tsunami warning, they are still plenty large enough to scare the bejesus out of a Taiwanese boat captain trying to winch in his nets. Large enough to rear up out of a calm sea and snatch away an unsuspecting reef walker in Fiji. Large enough to fling refrigerator-sized bricks of ice at a cruise ship off Alaska or to upend lanteen-sailed fishing skiffs beached along the coast of Mindanao. What causes a rogue wave is always a mystery. An infinitesimal shifting of the continental plates, perhaps. A sudden subsidence in the Marianas Trench. A grumbling concatenation of volcanic tremblors around the Ring of Fire. Or just a random agglomeration of water. Brownian motion with a motive. Whatever its cause, this wave, ten feet high, fifty yards wide, and three hundred miles long, proceeded in towards Waikiki Beach at a steady thirty miles per hour.

But even though he was staring straight at it, the massive disturbance was invisible to Gordon, nothing but an imperceptible swelling halfway out towards the horizon. He looked back down at his fortune. "You will die in September." This was January. If it was true, he had nine months.

"Who's responsible for this?" he asked resentfully.

────────

On the island of Borneo, in the Kanowit longhouse, four days upriver plus a twelve-hour hike from the nearest electric light bulb, Kip Stallybrass stood naked inside his sarong, the tube of cloth that served alternately as his pajamas, towel, and personal changing room, and stared glumly down at his private parts. A fat, black leech had affixed itself halfway up his inner thigh.

"Mundi, Tuan! Mundi!" an old Iban woman cried cheerfully, urging him to join the other men who were preparing to go down to the stream to bathe. She squatted in the semi-gloom of the *ruai,* a kind of covered veranda that looked like a big wooden shed and was the common area for the twenty or so families in the longhouse. Her withered, wrinkled dugs hung flat against her chest as she smiled encouragingly up at him, exposing a few black stubs of teeth and two rows of gums stained red from betel nut. She was squatting just a couple of yards away along with a dozen other old women, naked infants, and young children who formed a semi-circle around Kip and were watching him prepare for his bath with varying mixtures of approval, fascination, good humor, and revulsion. After twenty-five visits to some of the most remote longhouses in Borneo, Kip was used to this kind of attention. He was, after all, the first white man many of these children had ever seen. He was at least a foot and a half taller than any Iban. He wore thick, insect-like panes of glass in front of his eyes. And the hair that covered his arms and legs was a reddish blond shade not unlike that of an orangutan which, literally translated from the Malay, means "man" (*orang*) "of the jungle" (*utan*.) Kip knew that real orangutans were few and far between these days, their numbers having been greatly depleted by hunting and logging, so he was probably as close to the legendary "man of the jungle" as most of these kids would ever get. The irony of a newly minted Ph.D. with four years of college and six years of graduate school being mistaken for an intelligent ape was not lost on Kip. He was just bored with it.

Besides, right now there was the issue of the leech. After much trial and error, he had concluded that the Iban method of dealing with leeches was the best. This involved using a thin blade of polished bamboo and whisking them off with a quick flick of the wrist. The practice of burning them off with a match, while affording a deep sadomasochistic satisfaction, often caused a leech to try and burrow in deeper and increased the likelihood of infection. The difficulty with the quick flick method, however, was that it had to be done at just the right speed and angle, and this particular leech's choice of venue made that tricky. A downward flick would be extremely awkward to self-administer, but an upward flick might flick him right into leech heaven, so to speak.

"Mundi, Tuan! Mundi!" The old woman grinned at him.

If he was wearing underwear, Kip thought, he might be willing to attempt the upward flick. But he didn't have any underwear. He hadn't worn underwear since shortly after his arrival in Malaysia from Minnesota several months earlier. The sudden intensity of the climate combined with his Midwestern attire of Jockey shorts and long trousers had given him such a ferocious case of crotch rot that he had been forced to retreat to Kuala Lumpur's totally air-conditioned Earl Court Hotel. He had spent four miserable days there, alternately lying in bed, nude, with his legs spread, his scrotum bone-white with talcum powder, or else waddling like a duck in baggy shorts down to the hotel coffee shop where he had to make his way through shoals of immaculately groomed Asian businessmen in sharkskin suits. All the while, the hideously expensive Earl Court had sucked away precious dollars from the meager budget his post-doctoral grant allowed him, thereby endangering his field trip, his study, his paper, and his chances of ever finding a university job.

So he had sworn off underwear. It was a sound practice, notwithstanding his present predicament. It just meant he would have to go with the downward flick. Kip quickly cinched his sarong around his waist and squatted down to fumble in his pack for the blade of bamboo.

"Mundi, Tuan! Mundi!"

But the trouble with the downward flick, he realized as he groped around in his pack, was that it might not work the first time. Or the second. Or even the third. And the sight of "Tuan" standing nude on the ruai inside his sarong, lashing at his privates with bamboo, might tend to compromise his status in the Kanowit longhouse. Ibans loved to joke and tease, particularly the old women. And it was hard enough to gain the respect of the Tuai Rumah. Hard enough to get the old warriors to share their sacred rituals that laid the spirits to rest. They were unlikely to share them with a fool. Or with some perverse, visiting flagellant. And it was uncanny how stories about Kip traveled from longhouse to longhouse, as if the Ibans were all secretly carrying cell phones and calling each other up to gossip about him as soon as he left.

He would have to chance the upward flick.

"Mundi, Tuan!"

He nodded and smiled at the old woman. He wanted very much to *mundi*. They had started the hike in from the last longhouse at four a.m. when it was still relatively cool. After two hours on the trail, he was hot, sweaty, scratched, and covered with little flecks of dirt and scraps of wet leaves. The thought of plunging into a cool, clear jungle stream in the early morning hour was delicious. He grasped the blade of bamboo, withdrew it from the recesses of his pack and rose quickly.

"Tuan!" The old woman smiled in bashful, mocking appreciation of him as if he had just done something inordinately clever simply by standing up.

"Think that was good, watch this," Kip said under his breath. He smiled at his audience and uncinched his sarong. Glancing down, he spotted the leech again, bloated with blood and pulsating slightly, probably to the rhythm of Kip's own heartbeat. He clenched the edge of the sarong in his teeth, stretching his neck and pulling the tube of cloth taut against his back. Reaching down with his left hand, he shielded what mattered as best he could. Then with his right hand he reached down and, peering around the sarong, positioned the bamboo blade. He glanced up, giving one final smile through clenched teeth at his audience, many of whom were staring fearfully at him as if he were about to explode. Peering back down at himself, he took aim and flicked. The bamboo blade deftly whisked off the leech and continued to whisk right on up his inside thigh to give one of his testicles a smart crack.

———

"Hy-yea! Hy-yea! Hear! Hy-yea! Hear! Hear!"

The Minister holding forth at the Dispatch Box had said something particularly sly about the other side, but up in the gallery, Lady Gloria Ryder, only child of the Marquess of Sudbury, favorite of the Queen and darling of the tabloids, fought desperately to keep her eyes open. While it might be high noon in Hawaii and six in the morning in Borneo, it was eleven o-clock at night in London, a time when the British government often required its Members of Parliament to appear in the House of Commons and make some of their more important decisions. Lady Gloria thought this was bloody stupid. How could these men, many of whom had risen at four or five in the morning to plow through several red boxes full of briefing papers and then had spent twelve hours or more administering some vast, obstreperous bureaucracy, how could these men be competent to evaluate debate at eleven o-clock at night? Particularly on subjects entirely foreign to their own expertise? Particularly after slabs of roast beef and a bottle or two of House Claret in the Members Dining Room? The answer, of course, was that they weren't competent. Nor were they expected to be. All that was really expected of them while sitting in the House was to alternately shout, "Hear hear!" or "Rubbish!" depending on which side was at the Dispatch Box. And once all the fulminating was over with, they were expected to file through the lobbies and vote the party line, which they all dutifully did, producing exactly the result that all concerned could have predicted hours earlier. This, at least, was Lady Gloria's opinion as she stared down at them like a sleepy owl from the Distinguished Stranger's Gallery. "Get on with it!" she thought dully to herself.

"We shall throw the 'book' at them!" said the Minister at the box, getting off a good one.

"Hy-yea! Hy-yea! Hear! Hear!" Another great welter of vowel sounds rose up from the Solons and swirled about the chamber. To Lady Gloria, it was like the incomprehensible chanting of Tibetan monks or the distant throbbing of surf upon the shore, incredibly soporific. She blinked fiercely several times, her eyes actually watering with sleepiness. The Chamber was a surprisingly narrow but tall space, and staring down from the gallery at the green leather benches far below reminded Lady Gloria of staring down into a tranquil woodland pool. The indolent forms of the dark suited MP's, some of them lying almost prone with apparent indifference, were like the shadowy shapes of sleeping trout. Long, thin, silvery wires hung down into this pool, suspending microphones like fishing lures just above the members' heads. And like fishing lures, these microphones had hooked many an unwary MP whose uninformed comment or infelicitous turn of phrase had been reeled in by catty, bilious reporters who sat crouched and waiting by little speakers at the other end of this electronic tackle.

The thought of reporters caused Lady Gloria to stiffen. Their gallery was diagonally opposite where she was sitting, and several of them were no doubt watching her instead of the MP's. It wouldn't do if they spotted the Marquess' lovely, auburn-haired daughter nodding off. She was attempting to rehabilitate her image as an oversexed, over privileged party girl by feigning an interest in whatever it was they were blithering about down below. Something to do with education, she believed. Her nominal cause was literacy, and Ronnie had told her that tonight's debate was relevant. Literacy had seemed like the ideal thing to champion. It was a low-priority, passionless sort of good work that virtually no one objected to and which didn't involve any contact with unpleasant sights or communicable diseases. What Ronnie hadn't told her was that the cataclysmic dullness of it all was enough to fell an ox.

If pressed, Gloria would have granted that the sedative effect of House debate was exacerbated because she had gotten only four hours of sleep the previous night. And irritatingly enough, not because she had been out doing something worthwhile, like dancing. Her fatigue was the result of an attempt to become a "good girl," an ambition that had been inflicted upon her by an irate father who was threatening loss of allowance and disinheritance if he saw another revealing photo of her in the tabloids, "with a rock star, a footballer, a biker or any of the other pimply layabouts you seem to favor. Thank God your mother didn't live to see them."

With his standards in mind, she had spent the previous night at a peculiar, mostly female soiree hosted by Lady Hortense Crawley-Smith. Lady Hortense was just the sort of company her father wanted her to keep. Or so she had supposed. The evening had begun rather like a peculiar, upper-class Tupperware party, then evolved into a New-Ageish sharing of feelings, took a sudden lurch into the advocacy of blood sports, and by and by it became clear that Lady Hortense's real agenda was to solicit membership for a coven of witches. Being a healthy, no-nonsense sort of girl at heart, Gloria had told her to get stuffed.

But now she wished she could just lie down like Ronnie. She had spotted him on one of the back benches, virtually horizontal, his head crooked against the leather backrest. She thought of writing him a silly note on her pink, scented stationery, folding it up into a paper airplane, and trying to hit him on the nose with it. She imagined this winged missive, trailing whiffs of perfume, spiraling down past the oak wainscoting of the Chamber and fluttering round the stern, bewigged head of the Speaker. She giggled.

"Shhhh!" A cadaverous stranger who was sharing the Distinguished Stranger's Gallery glowered over at her. Unabashed, Gloria simply lifted an eyebrow and sniffed. She wasn't a Marquess' daughter for nothing.

Reawakened, she scanned the benches below for that Junior Minister Ronnie had introduced her to the other evening. The one with curly brown hair, a crooked nose and a jolting charge of sex appeal. To her surprise, she discovered him at the Dispatch Box. He was the one making the forceful speech that was eliciting all those angry hoots and approving "Hear hears!"

"He must have some post in Education," she thought, and this realization made her lean forward gracefully and gaze down at the hitherto dreary House of Commons with a look of pleasant anticipation. She had just thought of a way to make her interest in literacy far more interesting indeed.

_____

On West 44th Street in New York, the last of the matinee crowd was trickling out of the Shubert Theater into the chill, gritty, January dusk. Both the Shubert and the Majestic had turned on their marquee lights. The Broadhurst between them and the St. James and Helen Hayes across the street were shuttered and dark, the grime-streaked posters from old flops still marking their facades like rows of garish tombstones. In another hour or so, the twinkling lights of the Shubert and Majestic would be able to create small islands of giddy excitement in the night, but now the little bulbs still competed with the last gray light of day, and so from across the street, their yellow, nervous flickers seemed feeble, jaundiced, old, serving only to emphasize the encroaching gloom of the shadows that crept across the asphalt from the St. James.

One of these shadows moved, shifting its weight from foot to foot on the brutally hard, cold pavement. The shadow glanced over to its left at the corner of Eighth Avenue where the limo would appear, back to the front of the Shubert, then turned and began walking slowly along the sidewalk.

Mislov Rapolovitch dressed entirely in black. Black wool slacks, black peacoat, black turtleneck. His hair was black and so were his eyes and so was his beard. He had sleek, black eyebrows that extended into curly black sideburns. What little skin that was visible around his cheekbones and forehead was dead white. The only color to be seen on Mislov Rapolovitch was on his lips, which were full and fleshy and rosebud red.

He wiggled his toes inside his black Reeboks. When the moment came, he would have to move swiftly, and he was stiff with cold. He had been lurking in the chill, desolate shadows of the St. James for nearly twenty minutes. Now passing beneath the darkened marquee of the Helen Hayes, he glanced down at his Nikon, black of course, set on motor drive and ready to rip off six frames a second. The ready light glowed green on his super-charged flash unit, specially modified to be able to keep pace with the motor drive. He reached the row of metal garage doors of the old Times building directly across the street from the Shubert and paused there, glancing back over his shoulder at Eighth Avenue. It would happen any time now. He was certain. The other paparazzi were scattered up and down 45th in front of the Royale, the Plymouth and the Booth, where she usually appeared. She could even emerge over by the Minskoff Theater near Times Square. The warren of little alleys between the theaters on 44th and 45th allowed her dozens of options. But something told Mislov that tonight one of the most famous rock stars in the world, appearing for a limited engagement in Broadway's newest musical amidst rumors of the imminent breakup of her marriage, would choose the front entrance of her own theater, the Shubert, to make a dash for her limousine. Mislov licked his lips. He felt a sudden rush of saliva in his mouth. It would happen soon. And except for Nigel, he was the only one staking out the front of the Shubert. Nigel was, rather stupidly, swaggering up and down right in front of the Shubert box office, wearing his cleverly ripped jeans, faded bomber jacket, and swinging his Nikon about at waist level like a big black cock.

"Could I be wrong?" The black thought flooded through him. How could he and that fool Nigel be mutually of a mind? Could he, Mislov, be in agreement with anyone on anything and still be true to himself? His mouth went dry again. His eyes glittered blackly with contempt as they swept up and down the grimy, darkening street.

There! He spotted one of her bodyguards, a huge man seemingly the width of a mobile home, walking slowly along Shubert Alley towards 44th. Mislov slunk further back into the shadows as the bodyguard reached the corner of the theater, turned and quickly surveyed the remaining crowd still milling around under the marquee. The man noticed Nigel swaggering along with his back turned and quickly stepped back into the alley. He said something, seemingly to himself, but Mislov could see a tiny light blinking in the Bluetooth phone bud clipped to his ear.

Yes! It was going to be here! Again the saliva filled Mislov's mouth. He swallowed painfully and glanced over at Eighth Avenue. There was the limousine! Nosing around the corner. Making its way slowly down the narrow street. Nigel had seen it too and was eyeing it suspiciously. Long, black limousines were a dime a dozen in the theater district in New York. Likely it was just on its way to pick up some of the blue-haired dowagers still squawking and clucking under the marquee. Nigel might think that, but he couldn't see the bodyguard. Mislov checked his Nikon again. Medium wide angle for this job. Close work. Extremely close. The limousine was passing the Majestic now, slowing even more. Its opaque, black-tinted windows glittered at him, reflecting back the same contempt his eyes fired at them. There was no way of telling who was inside. It could be carrying a Japanese tourist, a Bronx mobster, an Arab sheik, a visiting mayor from Des Moines. But no, it was for her!

The bodyguard, moving like an NFL tackle, cut in under the marquee from the alley, threading his way through the dowagers and groupies towards Nigel. The limousine darted forward, then jerked to a stop with a squeal that merged with a chorus of other squeals and shouts that blew out of the theater as two doors burst open and a flying wedge of seven bodyguards rushed across the sidewalk towards the limo.

Mislov sprinted across the street from the Times building. He would only have a second at most. The first bodyguard was blocking Nigel, moving from side to side as Nigel tried to run around him. The wedge of other bodyguards had reached the limo, the first man yanking open the door, the last man closing the ring of protective flesh around her as she ducked inside. Nigel was hopping up and down, screaming with rage and frustration as he futilely tried to pop off shots above the guard's head. Mislov reached the limousine as he heard the door slam shut on the other side. He thrust his Nikon up to the black-tinted glass and POW! POW! POW! POW! POW! POW! POW! POW! The super-charged flash lit up the street, catching the faces of the startled guards with their mouths open, the dowagers gaping with shock and fear, the groupies frantic, screaming with excitement. And inside the limousine, Mislov's flash driving through its tinted glass, another private moment fell into the public glare.

———

To the employees of the Earl Court Waikiki, Gordon Coburn often seemed like God. Or at least like a god. As did Kip Stallybrass to the Ibans. And Lady Gloria Ryder to readers of the tabloids. And Mislov Rapolovitch to people like Lady Gloria Ryder. The four of them could appear to others as an unknowable force. A distant icon. An indifferent manipulator or unapproachable observer. They could even, on occasion, appear as a personally involved malevolent force or a forgiving, helping, Father-Mother figure. But an Omniscient Narrator – if such a being existed – would have to relate that none of the four actually believed in God or gods themselves. Not that they didn't think about the possibility from time to time. When passing a church, say, or looking up at the stars, or finding themselves alone and aware in an elevator, precipitously rising or falling, a brief moment of reflection might visit them: "Why? What's it all about? Am I missing out? Should I look harder? Try harder?"

Like most secular participants of the 21st century, Gordon, Kip, Gloria, and Mislov never added these moments up or counted them a significant portion of their lives, but the moments did come along fairly often. Daily in fact. Were they intimations of immortality? Or just intimations of . . . mortality? Never mind. On with life while we've got it.

Insulated by busy days, excellent health, and the iron certitudes of western science, the four could easily go half a year or more without entertaining serious thoughts about a deity. And none of them had any knowledge of each other, even if each of them was making decisions that could wildly alter another's fate ten thousand miles away. A chaos theorist could claim they were simply acting like a butterfly's delicately fluttering wing that precipitates a hurricane on the opposite side of the globe.

When he was about five, Gordon believed that his Sunday school teacher may have been God. He was a kindly old man with a lot of wrinkles who told wonderful stories. Gordon loved going to Sunday school and listening to stories about Jonah who lived in a whale and the little boy Moses who floated down a river in a basket of bulrushes, whatever bulrushes were. But then Gordon's parents started going to a different church, so Gordon had to go to a different Sunday school, and that shocked him. Could you just walk away from God like that? At his new Sunday school, nobody told stories, and the other kids liked to start spitball fights, and some of them talked dirty. Gordon began to lose faith in organized religion.

There was an introspective, spiritual side to him, but that got pretty well squelched by high school peer groups. In his freshman year, a huge lineman on the school football team caught him reading *Alice in Wonderland* for pleasure, and it took Gordon most of his sophomore year to shed the reputation of being a "bookworm fag," which he managed by lettering in track as a sprinter and dating a cheerleader. College fraternity life and a demanding business career paved over any remaining spiritual or religious interests. Musings on the meaning of life were not rewarded in those environments.

Gordon matured at a time in America when entrepreneurial verve seemed to justify greed. CEO's were heroes and appeared on the covers of magazines. They were the role models he was told to emulate, and since he was likeable, good-looking and hard working, the role models he encountered thought they saw themselves in Gordon, and he was rapidly promoted up the ladder.

A little too rapidly he occasionally confessed to himself. He was now the youngest General Manager in the entire Earl Court chain, and it made him nervous. He had those role models, of course, and he knew how to act like a seasoned executive in theory, but he really wasn't a seasoned executive, and deep down he knew it. That insecurity sometimes informed his tone, so his efforts to be decisive could make him appear arbitrary. Kindness could come across as condescension. Knowledge as arrogance. He knew this too, and aside from just trying to be nice, he found the best way to keep from feeling nervous was to move quickly, stay busy, and stick to his guns even if he often felt like a little boy floating aimlessly in a basket of bulrushes. Death, the primary occasion for thinking about a Creator and the afterlife, had never crossed his path in all his thirty-two years.

So thoughts of a possible deity were far from Gordon's mind as he strove to take charge of the fortune cookie challenge. He stood, Jove-like in the glass walled magnificence of his office eyrie at the Earl Court, and used his speakerphone to hurl thunderbolts down at his staff.

"Who supplies our fortune cookies?" boomed his voice in the Food and Beverage Manager's office.

"Send a bag of them to my office right away," came the command in the restaurant kitchen.

"Give me a list of who was working there last night," was the order to the maitre d' who assumed this a preliminary to a kind of human sacrifice.

The speakerphone blinked an amber eye and interrupted his barrage in prim, female tones. "Carol Nickle is here."

"Send her in." Gordon resumed his seat in his leather executive chair behind his koa wood desk. Carol Nickle, his new Public Relations Director, entered, smiling easily. Gordon greeted her with a serious frown.

"Carol, did you get a fortune cookie last night?"

"Excuse me?"

"A fortune cookie. Did you get one at dinner last night?"

Carol replied slowly, holding her smile. "Yes."

"What did it say?"

"A stitch in time saves nine. Something like that. Why . . . ah . . . why is this important?"

Gordon handed her the little ribbon of paper and swept the fortune cookie crumbs off his desk. "I didn't open mine till just now," he said, and dabbed one of the cookie crumbs to his tongue. It tasted of rice flour and sugar. Dry, stale, and sweet.

"You will die in September," Carol read aloud. "Well, I'm glad I didn't get this one."

"I'm just glad Suzuki-san didn't get it. It might have queered the whole deal. He might have thought it was a prediction about the renovation." Gordon squinted through the heavily tinted slabs of glass at the coruscating sparkle of the sea as, three miles away, the rogue wave passed beneath a massive Matson container ship, which happened to be carrying the things Carol had packed up and shipped from Atlanta the month before. Almost any other vessel would have experienced a noticeable pitch and yaw, but the container ship was so vast — nearly nine hundred feet long and displacing almost thirty thousand gross tons — it was virtually an island unto itself. In addition to things like Carol's silver service and her childhood teddy bear, it was also transporting fifty Nissan trucks, three tons of cantaloupe, two hundred thousand swizzle sticks, and a million other items required to sustain the needs and whims of paradise. It sailed serenely on at a steady twenty knots with a barely noticeable rise and fall along its length as the rogue wave, which was roughly the size and weight of the Santa Ana Freeway, passed under it, moving just slightly faster than the ship in towards Gordon and his guests.

Gordon's eyes, usually a sparkling blue like the sea outside, assumed the darkened shade of his office windows as he envisioned the distant autumn season. "September is when we should begin the renovation, not when we have to finish it."

"Why don't you tell Earl?"

"Won't do any good. Suzuki-san's the one who's paying for it. He wants to get started."

The day before, Gordon had convinced Mr. Suzuki, the actual owner of the Earl Court Waikiki, to commit forty million dollars to the hotel's renovation. Gordon's haphazard but boyishly enthusiastic presentation had impressed this Osaka billionaire who knew that while top Japanese executives should be old, top American executives are supposed to be young. Gordon looked even younger than his thirty-two years. He looked like a college fraternity president. But now, Gordon's head sunk down till his chin rested on his carefully knotted Italian silk tie, and he soberly contemplated the smooth roll of fabric his English wool trousers made above his crotch. He looked like a fraternity president with serious pledge problems.

"He's cute," Carol thought. This thought often occurred to her. It was her first thought on the job when she assumed the post of Public Relations Director a month before. Gordon had asked her then to listen to the presentation he was preparing for Mr. Suzuki. General unfamiliarity with the hotel's operations had caused her to miss most of the non-sequiturs in his arguments. Like Suzuki-san who had only an erratic grasp of spoken English, she concentrated on the overall impression. Gordon was cute.

The overall impression had worked, but with success came difficulties. Mr. Suzuki, having made the forty million dollar commitment to the renovation, wanted the job done immediately. To meet his September deadline, the work would have to go on throughout the summer months, normally one of the peak seasons. Several wings of the hotel would have to be closed off. Some reservations already on the books would probably have to be canceled, many more refused. And hotel General Managers, no matter how cute, are ultimately judged by the occupancy rates they are able to maintain. The renovation would provide Gordon with an excellent excuse for low summer numbers, of course, but still.

Carol watched emotions of gloom, determination, fear, and cordiality page across Gordon's face as he considered the months ahead. She knew her new boss well enough by now not to try and predict what was going to pop into his head next. That was impossible. But discerning what was on his mind at any given moment was duck soup. Gordon's face was the most open of books. Carol wished she could get him into a game of poker. Strip poker.

She relished that idea, turning it over in her mind behind her own, more impassive, Chanel-shielded features as Gordon brooded over his renovation. They would play five-card stud. Queens wild. First she would wager and quickly lose her silver starshell earrings and ebony and silver headband, releasing her long, ash-blond hair that would cascade down over her shoulders. Next, she would risk her black silk jacket overlaid with a discreet, white, tapa-cloth pattern that was so classically stylish as well as culturally appropriate here in the islands. Removing this imposing, wide-shouldered garment would reveal her in a simple, white, rough-silk shift, still fully clothed but achingly vulnerable. Gordon, now thoroughly inflamed, would gamble impetuously, and she would take from him in rapid succession his worsted wool suit coat, that darling tie, his pima cotton shirt. (Did Gordon have hair on his chest? Never mind.) His belt. His pants. Wait! His shoes first. Force him to bet his Italian loafers, French socks, and English trousers all on a single, doomed card.

Carol had Gordon down to his skivvies, which she pictured as white boxer shorts decorated with yellow bananas, and she was filling an inside straight while smiling a Cheshire-Cat smile when the Gordon in front of her suddenly sat bolt upright behind his desk with a look of panic.

"My God!" he shouted. "They'll both be here at the same time!"

"Who will?" Carol asked.

"Earl and Suzuki-san. They'll both be here at the same time. For the grand opening. The re-opening."

"Yes. Well? So what?" Carol asked somewhat petulantly, wanting to get back to her inside straight.

"They'll both be here at the same time! Who's going to get the Presidential suite?"

Now she understood. Gordon, absolute ruler of his fiefdom in Hawaii, still had to pay obeisance and send tribute to those two distant emperors, one in the east and one in the west. Earl Pressler was the second-generation Chairman and Chief Executive Officer of the international Earl Court hotel chain founded by his father fifty years ago. Mr. Pressler senior had named the enterprise after his son Earl while the boy was still in the cradle. Earl Court International, Inc. now managed more than five hundred hotel properties worldwide, from New York to Rio de Janeiro, from Hawaii to Abu Dhabi. For a variety of reasons, the chain found it more profitable to simply manage the hotels under long-term contracts, and the majority of them were in fact owned by independent entities such as insurance companies, retirement funds, and Osaka billionaires. These owners ordinarily took only a passive role in management, unless something like a forty million dollar renovation was called for.

Both Earl Pressler and Kenji Suzuki were international tycoons. Both traveled with a large entourage. Both possessed punctilious manners punctuated by astonishing spasms of rudeness, cruelty, and indifference. They both had a passion for the finer things in life and the intelligence and breadth of experience to know what they were. This was the first occasion when they both would be in residence at the Earl Court Waikiki at the same time, and in the past, each had always stayed in the Presidential Suite.

Gordon's sensitivity to this potential contretemps and his foresight to panic over it well in advance were exactly the sort of qualities that made him such an exceptional hotelier. As with the fortune cookie a few moments before, he sprung into action, swiveling around in his leather, executive chair, leaning over his broad, koa wood desk, and stabbing at the black box of his speakerphone with an agitated forefinger. The speakerphone winked its amber eye and spoke in the shy, lilting, affectionate tones of a girl born and raised in the Hawaiian Islands.

"Reservations. This is Cynthia."

"Cynthia, this is Gordon Coburn. Is anyone booked into the Presidential Suite during September?"

"Oh, yes Sir."

"There is?"

"I mean, I'll check." "The speaker phone sounded flustered. "This coming September?"

"Yes. Nine months from now."

"Just a minute."

The speakerphone went silent. Gordon, wide-eyed, tense, stared over at Carol like a submarine Captain waiting for the muffled thump of a depth charge as offshore, the rogue wave rolled ineluctably towards them.

"No sir, no one's booked the Presidential Suite in September," the shy voice announced. "It's available."

"Damn!" Gordon said. "There's nobody in there the whole month?"

"No sir. Do you want to reserve it?"

"No. I want someone else to reserve it. Let me know if anyone does. In fact, put it on special. The whole month of September, the Presidential Suite will be available for . . . let's make it . . . eight hundred a day."

Eight hundred dollars a day represented a twelve hundred dollar reduction off the standard rack rate for the Earl Court's Presidential Suite. The speakerphone responded to this news with a brief pause. "Yes, sir," it said doubtfully.

"See that gets entered in, would you Cynthia?" Gordon said courteously. "And try to move it for me. I want that suite booked solid all September."

"Yes, Sir."

"Good work. Thank you, Cynthia." Gordon poked at the black box on his desk, and the amber light winked out. He leaned back in his executive chair and looked proudly over at Carol. "If we get some solid reservations in there, we can put both Earl and Suzuki-san somewhere else."

"So they'll both be pissed off?"

"A lot less pissed than one of them would be if the other was in there, and he wasn't. They'll appreciate that paying customers come first. Specially after the lousy summer we're going to have." Gordon's face darkened again. "We better be full in September."

"You better get some groups in, then," Carol said. "You'll never do it with F.I.T.'s in September."

"I know. I'll have to speak with Howie," Gordon said, and somehow, thinking of speaking with his Director of Group Sales made Gordon realize that he was currently speaking with his Director of Public Relations. She was right there in front of him. Gordon smiled appreciatively at her. Carol smiled appreciatively back and re-crossed long legs sheathed in translucent white hose. She glanced at her watch, a heavy, broad band of silver and gold with an elegantly simple face of pure black with no numerals, just a gold dot instead of the twelve. Gordon smiled appreciatively at her watch, too. He was an excellent judge of style, of the multitude of little touches that created an ensemble, and his new Public Relations Director knew how to create beautiful ensembles of herself. Gordon, for perhaps the twenty-thousandth time in his career, imagined what it would be like to go to bed with one of his hotel employees. He hadn't done it as often as he had imagined it, but he had done it. He was doing it at the present time, in fact, with another woman employed at the hotel. A risky business. Should he chance doing it with

Carol, too? Was it even possible? He took a deep breath. Paused. Considered. And wrinkled his nose. There was something stale and musky in his office. He would have to tell Gail to tell the cleaning people. He exhaled, sighing, and spun sideways in his chair to stare out the window just as the rogue wave broke over the reef a half-mile off shore.

Nathan Kahaano saw it first. A sixteen-year-old surf addict who was playing hooky from McKinley high school that day, Nathan had paddled way out beyond the break. He wanted to be alone with his thoughts. They were the same thoughts that prey on most sixteen-year-old minds, thoughts of sex, the presence or absence of parents (both equally upsetting), the meaning of life, and what the hell was the point of anything. For Nathan, more fortunate than most sixteen year olds, the point of everything was suddenly made clear as the wave, a grand, glassy, annihilating wall of water surged mountainously towards him. For Nathan, it was the Perfect Wave, the Wave other surfers search for all their lives. Come to him, him alone, after only sixteen years. He whooped a wild, passionate cry, turned on his board, flat on his belly, and dug with all his might, arms and shoulders pinwheeling white spray from the blue sea.

For Kimo Hart, Captain of the catamaran, Waikiki Sun, Nathan's wave was not so wonderful. He was taking twenty-five tourists out for the standard twenty-minute turnaround cruise when he saw this crazy kid jump up on a wave that belonged out on the North Shore somewhere. Somewhere out at Waimea or Sunset during the long board championships, not rolling in towards his cat when he had a load of pink-skinned children, roly-poly Midwesterners, and a couple of grandmothers on board. He had enough time to shout to everybody to hold on and thank his stars that his insurance was paid up before the wave surged underneath his cat, taking it up almost vertical with both prows pointing five feet up out of the water and letting it hang there for what seemed like about fifty years, deciding whether or not to flip them over backwards while that crazy kid, whooping like an Apache, zoomed past them to his apotheosis, hanging five on the curl.

"Great ride," said Gordon. He was standing up now, staring out his tinted windows, one hand grasping the drapes in a classic executive pose. He gazed benevolently down at his guests and at this local kid who was cutting back and forth on a big wave that seemed to be giving everybody a lot of fun. That catamaran must have jumped twenty feet. What a thrill!

Down on the beach, Sidney Kramer, a litigious man from Passaic, New Jersey, stalked angrily along at the edge of the water. He was suffering postpartum depression from the successful conclusion of a five-year lawsuit with his ex-wife's building contractor, and all the giddy shrieks and banal happiness, all the sparkling water and golden sunshine that surrounded him, he found irritating in the extreme. Pot bellied and spindle-legged, he looked like a large, suspicious shorebird patrolling the beach, a flamingo, given the painfully pink hue of his skin. He stared out at the laughing scene, the rolling surf, the picturesque view of Diamond Head, and snorted in disgust. Resolving to cut his trip short and return to Passaic, he turned his back on the ocean, always a dangerous thing to do, and was struck about butt-high by the remnants of the rogue wave. It threw him violently forward onto the sand, breaking his arm and so giving him a new purpose in life.

Gordon chuckled. From up in his office, Mr. Kramer's painful experience appeared as a humorous little spill. He smiled down at the man thrashing about in the water and then gazed back up at the distant horizon as the invisible energy of the rogue wave, carried now by the air, gusted through him and past him and on around the world. He felt a brief chill and shivered. "You will die in September." What if it were true?

CHAPTER TWO

"One Club Sandwich, one Chicken Salad, one Papaya Boat!" Evelyn Fujii shrieked. "This for Coburn! You make 'em good!"

Benjamin made a face at her. "I make 'em all good."

"Hey, this no order Black Dog for your friends, this for the big boss. Gimmie three iced tea."

"I no make Black Dog for my friends, my friends all eat fugu."

"Your friends all dead!"

The kitchen erupted in laughter. Benjamin, because he was Filipino, was supposed to cherish black dog above all other culinary delights, and Evelyn, a Nisei, or second generation Hawaii Japanese, was supposed to relish fugu, a poisonous blowfish that was notoriously tricky to prepare and which every year killed a number of adventurous gourmets back in Japan. Neither of them had ever tasted black dog or fugu.

Evelyn quickly selected three long, succulent wedges of pineapple and thrust them down into the iced teas. Her hands moving in a blur of precise actions, she arranged a sprig of mint, a slice of lemon and a lavender orchid blossom around the rim of each glass, then turning, tray held aloft, and shouting "Otta way!" she swept out of the kitchen.

And despite his show of indifference, Benjamin split open three papayas before he found one with just the right firm but creamy texture. With a deft twist, he spooned out its nest of black seeds, leaving a perfectly smooth, glowing, orange-yellow cavity wherein he positioned a generous dollop of large-curd cottage cheese.

This sort of meticulous, aesthetic care circled around Gordon constantly, twenty-four hours a day. He was well aware of it, and he tried his best to appreciate and compliment every act no matter how small. He was naturally inclined to do this anyway, but it was also an important part of his job. He was supposed to be coddled and fed and served and entertained and have his every whim anticipated with just the right degree of gracious attention. Few people in the world lead a more luxurious and sophisticated material existence than the General Manager of a first-class resort hotel. The Earl Court Waikiki had eighteen hundred employees, all of whom were, in effect, highly trained servants whose single, unified goal was to please and delight. There were masseuses and dancers and ice carvers, translators and musicians and sommeliers, pastry chefs and scuba instructors and fireworks experts. There were three hundred maids and two hundred waiters and waitresses. There was a man who did nothing but create new and ever-changing fresh flower displays, a woman who cared only for the exotic birds that swung from trapezes in the lobby, and a devoted old fellow whose whole life consisted of pampering schools of plump carp that swam through meandering streams about the grounds in mesmerizing, multi-colored swirls of flesh. The Earl Court Waikiki had seven different restaurants and a dozen bars including a nonalcoholic one that floated in an acre-sized pool. The sushi chefs spent two weeks in Tokyo every six months in order to keep up with the latest styles in raw fish. The Italian waiters could discourse passionately on their chef's method of preparing the catch of the day. The French maitre d' in the Zebra Room never forgot a face, and one of the bartenders in the Beachboy Lounge could mix five hundred cocktails from memory while his pet parrot, an African Grey, recited amusing dirty phrases in English or in Japanese. The Earl Court Waikiki had a spa with Personal Trainers to assist in "body shaping," a staff of Party Coordinators to stimulate the imagination, and a Chinese Fortuneteller in the Red Dragon Restaurant who could tell you what was going to happen. The resort offered afternoon classes in quilting and lei making and an after-hours nightclub called Cuffs where nearly nude waitresses in black net stockings imprisoned guests in a cage behind the bar. A glass-enclosed elevator could whisk you from the steel guitars of The Earl Court Luau down on the beach to the latest rock music in The Lighthouse dance club forty stories above it. There were Hawaiian storytellers and professional astronomers, Mozart String Quartets and New Orleans Jazz Bands, authentic Tahitian hula and superb French champagne. The selection of pleasures drew from all cultures and all times. No Sultan of Byzantium, no Emperor of Rome, no Mogul or Maharaja or Khan had ever assembled so diverse and skilled a court of entertainments. Gordon was prince of it all.

As General Manager, he lived in a suite on the thirty-fifth floor and commuted to his office on the fourth floor in a teak and brass-lined elevator. The constant surfeit that surrounded him might have caused even a Mogul or Maharaja to burst into tears at some point, but Gordon had a unique hedonistic advantage. He was supported by the Puritan work ethic. On any given day, up to twenty-five hundred guests were depending on him to maintain standards, so it was his Calvinist duty to have the girl behind the front desk smile sweetly at him. It was his hard responsibility to taste the mints placed upon the pillow at night. He was managerially tasked with enjoying the melodies of the pianist in the cocktail lounge and experiencing the fluffiness of the towels left out by the sauna. He had staffs of experts and administrators to assist him in all this, of course, but ultimately, quality control was up to him, and every one of the eighteen hundred employees at the Earl Court Waikiki knew it.

"Thank you, Evelyn," he said graciously, as their waitress served them their three, baroquely decorated iced teas. Evelyn's plump, middle-aged face burst into a smile, revealing a gold filling that glinted in the sun. They were lunching casually in the Surfside Coffee Shop, an attractive, open-air restaurant with a low ceiling and semi-circular banquettes that faced a row of planters exploding with pink and purple bougainvillea. Immediately beyond the bougainvillea, the golden sands of Waikiki Beach fell away to meet the surf. The aptly named Surfside Coffee Shop was one of the few restaurants in the hotel without a carefully wrought personality or theme that portrayed some other time or place. The Surfside Coffee Shop pretended to be nothing but what it was, and Gordon had selected it because considering both view and price, it was the best value they offered. Not that he or anyone else at the table would actually pay for what they ate, but it was important to demonstrate that meals at the Earl Court could be, if not inexpensive, at least reasonable. He was hosting Howie Berg, his Director of Group Sales, and Janet Sorenson, a woman who was apparently capable of bringing as many as twelve hundred people to the Earl Court Waikiki in September. She was the local representative for something called the Seventh Annual Conference on Shamanistic Practice.

"Who actually participates in your conference?" he asked.

"Largely academics," she replied. "About half are from the U.S., but the rest come from all over the world. That's why we're considering Hawaii. It's more centrally located than California, given our attendees."

"This is the crossroads of the Pacific," Howie said happily.

Gordon blinked. Howie liked to use phrases from the Meeting Sales brochures in a rather ironic way, a habit that often made Gordon feel uncomfortable without quite knowing why. Ms. Sorenson nodded in polite agreement, and there was a brief pause as Evelyn reappeared with their lunch. As they were being served, a fat, self-important-looking white pigeon fluttered down to roost on the planter next to Gordon and cocked a hungry red eye at their table. Gordon crumbled a bit of crust from his roll and tossed it out onto the beach. The pigeon flapped heavily once, dropped down behind the planter and disappeared.

The General Manager of the Earl Court spooned up some cottage cheese and watched the potential savior of his September pick at her chicken salad. Ms. Sorenson was a woman of about thirty-five or forty with frizzy hair, a comfortable face, and an alert, attentive way of listening. She was pleasant and undoubtedly intelligent, but Gordon suspected she was out of her depth negotiating what could amount to a half million-dollar deal. She taught at the university just a couple of miles away, and when he had discovered from Howie that they were in negotiations with her regarding a possible September booking, he had immediately called her up himself and asked her over for lunch. Howie probably wasn't happy about his horning in, but the prospect of an empty hotel in September made Gordon nervous. A possible convention booking was too important for him not to get involved.

"Oahu is the island known as The Gathering Place," Howie said and crunched down into his club sandwich.

Gordon blinked again. "Will any actual shamans be coming to your conference?" he asked.

"Oh, yes. We encourage that. As many as can make it. We had several dozen last year."

"What are shamans, exactly?"

"Well, our culture has a variety of names for them. Witch Doctors, Juju Men, Faith Healers, Medicine Man. But in their own cultures, these people are sort of a cross between a Doctor and a Priest. They're the ones who negotiate between what we call the 'real' world, the physical world, and the world of the spirit."

"Ah," Gordon said and felt a twinge of discomfort. A phrase like "world of the spirit" made him think of the after-life. The afterlife made him think of death. Death made him think of that damn fortune cookie. His death. What if . . . ? He glanced out towards the ocean and saw that the fat, white pigeon had returned and was glaring redly at him from the edge of the planter. "But most of the participants are like you?" he asked quickly. "Academics. Professors."

"Yes. That's one of our problems, really."

"How's that?"

"Most academics have to apply for individual travel grants in order to attend a conference. A lot of the papers will be published, at least their authors want them to be. So, it's very important that our conference be perceived as a seri-ous endeavor."

"Yes?"

"Well, Hawaii isn't a serious place." Ms. Sorenson gestured out past the pigeon and the bougainvillea towards the beach where several thousand tourists in Day-Glo swimsuits were dozing and frolicking in the sun. "That's what the rest of the world thinks."

"Believe me," Howie said gravely, "We take this very seriously. Nothing is more important to us than the success of your conference."

"Yes," said Ms. Sorenson. "Thank you. But the problem isn't with you. It's with some university administrator in Chicago or Ithaca. If their people are going off to Pittsburgh for a conference, the administrator thinks they're probably going off to do some real work. But if they're going to Hawaii, everybody winks and nudges each other and talks about hitting the beach. Believe me, it's a real problem. Although, it's not our biggest problem."

"What's that?" Gordon asked.

"Well, cost. Academics don't have much money. As I told you on the phone, ordinarily we wouldn't even consider the Earl Court, but if special rates are available . . . " Ms. Sorenson let her hypothesis hang delicately in the air and smiled apologetically.

"What sort of rates were you hoping to get?"

"University people can't afford anything, really."

"You mean you'd like us to put you up free?"

"That would be nice." Ms. Sorenson giggled a girlish giggle. Howie quickly joined in, laughing jovially. "We've been working towards something we can both live with," he said, finishing off the topic.

But Gordon persevered. "What's the most you'd be able to pay, per room?" he asked.

"I don't really know. Everything has to be approved by committee. How low are you able to go?"

"How many guests are you able to guarantee?"

"That's hard to say until we know how much it is."

Gordon took refuge in his papaya boat and spooned up some more cottage cheese. He wished this woman was a professional meeting planner, someone he could negotiate with. Try as he might, he couldn't seem to get the ball out of his court. He was wondering if he should just offer her a low-ball rate when Howie, whose eyes had been flickering nervously back and forth between them, suddenly pointed out towards the ocean and blurted, "Looks pretty flat out there. That kid won't be breaking any more records today."

"I saw him do that, you know," Gordon said.

"Saw who do what?" Ms. Sorenson asked.

"An hour or two ago, just before I called you, a local kid caught the longest ride off Waikiki since Duke Kahanumoku. Surfed in and crossed nearly the whole length of the beach from Diamond Head to Ala Moana. I saw him."

"Some freak wave," Howie said. "People thought you couldn't do that any more since they did some dredging out there after the war."

"Really. That's interesting," Ms. Sorenson said mildly and added, "What kind of rates do you think you could offer us?"

"Hundred a night," Gordon said.

There was a loud crunch as Howie took a fierce bite out of his club sandwich, and the fat, white pigeon flew heavily away, its flapping wings sounding like a round of applause.

———

Like a bat come to rest in a lavatory, Mislov Rapolovitch leaned against the back wall of Sid's One Hour Color Developing and waited in its dirty, florescent glare. Sid's was a one-man, hole-in-the-wall operation on Eighth Avenue a few blocks from Port Authority. A traditionalist in his craft, Mislov still preferred to use film rather than digital cameras, partly because he believed film still provided higher quality images, and partly because original, unretouched negatives could be useful in a court of law in case the subjects of the photographs decided to sue. If Mislov could have shot in black-and-white, a medium he far preferred, he would have developed his own film. But his clients all demanded color, and so he was compelled to utilize places like Sid's. He found Sid's amusing, however. It was frequented by sweaty, furtive businessmen in a rush to catch a bus out to Jersey or Connecticut. They would dodge in from the hostile blare and hustle on Eighth Avenue to download images from their phones or drop off disposable cameras with film they had shot up in one of the seedy hotels nearby. So many of them wrote the name "Smith" on their claim check, Sid had taken to asking them for their first name as well in order to avoid confusion. But this simple request often flustered them. So impoverished were their imaginations, they couldn't think of a phony first name to go with "Smith," and they were too paranoid to give their real one. Half of them never came back to pick up their prints.

Sid was dealing with a Mr. Smith now, a short, balding man with a pendulous nether lip and puffy white cheeks that were spotted with unhealthy florid patches as if he had just engaged in some unaccustomed exertion. His layers of clothing, shirt, tie, suit coat, topcoat, were all loose, untucked and flapping about him, adding to a general air of distraction and suppressed panic. He scowled and squinted at the claim check, held the pink tip of his tongue between his teeth, and scribbled something swiftly with Sid's ballpoint.

"First name?" Sid asked, taking the claim check. Sid's flannel shirt was unbuttoned, and his hard, basketball-sized gut, encased in a dirty white tee shirt, protruded aggressively out over the counter.

"What?"

"I need your first name, too."

"Why?"

"I get a lot of Smiths in here. You want somebody else to get your pictures?"

"No! No, it's . . . ah . . . it's . . . John!"

Sid sighed. "You're John Smith, huh?"

"Yeah."

Sid shrugged and started to add in the name

"No. No, it's Hector," the man said.

"Hector? So are you a Hector or are you a John?"

"Hector John. I'm Hector John Smith."

"Hector John Smith. OK, we don't get too many of those." Sid wrote on the claim check. "You want mat or glossy?"

"What?"

"Mat prints or glossy prints?"

"Ah, glossy." The man's eyes flitted nervously over Sid's shoulder to bounce off Mislov's black, ominous form leaning against the back wall. His gaze skittered around the shop, returned to Mislov, bounced off again.

"Oversized?"

"What?"

"You want oversized prints?"

"No. Yeah. Yeah."

"Doubles?"

"No."

Mislov's unmoving presence was like a black hole, sucking at the man's attention. His eyes kept returning for longer and longer periods, staring with growing fear and fascination. Sid finished checking the boxes on the claim check and turned to ring up the sale.

"That's twenty-two fifty. In advance."

The man thumbed bills out of his wallet, glancing up at Mislov every other second as if he couldn't bear to look at him and couldn't bear to look away.

"Two fifty back," Sid said.

Almost in a frenzy now to escape, the man snatched at his change and fled back into the night, forgetting the claim check stub still lying on the counter.

Mislov smiled. Yes, he liked Sid's. The place renewed his peculiar faith in human nature. Once or twice he had even been able to place a couple of the abandoned photographs at Sid's with one of the tabloids. Mostly, however, these snapshots were both too explicit and too boring. And they lacked the *sine qua non* of his work, celebrity. There was a time when Sid had been able to take unclaimed prints that weren't too fuzzy and were more or less properly exposed, bundle them up into packs of a dozen, and sell them to pimps and street hustlers for ten dollars apiece. They in turn would resell them on the street to other nameless men for up to fifty dollars a pack. Mislov had regarded it as a form of desktop journalism. Sort of the people's tabloids. Alas, it was another fine old custom that had drowned in the rising tide of the Internet where anyone could swim in an ocean of pornography for free.

The developing machine burped, and his own roll of film began spooling out, a long, dark band of celluloid dripping fluid off its orange edges. Mislov turned to study it. Experience had made him proficient at interpreting the ghoulish, Halloween images of color negatives. He didn't really expect too much. A little tit falling out maybe, depending on what that rock star at the Shubert had been wearing. He peered down at the wet film and felt a sudden, electric shock of excitement. Looking out from the cave of their limousine were not one but two, tiny, cyan and magenta goblins trapped there on his film. Their purplish faces were locked together in a kiss, but their white eye sockets stared fearfully askew, not at each other, but back up at him.

———

In Borneo, far fewer events intruded upon the even flow of time, and a week or ten days passed before Kip was again as conscious of himself as he had been at the Kanowit long-house. They were days spent chugging up rivers in narrow wooden launches powered by ancient, single-cylinder engines that thumped like a slow, sleeping heartbeat against the walls of jungle. Days of sitting cross-legged on finely woven rattan mats, his eyes tracing and retracing their intricate patterns as he listened to the idle chatter of old Iban women discussing matters like the angle of sunlight, the flavor of rice, and how they had just walked from, or might walk to the stream. His time was filled with endless invitations to "mundi," all gratefully accepted as even on the hottest days, the jungle rivers were cool and clear and made the flesh tingle with goose bumps and the mind fresh with uncomplicated thought. "Kini nuan?" the Ibans would say when they met each other going to and fro. It was a polite greeting that meant, "Where are you going?" to which the proper response was "I am going to bathe." "Oh, are you going to bathe?" they would say. "Yes, I am going to bathe," the exchange went on, "Where are you going?" "I am going to the longhouse." "Oh, are you going to the longhouse?" "Yes, I am going to the longhouse." And all this would be repeated a half hour later as the two parties passed each other once again on the path, going in opposite directions. Since he was a "Tuan," everyone was especially polite to Kip, which meant he spent many of his waking hours describing where he was going and where he had been, when he was bathing and if he had bathed, if he would eat and when he had eaten, when he would sleep and if he had slept.

But he kept notes. Careful notes with a blue ballpoint pen slippery with sweat. He filled steno pad after steno pad, wrapped them carefully in triple layers of plastic and stored them deep in his pack along with digital recordings of the stories and legends the old men told him. These notes and stories were the raw material for his talk at the next Conference on Shamanistic Practice. His talk would become an article. His article would make his reputation. His reputation would secure him a job, a job at some world-renowned university like Harvard or Stanford.

"Or Podunk U.," Kip said to himself, coming back to earth. He was well aware of how problematic his career path was. It could easily turn out to be like the false trail they had followed one day in search of a longhouse. That path too had started off wide and smooth and unmistakable, but it had wound on through ever more hilly and difficult terrain and had finally just petered out in thick secondary jungle with no spurs, no side trails, no rhyme or reason for its existence. It was just a trail that led nowhere.

There were at least a hundred Ph.D.s in anthropology for every job opening in the academic world. Perhaps two hundred. And if you didn't get a job that first year after you got the degree, the odds increased to four hundred-to-one against your getting a job the next year since you were then competing with that year's crop of Ph.D.s as well. After three years and six hundred-to-one odds, most everyone abandoned hope. Some returned to the head of the trail to start all over again in law school or study for some sure-fire trade like X-Ray Technician. Some struck out blindly through the jungle, thrashing their way through thorns and thickets, and a few of these stumbled into executive careers in business, high speed freeways down which they rapidly disappeared. Others never left the end of the trail. They just camped there where it petered out, making do as over-educated cab drivers, despairing tire salesmen, cynical wait-resses. The groves of academe, Kip knew, could be very like the jungles of Borneo.

No university had offered him a position during his first round of interviews after the degree, but Kip had won a reprieve from the otherwise inevitably heavier odds. His post-doctoral grant ran for a year and would allow him to take another stab at the job market as a first-time candidate. Actually, he might have even slightly better odds since a post-doc lent a certain small prestige, and if he could get an article accepted out of it, he would definitely have a leg up.

This was his argument to Barbara, the woman he had lived with for two years while he was finishing his disserta-tion and she got a Masters in Sociology.

"You're going to go live with headhunters!" she had cried when he came home from work one night and made his announcement.

"Well, you've been telling me to go see a headhunter," Kip said wryly, unclipping his taxi-driver's identification badge.

"I've been telling you to go look for a job. A real job. Not driving a hack part time. Eddie found one."

"Ah, yes," Kip said, cocking his head and frowning with mock sincerity. "But ask yourself this. Is Eddie *really* happy?"

"Eddie's ecstatic. He's euphoric. He's on Cloud Nine."

"I thought he was in Chicago."

"Be serious! It's better than Borneo."

"Not for an anthropologist."

"There are plenty of weird people in Chicago."

"But no headhunters. At least no socially acceptable headhunters."

"My God."

"And the truth is, there are hardly any socially accepted headhunters left in Borneo, either. Headhunting was outlawed by the White Rajahs—"

"White Rajahs?"

"Englishmen. Then the Malays. Headhunting's been illegal for over a hundred years, but in the Iban culture, only a man who has taken a head can perform the ceremonies that lay the spirit to rest after someone dies. It's important to have a couple of these guys around, otherwise spirits just roam all over, unhappy, scaring people. So whenever there's been a socially acceptable way to take a head, like World War II for example, a few Ibans used to slip off and try to participate. These opportunities have been few and far between lately."

"How sad."

"Isn't it. This grant of mine could be one of the last chances to record these—"

"Kip!" Barbara's brown eyes were suddenly wet with tears. "It's dangerous."

"No it's—"

"It's dangerous and awful and crazy, and I won't see you for months, and I may not see you ever again." Her tears welled over and ran down her cheeks.

"Hey. Sure you will," he said, hugging her close. "You'll see me." He kissed her and tasted salt. "You'll see me. Come on." He tilted her chin up. "I can't give up this soon. I can't. And this is a really good thing for me." He smiled. "I'm only trying—"

"To get a head," she said, stealing his punch line. She shook her head, blinking away the tears. "I'm going to miss your lousy jokes."

They were wild together that night, gay and sad and keen with loss, crying and laughing as they made love three times, the last time in the solemn, gray, half-light of dawn. And that last time proved to be the very last time, as Barbara went off the next day to visit with her parents. What with one thing and another, they just never got together again until that awkward moment at the airport when he was leaving and she got the flight time wrong and nearly missed saying goodbye altogether. He was not really surprised when he received her letter two months later with the news that the lease on their apartment had expired along with, it seemed, their relationship. The good news was that his refund on the rent deposit was enclosed. Kip had wept a little and cashed the check.

And as it happened, that night five months ago was the last time that he had had sex, period.

"Period," he said aloud.

"Tuan?" one of the Iban boys asked.

He smiled and shook his head. Sex and abstinence were much on his mind, which was natural enough after five months, especially tonight as it appeared that the teenage boys he had hooked up with in this longhouse were setting him up to get laid. The Ibans had turned out not to be anything like what one imagined headhunters to be like. While they could sit and discuss a subject for days, they never seemed to argue over anything, much less fight over it. The longhouses that Kip sought out were far enough back in the interior so the people there still grew hill padi rice, raised a few semi-wild pigs and chickens, and traded down river for whatever else they needed. The beverage of choice was *tuak*, a cloudy rice wine. Or if they were in for a serious night, *arak*, which was a distilled rice moonshine that burned with a clear, blue flame and would burn the hair off your chest if you spilled any of it. After a few rounds of tuak or arak, out would come a set of gongs, sort of a rude gamelan, and the men, one by one, would get up in the center of a big circle and dance slow, taut, graceful dances that looked like the flights of birds.

The Ibans loved to tell stories. They loved to joke. They loved to tease, especially about sex. With Kip, the joke usually revolved around *ngayapping*, which was a courtship custom traditionally intended to lead to marriage. Like any such custom in any society, since it offered the potential for sexual congress, the custom of ngyapping was often joyfully abused by hormone-charged teenagers and, perhaps, by horny anthropologists.

In an Iban longhouse, the young men usually slept out on the covered verandah of the ruai, while the young women slept inside the individual family billets that led off from it. Everyone slept inside individual mosquito nets, which were made of gauzy white cloth and suspended in oblong box shapes over the sleeping mats. Ngyapping involved a young man stealing out of his mosquito net in the dead of night and making his way across the utter darkness of the ruai floor to the family apartment of the girl who, through many mutual jokes and teases throughout the day, had indicated that she might welcome his attentions. Upon reaching the family's closed and locked door, the young man somehow had to climb over a flat board wall about ten feet high with no purchase on it but splinters and knotholes. Descending the other side, he then had to make his way through the darkened, unfamiliar geography of the sleeping household and slip underneath the girl's mosquito net, distinguishing it somehow from the mosquito nets of all the other members of her family, especially the one of her parents. He then had to hope the girl wouldn't scream. In fact, the whole enterprise theoretically had to be carried out without a sound or else the father, hearing the intruder, would be justified in snatching up a *parang*, which was a long machete-like knife, and chopping the young man's head off. Since longhouses were lashed together on log stilts about twenty feet off the ground, the least pressure on any board conveyed creaks and vibrations to all the others, and soundlessness was plainly impossible. The truth was that pretty much everybody in a longhouse knew when some ngyapping was going on, especially the parents of the girl involved. On the young man's first visit to her mosquito net, all that was supposed to happen was nothing more than intimate conversation. On the second visit, heavy petting might take place. And with the third visit, the couple was basically engaged and entitled to do what they liked.

Frequently, of course, the third visit never took place, and what actually happened beneath the mosquito net on the first and second visits only the young couple knew for sure.

To Kip, ngyapping appeared to require a preternatural level of athleticism and sexual desire. He had never even attempted it. But tonight seemed different. Tonight, the young men of this longhouse were not leading him off to sleep on the ruai, but instead they had taken him behind the wall that marked the line of family apartments to what seemed a sort of empty storage area with raised platforms. The five of them were setting up their mosquito nets down on the floor, and up on one of the raised platforms, illuminated by the flames of two small, flickering brass lamps, a beautiful young widow was setting up hers.

The widow had been pointed out to him earlier in the day, although that had hardly been necessary as she truly was beautiful with flashing white teeth, creamy coffee skin, thin graceful arms, and full heavy breasts. She was only about twenty-two, younger than Kip but older than the teen-age boys that were with him, and she had the sure, languid movements that signaled mature, confident sexuality. Kip was surprised that she was still in the longhouse and hadn't made her way to one of the coastal cities. There couldn't have been much of a life for her here. The young men seemed both cowed and excited by her, and she was clearly bored with them. But she had smiled invitingly at "Tuan" that afternoon as he came back from his bath in the stream, and she had said something quickly that his rudimentary under-standing of Iban couldn't catch but which caused everyone else to snort and laugh. Now the boys were again snort-ing and laughing, speaking in quick, slang phrases he didn't understand, joshing and shoving each other, their smooth, golden limbs tangling in the lamplight as they readied for sleep. Up on the raised platform against a backdrop of leaping shadows, the beautiful young widow moved like an houri inside her translucent white mosquito net, its diaphanous folds alternately concealing and revealing as she stretched out those long, graceful arms, smoothing her skin from shoulder to wrist. Inside his own mosquito net, Kip curled on his side, rigidly feigning sleep, watching her through half-closed eyes. Five months! It was clear, wasn't it? What everyone wanted? Should he? What was the risk? It was like a stage set. The little lamps up there. Everyone would be watching. So what. They wanted him to. Should he? Five months. The folds of the mosquito net parting. Her smile. Her graceful arms. Those rich, full breasts. Should he? The folds of the net. Five months.

———

The mockup of the poster in Lady Gloria's London flat was the same size as the ones plastered up in tube stations, and it nearly filled the space between the heavy damask drapes and her massive stereo speakers. The poster's design featured bold, red, Helvetica type printed on a gray background of random letters and nonsense words. The message was, "Illiterate? Can't read? Call this number: 944-READ."

"I believe your contribution could be more wisely employed, Lady Gloria," Glynis Mortimer said.

"Really? Don't you like it?" Gloria asked. She studied the poster for a moment. The bold red type seemed to vibrate between her eyeballs, enlarging a rather nasty champagne hangover. She looked away quickly. It was more restful to ponder Ms. Glynis Mortimer's deep blue, woolen suit. More restful still to close her eyes altogether. They were seated at either end of a puffy, white sofa, and Gloria took a moment to lean back amidst the cushions and essay a light massage of the temples. Ms. Mortimer maintained an admirably erect posture.

"I think the medium of radio might be more efficacious," she observed.

"Really Glynis? May I call you Glynis?"

"Yes, M'Lady."

"A great many people ride the tube, you know."

"Yes, M'Lady."

"There's nothing to do while you wait for the train but look at those bloody posters."

"Yes, M'Lady."

"This one was designed by a rather famous artist friend of mine. It cost a bomb, actually."

"That is unfortunate, M'Lady."

"What makes you think radio might be better?"

"Your target audience can't read, M'Lady."

"Well yes, that's rather obvious, isn't it?"

"Yes, M'Lady."

"So what's your point?"

"They won't be able to read your poster, M'Lady."

Gloria's eyes flew open, her hangover temporarily suspended. She stared at Glynis. Stared at the poster. Stared back at Glynis. And uttered an expression favored by her father, the Marquess, when he fell off a horse while riding to hounds.

"Beg pardon, M'Lady?"

"I mean, crikey. You're right."

"I'm afraid so."

"Why didn't anyone tell me this before?"

"I can't say, M'Lady. Perhaps it's like the Purloined Letter."

Gloria felt her hangover returning with renewed intensity. "Why is it like a letter?"

"The Purloined Letter, M'Lady. A short story by Edgar Allen Poe. The plot centers on the fact that the thing that is the most obvious is often the thing most easily overlooked."

"This wretched thing cost me twenty-five hundred quid."

"In The Purloined Letter, I believe the sum was twenty-five thousand."

Gloria squinted at her. "You're well-read, aren't you Glynis?"

"Much have I traveled in the realms of gold."

"What?"

"I have read a little, yes."

"Good." Gloria squinted at her some more. Glynis Mortimer was a woman of indeterminate age, perhaps forty, perhaps fifty, with a high forehead, steel gray hair, and steel gray glasses. The glasses sharpened the gaze of bright blue eyes in which, Gloria suspected, there presently danced a certain hint of amusement. "She's terrific," Ronnie had declared. "An absolute prize. If you scoop Glynis Mortimer, you'll beat out several multi-nationals." Glynis Mortimer was, according to Ronnie, the world's foremost Executive Secretary, possessing lightning shorthand, a steel-trap mind, and exceptional skills in the arbitration of corporate politics. She could take dictation in French and German as well as in English, and she was conversant in Japanese to boot. She was also proficient in virtually all word-processing programs and accounting spreadsheets. Her former employers included the Chief Executive Officers of several different billion-dollar companies, and none of them had long survived her departure. Some had opted for early retirement. One had attempted suicide.

"I understand," said Gloria, "that you are accustomed to ruling vast corporate empires."

"I have worked for some large organizations, M'Lady."

"I am told that at your passing, strong men tremble, industries totter, and thousands of minions press their noses against grindstones."

"An overstatement, I'm afraid."

"What I'm getting at is that the employment I can offer you is rather lower key."

"I would find that appealing, Lady Gloria. The world has been too much with me, of late."

"Is that a quote?" Gloria asked sharply.

"A paraphrase, M'Lady. Wordsworth."

"Good," Gloria said, rather pleased with herself for catching it.

"I would enjoy a respite from the pressures of business," Glynis explained. "I am also seeking a change from what is, I believe, an excessively male-oriented realm."

"Don't you like men?" Gloria asked somewhat worriedly. "I do, you know. Rather."

"I like some men, M'Lady. My husband, Clyde, in particular."

"Oh, yes? What does Clyde do?"

"He's a potter, M'Lady. It was my wish to spend more time at home with him that led me to resign my previous employment."

"I see. Well, Glynis, the task at hand here is partly social, partly business, and partly catch as catch can. I'm making this big push to get everyone in the country reading, you see. Reading something, even if it's the wretched tabloids or beer labels."

"An admirable cause, Lady Gloria."

"Yes, well I have to do something admirable or my father will cut me off without a penny. But there's rather a lot to this literacy business, once you get involved. You wouldn't believe the number of committee meetings, for example."

"Indeed, M'Lady."

"And how long they go on! Really! Quite incredible! At any rate, I need someone to, ah, coordinate my various involvements in this area and stand in for me from time to time. As my representative."

"I see, M'Lady."

"There would be a fair bit of telephoning, a bit of letter writing. I expect half-days would be sufficient in the normal turn. Although some of these meetings do go on for a hundred years. I have a study off the hall where you could set yourself up. There's a desk. We'll put in a separate phone line if you like. I expect you'll want a computer. I'm told you're a whiz with them."

"Perhaps, M'Lady."

"Perhaps you're a whiz? Or perhaps you don't want one?"

"Perhaps I'll consider the position, M'Lady."

"If it's a matter of salary . . . "

"Salary is quite sufficient, Lady Gloria. I would simply want to confirm my suitability for the position."

"I'm sure you're quite suitable."

"Thank you, M'Lady. But if I might suggest, perhaps a trial period might be advisable."

"I see. For how long?"

"Two weeks, perhaps."

"Yes. Well. Do you think you could make it a month, Glynis? You see, that would take me through this party I've planned for a variety of literate people. That is, I'm having a number of people in, including one or two MP's. One of them is a Junior Minister at Education. I had planned to present the government with the gift of this, this thing. But now . . ." Lady Gloria stared with mounting dismay at the huge poster leaning against her wall. Its red letters vibrated aggressively at her. "God, what will I do? That was supposed to be the *raison d'être* for the whole occasion. But I can't give him this wretched thing. I'll look like a . . . like a . . ."

"Like the east end of a west-bound horse, M'Lady."

"Yes. Excuse me?"

"If I might suggest, Lady Gloria," Glynis continued smoothly, "you mentioned that the artist is famous?"

"Oh yes. He gets paid bundles of money for just throwing up on a canvas. You trip over his stuff in every drawing room in London."

"Well then, perhaps other artists might also be invited to contribute some original work. The theme being a utilitarian one to combat illiteracy. There are one or two of my husband's friends who might be persuaded. Your party could then be an occasion to display the art and perhaps offer it for sale, the proceeds going to, ah, one of your committees."

"Glynis! That's brilliant!"

"Thank you, M'Lady."

"Then you will take the job?"

"On a trial basis, yes."

"One month. Oh, yes! Oh, Glynis, you're a life saver! I'm so pleased!" And disregarding her hangover's sensitivity to sudden movements, Lady Gloria leaned over on the sofa and gave Glynis Mortimer a warm and honest hug, an impetuous but sincere gesture that made that formidable woman blush an unaccustomed shade of pink which went very well with her dark blue suit.

"If I might ask, Lady Gloria," Glynis said, regaining her composure and nodding over at the poster, "what happens when one calls that number, 944-READ?"

"I don't know, really. I think the artist just put it in as an example, you know. An example of a phone number."

CHAPTER THREE

"**B**EEEEEEEEEP!"

The answering machine on Janet Sorenson's home phone concluded its duty of playing back her messages with an imperious tone and then a series of officious little clicks and whirs as it rewound itself into readiness. The thin, harsh, mechanically flavored intonations of the recordings faded away, and the full, wet, warm ambience of night in Manoa Valley returned to her. Outside, water dripped from the eves onto the broad leaves of the crotons. In the distance, a single moped whined its way back and forth up one of the winding side streets on the valley wall. She stared at the dark blank of the open window in front of her and sighed.

Well, she had done it. The Seventh Annual Conference on Shamanistic Practice would be held in Honolulu at the Earl Court Resort in Waikiki in September. Confirming letters had been faxed from the committee in California. Authorized signatures would be exchanged in the mails. A local bank was arranging for transfer of funds to an escrow account. It was a done deal, and she had done it. The recorded messages, while tinged with understandable worry and concern, were nonetheless filled with gratitude and praise. The base deal she had negotiated was for seventy dollars per person per night for a minimum of a thousand people for four nights.

On top of that two hundred and eighty thousand dollars for room nights was another fifty thousand dollars for conference meals and convention services. Total cost: three hundred and thirty thousand, excluding what the attendees would spend themselves on food and beverage.

Janet smiled a wry smile. She supposed food and beverage must be where the hotel was planning to make their profit, since it wouldn't be hard to spend a hundred bucks a day on meals and drinks at the Earl Court. But Janet knew her fellow scholars. They were far more likely to be found in a nearby Pizza Hut than in the Earl Court's Zebra Room. Anthropologists, especially, would delight in ferreting out Honolulu's innumerable little ethnic restaurants. No, the Earl Court was going to take a bath. Negotiating with the General Manager had been ridiculously easy. Nothing like arranging a bride price in India, for example. She remembered assisting in the exchange of an ox, four saris, and three pots between a couple of peasant families in northern Bengal. That had taken weeks of ritualistic feint and bluff. Or the time she had driven a hard bargain with a tribe of African pigmies for an elephant's foot. She could have gotten a poison dart in her back as she walked away from that one. By comparison, dickering with Gordon Coburn was like offering a selection of lollipops to her three-year old nephew. Seventy a night was a steal. The cheapest rack rate at the Earl Court was a hundred and ninety. And last year, participants at the conference had paid eighty dollars per night for a much less luxurious hotel.

But they couldn't go back there, even if everyone was willing to pay twice as much. The previous year in California, one of the conference organizers had been foolish enough to invite the local Catholic ministry to send a representative to speak on the subject of exorcism. Word of this had filtered up to the very conservative local Bishop, who did not appreciate his men of the cloth being equated with Haitian witch doctors. In his view, the authority and respect due the Church were undermined when a bunch of agnostic, atheistic academics set about comparing holy rituals to those involving a severed chicken's head. The Catholic Church performed a great many wedding ceremonies in the city every year, and the Bishop let it be known that any hotel in his diocese that ever hosted such a crowd of devil-worshippers again would never, ever host another Catholic wedding reception again, so help him, Hail Mary Full of Grace!

This opposition very nearly scuttled the conference altogether. Long term planning rules the academic world, and six months notice is considered hardly any time at all. A change in venue to a wholly new city would have been impossible if Janet had not been able to secure such excellent terms at such a superior hotel. As it was, an urgent email blast with notice of the change was going out worldwide by the end of the week. As an enticement for the prospective participants, the email included a link to the Earl Court Waikiki website which was replete with photos of idyllic beaches and luxurious accommodations. The email also had a PDF attachment with a dour, typed list of numerous "serious" conferences that had been held at the Earl Court. This was for forwarding along to Deans and Department Chairs and other dubious parties.

The night tradewinds stirred the plumeria tree outside Janet's open window and wafted its voluptuous perfume through the screen. The plumeria tree was Janet's closest friend, and she was always gladdened when spring came round and her friend bedecked herself in a thousand, milk-white flowers. A Hawaii snowfall, she called it. The blossoms would last for weeks if no one picked them, each flower astonishingly perfect, intensely fragrant, velvet to the touch, with five, simple, broad petals that spiraled inward toward a delicate gold sunrise in the center.

"What do you think?" Janet asked aloud of her friend outside in the darkness. "Did I do good?" She breathed deeply, inhaling her friend's reply. It smelled wholly approving and supported by a bracing scent of rain coming down towards them from out of the valley. "How about her?" Janet inquired, referring to Carol Nickel, the hotel's blond Public Relations Director who had been assigned to help develop the list of "serious" conferences. The reply that drifted back through the window carried an odor from the litter box the neighbors kept outside for their cat. "That's what I think," Janet said. "What about him, though? So innocent. Like a kid in a sandbox. I hope I wasn't too hard on him, but heavens, he's the General Manager, he ought to know what he's doing." The effulgent opinion of a thousand plumeria blossoms returned. "He can't possibly be as young as he looks, can he?"

Like most anthropologists or anyone who spends long periods of time in lonely, isolated pursuits, Janet was quite comfortable talking with herself or with trees or with walls or rocks, and she would have been happy to continue this conversation. But now a sudden, gusting rain shower quelled her friend's loquacious fragrance, and Janet turned away from the open window to eye a stack of undergraduate papers on her desk. They had to be graded before the next day. She sighed again and cast a jaundiced eye over the confines of her tiny, one-room cottage. Even for an experienced anthropologist, it was quite a culture shock to go from the chandeliered splendor of the Earl Court in Waikiki to the academic digs of a professor in Manoa Valley. Hawaii's absurd housing costs meant that even a tenured faculty member like herself with an international reputation and a respectable salary could never really afford to buy a home. Not unless she finally married someone so they could put two incomes against a mortgage. Instead, she paid an exorbitant rent for this tiny cottage, which was about the size of a one-car garage and possessed a similar degree of architectural nicety. Aside from the plumeria tree and a small private yard, the cottage's chief asset was proximity to the university and a location within the nurturing green clefts of Manoa. Janet pondered the difference between the genteel, tropical dishabille of her lifestyle up in the valley and the glitz and opulence that surrounded Gordon Coburn down in Waikiki. The physical distance was only two or three miles. She wondered briefly how the General Manager of the Earl Court spent the late hours of his Tuesday evening.

In fact, the General Manager of the Earl Court had himself spent the previous few hours in unaccustomed self-reflection, feeling alternately lonely and lustful. What he needed most, he thought occasionally, were some good friends he could talk to, preferably ones not in the hotel business. But the Earl Court chain made a practice of transferring their rising young executives from one resort to another every year or two which made it hard to cultivate lasting friendships. Gordon didn't have any friends in Hawaii, just employees. He didn't even have a plumeria tree to talk to. The pressures of his job were intense, and there was no way to really speak his mind to anyone and let off steam, so every once in awhile, he did something kind of stupid. He knew it was kind of stupid. Quite risky, in fact. But it was also thrilling and very pleasurable.

So could a trained anthropologist like Janet Sorenson or Kip Stallybrass have observed Gordon at that moment, they would have recognized that he was engaged in a luxury hotel manager's version of ngayapping. Ominous fortune cookies forgotten, Gordon was striding down the corridor of the twenty-first floor of the Earl Court Waikiki, a smile on his lips, a condom in his pocket, and jingling his General Manager's universal pass key along with his change.

———

In Bangladesh, a ferry capsized, killing hundreds. In the Amazon, an area of rainforest the size of Rhode Island was destroyed. Coups threatened the governments of five African countries and one in Central Europe. A new Middle East peace mission was underway, and in a Winn-Dixie super-market near Orlando, Florida, Beth Phillips stood in line at the checkout counter, riveted by the news. The tabloids at the supermarket checkout line carried none of that news, of course. What sent their headlines screaming was the extra-marital affair of a famous rock star. One tabloid actually had a picture of the star in her limousine, kissing a young man who was not her husband. The camera had caught them with their lips still pressed together but with their eyes rolling away from each other out towards their avid public. They stared out at Beth, standing in line there at Winn-Dixie supermarket, with a mixture of fear and loathing.

Beth stared back at them with the same expression. Every time she shopped, she was both disgusted and astounded at herself for being gripped by these lurid front pages. Why did she want to know about this celebrity's diet and that one's cancer and another's abused wife/child/lover? She didn't want to know about them. She didn't want to care about them. All these overripe people in sequined dresses, both men and women. They were always in agony, suffering a tragedy, fighting for custody, battling a disease. Why was she compelled to participate in their squalid discoveries simply because she needed to buy some bread and soup?

Still, trying to look away from them was like ripping off an adhesive bandage. With a stern act of will, Beth bent her gaze downward to study the sheaf of coupons she clutched in her right hand. She and her husband were retired on a disability pension. They had very little money but a great deal of time on their hands, and Beth purchased virtually nothing that wasn't discounted or on sale. Nothing, that is, except medicine and doctor's treatments. Those were never on sale, but they nonetheless required that she clip the coupons of Medicare and Medicaid, the multiple forms for government and insurance reimbursements that were so tortuously conceived and confusingly written that they frequently reduced her to silent tears out in the kitchen. "What are you doing?" Frank would call from the TV room. "Clipping coupons," she would call back. "Well, take a break and come help me play Jeopardy." And wiping away tears, she would come out to him with the news that Jell-O was on sale at Winn-Dixie, and this Sunday, she would make him his favorite lime and carrot Jell-O. And Frank would look up from his wheelchair, his sweet, wrinkled head bald as a baby's and smile such a happy, grateful smile, that she couldn't help but bend down and kiss him just as tenderly and with the same devotion as on their wedding day fifty-nine years ago. Frank didn't know that the real surprise she had in store, the real reason she clipped coupons so carefully, was that she was saving for their sixtieth wedding anniversary present in September. She was going to take them both on a vacation to Hawaii. Frank had served there during the war, and he hadn't been back since. She imagined the incredibly sweet, happy smile on his face when she finally told him about the trip, and she couldn't help but look back up while standing in the line there at Winn-Dixie, smiling to herself.

And was slapped again with the loathing, loathsome stare of the rock star and her lover. It so infuriated her, she rattled her shopping cart and sniffed audibly. Who was responsible for this imposition, this nastiness? She resolved to write a letter to the manager about it.

Meanwhile, a more directly responsible party than the store manager, namely Mislov Rapolovitch, drank ouzo in a booth in a scrofulous Greek restaurant on the west side of Manhattan. He was waiting for another responsible party, an expatriate Australian who worked for the tabloid that had purchased his photograph of the rock star and her lover. Greek was one of Mislov's languages, and he liked to arrange rendezvous with his clients at this restaurant. A sudden, explosive exchange with one of the sullen waiters in the incomprehensible Greek tongue helped to place a prospective buyer at a disadvantage. It made him nervous, suspicious, and all the more in awe of Mislov and his remarkable ability to get the shots that no one else seemed to be able to get. Mislov was one of the few completely free-lance paparazzi in the world. He sold to all the rival tabloids. Often he would send defaced, unreproducible, black and white Xeroxes of his shots to several of the tabloids at the same time and force them to submit telephone bids if they wished to publish the

scandalous original. He would receive the bids at a specified hour at an anonymous phone booth and call the winner
back with the arrangements for the exchange. He always
demanded payment in cash.

Only a rare talent could enforce such humiliating procedures upon the leaders of an industry who were themselves
experts in humiliation. But quite simply no one else captured the kind of material that Mislov did. He was skilled,
fearless, totally without scruple, and most importantly, he
was eerily prescient. Other paparazzi had to chase after their
quarry. Mislov seemed able to position himself so his victims
came to him.

Now he sat, still as a crow on a branch, and waited for
the editor to appear. The man had requested this meeting
on his own initiative, which was rather unusual. Mislov supposed he wanted to propose an assignment. That would be
fruitless, of course. Mislov never worked on assignment. He
never worked for anyone under any circumstances. He only
hunted.

His Nikon was set out on the stained Formica table
beside his glass of ouzo, and this was another of his exercises
in one-upmanship. He had fitted the camera with a zoom
telephoto and positioned it so the barrel of the lens pointed
directly at whoever would sit down opposite him. The big
glass eye of the lens would stare at the Aussie editor while
Mislov stroked and petted its black barrel. Occasionally he
would twist the knurled ring that made the lens expand,
making it longer, bigger, the glass eye pushing forward at
the man as Mislov fixed him with his obsidian gaze and
pursed his rosebud red lips. If Mislov knew the insecure,
homophobic mind of the Aussie, the man wouldn't last five

minutes in the booth. That would teach the fool to try and offer him a job.

Mislov smiled at his Nikon. He was bisexual himself in the sense that that he found the prospect of physical intimacy with anyone of either gender equally repugnant. He understood the sexual fears of others very well. He knew what his camera looked like and what it represented to most people. It was his lance, his sword, his automatic assault weapon, and it looked phallic like all those other male toys. But Mislov also knew that his camera's real nature was female. In his hands, she was a weapon, but she didn't spew projectiles out. She sucked her victims in. She magically inhaled their essence and then in a fearful fecundity, multiplied that essence a thousand, a million, a billionfold, making her victims permanently her creatures, imprisoning a certain moment of their time for all time. The still camera and her many sisters in video and motion pictures were the most powerful weapons in the world, and they were female.

"Mislov! You Grim Reaper, what are you drinking?" The Australian editor, Garth MacLeod, slid into the booth opposite Mislov and his camera. He was a slovenly, paunchy man with watery blue eyes and a nose that looked more like an internal than an external organ. Most of its capillaries had burst from either hard liquor or angry fists.

"Ouzo," said Mislov.

MacLeod made a face. "I'll have a beer."

Mislov made no response to this, so after a moment, MacLeod twisted around in the booth and shouted in his harshest Australian, "Aye! Bring us a beer, will ya!" He twisted back and regarded the black clad photographer with wary amusement. "Always a pleasure to see you, Mislov," he said, his smile exposing a set of nicotine-stained false teeth.

"Why?" Mislov asked, starting to fondle his camera.

"Can't say, really. Same pleasure I get walking by a graveyard, I suppose. Makes me realize I'm not under yet. Fella gets depressed, you know, from time to time. Specially in our line of work. All these human foibles."

A waiter appeared, looking like an assassin and bearing an American beer. MacLeod made a face at it. "That's not beer. That's weasel piss."

Mislov ripped out a sudden, hostile stream of guttural Greek syllables. The waiter darkened and responded in kind. Mislov came back at him again. It was like the beginning of an Adriatic knife fight.

"Never mind! Leave it! It'll do!" MacLeod grabbed the beer and splashed it into the glass, getting mostly head. "There, that's the problem, you see. All gas, American beer. Makes you fart like a teakettle. Never mind. Cheers." MacLeod hoisted his glass, knocked back half of it, and wiped off the foam with the back of his wrist. The waiter returned to the bar, muttering dark imprecations.

"Yes, whenever I'm feeling blue, I think of you," MacLeod went on. "Makes me realize what a bloody cheery bugger I am."

Mislov pursed his lips and twisted the knurled ring of his telephoto lens. "Is that why you wished to see me?" he asked.

MacLeod winked at him. "Your Nikon's getting a hard-on, Mislov," he said and took another sip of beer. Mislov's eyes narrowed in irritation. "Actually," MacLeod went on, "I want to do you a favor."

"I don't want favors," Mislov snapped.

"Oh, yes you do.

"I don't accept them."

"You'll take this one. I'll scratch your back. You scratch mine."

"I don't scratch backs."

MacLeod leaned across the table and affected a terrified, conspiratorial tone. "She's out to get you."

"Who?"

MacLeod leaned back in the booth. "The little tart you shot in the limo with her toyboy. The one we put on the front page this week. She has let it be known to certain of her admiring fans that when next they see you on the street, they are to break your camera along with your legs, arms and other extremities."

Mislov smiled in contempt. "I do not worry about those kinds of threats."

"Yes, I know. Black belt in karate and all that. Although I always thought for you it might be just a fashion accessory. Think though, Mislov, just how many fans she has. And how many of them wear barbed wire earrings and swastika nose studs. Are you really up to dealing with them in packs of ten or twenty?"

Mislov remained expressionless. MacLeod shrugged and finished off his beer.

"Well, a word in your ear is all. If I were you, I'd see what the hunting is like in Europe or the West Coast for a while. Till her ardor cools. And if you come up with anything good, Mislov, I hope you'll give us first go at it.

———

WHAT DOES IT MEAN?
WHAT DOES IT MEAN?
IF YOU CAN'T READ IT,
YOU CAN'T BE SEEN!
I was trapped in a page cage
Stuck at the cross word
Minimum wage rage
When the Big Boss heard
I was just fakin it
Couldn't read the recipe
Never be a makin it
If you got illiteracy.
TRY AND FIND A JOB WHEN YOU
CAN'T READ THE WANT ADS!
World's not considerate,
When you're illiterate.

The huge speakers in Lady Gloria's flat shook and trembled, the sub woofers laboring like galley slaves under the lash of the rap beat.

So if you can't read,
Listen to me,
Call nine four four,
Seven three two three.

Severed from any possibility of conversation by lyrics seemingly enunciated by a pneumatic drill, Lady Gloria's guests wandered between the drinks and the canapés while wearing the pained smiles of martyrs. A few demonstrated the sycophantic raptures the upper classes frequently exhibit for lower class culture by huddling around the throbbing speakers, bobbing and jiving and risking permanent hearing loss.

> *Nine four four*
> *Seven three two three*
> *That's the ticket*
> *To literacy!*
> NINE FOUR FOUR, READ!
> NINE FOUR FOUR, READ!
> NINE FOUR FOUR, READ!

And silence. The speakers emitted an electronic pop followed by a faint hiss. The deafened guests cast appreciative glances at one another, whether for the rap or for the silence being an open question. There was a pattering of applause.

"And so we learn our ABC's," said Ronnie, emerging with a fresh vodka gimlet from the furthest corner away from the speakers. The tinkle of conversation and glassware picked up around the room.

"What did you think?" Gloria asked.

"I think the Americans are far ahead of us in illiteracy, as in so many other things," Ronnie said. "The real question, however, is what the Minister thinks. Eh, Tom?"

"Yes, what does the Minister think?" Gloria asked.

Thomas Leary, Junior Minister at Education, grinned and thumped the side of his curly brown head with the heel of his hand like someone with swimmer's ear. "The Minister feels like he's under water," he said. "I think I may be deaf for life."

"Do you think it's of any use, though?" Gloria asked.

"Absolutely. Personally, I find it bloody awful, but I also think it's exactly the kind of thing we need. I'd like to get it on the air."

"DT would be thrilled."

"Deidre?"

"DT, the rapper. The singer." Gloria nodded over at the speakers where a black man in an orange suit was accepting admiring comment from several of the guests.

"Right," Thomas Leary said. "But what happens if you actually . . . ?" He paused and looked at her thoughtfully.

"Yes?" Gloria said brightly.

"Lady Gloria, is there a place I could make a call?"

"Of course. Try the study. Off the hall."

"Thank you. Excuse me, won't you."

Pulling out his cell phone, the Junior Minister disappeared down the hallway. Gloria and Ronnie watched him depart.

"He's got a cute bum, too, don't you think?" Ronnie asked.

"Behave yourself, Ronnie," Gloria said. "Save that kind of talk for your constituency."

"Gloria, dearest!" Lady Hortense Crawley-Smith swooped down on them and fixed Gloria with rapturous, devouring eyes. "I simply must have that vase!"

"Well, put up a jolly good bid, then, Hortense. All for a good cause, you know."

Lady Hortense executed one of her odd, discomfiting, long silent pauses, staring at Gloria as a glutton might stare at a chocolate cake. "I love your hair," she said at last with grand irrelevance and swooped away. The image of her horsy, hungry face with its rapturous, devouring eyes seemed to hang in the air after she left. Gloria felt a delicate shudder crawl along her shoulder blades. She had asked Lady Hortense to the party because Lady Hortense was the sort who really might put up a jolly good bid for something. Gloria certainly felt no need to repay a social obligation. Being duped into spending an evening with the woman's coven did not fill her with the urge to reciprocate. She observed Lady Hortense filling out the silent auction card by the vase and rather wished she had left the unsettling Viscountess off the list. The vase that she so desired was the donation from Glynis' husband, Clyde, who had created the piece specifically for the occasion, but who had chosen not to attend the party himself. Gloria still hadn't met Clyde, and she was beginning to think of him as something of a mystery man. The vase he had fashioned was really more of a wide shallow bowl that glistened with a rich, mottled glaze. It was supported by a tripod, each leg being in the shape of the letter "R." Glynis had explained that the base represented "The Three R's" of "Readin, 'Ritin, and 'Rithmatic," and from this Gloria had deduced that Clyde must be American. The wide shallow bowl itself presumably represented the welcoming receptacle that literacy provided for knowledge. Either that or the hollow emptiness of it all. Gloria wasn't sure. She briefly imagined the uses that Lady Hortense and her coven of fellow witches might have for that wide shallow bowl on its tripod stand, but this train of thought proved quite unsettling indeed, so Gloria quickly bustled off to replace the deadening background silence with some new music.

The party seemed to be going well. A number of the silent auction envelopes were piling up on the coffee table. The wall hanging by a well-known weaver appeared to be popular. It incorporated yarn, twigs, and half-torn pages from Shakespeare and various cookbooks. A handsomely illustrated rebus, suitably proportioned for reproduction as a bumper sticker, was also a big hit. The drawings from left to right were that of a weeping eye, a heart, and a book, and below them the ubiquitous phone number, 944-7323.

Gloria smiled with parental satisfaction at the little pile of auction cards. The proceeds were going to the UNICEF worldwide literacy program. With typical business acumen, Glynis had pointed out that continents like Africa and Latin America offered vast, untapped markets for literacy investments, whereas in England the literacy rate was exceeded only by one hundred percent achievements in places like Luxembourg and so offered only low, marginal rates of return. Gloria hoped that they might raise a total of several thousand pounds for UNICEF, which combined with the constellation of political, social, and artistic celebrities she had assembled for this affair was almost certain to gain her an approving mention in one or another of the columns that her father liked to read. This was all quite fine, of course, but it was really only Gloria's secondary objective. The primary purpose for this party, as far as she was concerned, was a closer acquaintance between herself and the curly-headed, broken-nosed Junior Minister at Education with the charming grin. Discreet inquiry had produced the information that the Minister was currently estranged from his wife and living in a small flat in the city. That was when Gloria's party plans had really swung into high gear. She was shuffling happily through her collection of CDs, looking for something appropriate to follow the "Literacy Rap," when none other than Tom Leary, the handsome Junior Minister at Education, reappeared.

"Well, that's bloody brilliant of you," he said. "A literacy hotline. That's why this phone number is plastered all over everything. But tell me, what was the stuff about schnauzers and parakeets?"

"On the recording? Yes, isn't it clever. I have to confess it was Glynis' notion. The number, 944-READ, it's actually the number for a pet shop, you see. It's run by this quaint, dear, old couple who as luck would have it simply love to read. Our artists – well, one of them really – had already used that number in his work, so Glynis called it and struck up an acquaintance with the woman who answered, and then we both went over and invited her and her husband out to tea. Glynis explained how this really might be quite a good thing for their business. Sort of a traffic builder. So at the moment we have this combination pet shop and literacy hot-line. Eventually, we hope to staff it with live volunteers."

Tom Leary stared at her, grinning an exceptionally charm-ing grin.

"Oh," Gloria added, "we've also taken on trying to find homes for some schnauzer puppies. Would you like one?"

Tom Leary continued grinning, and after a moment, an irrepressible laugh started to burble up.

"Well, I think it really might work," Gloria said defen-sively. "Illiterate people are easily embarrassed and intimi-dated, you know, and cute, furry little animals help one to get over that. And most people do understand phone numbers even if they can't read."

"I agree. I think it will work. I think it's charming, brilliant, wonderful, and perfectly bizarre. I'm enchanted, frankly."

"Oh. Well. Thank you."

"But if you are able to plaster this number everywhere–"

"Glynis says we'll put in a call center."

"Right. Well, it will be a marvelous contribution!"

"Well, not that significant, probably. Not compared to what you do."

"I disagree."

"I saw your speech, you know, in the House several weeks ago. Now, that's a contribution."

"To Global Warming? Lot of hot air, probably."

"No! It was quite impressive. The Members appeared impressed, too. At least some of them. It was rather late and a few of the back benchers, like Ronnie I must tell you, appeared to be asleep."

"Really? He gave me an excellent summary and response after."

"Well, he was lying virtually prone with his head against the backrest."

"Oh that's what you have to do on the back benches sometimes. There are little speakers embedded in the backrests, you see, so you can hear the actual speech over all the hubbub."

"Oh," Gloria said, somewhat abashed.

"Lots of people think we're dozing off when they first see us. Where were you? In the Public Gallery?"

"Distinguished Strangers. Up above, though, looking down on your head."

"Well, if you'd like to come again sometime, I might be able to slip you into another gallery down below. It's on the same level with us. Gives you a different point of view."

"That would be wonderful!" Gloria said, trying not to gush. To cover her delight, she popped in a CD at random. It proved to be a jazzy, upbeat version of Bach's "Ode to Joy," which rather embarrassingly replicated her feelings. She quickly dialed down the volume. "When will you be speaking next?" she asked.

"Not for awhile, I'm afraid. But don't come just for that for heaven's sake."

"Let go! Unhand me! You vile shrew!"

Fairly spitting with aristocratic rage, Lady Hortense Crawley-Smith frog-marched up to them. Behind her, forcing the march and twisting the Lady's wrist into a discreet but painful armlock was a stern and commanding Glynis Mortimer.

"Release me!" Lady Hortense hissed *sotto voce*. "Gloria! What's this ridiculous–? Unh!"

Glynis gave Lady Hortense's wrist an extra twist, causing her to issue forth a distinctly unladylike grunt of pain.

"Whatever is the matter? Gloria asked, glancing about the room and smiling fiercely at her curious guests. She reached down quickly and dialed the volume back up on "Ode to Joy."

"I observed this woman, Lady Gloria, going through your things in the bedroom. She has made off with your silver haribrush and manicure set."

"Nonsense!" said Lady Hortense. "What would I need with more silver?"

"Yes, Glynis, what would Lady Hortense need with more silver?"

"I do not know, Lady Gloria. Nonetheless, it is there now in her handbag." Glynis nodded down towards a capacious black leather bag hanging from a strap on Lady Hortense's shoulder.

"Is it, Hortense?"

"Certainly not!"

"It certainly is," said Glynis.

"What do you propose then? To search me? Walk me through a metal detector? Is this how you treat guests, Gloria? Like Heathrow security? Who *is* this woman?"

"Glynis is my literacy assistant."

"I expect you need one, to assist in a reading of basic manners. But why then is this, this librarian assaulting me?"

Gloria glanced around again at her guests, many of whom were sidling closer and craning their heads in an attempt to overhear this conversation through the crashing, inspirational harmonies of "Ode to Joy."

Lady Hortense stiffened in a full flowering of imperious, aristocratic hauteur. "Take your hands off me!" she said, biting out each word while staring directly at Gloria in front of her. Gloria hesitated and glanced over at Tom Leary, who also hesitated, and then nodded slightly.

"Glynis, perhaps you'd better," Gloria said.

Glynis Mortimer gave Gloria a cool look through her steel gray glasses. "As you wish, Lady Gloria," she said, and released Lady Hortense's arm. But in the same instant, she reached quickly over, snatched the black handbag, unzipped it and upended it in one smooth motion. Out spilled wallet, pen, cell phone, coins, compact, two twisted roots, vials of pills, and a silver hairbrush and manicure set. The whole party stared down at the brush, gleaming there on the carpet, long strands of Gloria's lovely auburn hair clinging to its bristles.

"Well, Hortense," said Gloria. "What do you have to say for yourself?"

"I don't want your ugly brush!" Lady Hortense snarled. Reaching down, she snatched it up and waved it back and forth so the auburn strands of Gloria's orphaned hair floated off through the room. "I want your hair!" And then she cackled, cackled as wildly as any witch in her coven, staring at Gloria with her ravenous, devouring eyes until Tom Leary grabbed her wrist so tightly her grip on the brush loosened and he could firmly withdraw it from her grasp.

———

For Kip, who was penetrating ever deeper into the equatorial jungles of Borneo, curious moments and strange tableaux were no longer unexpected. They simply passed by, blandly observed and quickly forgotten, like colorful floats in a parade with some unexplained theme. Immersed as he was in a sea of unaccustomed customs, only a few scenes had such brilliant hues and were so oddly freighted with meaning as to imprint themselves on his memory. He did recall a tattooed Iban standing in the prow of a narrow, wooden longboat. Iridescent dragonflies were escorting them up the river that day. Blue green gemstones with diamond wafer wings, they darted to and fro or hovered dead still just ahead of the boat. Suddenly, with reflexes too fast to calculate, the Iban actually plucked one out of the air. He smiled down at it for one humming, sunstruck instant and then popped it in his mouth, crunching down on that exoskeleton of light and air with evident relish.

And the fruit bats made an indelible impression. Every evening, black squadrons of them would stolidly plow through the sunset sky on their way from their caves to feed. They flew as machines might fly, not riding up and down the air currents as birds do, but instead trudging through the atmosphere at a constant altitude with heavy, unvarying wing beats. They looked like construction paper cutouts against the rose and mauve clouds. It wasn't until he had watched them make their twilight journey a dozen times that he realized the reason the scene gripped him so was that it looked exactly like the movie scene in *The Wizard of Oz* when the Wicked Witch of the West sends her bat-warriors off in pursuit of Dorothy, and swarms of them go flying out of the castle across a Technicolor backdrop.

And there was the night he and his guide started upriver at three in the morning. They did it in order to take advantage of the tidal bore, the sudden, powerful current sweeping in from the ocean that makes Borneo rivers run in opposite directions every twelve hours. It was pitch dark, and the tide was running so strongly, they had no need to paddle, only to steer, when suddenly there loomed before them a huge, silvery, glowing ghost. It was a tree, which on that night was the chosen rendezvous for some kind of firefly. The swarm had covered every leaf and branch and scrap of bark so the whole organism glowed pale silver. It clung to the edge of the bank like the ghost of all the felled trees in all the logged rainforests, watching Kip glide past in the little longboat as the tide swept him up into the dark unknown.

But of all the strange sights he had seen, none struck him as so odd, so peculiar, so fundamentally other, as the little, ten-year-old boy who sat across from him now. This longhouse was the most remote and isolated Iban community he had yet visited, reachable only by a three day longboat journey plus a difficult, four day hike up and down the steep jungle hillsides. The last hillside was the most difficult of all as it was crisscrossed top to bottom with a latticework of wet, slippery roots that seemed to nourish no tree but only served to trip and to trap and to break the ankles of whoever might try and climb the hill. On the apex of this hill stood the longhouse, and within the longhouse lived this strange little boy. Kip was certain that he was the first white man the boy had ever seen, and perhaps that was why the boy bothered to notice him.

Chronologically, the boy was only ten, but you knew as soon as you looked at him that he was at least a thousand years old. His body had none of the evolving softness of childhood. His muscles were cut and defined and hardened like those of a highly trained athlete in middle age. But it was his face that was really the clue. Worldly, cynical, bored, powerful, it was the face of someone who had traveled further than all the astronauts, received more adulation than all the movie stars, had plumbed deeper mysteries than all the Einsteins. Beneath a cap of jet-black hair, this face of a ten-year old innocent deep in the jungle fastness of Borneo was the most sophisticated face Kip had ever seen.

As a professional anthropologist with an interest in shamanism, he had read of a number of cases where an individual in some remote corner of the world was reputed to have supernatural powers. It always seemed to occur back of beyond somewhere in rural Ireland, or upper Amazon, or northern Tibet. Never in Scarsdale or Evanston or Pasadena. As a consequence, the powers of these individuals were hardly ever subjected to rigorous scientific analysis. On the few occasions when this had been possible, the powers in question seemed to shrivel up or simply disappear. Like most western believers in the scientific method, Kip figured this was because such powers never really existed. All the anecdotal evidence of their existence could eventually be explained away through references to swamp gas or mass hysteria or simple charlatanism. Upon the conclusion of all this comforting debunking, however, there still remained a smidgen of doubt. What if these supernatural powers were like the sub-atomic particles of modern physics, incapable of being observed without being affected? What if the very nature of modern civilization with its hyperactivity and electronic media were inimical to these powers, suppressing them somehow or causing them to suppress themselves? What if the individuals who really had such powers simply didn't want to be noticed? What if they had more important things to do? What if they preferred surfing on quarks and neutrinos or inhabiting the bodies of dolphins and sequoias or time traveling or philosophizing with beings of a fifth dimension or any of an infinity of other options available to them? What if they preferred those things to appearing in clumsy laboratories or on afternoon talk shows? Wouldn't such individuals naturally flourish in places like northern Tibet and central Borneo? Besides, most of the people who did become famous for supernatural powers did so because they were healers. They cured the sick, so people came from all over, and so naturally the healers became famous. What about certain beings who didn't care about being healers? Who couldn't be bothered? Like this little boy, for example. He didn't look like a healer. He looked like an emperor.

Kip couldn't explain why he was so certain of the powers of this tiny, half naked being that suddenly confronted him on the blond rattan mats in the lazy afternoon sunlight, surrounded by the gentle, murmuring life in the longhouse. In that moment, he just was certain. Absolutely certain. Indeed, the boy was such a powerful presence, Kip didn't understand why all the other Ibans didn't stop whatever they were doing to turn and stare at him. Perhaps they had grown accustomed to his presence over the years as he was growing up. The dull film of familiarity could blind people to almost any wonder. Villagers living all their lives beneath Mount

Vesuvius didn't pay much attention to that, either. Or perhaps the little boy didn't want to be bothered by the other Ibans in the longhouse and so screened himself off from their notice somehow. At the moment, he did seem mildly interested in Kip and in Kip's awareness of him. Not, Kip felt certain, because of any exceptional qualities he himself possessed. It was just that Kip was the first person the boy had come in contact with who had flown in airplanes, traveled in elevators, walked through museums, and had read many books. Kip had wider points of reference than anyone who had ever seen the boy before, and so Kip was better able to apprehend the phenomenon, in the precise sense of the word, of the boy's existence. The boy found this mildly interesting. And so he was reading Kip's mind.

Kip could feel him in there, paging through his memory file, and there was nothing he could do about it. It was a realization at once so alarming and so enfeebling, it left him motionless, a helpless spectator of himself. Here he was, an emissary of the all-powerful western culture, one of the culminating products of the civilization that created skyscrapers and libraries and moonwalks, one of the educated elite who possessed a historical perspective of dozens of other civilizations extending over dozens of millennia, one of the winners in the human race, a supremely confident, rational and rationalizing, walking success story. He, Kip Stallybrass, Ph.D., had for months favored these primitive jungle people with his academic attentions, observing and cataloging their most sacred beliefs and foibles in his anthropological bestiary, and now deep in their furthest, most remote and backward corner, he suddenly discovered that in addition to his benign and godly role, he was also playing the part of a cowed puppy before the kennel master. Or perhaps even more accurately, that of a fly in the hands of a boy intent on sport.

And in one way at least, this boy was a typical, prepubescent ten-year old, because what seemed to interest him the most was sex. He rapidly tossed aside Kip's memories of dragonflies and fruit bats and went looking for the good stuff. Unfortunately for them both, however, Kip's sex life had been nothing but an arid desert littered with an occasional car wreck for months. Sitting there on the rattan mats in the sunlight, feeling the boy leaf through his few, excruciating moments of sexual self-awareness, Kip could see that worldly, cynical, infantile face grow progressively more disgusted and more contemptuously amused.

There Kip was, waking up that morning after his opportunity to go ngayapping with the beautiful Iban widow, feeling sticky, and realizing that he hadn't really taken the opportunity to go ngyapping the night before, he had just fallen asleep and dreamed about it. And now there he was surrounded by spectators in the Kanowit longhouse an instant after whipping his own privates with bamboo, howling in pain and dropping his sarong down around his ankles. And there he was, waddling like a duck through the hotel lobby in Kuala Lumpur, and lying spread-eagled in bed with the talcum powder.

The most humiliating, ignominious, god-awful moments of his time in the country were being thumbed through and snickered over by a telepathic, ten-year old resident of it. It was too awful, too degrading. How could anyone so knowing and so powerful be so intrusive? So wantonly, cruelly insensitive? Kip wouldn't do anything like this, would he? Or had he? Were his anthropological investigations really any different? Did the Ibans he was studying think of him as some imperious, dirty-minded being with godlike powers? He suddenly felt flooded with guilt. The little boy smiled and burrowed deeper.

In desperation, Kip threw his mind back to Minnesota, to that last night with Barbara and that last time they made love in the gray, half-light of dawn. That moment, at least, had been honest and passionate and consummated. He thought of it, clung to it, and was rewarded with a fleeting look of surprise and grudging admiration that passed over the little boy's jaded, contemptuous countenance.

And suddenly everything was ordinary again. Kip was just a guy, sitting on a mat in the sunlight, listening to other people talking. He smelled the wet charcoal smell from the cooking fires and heard the semi-wild pigs grunting and squealing under the longhouse. That strange little boy must have gotten up and left when he wasn't looking. The weather seemed pleasant, not too hot. Later, they all went down to the stream to bathe. That night, he made some desultory conversation with his hosts, didn't bother to record anything or take any notes, strung up his mosquito net early, crawled inside, and slept a blank, dreamless sleep.

CHAPTER FOUR

"F.I.T." is a travel industry term that refers to the "Free, Independent Traveler." Individuals who merit this euphoric designation are the most desired of all guests because what is really meant by "Free, Independent Traveler" is someone who pays full rate. The "Free, Independent Traveler" is affiliated with no group and, as a consequence, receives no group discount. After all, freedom and independence always come at a price.

It was the pursuit of the free-spirited, free-spending F.I.T. that saw Carol Nickle up at seven a.m. one morning, escorting a group of California travel agents along the fourteenth floor corridor of the Earl Court Waikiki. Mostly women, these were all top-producing travel agents who collectively sent thousands of F.I.T.'s vacationing on their merry way every year. It was critical to the continued success of the Earl Court that travel agents like these pass along favorable impressions of the hotel to their clients, so it was a regular part of Carol's job to take visiting agents on familiarization or "Fam" tours of the property. The early morning hour of this tour was only partly due to diligence. The travel agents had just arrived the night before and were operating with a two-hour jet lag. It was like nine in the morning for them, and Carol had been required to meet them for breakfast at six a.m., her time. Being chipper and well turned out at ungodly hours was an important part of her job, and she was generally able to create the impression of fresh, eager intelligence while really half asleep. On a Fam tour, her duties were similar to those of Vanna White on "Wheel of Fortune." She dressed great, walked good, and threw open a succession of doors. The hardest part was staring at all those beds in the various rooms and suites and thinking of how she could still be asleep back in her own.

"What I'm going to show you next is one of our Mauka View rooms," she said. "'Mauka,' means 'mountain' in Hawaiian, and these have mountain views. I know everyone always requests the ocean view, but I think the mountain view is really more interesting."

"You don't get the sunset, though," said one hard-faced old pro. Carol had privately dubbed this woman "The Inspector General." At breakfast, "The Inspector" had noted an incorrect placement of silverware by her fruit compote. The way her eyes had widened and then narrowed at this *faux pas* made it clear that the Earl Court was going to have to scramble to get her recommendation.

"That's right, no sunset," Carol said. "But once the sun goes down, you do get the city lights, and that's quite romantic." Carol gave a perfunctory rap on the door of Room 1410, used her pass key to open it, and stood aside so the travel agents could file in.

"Oops!"

"My God!"

"Wow!"

This was not the usual response to the Mauka View. Carol turned to look inside. A tight jam at the door made it difficult as some of the women in the front of the group seemed to be backpedaling while the women at the back strained forward to see. A gap opened suddenly, and Carol saw the cause of all the effusive comment. It was Gordon Coburn, General Manager of the Earl Court Waikiki, standing stark naked and open-mouthed in the center of the room and demonstrating to the travel agents by means of an impressive erection just how romantic the Mauka View could be.

"Wow!" the Inspector General said again.

Carol heard a shriek and saw a naked blur moving in the direction of the bathroom. It looked like one of the women who worked at the Concierge Desk. Gordon's eyes met Carol's for an instant, and then he too turned and fled toward the bathroom. The rest of the travel agents spilled back out into the corridor, and Carol slammed shut the door to room 1410.

A few minutes later, Gail Takahashi, Gordon's secretary, received a brusque phone call from her boss, interrupting her early morning, coffee-and-Danish chat with Howie Berg, the Group Sales Director.

"Gail! What's on my calendar this morning?"

"Well, you've got a seven-thirty with Howie. He's here now."

"Cancel that," Gordon barked. "What else?"

"Ah, there's an eight-thirty with the attorneys about that lawsuit, a nine-thirty conference call with Suzuki-san and the interior designers in L.A., a ten-thirty with Christine Larren and her son. You've got lunch with Carol Nickle and a group of travel agents from Orange County—"

"Cancel that. I won't make that. Tell Howie to take them to lunch. I have to do the rest, though. I'll be in by eight-thirty."

Gordon hung up abruptly without a goodbye, an impoliteness that was quite unlike him. Gail raised her eyebrows a millimeter above the large, plastic frames of her glasses and glanced over at Howie who was blowing heavily into his coffee cup. Gail and Howie were old-timers at the Earl Court. Both had started when the hotel had opened in the nineties, and they had seen three General Managers come and go before Gordon. Gail was the cool, efficient gatekeeper. Howie was the ruddy, gregarious salesman. After fifteen years of shared middle age in the hospitality trenches, they understood each other pretty well. Howie enjoyed teasing Gail and trying to uncover management secrets. Gail enjoyed being teased and pretending to know more than she did.

Howie puffed again at his coffee, wreathing his pleasant, baggy face in clouds of steam. "What's up?" he asked.

"Gordon can't make it, Howie," Gail said.

"What?" Howie stopped blowing into his coffee. "This seven-thirty thing was his idea."

"I know."

"My God, I've got a forty-five minute commute. Can't he even take an elevator on time? He's worse than my ex-wife."

"Something came up."

"What? Did he open another fortune cookie?"

Gail giggled, then clamped her mouth shut primly. The fortune cookie story had become the favorite explanation around the hotel as to why Gordon did anything. "I'm sorry, I can't tell you. Oh, and he asked if you could fill in for him at lunch today. It's those travel agents Carol is taking around."

Howie flushed and set down his coffee cup. "I can't. I've got my own lunch date."

"These are the top agents in California. We ought to treat them nice."

"Then he ought to follow through on his commitments. I'm taking Janet Sorenson to lunch."

"Who's she?"

"She's our contact for a September group. The Boy Wonder screwed up my negotiations with them, and we're losing our shirt."

"Can't you take her to dinner, instead?"

"I've got . . . " Howie took a deep breath. "OK. I'll call her and see if I can reschedule."

"Thank you, Howie. I'll tell Gordon. I'm sure he'll appreciate it."

Howie stood up. "I'm not," he said.

And indeed, all Gordon could appreciate at that particular moment was his own particular situation. Those were the Orange County travel agents! Good God! They had got a "Fam Tour" of the hotel all right. An unprecedented degree of familiarization with the General Manager himself. Had they recognized him? Carol had, once she looked up at his face. What had she told them afterwards? What if she told them who he was? What if the travel agents complained to Suzuki-san or Earl Pressler? What if one of them wrote a letter saying the General Manager of the Earl Court Waikiki had flashed them on a Fam Tour? While screwing an employee. In an unoccupied room.

Gordon felt actual beads of sweat popping out on his forehead as he waited on the fourteenth floor for an up elevator. Melanie Kalanikoa, his *in flagrante* partner from the Concierge Desk, had taken a down elevator about five minutes before. She had been giggling uncontrollably, and Gordon, realizing that her job was on the line too, had told her to take the day off. She worked up in The Earl's Club on the thirty-fourth and thirty-fifth floors, and that's where all the travel agents were staying. They might recognize her behind the desk. Especially if she started to giggle at them. "I better tell her to call in sick for the next few days," he muttered as he waited.

But while it was relatively easy to protect Melanie, how was he going to protect himself? He lived in The Earl's Club. That's where his suite was. He was likely to run into the travel agents up there walking along the corridor or riding the elevator. Maybe this elevator!

"Bing!"

Gordon stared at the elevator doors as if they were the portals to hell. They yawned open at him but revealed only a small, teak and brass lined room. Inside was an elderly couple with flowery aloha shirts, baggy swimsuits, and white, knobby knees which looked rather like their white, knobby faces. Gordon stared at them. They stared at Gordon. And the elevator doors nearly closed on him before he snapped out of his trance and jumped inside.

This was impossible, he thought to himself as he stared up at the flickering digital lights of the floor markers. How was he supposed to run a hotel if he was afraid to ride the elevator? Besides, it wasn't as if he had actually done something wrong. He and Melanie were consenting adults. They were the ones who had been disturbed. Somebody else should be sweating right now, not him.

This self-righteous spasm lasted about two floors. If Earl Pressler found out about this, he was dog meat. Earl Pressler had been known to fire a General Manager for wearing a bad tie. Relations between hotel management and staff in the Earl Court chain were officially frowned upon. Using unoccupied rooms for illicit liaisons was technically theft. Pressler was a randy old goat himself, and he might forgive those transgressions if he was having a good day, but he wouldn't forgive offending the top travel agents in California.

"But hell!" Gordon said aloud. "That wasn't my fault!"
"Bing!"

The elevator had arrived at the thirty-fifth floor, and Gordon realized he was now alone. The elderly couple must have gotten off at some other floor without his even noticing. He peered cautiously out into the corridor to see if any travel agents were lurking there, saw none, and hurriedly quick-stepped down the hall to his suite.

As General Manager, Gordon rated a spacious corner suite possessing a panoramic view of Waikiki Beach and Diamond Head. He had his pick of furnishings from a huge collection of exquisite pieces available at the hotel, and with tasteful eclecticism, he had mixed items like a gilt and green Rothschild Console and a satin-finished Charleston Pie Crust Table with brightly colored Hawaiian print fabrics, comfortably masculine leather armchairs, and original oils of voluminous Polynesian women by Madge Tennant and Pegge Hopper. From his king-size bed, with the assistance of two shrewdly positioned mirrors, one could see both the sunset and the sunrise as well as those romantic city lights. And each of these rose or gold or ebony vistas was accented by a graceful, elongated Giacometti sculpture set outside on the lanai. This was, in sum, the quintessential bachelor pad, and it was the chief frustration in Gordon's life that he was unable to put his quarters to their best use.

Just down the hall from his suite was the Earl's Club Concierge Desk, which was staffed twenty-four hours a day. It was nearly impossible for anyone to enter or depart Gordon's suite unobserved. And even if that were possible, the sharp-eyed maids who cleaned his suite and made his bed every day would spot the telltale signs of an overnight visitor. A single strand of blond or brown or brunette hair was all it would take. The eighteen hundred employees of the Earl Court Waikiki found every activity of their General Manger of interest, but nothing was more gripping than his love life. Gordon knew this from personal experience working at other hotels. News of a General Manager's affair spread like wildfire, especially if it was an affair with an employee. And if the General Manager chose to enjoy an affair with more than one employee at the same time, it didn't take long before the two or three or four or five women found out about each other. And that made it damned difficult to manage them. Gordon himself felt perfectly capable of keeping his affections separate from his management decisions, but no one else would believe that. Even a single affair with an employee generated rumors of favoritism, secret cabals, and tearful confrontations. All the usual management problems were magnified tenfold.

"If I wasn't so damned responsible. So damned conscientious!" Gordon said aloud to himself as he hopped into his Italian marble shower. He soaped himself with the mink oil and lemon grass body gel provided fresh for him each day by the maids and reflected bitterly on how the same Puritan work ethic that compelled him to sample any number of pleasures not particularly to his taste also forbade him from indulging in the one activity any vigorous, powerful man found most pleasurable. He was surrounded by beautiful women. It was part of his job to hire them. Roguish, laughing women with bold, inviting glances. Pale, demure women with flatteringly downcast eyes. Liberated California girls with a stunning freedom from inhibition. Hawaii's multi-racial society produced women of astonishing, legendary beauty. They were chocolate and blond and tan and cream and all the exquisite, hapa haole, chop suey mixes in between. He was prince of a damned harem and he wasn't supposed to touch anybody. It was unnatural and unfair, he concluded, and sluiced himself off with the shower massage set on heavy pulse, feeling each throbbing jet of water as another erotic temptation he had to resist throughout his tortured day.

"If I wasn't doing such a good job, I wouldn't be in this fix," he said aloud and wrenched off the water. In fifteen minutes, his emotions had passed from shock to fear to guilt to self-pity and now marched on towards self-righteous indignation. He had looked into living outside the hotel. He couldn't do it. As General Manager, he was required to live on property. Not only was he expected to be "on call" twenty-four hours a day, there was also a little known law specifying that if a hotel's General Manager actually lived on the premises, then the hotel was entitled to refuse service to anyone who might want to stay there. This legal quirk had probably originated in the previous century during the days of four-room hostelries, but it still proved quite useful in getting rid of drunks, druggies, crazies, and prostitutes. So he had to live in this damned suite. This damned gilded cage. This damned fishbowl. And living on the property all the time, how was he supposed to meet anybody but staff or guests? Who was he supposed to go to bed with?

"They expect me to be celibate?" he asked rhetorically of the man shaving himself in the mirror. The man snorted.

The solution Gordon had finally found to his sexual imprisonment was right on his key ring. For several months, he had arranged trysts, first with one, and then with two different women in one or another of the hotel's unoccupied rooms. His General Manager's passkey afforded universal access, and there were usually two or three hundred vacancies among the hotel's twelve hundred rooms and suites. He and his partner of the evening would arrive and leave at different times, either entirely unobserved or else mistaken for normal guests. It was anonymous and adventurous and gave him a pleasurable feeling of invisible omnipotence. He always chose a different room, and the rooms were always exactly alike. In the morning, the maids unknowingly cleaned away all traces of their passage. It was as if the sex had never happened. If Gordon's partner didn't talk about the affair, no one would ever know of it. And Gordon made it very clear how talking about their affair would be equally damaging to the two of them. Although to have been precise, he should have said to the three of them. Or even, he had been thinking lustfully, to the four of them.

"And then of all the damned luck! A damned Fam tour!" Gordon realized he had a bad headache. He almost never got headaches. He jerked open the medicine cabinet and pulled out an unopened box of Tylenol. He ripped it open, shook out the tiny bottle, and a little note fell out of the box. It wasn't the usual minute instructions. The type was too big. Gordon unfolded the note and read, "Take these when you're feeling bad, but you should feel bad, so they probably won't do any good, and you'll die in September anyway."

The little plastic bottle of Tylenol fell out of his hands and caromed around inside the washbasin. "You'll die in September anyway?" What was happening here? What was going on?

The medicine cabinet mirror slowly swung shut in front of him. Gordon looked up and saw his reflection revolving into view. He looked naked. Fearful. Mortal.

"I'm getting death threats," he said aloud.

From who? How? Why?

But, no! He couldn't worry about that now. He had the travel agents to deal with. He had appointments. He had a job, at least for the time being. And he sure wasn't going to take that Tylenol. To hell with it. And to hell with his headache, too.

Gordon stormed out of his Italian marble bathroom and over to his cedar-lined closet. As he padded nude past his lanai and its million-dollar view, he heard a raucous "cooing" sound and nearly jumped out of his skin. That familiar, fat, white, pigeon was perched out on the lanai railing, bobbing and bowing and cooing at an utterly indifferent female pigeon. The male puffed up its neck feathers, rotated precariously, full circle on its narrow perch, and hopped on down towards the female. "Coo! Coo!" he boomed. The female hopped further away. The male bobbed and cooed some more. His red, lustful eye swung past Gordon's as he executed another display of his magnificent rotating ability.

What the hell was he watching pigeons for? Gordon stomped on towards his closet. He glowered at his wardrobe and grabbed a pinstriped, double-breasted suit. He wanted to look as intimidating as possible today. He threw it on, glowered at himself in the mirror, glowered at the door to the corridor, then opened the door and peered out warily, on the lookout for marauding travel agents.

By the time Gordon strode into his office, glowering, he was in as foul a mood as he had been since the start of his career in the travel industry. He had concluded that it must be one of his employees at the hotel who was making these death threats, but he had absolutely no idea which of the eighteen hundred ones it could be. And halfway down on the elevator, he realized that he didn't know what the travel agents looked like, either. It had all happened too fast. There was one with eyes like searchlights who had kept saying "Wow!" He remembered her. But he might encounter any of the other travel agents anywhere in the hotel and never know it until they started laughing and hooting at him behind his back. He had passed by twenty women on the fourth floor on his way from the elevator to his office, and any one of them could have been a travel agent. A travel agent capable of wrecking his career. He had also passed by two hotel employees and had glowered at them suspiciously. Suddenly, instead of enjoying a feeling of invisible omnipotence, he felt himself surrounded by invisible powers. He didn't like it. Not one bit.

"Let's get started," he snapped at the two attorneys, John Wong and Ed Fernandez, who were waiting for him by Gail's desk. He strode past them into his office and assumed his place in his leather executive chair behind his broad, koa wood desk. The two lawyers followed after him, fumbling with briefcases and half-finished cups of coffee. Gordon's pinstriped glower flustered them. Like most businessmen in Honolulu, John and Ed were wearing aloha shirts, but when they were in court, proper decorum required that they wear suits. Right now, Gordon reminded them of a mean judge.

"How much does the son-of-a-bitch want?" Gordon asked.

"Half a million," John Wong said with a nervous laugh.

"He'll come down," said Ed Fernandez. "I bet he'll settle for two. Maybe one-fifty."

John Wong was short and broad-shouldered. Ed Fernandez was big and hairy. Two "local boy" attorneys, they both spoke in the loud, flat, locker-room shout of lifelong jocks. They spent their lunch hour every day lifting weights in a gym downtown, and they tended to talk about their cases as if they were handicapping an NFL football game.

"Ed's more optimistic than I am," said John, "but hey, he'll come down. Maybe three."

"Maybe two fifty," said Ed.

"Maybe nothing," said Gordon. "Maybe zero. Nada. Zip. Hold on a second." Gordon stabbed at his speakerphone. "Gail?"

"Yes?" the speakerphone replied.

"Send somebody to track down Carol Nickle. She's with those travel agents. Tell her to break away and come see me. I need to talk with her." Gordon chopped off Gail before she could reply and turned back to John and Ed.

"Why should I settle with the son-of-a-bitch at all?" he asked.

"Well, you don't want to go to a jury," John cautioned in his semi-shout.

"You never know what a jury's going to do," Ed agreed at equal volume.

"It gets into court, he'll ask for ten million."

"Jury might give it to him."

"Why should this go to court?" Gordon asked, his voice rising involuntarily in response to the decibel levels of counsel. "What's there to settle? This was an Act of God."

"Well, maybe it was and maybe it wasn't," John said.

"Hell if it wasn't!" Gordon said. "A freak wave like that? A tsunami! If that isn't an Act of God, what is? This guy Kramer is just a sorehead. Let him go sue somebody back in Jersey."

"Well, you know, I think it was an Act of God," John said. "Of course! I mean, everything's an Act of God, right?" He laughed a loud, staccato laugh. "But legally speaking, it may not have been an Act of God."

"There was no tsunami warning, you know," Ed reminded them all in a voice suitable for calling hogs. "No record. Tough to prove an Act of God without any record."

"There were ten thousand witnesses!" Gordon cried in a near shriek. "There were ten thousand people on the beach. Get them to testify it was an Act of God."

"Don't want to go to a jury," Ed bellowed.

"Never know what a jury's going to do," John roared.

"I know what I'm going to do," Gordon screamed. "I know what I'm not going to do, too! I'm not going to pay some sorehead son-of-a-bitch half a million dollars. I'm not going to pay him ten cents! I'm not going to see my insurance premiums go through the roof for a measly broken arm. I say that was an Act of God, and I'm not liable for Acts of God. This hotel is not liable for Acts of God. Particularly on a public beach that we don't even own! Now get out of here and tell that son-of-a-bitch to back off!"

John shook his head. "He may take you to court."

"It's your job to keep me out of court. Now, I've got another appointment, so good-bye. Aloha!"

Gail Takahashi kept her head down and her eyes glued to her computer screen as the two lawyers filed past her desk, still holding their half-finished cups of coffee. They looked about distractedly for a place to put them.

"Just leave them here," Gail said, looking up with her best, blandly polite manner and smiling as if she hadn't heard a thing.

"Gail!" Gordon called sharply from inside his office.

Gail started up from her chair like a spring-loaded toy and trotted into the presence. Her expression of impervious politeness clicked off. She stared at Gordon with a look of fierce dismay.

"Where's Carol?" Gordon barked.

"I left her a message. I think she's turned off her cell phone!" Gail announced, stiff from the insult of this shockingly irresponsible act.

"Well, send somebody after her."

"I did. I sent Susan."

"All right. Send her in as soon as she gets here. No! Have her wait. Just let me know."

Gail nodded sternly and trotted out, closing the door behind her. Gordon glowered around his empty office, which was filled with the mementos, and honors that accrued almost automatically to the man who was General Manager of the Earl Court. There was a Stuben crystal dolphin, a gift from a visiting sheik. A bronzed golf ball from his birdie in the Senior Skins Pro-Am. Framed certificates from the Sales and Marketing Association, the Hawaii Visitors and Convention Bureau, the American Red Cross, and the Boy Scouts of America, all of them in honor and appreciation and gratitude. And all of them, Gordon knew, a result of his job. His job was one hundred percent of his life. There wasn't anything else. He wasn't anything else. "You will die in September anyway," the note had read. In September? Did he even have that long? If he did die, what would all this matter? Never mind that nonsense! Think of the job. Saving the job.

Gordon began to pace up and down in front of his tinted glass windows. He had to get hold of Carol and start to exercise some kind of damage control with the travel agents. How had she handled it? Had she told them who he was? Why had she turned off her phone? Where was she? This was a hell of a day for all this to happen. He glanced at the notes on his desk. He had to review them before his conference call with Suzuki-san. It was a crucial call. Where was she?

By ten-thirty, Gordon had stewed himself into a near frenzy. He had summoned Gail three times to ask the whereabouts of Carol but without success. Carol's phone was still off. She wasn't in her office, and Susan had finally returned with the news that the travel agents had been released after their room tour and they would be at large within the hotel until they gathered again for lunch. That meant Gordon couldn't even risk leaving his office for fear of being seen. He was trapped, distracted half out of his mind, and now he had to get on an international conference call with the hotel owner in Japan and a supercilious interior designer in Los Angeles and make a forty million dollar decision. The decision was what color they were going to make the hotel.

Like many hotels, the existing color of the Earl Court Waikiki had been determined by a little known but awesomely powerful group in New York called The Color Association of the United States. This assembly of interior designers, fashion designers, industry executives, and color consultants meets every year to "forecast" what colors will be popular in the coming months. Since the same people also make the decisions as to what color their own products are going be, their "forecasts" are certain to come true, at least in part. Fifteen hundred companies subscribe to these forecasts, including textile mills, paint manufacturers and design firms. As a consequence, the Color Association's forecasts really are edicts. No one making washing machines, for example, would want to continue heavily in an avocado green mode if all the other appliance manufacturers were going to move to almond or stainless steel and all the linoleum companies and all the wallpaper companies were going to be making their products in colors complementary to almond or stainless. An avocado green washing machine would rapidly become an incompatible ugly duckling on the appliance store floor.

At the time the Earl Court Waikiki was built, the Color Association was recommending a "Classical Tempo" color palette consisting of "Subtle Taupes," "Dusty Mauves," and "Etruscan Browns." The Subtle Taupes were gray, the Dusty Mauves were sort of purplish rose, and the Etruscan Browns were, well, brown. Overall, it was a very sober, a very corporate color palette, and the colors rolled out over the world in the form of hundreds of acres of draperies, thousands of city blocks of upholstery fabric, whole continents of carpeting and tile. The corporate grays and browns and mauves influenced everything from the uniforms of flight attendants to the packaging of Kleenex to, some might say, certain Republican presidencies.

The exterior color of the Earl Court Waikiki was Etruscan Brown. The carpeting in the corridors was Dusty Mauve with accents of Subtle Taupe. The wallpaper and the bedspreads were in complementary "Classic Tempo" colors with shades like "Gulfstream Beige," "Indian Green" and "Caribbean Blue." But the paint had started to peel and the carpeting was worn, and Gordon had convinced the owner, Mr. Suzuki, that it was time for a change. The question was to what. It was likely that the Color Association would be forecasting some major changes. But the difficulty was that the Color Association wouldn't meet until the middle of June, and their charts displaying the forecasted colors wouldn't be in subscribers' hands until September. September was when Gordon had to be finished with the renovation. If he acted immediately, there was barely enough time to order the custom designed carpets, wallpapers, fabrics, bedspreads, and all the other requisite items. He and Mr. Suzuki had to agree today what colors the hotel should be without any forecasts but the one supplied by their interior designer in Los Angeles.

Gordon stared down at the collage the designer had expressed to him. It was a three-foot by four-foot bas-relief made up of scraps of carpet, snips of fabric, shards of tile, swipes of paint, vignetted photos, and odd, little found objects. It represented the proposed colors and materials for the hotel, and Gordon thought it looked like puke. He wondered, in fact, if the color of puke was the basis of this designer's inspiration. The foundation color, recommended for painting the hotel's exterior and atrium spaces, was something called "Tamarind Summer." It was a sort of dull orange puke color. The major contrasting or complementary shade was an indefinable, mottled, greenish tinge that Gordon might have dubbed "Regurgitated Pear," but which the designer called "Faded Moss." Gordon occupied himself with renaming the other colors in the collage as Gail set up the conference call and his speakerphone lit up with little green and amber lights. He had come up with "Expectorant White" and "Vomit Grey" when Gail connected with the interior designer in Los Angeles.

"Hello, Timmy," Gordon said.

"Hello, Gordon," said the speakerphone. "How's the weather?"

"Beautiful. It's always beautiful."

"Very good, Gordon. Keep it up."

Gordon managed to snort out a laugh. He had never liked Timmy's attitude. The man always sounded as if he was deigning to instruct the feeble-minded. Gordon didn't feel as if he needed instruction from someone who wore miniature bow ties and had a rhinestone in his ear. He couldn't really tell Timmy off, however, because Mr. Suzuki had hired him.

"Go ahead, Gail," he said, "call Suzuki-san." Protocol required that both he and Timmy be present, waiting for Mr. Suzuki to enter the telephonic audience chamber, before they called Japan. The electronic beeps and pauses bounced off satellites and sped through undersea cables, and as he waited, Gordon tried to name what he privately termed the "Barf Browns" in Timmy's collage. He had come up with "Dog's Breakfast," and "Baby's Bib" when he heard, "Mushi Mushi," followed by "Gordon?"

"Suzuki-san!" Gordon cried at his speakerphone. "Ohio!"

"Ohio-mas, Gordon," the speaker phone responded.

"It is very early in the morning for you."

"It is five-thirty."

"Yes. Very early."

"Yes. We are early birds to catch the worms."

The speakerphone tittered which was presumably a response from Los Angeles.

"Timmy and I are both here," Gordon said hurriedly so Suzuki-san wouldn't think he was the one tittering. "Timmy's in Los Angeles, that is."

"Hello, Timmy," the speakerphone said.

"Hello, Suzuki-san," the speakerphone replied to itself.

"Did you receive Timmy's . . . thing?" Gordon asked.

"Yes. I am looking at it now."

"So am I," Gordon said. There was a long pause.

"What do you think of Timmy's thing, Gordon?"

Exactly the question he had feared. Should he tell the truth? He thought it looked like the bottom of a toilet bowl after an all night drunk. They were about to take a half-billion dollar hotel and swish it around inside a giant airsickness bag.

"Yes, what do you think of my . . . thing, Gordon?" the speakerphone tittered.

Suzuki-san had hired Timmy. Japanese tastes in color were different. Suzuki-san probably liked and admired Timmy's work. If Gordon objected now, the renovation would be delayed until months after the September deadline. Suzuki-san would be displeased. That would displease Earl Pressler. What if Gordon's affair with the Orange County travel agents came to light under those circumstances?

"Well," Gordon said, "if you like it Suzuki-san, I think we can go with it."

"Do you like it, Gordon?"

"I think. I think it's very good," Gordon found himself saying. He could feel his gorge rising as he spoke.

"I am glad you think so, Gordon," the speakerphone intoned solemnly. "This is very serious decision. You know the market best."

Damn! Now it was his decision. But he couldn't back out. "Yes. I say go with it," he said, committing himself to puke.

"Then we go. Good work, Timmy."

Gordon stared down at Timmy's work and felt near to adding his own thematic contribution to it. "Yes, Timmy, good work," he croaked.

"Thank you, Gordon. Good of you to say so."

"Gordon, Timmy, I must go now," the speakerphone said cheerfully. "I have more early worms to catch."

"Good bye, Suzuki-san. Thank you."

The forty million dollar conference call was rapidly concluded with Gordon trying to sound cheerful and complimentary and Timmy graciously accepting the compliments as merely his just due. Gordon finally got rid of him, threw himself back in his leather executive chair, and stared up at the ceiling. "I'm going to be General Manager of The

Upchuck Resort," he said aloud. Then tilting forward, he stabbed at the speakerphone again to ask Gail about Carol Nickle.

Gordon's pessimism over the colors was not allayed by his meeting an hour later with Christine Larren and her son George. Christine Larren was a ferociously elegant international art dealer specializing in Pacific art and Oriental antiques. She was based in Honolulu but traveled constantly, usually on assignment. Elaborate and splashy art collections had become fashionable amenities for first class resorts in Hawaii. Art was like the flowers and the parrots and the koi. The upscale traveler expected to see it in the lobby. Preferably big art. Preferably big art that looked classy but didn't make anyone think too hard. Pacific carvings and Asian sculpture filled the bill perfectly. Nobody had the foggiest idea what they symbolized, but they looked beautiful and exotic and big. A number of hotels had hired Ms. Larren to furnish them with a collection, and Mr. Suzuki had contracted her to assemble one for the refurbished Earl Court. She had a budget of three million dollars with which to do it.

When faced with Timmy's "Tamarind Summer" collage, however, Ms. Larren gave it a long, hard look and suddenly announced that her twenty-two year old son, George, would actually be doing most of the buying. This appeared to be news to George, who looked over at his mother with an expression of shock, mixed with fear and gratitude.

"I think primitive, New Guinea art from the Sepik river region would fit in nicely against that background," she said. "Lots of dark, natural woods and earth tones. George would enjoy an expedition up the Sepik, wouldn't you George?"

"Oh? Yes, mother," George said. He dressed as elegantly as she did and wore almost as much jewelry.

"You're going to get some Buddhas, too, aren't you?" Gordon asked.

"Every Hawaii hotel has Buddhas," Ms. Larren said dismissively.

"Well, yes. Exactly," Gordon replied.

"Oh yes, I suppose we can pick up some Buddhas," Ms. Larren sighed. I'll get them in Hong Kong. And I'll go to Bali, too, and find you some murals of nude nymphs. But George, after the Sepik, why don't you go to Nepal. Maybe you can find something Tibetan. A row of prayer wheels would be nice, don't you think? Tinkling in the wind?"

Gordon decided he didn't give a damn. The important thing was to get rid of these two and make sure he was still going to have a job by the time the tinkling prayer wheels arrived. It also occurred to him that he could secure some small revenge on Timmy by inflicting Ms. Larren on him, so he exacted a commitment from her to fly to Los Angeles for a personal conference with the interior designer before she and George began their global shopping spree. Ms. Larren agreed reluctantly and only after Gordon told her that Mr. Suzuki had specifically requested it. Casting a final, dubious glance at the "Tamarind Summer" collage, she swanned out of the office, her son fluttering behind her like a eunuch in the wake of the Dowager Empress.

Gordon escaped to the spa. It was nearly noon, so he assumed the travel agents were safely corralled at their lunch with Howie. Carol Nickle still hadn't been found. He was nearly crazy with worry. And the truth was, he had been suffering all morning from a bad case of blue balls as a result of his *coitus interupptus* in room 1410. That was probably why he had such a hellacious headache. He needed to work it off.

So naturally, he ran into Carol in the spa gym.

There she was, wearing a hot pink, Lycra spandex thong leotard over second-skin, translucent-white biker shorts. She was lying on the floor and thrusting her pelvis at him. Actually, she was doing this along with a dozen other similarly dressed women who were all taking the hotel aerobics class. Gordon was toiling away in lonely splendor on the Stairmaster, climbing endless steps to nowhere in the frigidly air-conditioned workout room, when the women all pranced in, set up a boom box, and started writhing around on the floor in front of him to the accompaniment of an old tune by Rod Stewart.

> *If you think I'm sexy,*
> *And you like my body,*
> *Come on baby tell me so!*

It was not a spectacle calculated to alleviate his blue balls. To make matters worse, one of the other women in the class was Cynthia Tanaka, the darling reservationist with the little-girl voice who, like the laughing, fun-loving Melanie, had also become his secret trysting partner in the anonymous bedrooms of the Earl Court. Cynthia was wearing a rose-patterned thong leotard over midnight blue, second-skin biker shorts. Cynthia was very good at aerobics, demonstrating great flexibility. Particularly with the splits.

Workout room decorum prescribed that he take no notice of the women stretching and jiggling in unison before him. And they, of course, completely ignored him. Anyone in the workout room was supposed to be totally dedicated to the Grail of Personal Fitness. The mirrored walls were for looking at yourself, not at others. Ordinarily, Gordon would have kept on at the Stairmaster for only a couple of minutes more, then discreetly stepped down, toweled off, and walked away. But if he did that now, he might lose Carol again. She might disappear into the women's locker room. And he couldn't very well pull her out of the class in front of all the other women to talk about his sex life. Not with Cynthia there, too. The only thing to do was to keep stepping away on the Stairmaster until the class broke up. Then he would pretend a casual encounter, get her off into a corner, and find out what the hell was going on.

Gordon had already been on the Stairmaster for twenty minutes when the aerobics class started, and it was a forty-minute class. He had climbed the equivalent of three and a half Empire State Buildings before it was over, watching his face in the mirrored walls getting steadily redder and sweatier. Halfway up the third Empire State building, he caught a vicious charley horse in his calf, but he toiled grimly on, hitching his way up into the hypothetical stratosphere. The spandexed women pranced and jiggled in front of him, bright thongs cleaving their Lycra buttocks.

If you think I'm sexy,
And you like my body,
Come on baby tell me so!

Throughout the morning, Gordon had been obsessed with what various women might be thinking about him. But now as he neared the twenty-second floor of his fourth Empire State Building, his pretended obliviousness to the women in front of him became real. There was a roaring in his ears. The workout room seemed veiled in black gauze and filled with tiny sparks. He barely heard the round of clapping that signaled the end of the class.

"Real good, ladies! Thank you!" cried the aerobics teacher.

They were leaving! Gordon reeled dizzily out of the Stairmaster and hobbled after them past an empty row of high-tech, chrome-plated exercise machines. The pain in his calf was intense. It was like someone had planted a knife in it. Fortunately, Carol seemed to be walking slowly off by herself. None of the other women were near her.

"Carol!" he cried hoarsely. "Have you got a second?"

She stopped and turned, waiting for him by an obscure, Torquemada-like device with shiny, curving bars and dangling, black straps. He limped up to her.

"Hi," she said with a funny smile. "Have a good workout?"

Suddenly, Gordon was hit with a terrific gust of Carol's body odor. It was the same stale, musky scent he had noticed before but had never really identified during meetings with her in his office. Now, after a forty minute aerobics class, it was almost overpowering. This was hardly the moment to mention it, however.

"Carol," he said, reaching unsuccessfully for an authoritative tone, "about this morning. What did you . . . ? Do they, the travel agents, know who I am?"

"They know a lot about you," Carol said, her funny smile getting wider.

"Do they know I'm . . . I'm the General Manager?"

"Not yet."

It stopped him. He was coping with the multiple implications of this statement, his exhaustion, the pain in his leg, her overpowering smell, when she smiled even more widely.

"Let's talk later," she said. "I've got to hit the showers."

He tried to speak, but she overrode him, her eyes flashing

with an imperious confidence that filled him with dread. "I'll see you in room 1410 tonight," she said. "Around nine."

And she turned and disappeared around a corner into the women's side of the spa, a mysterious series of marble chambers where even the General Manager of the Earl Court could not follow her.

CHAPTER FIVE

Mislov arrived in London in a black mood. This, of course, was normal, but he had occasion for a particularly pitch black gloom. Because of that meddling, beer-swilling Aussie editor, Garth MacLeod, some people in his profession might think he was afraid. They might think he had heeded MacLeod's warning and was running away from New York. They might think he was actually intimidated by that amplified rock-star bitch he had photographed with her boy-toy in the limousine. Afraid of her and her half-deaf, heavy metal fan club. He wasn't, of course. He was not leaving New York. He was coming to England. England was where the action would be for a paparazzo this summer. Mislov was confident of this. There were rumors of further riffs in the royal family, and the British public seemed to have developed a desire for scandal akin to that of an addict's for heroin. The more the news in the tabloids sickened them, the more they craved it. It was to these Elysian Fields that Mislov traveled.

Still, it was galling that MacLeod and others might believe he was heeding a warning. Even more galling was the possibility that it might be true. A few days after his conversation with MacLeod in the Greek restaurant, Mislov had spotted five androgynous toughs walking towards him from the Shubert on 44th street, and he had actually turned aside. He, Mislov Rapolovitch, the fearless black nemesis, had altered his course. He despised himself for it. Almost as much as he despised everyone else. All the way across the Atlantic, he privately castigated himself, MacLeod, and his fellow idiot passengers in first class. He arrived in a fuming rage. After deplaning at Heathrow and establishing himself at an anonymous hotel, he went immediately to Covent Garden and the Mechanical Cabaret Theater.

The Mechanical Cabaret Theater was an odd little museum located on the lower level of Covent Garden. The exhibits were of two general kinds. One was represented by elaborate Rube Goldberg machines with cheerful colored balls, levers, screws, balance beams and myriad other devices, all perfectly visible and understandable and yet all interconnected in unexpected ways. Once a tiny action was initiated, like a ball rolling down an incline, a concatenating series of events took place. The ball might trip a small weight which in turn might trip a large one, and that would make the ball shift direction and spiral down a ramp which would cause a lever to ratchet up on the opposite side of the contraption and that would make a series of dominos cascade back across to the first side to trip another lever which would unexpectedly lift the spiraling ball back up to the top to start down another incline and so on in a continually surprising succession of causes and effects. Once begun, a wave of energy moved through Rube Goldberg's creation, and while each ball or lever or tumbling domino contributed its own unique energy to the wave, it was clear they were not the wave itself. Nor did they have any idea the wave was coming. Like the water molecules that rose and fell off Waikiki Beach and perhaps like Gordon and Kip and Gloria and Mislov, they participated in something that was not them. In this three-dimensional metaphor, everything was connected and everything affected everything else while still preserving its own unique identity. There was something about this that made nearly everyone who saw it smile.

It did not make Mislov smile, however, and those exhibits were not why he made a pilgrimage to the Mechanical Cabaret Theater whenever he was in London. He returned in order to see certain glass cases that housed elaborate cuckoo clock scenes resembling the transformational cartoons of *Monty Python*. Many of these scenes were obscene, perverse or scatological, which he naturally found appealing. And for him, these other exhibits delivered an altogether different kind of message. In them, little men ran up towers. Little camels trudged across deserts. Little dancers whirled and jigged, and one thing became another thing, which became another thing. But at the end of all this arduous or frenetic activity, each elaborate device returned to square one. All the little creatures came back to exactly where they started, ready to undergo the same trials once again, endlessly, at the bidding of whoever put a coin in their slot. For Mislov, the message of the Mechanical Cabaret Theater was one of futility. Absurdity. He found this invigorating.

One exhibit in particular spoke to him. It began with a mystery, a medium-sized glass case that was completely empty except for a layer of gravel at the bottom. The gravel was slate-gray, sharp-edged and very clean, and each stone was of uniform size. Upon insertion of the coin, at first nothing occurred. Then, a slight stirring could be perceived in the center of the gravel floor. Then, something began to emerge, and one braced for something awful, something grotesque. But what slowly began to rise above the gravel was the bowler hat of a City Gentleman. And following that, the proper face and moustache and tie of a City Gentleman. And then the proper jacket and slacks and brolly of a City Gentleman. And everything about him was in the proper shades of gray, which seemed exactly right, for it was as if the slate gravel was indeed becoming the City Gentleman. And he slowly rose up to his full height and stood there in full possession of the glass case, and that seemed to be that.

And then his bowler hat split open, and inside his head there rose up a pink and orange naked woman. A voluptuous, naked, pink and orange woman with jutting, red-tipped titties and curving, naked thighs, and she rose up inside his head and stood there smiling, and that appeared to be that.

And then the naked woman split in half to reveal a gross, green frog.

And after a certain pause, the woman swallowed the frog, and the man swallowed the woman and the gravel swallowed them all, and the mysterious glass case returned to a vacuity with a slate gray floor. Mislov only had to expend one coin. Inspired and refreshed, he went off to find something to photograph.

And across the city, Lady Gloria Ryder went back to her closet for the fourth time. She was desperate for something to wear.

"Glynis!" she cried. "Please come help me. Tell me what you think." Gloria held up a houndstooth suit with a long pleated skirt in front of her and stared into the closet mirror. It was wrong. She cast the suit aside and reached instead for cream-colored linen slacks and a dark blue jacket. Wrong again. Perhaps her green dress. It went well with her auburn hair. She burrowed deep into the recesses of her closet. Gadfry, she must not have worn that dress for quite a while. How old was it? "Glynis!" she cried fretfully.

"Yes, Lady Gloria?" Glynis Mortimer appeared in the bedroom and addressed the open closet, which was emitting various whimpering and scratching noises as if it also doubled as a puppy kennel.

"Glynis!" came a muffled cry. "Where is my green dress?"

"I haven't the faintest idea, Lady Gloria."

"Ah ha! Here it is, all along." Gloria emerged from the closet holding a green dress with a high neckline up in front of her. "What do you think?"

"I think it is a very nice dress."

"So you think I should wear it?"

"That depends on what your objective is, M'Lady."

"I want to look nice."

"Yes, but to what end?"

"To what end? To the end of looking nice. What else is there? Oh well, I suppose my real objective is to get Tom Leary to join our country weekend at my father's. Oh, and to look good in your news photos, of course. How many will be there?"

"I have been assured that at least three newspapers will send photographers. Perhaps as many as six."

"Super!"

"But if those are your objectives, M'Lady, then that dress is not suitable."

"It isn't? Why not?"

"Well, as regards the first objective and Mr. Leary, it doesn't cling to your figure or show enough skin."

"Glynis!" Gloria giggled. "I'm shocked."

"And as for the newspapers, that solid green color will not reproduce well in black and white. I doubt that we'll make the color supplements. You need something with more contrast."

"Well, in that case." Gloria dived once more into the depths of her closet. "I have this little thing. You've seen it before." She reemerged holding a filmy, low cut, white satin, summer frock with a pattern of big blue polka dots. "I wear it with a big, faux pearl necklace and earrings. But really, I couldn't wear this to Parliament, could I? He's getting me into a special downstairs gallery. I don't want to exhibit myself to all the Members. Wait! My blue silk shawl!"

Gloria disappeared once again and after several moments and a loud clattering noise of hatboxes cascading to the floor, she reappeared with a large silk scarf, which was the same shade of blue as the polka dots.

"I wrap this so, with a brooch, and it looks quite formal. Then at the appropriate moment, I unpin it and just sort of fling it back."

"Ideal, M'Lady."

"You think so?"

"Yes. Ideal. If I may be excused? I have three more newspapers to call and reconfirm."

"Oh, yes. Thank you, Glynis, you've been a dear."

Glynis returned to her study off the hall, and Gloria turned to selecting a brooch to go with the scarf. Tom Leary was coming to pick her up in his government car, and while she had begun dressing well before the appointed hour, by the time the brooch was selected, the hair dried and combed, the makeup applied, and after a frantic search for white pumps to go with the summer frock had been concluded – which required another appearance by Glynis at the open, whimpering closet – she was late. Crying out her thanks and a "See you in the East End" back over her shoulder, she dashed outside to where the Junior Minister was waiting with his car and driver.

Being chauffeured about London was hardly a new experience for Gloria, and usually it was in a Bentley or a Rolls, whereas the Junior Minister at Education only rated a Rover. Still, it was an official government car, and it gave her rather a thrill to be able to whisk past all the security barricades and the nodding Bobbies and into the many-spired Palace of Westminster, slipping smoothly through a narrow stone passageway originally designed for horse and carriage and probably too narrow for a Bentley anyway, and ultimately arriving at an interior courtyard where one of the House staff was waiting to escort her to the special gallery.

This gallery, Tom had explained on the way, was generally used only for rather important advisors to the opposition front bench. Being a Minister, however, he was able to instruct the Sergeant at Arms to admit Lady Gloria for a few minutes, and as it happened, she had it all to herself. It was a small, low-ceilinged chamber with just two little wooden benches. It was positioned diagonally opposite the Speaker, on the same level as the Members, and about halfway up along one side's rows of green leather benches. Gloria could look along their length at the fidgeting or drooping profiles of one set of MP's as well as directly across at the faces of the opposing side. Because of the gallery's low ceiling and deep setback, she was invisible to anyone in the public galleries above her, although she probably still could be glimpsed by the journalists peering down from their place over the Speaker's head.

What struck her first were the slivery wires holding the microphones. Looking down at them during her previous visit, these wires had seemed like fishing lines suspending lures above the Members' heads. Now from below, she could see that there were other, even thinner wires that radiated out horizontally from each microphone to all the others. The function of this grid was probably to keep the microphones from swaying distractingly back and forth. The result, however, was that the British House of Commons appeared to be enveloped in a gigantic, glistening spider web. Whether the Members who labored there took the part of spiders or of flies, Gloria could not be sure.

The next surprise was the irritation, the contempt, the genuine animosity that the Members on one side seemed to have for the Members on the other. In the newspapers, or even from the public galleries, their mutual antagonism had a generalized quality. And their many petty rules of behavior and parliamentary procedure contributed to an overall impression of some complicated team sport. If it was a sport, then of course one supposed that these men would be "good sports" while playing it. From these close quarters, however, it didn't look that way. From above, their various rude remarks and interruptions blended into one guttural male roar. Now down on their level, one could identify individual speakers. One could distinguish individual comments. One could see lips curl. Watch backs stiffen. The Members of Parliament were shockingly rude and nasty to each other.

"If the Member would simply . . . "

"Rubbish!"

"Perfect rot!"

" . . . simply listen to what . . . "

"Listening to you is bad enough!"

" . . . to what his own constituents are saying . . . "

"I speak for my constituency, not you!"

"Hear! Hear! Hy-yea! Hy-yea!"

" . . . he would discover that this proposal . . . "

"Is indecent!"

"Hy-yea! Hy-yea! Hear! Hear!"

Perhaps all men's sports were like this. Gloria had never observed the inside of a rugby scrum before either, but she decided she was glad that Tom wasn't speaking. She didn't want to hear him subjected to such abuse. He slipped in after a few minutes and took a place over on one of the benches near the Speaker, ignoring her completely as he warned her he would do, and looking manly, relaxed, and faintly amused. He looked perfectly at home in this whirlpool of power beneath the glistening spider web, and to Gloria, he looked perfectly desirable. Between her shock at the general level of vitriol on the floor of Parliament and her passionate interest in how Tom's hair curled around his ears, she never quite tuned in to the actual subject under debate. The Sergeant at Arms had only granted her a fifteen-minute audience in the special gallery, and before she knew it, her escort was at the little side door, waving to her that her time was up.

Her arrangement with Tom was to wait for him in the rotunda of the Central Lobby, which was the normal place for constituents to rendezvous with their representatives. He would join her there as soon as he decently could, and then they would go off to the East End together in his car. Her escort led her along the passageway from the Chamber and through a small rotunda called the Members Lobby where only Members and accredited journalists could linger. It was empty except for a peculiar, bearded man dressed all in black.

Upon reaching the Central Lobby, her escort managed to secure her a seat on a stone bench underneath the mosaic of the patron saint of Scotland. Murmuring good wishes and the belief that Mr. Leary would be along shortly, he left her there to observe the other side of the political coin.

Here, everyone loved each other. And there didn't seem to be any sides, either. Everyone just milled about, nodding, being polite, scanning the crowd for the familiar face, and then bursting into smiles and bonhomie when the familiar face appeared. It was rather like a dance, Gloria decided, with the constituents waiting to be asked to waltz by their elected representatives. Some constituents stood and waited in the center of the rotunda, slowly revolving as the crowd milled about them. Others toured the perimeter, pausing beneath the mosaics of the patron saints of England, Scotland, Ireland, and Wales and looking anxiously down the corridors leading off from each of the four entrances. And some, like Gloria, took the part of wallflowers and waited demurely on the stone benches. While many of the people waiting appeared to have been there for some time, the Members themselves rarely seemed to spend more than a few moments in the Central Lobby. They were adept at surveying the mob and knifing through it to greet their elector, often appearing without warning, genie-like, with a wide smile and a gracious hand extended.

"Hullo Gloria! Sorry to make you wait. Are you all right?"

Gloria looked up, startled, at the charming, broken-nosed face of the Junior Minister at Education smiling down at her. She felt her heart flutter and a schoolgirl blush rise up through her cheeks.

"Oh, yes," she said, taking his extended hand and standing up. "Quite all right. It's been fascinating, really."

"Good. I'm glad it hasn't been too boring for you. That's a charming brooch, by the way," he said, nodding at the gold pin in the shape of an open book that fastened her blue silk shawl. "Most appropriate."

"It seemed so, yes."

"So," he said, taking her arm, "it's off to Hackney, then."

"Yes. Glynis says as many as six newspapers may turn up."

"Really? If she can bring that off, I'll be astonished. We usually have to be discovered sleeping with a spy or a goat to merit that kind of attention."

Turning, they nearly collided with the peculiar, bearded man dressed all in black that Gloria had seen in the Members Lobby, but she didn't notice him at all this time. All she could see was Tom Leary.

The trip to Hackney in the back of Tom's Rover passed quickly amidst a buzz of legislative news and gossip. Tom was energized from the debate that turned out to have been over one of the measures in the Finance Bill, which was slowly making its tortuous passage through the House. There were several other bits of legislation that he was intimately involved with as well. Gloria found it all novel and exciting. Not that she cared beans about the Finance Bill, but it was surprisingly thrilling to be with someone for whom so many things did actually matter. Someone who really cared, quite passionately, about public issues and seemed to believe that something could be done about them. Ennui and cynicism were the expected attitudes in Gloria's set. Most of her friends were ignorant of issues in the fields of health and education and contemptuous of those who tried to effect any progress, but Tom not only cared about things, he did things. So as he burbled on, Gloria listened attentively, and neither of them paid any attention to the black taxi that followed closely behind them all the way out to Hackney. London was full of black taxis.

"By the way, heard anything from the witch?" Tom Leary interrupted himself to ask.

"Hortense? No. Well, not really. I believe she called Daddy up."

"Your father? What for?"

"Something to do with hunting. She made a passing reference to Glynis. Called it a misunderstanding."

"Cheek."

"Yes. Speaking of Daddy," Gloria said, fiddling with her brooch. She had decided the moment had come for the unpin and fling maneuver with her shawl.

"Yes?"

"Damn." The brooch was being difficult. Gloria abandoned the effort and plunged ahead. "Sorry," she said, "I'm just afraid you're going to be too busy."

"Too busy for what?"

"Well, I wanted to invite you for a weekend visit at my father's country place a fortnight from now. Glynis and her husband Clyde are coming, and my father's having one or two people down. It's often quite lovely this time of year."

"That's awfully kind of you. Actually, I do have a constituency garden party that weekend."

"I was afraid you'd have something."

"But perhaps I could beg off. Ah. I think we're here."

And before Gloria could elicit any fuller commitment, the world outside the Rover swept them up. It was called Story Hour.

The concept of Story Hour was simply to have adult volunteers read stories to young children in one-on-one situations, much as their parents ought to have done, but for one sad, contemporary reason or another, never seemed to get around to doing. The purpose of Gloria and Tom's appearance was to publicize the program and drum up more volunteers. Glynis Mortimer was there as they stepped out of the Rover, and she smoothly set up photo opportunities for three bored news-paper photographers. Gloria, Tom, and the ecstatic woman who ran the program were positioned in front of the grim, Victorian brick walls of the Hackney Public Library along with a small group of cowed children. Glynis apologized for there being only three photographers, but Tom assured her that securing even this number was a minor miracle. And a fourth photographer dressed all in black turned up a little late and actually took a real interest in the scene, clicking off a series of shots using a motor drive camera. After a few more minutes of polite chitchat and effusive thanks from the Program Director, Gloria and Tom were ushered inside the library to actually read something to a child.

The Program Director, a middle-aged woman who was fairly giddy with excitement from the presence of both a Lady and an MP in her library, squinted nearsightedly at the small knot of children who had followed them inside, reached in more or less at random, and pulled out a thin, blond, little girl named Sadie.

"Lady Gloria Ryder is going to read you a story!" she announced grandly, and bustled the both of them off to a corner with a hard wooden bench that had been specially furnished for the occasion with a little pile of cushions and embroidered pillows. "What would you like to read?" she asked Gloria.

Gloria suddenly realized she was utterly unprepared for this question. She looked blankly at the librarian, then turned to look down at Sadie. "What would you like to read?" she asked.

"I don't know," Sadie said.

They both looked blankly at the librarian, who after a pause, suddenly spouted, "I'll get you a copy of *Where The*

Wild Things Are, that's always popular." She bustled off, and Sadie and Gloria were left to size each other up on the wooden bench.

"Have you read *Where the Wild Things Are* before?" Gloria asked.

"No," said Sadie.

"Neither have I. I hear it's a very good story."

Sadie stared up at Gloria as if making a careful evaluation. She was a thin little thing with large blue eyes and flat, lifeless blond hair that looked ragged and uneven as if she had cut it herself. She was wearing a white, giveaway sort of tee shirt celebrating a bank picnic. It would have hung down below her shorts except that she had bloused it and cinched it in with a cheap, fanny-pack belt that she wore round her waist with the pouch in front, marsupial fashion. "I can't read," she said after a time.

"But you're going to learn in school, aren't you," Gloria said.

Sadie paused again for a careful evaluation. "I don't go to school very much," she said finally. "We move a lot."

"But you have to learn to read," Gloria said. "It's very useful. How can you find your way around, for example, if you can't read the street signs or the bus destinations?"

"I ask people."

"How did you get here, today? Did your Mother bring you?"

"No. I asked people."

"*Where the Wild Things Are*, here it is!" The librarian bustled back to them, clutching the slim volume that was more pictures than words. The cover was brightly illustrated with drawings of friendly monsters in a dark, leafy jungle.

"I'm sure you'll both enjoy it," she said, handing the book to Gloria. "Have a good read."

The woman pattered off. Gloria and Sadie looked at each other.

"Well, shall we?" Gloria asked.

"Could you read this, instead?" The little girl asked suddenly. She unzipped the pouch at her waist, fumbled in it for a moment like a baby kangaroo, and withdrew an envelope marked with the simple address, "To Sadie."

"It's from my father," she said, holding it up to Gloria.

"Well," Gloria hesitated, "All right. I don't see why not. If you like, we can read them both." She took the envelope, which was unsealed and withdrew several sheets of paper covered with smudged, blue handwriting. "'Dearest Sadie,'" she read aloud, "'Long before you are able to read this, I shall be dead.'"

"Oh my!" Gloria said. "Oh dear, Sadie, I don't think I should read this."

"Why not?"

"It's too private. I think your mother should read it to you."

"She can't. She's dead, too."

"Oh, God. But who do you live with, then?"

"My Aunt. And my Uncle sometimes. But I don't want them to read to me. They don't like my Dad. They don't read anyway. My Aunt watches telly."

"But–"

"You're supposed to read to me," the little girl said with iron determination.

"Yes, I am. But. Yes. Well, all right, then." And Gloria took a deep breath and began again.

"'Long before you are able to read this, I shall be dead. I hope you can forgive me for leaving you. I am writing now as you sleep, and I can't believe I won't be here to see you in the morning and for many, many mornings more. Perhaps I will. The doctors sound hopeful. But if you are reading this, then I will be gone.

"'Still, I will be here in your mornings. You just won't be able to see me any longer. I found a yellow tulip in a shop this afternoon. I put it in a little pot by your bed so you can have some bit of sunshine when you wake up. I know you love sunshine.

"'Know that I love you. I would not leave you now, even with the pain, but despite what they say, I feel that something is ending. But only a chapter in a book, not the book itself.

"'Hopefully, you and your mother will have a little money to live on.'"

Gloria looked up. "But you said your mother was . . . ?"

"She was in an auto accident. She died the month after my Dad. My Aunt says she wanted to."

"Oh. Oh, poor Sadie."

"Could you read the rest, please?"

Gloria bit her lip and continued. "'I shall do my best to guard and care for you both, be it in this life or the next. I have no great thoughts or advice for you now. Only love. And a bit of sunshine in a pot. Live your life in the sunshine. I will see you there.'"

CHAPTER SIX

Kip crawled out of his mosquito net and looked up cheerfully at a basket of skulls hanging from the crossbeam above his head. For an anthropologist, it was a happy sight. Skulls in a longhouse meant that once upon a time, men living here had taken heads. If he was lucky, one of these men might still be alive and willing to talk about it. There were six or seven skulls up there. Old ones of course, covered with soot, and bound together all higgledy-piggledy by a thick, dried vine that wound around the various jaws and craniums as if it had grown that way. A shaft of early morning sunlight slanted across the ruai to light up the scene, and for a moment, Kip had the unsettling impression that one of the skulls was winking at him. It proved only to be a spider, however, out for a morning stroll along its web that was strung across one of the eye sockets.

"Top 'o the mornin to you," Kip said aloud, and strolled off himself for a morning bath down in the stream. He whistled as he made his way down the path. It was amazing how good he felt. He had slept like a rock. He suspected that he might have had a touch of sunstroke or heat exhaustion the previous afternoon when he arrived. He had a vague, confusing memory of some peculiar little boy, but what he could remember of the encounter was certainly nonsense.

"Mundi, Tuan?" an old woman asked him as he passed her by on his way to the stream with soap and towel in hand.

"Eeya, mundi," he replied.

"Tuan mundi," she chortled affirmingly.

The shallow stream was crystal clear and bordered by towering jungle hardwoods festooned with creepers and climbing orchids. It was also alive with butterflies, butter-yellow, firecracker-crimson, and midnight-blue butterflies that batted happily back and forth, alighting harmlessly on the backs and heads of the bathers to suck their sweat. The men and boys bathed in one small pool, and the women and young girls bathed in another about forty yards downstream. There was much ribald hooting and joking going on between the two pools, and the whole scene resembled a gathering of roguish fauns and nymphs in a painting rendered by a children's book illustrator. Kip splashed in and spent half an hour, laughing and soaping himself in the gurgling, silvery water amidst the orchids and the butterflies, the slippery limbs and the darting eyes.

Back in the longhouse, he was pleased to see an ancient old Iban man, hunkered down on his haunches and waiting for him, alone beneath the basket of skulls. If ever there was a kindly old headhunter, Kip thought to himself, this was the fellow. The old codger looked to be in his sixties or seventies. He had distended ear lobes that hung down almost to his shoulders and complicated, purple-black tattoos covering all the most difficult, painful places, ankles, knees, elbows, even his throat, which was the most difficult and painful of all. Traditional Iban tattoos were inflicted with a needle at the end of a stick. A second stick was used to tap, tap, tap the first. It took days or weeks to create tattoos this way. Few modern young Ibans wanted them, but for the old men, they were signs of status and courage.

"Sudah mundi, Tuan?" the old man asked.

"Eeya, sudah," Kip replied and squatted down next to him. The old man smiled a toothless smile that made his eyes disappear amidst many crinkling wrinkles. A rooster crowed off in the distance.

"Tuan nemo antu?"

Sure enough, this was one old headhunter. The previous night, Kip's guide had put out the word as to what "Tuan" was looking for, and first thing next morning, this old man turned up asking if he knew any ghosts. His name was Agak. It took about an hour of bargaining, and the old man never did admit to actually taking one of the heads that dangled above them, but he eventually agreed to describe his understanding of the world that awaited "antu" or departed spirits and how he might assist a spirit who had recently departed to make the transition. He even created a map of the departed soul's journey using sticks and pieces of rattan. Agak's story of this journey bore interesting parallels to various western versions. Like the Greeks, Agak said that there was a River of the Dead that the soul had to cross. Instead of the Styx, the Ibans called it *Long Bali Matei.* Like Virgil in Dante's *Inferno,* Agak showed the way to certain specific destinations where a soul spent the rest of eternity depending on how the individual had lived his life and how he had departed it. There was a place for warriors and heroes. A place for stillborn children. A normal place for those who died of normal causes, another, unpleasant spot for those who committed suicide. Kip had already recorded most of this information from his other interviews, so he and Agak were able to spend a happy

couple of hours swapping stories and theories about the after-
life. The whole interview cost him ten yellow beads and two
packs of cigarettes. When he had first begun interviewing in
longhouses, he had found it embarrassing to purchase information about the Iban spirit world with the same currency
that had once secured Manhattan Island for the Dutch, but in
the interior of Borneo, beads and tobacco were far more useful
and valuable than paper money. And from the way the old
man's eyes disappeared behind a wealth of smiling wrinkles,
he clearly felt he had the best side of the bargain.

When he and Agak finally finished their theological discussions, Kip put away his notepad and digital recorder. This
acted as a signal, and the typical longhouse crowd quickly
gathered round him in a circle and began asking the usual,
endless series of questions. How far was it to America? (Five
hundred days walk.) Did people eat rice there? (Yes, but not
always.) What was it like to ride in an airplane? (Like a bus.)
What was it like to ride in a bus? (Boring.) Was he married?
(No.) Was he lonely? (Sometimes.) Would he like an Iban
wife? (Much laughter.)

The morning stretched into the afternoon and then into
the evening. The questions and laughter were interrupted
only by more walks to the stream to mundi and by several
identical meals consisting of mounds of long grained, hill
padi rice that was purplish in color and had a delicious, nutty,
chewy flavor. Condiments were tiny, dried silver fish no bigger than paper clips, fresh slices of green mango, and a bit
of tinned corned beef that he contributed. The questions
and laughter burbled on like the stream. The distant cries of
roosters blended with a steady thumping sound from women
pounding newly harvested rice with wooden posts. As night
fell, this rhythm merged into the rhythm of gongs, and with

the encouragement of a few glasses of tuak, even Kip eventually stood up in the center of the circle, and amidst admiring eyes and the flickering flames of dozens of small lamps, he danced a dance he imagined to be as smooth and elegant as the flight of a magic bird.

The next day was like the one before and also like the one that followed. And after three days, or was it four, it was time to leave. He was to have different guides for the return trip, however, and a different route. He had learned that a new logging road had been cut through the jungle. Instead of a difficult four-day hike and five cramped days in a narrow longboat on a minor tributary stream, just six hours walk could now bring him to the road. Once there, it would be easy to hitch a ride on one of the logging trucks that roared along at fantastic speeds toward the mighty Rejang River. The journey that had taken nine days, coming in, would be over in one, going out.

They were up with the first rooster and had a last, shivery mundi down in the stream. After rice, corned beef and mango for breakfast, he was ready to go. Virtually the entire longhouse turned out to see him off, grouping themselves in a loose crowd out on the uncovered portion of the ruai. Kip and his two guides climbed down the notched wooden pole that served as the longhouse staircase, took a few steps down the trail, and turned to wave goodbye. And only then did Kip see the strange little boy again. His presence was like a blow to the heart.

He was a seemingly inconspicuous little tyke, standing there half-naked, just one of the crowd of a hundred or so Iban villagers. But to Kip, the sight of him was overwhelming. It was true! The boy was real! He wasn't the figment of a heat-stunned imagination. Kip was fresh, now. Rested. And there was the same soul-destroying little face. Age-old, worldly-wise, imperious, all knowing and vaguely contemptuous. Beneath the cap of jet-black hair, the two black eyes were two openings to an incomprehensibly infinite universe. Kip felt the same sense of helplessness come flooding back, the same enfeebling sense of embarrassment before an immeasurably greater creature. The little boy sat down suddenly, cross-legged on the ruai, and something clicked. A curious shift in space. Now, the random gathering of primitive villagers appeared as formally ranked retainers in the court of some oriental potentate. The tattooed men with their parangs, the women in their brightly patterned sarongs, the infants carefully placed for picturesque effect, all of them chatting and laughing, and all of them unknowingly positioned about the little boy in certain, particular, peculiar patterns, perhaps for no other purpose than the casual, aesthetic whims of this anonymous little chieftain who sat cross-legged among them.

Kip felt the little boy's mind casually riffle through his own. There was nothing more there. Nothing new. He was released. He turned and stumbled after his guides into the jungle.

For the first few hours, he traveled like a sleepwalker through the rainforest. One guide walked before him, one behind. He floated between them, numb, slowly comprehending the depth of his incomprehension. What was he to make of this experience? He felt as if everything were changed, all grounds and assumptions for daily life yanked away. If that little boy existed, and he did, then all of Kip's rational explanations for how the world worked were worthless, matchstick toys. Like Paul on the road to Damascus, he was struck down with revelation. But unlike Paul, he had not been lifted up. He felt no new sense of direction. No transcendent, selfless goal. The potent presence that had been revealed seemed largely indifferent to him. Kip was an item of passing, perhaps prurient interest, nothing more. How was he to share this humiliating discovery? Who would want to share it? It was isolating, debilitating, and it led nowhere. He had no physical evidence for it. He did not even have an entertaining tale to tell, one with cataclysms and thunderbolts and dragon apparitions. All he had was this subtle apprehension, a shift in view, resulting from the most personal of personal communications. Was this, he wondered, how the first Iban who saw the first white man had felt?

As the hours went by, he slowly became aware again of the vast, breathing jungle that enveloped him. Families of gibbons hooted off in the trees. A Malaysian thrush trilled its liquid, elusive notes. The rainforest was a huge, living organism, and the narrow path they followed was one of its capillaries. They traveled along it like bacteria or antibodies in the bloodstream. An incredible profusion of living things surrounded them. Scientists counted the Borneo rainforest as the richest, most complex ecosystem in the world. Kip had read that in one ten acre sample, researchers had found more than 800 different species of trees, more than existed in all of Great Britain. The butterflies that tagged along after him had probably yet to be cataloged. The lichens on the tree trunks no doubt harbored mysterious, life-saving compounds no one had identified. The whole buzzing environment contained a billion unfathomable wonders he would never understand. None of that upset him. Why should the little boy? Why should his exploitative indifference trouble Kip any more than that of the butterfly that sucked the sweat from his neck?

The answer that came to him as he trudged through the rainforest was that like most members of western civilization, he privately considered all other creatures on the planet to be inferior items of creation. Or at least, they weren't self-evidently superior like the strange little being back in the longhouse. And while the billion other buzzing wonders in the rainforest might not be understood, they could be. Would be. Eventually. They played by the rules. The little boy was outside the game.

Because of the dense canopy overhead, little direct light filtered down to the forest floor. It was hard to tell by the angle of the sun what time of day it was, but his watch said they had been on the trail for five hours, and now a new mystery overtook them. The jungle became quiet. He missed the gibbons first. Their distant but companionable hooting faded away. Then the birds, one by one, ceased their trilling, territorial claims. Finally, even the insects fell silent, and all around them, the only sound seemed to come from the plants themselves, as if in the act of photosynthesis their leafy respiration was audible, an imperceptible whispering in the perfectly still air.

It was then they heard the roar of the beast. A long, drawn out, rumbling howl that seemed to travel from one side of the world to the other. A groan of greed and monotonous, self-absorbed avarice that rose to an all-consuming shriek and then impossibly louder still, and then seemed to take an eternity to fade away, growling off below an unseen horizon, and when at last it was gone, even the millions of whispering plants were shocked silent.

The path they followed led straight towards it. In fifteen minutes, they saw the first sign of its passage, a raw, shattered stump nearly ten feet across. The stump was all that was left of one of the towering rainforest hardwoods. From the roughly circular area of devastation that surrounded the stump, they could see that the tree had once been more than a hundred feet tall. It had crushed a hundred smaller trees when it fell, and the mechanized creature that had dragged it off had mangled a thousand more. There was a hundred-foot wide swath of destruction that led off towards a strip of raw red earth a quarter mile away. A million shattered plants lay before them, torn and gouged and ripped from the earth, their broken branches interwoven with each other to create an impossibly treacherous tangle of trash. It was inviting a broken ankle to walk more than a few steps through the mess, and besides, his guides informed him, the tangle was filled with innumerable angry, newly disenfranchised snakes. The guides turned aside and led the way along a new path that looped around the first broken swath of forest, but soon ran into a second and then a third, and finally, the guides had to take out their parangs and chop their way twenty feet through a grasping thicket of sticks and vines in order to reach a deep gouge that one of the fallen giants had carved in the earth as it was being dragged away. The torrential rains that commonly arrived every late afternoon had dug this trench even deeper, widening it, and washing away the topsoil to reveal hard, red clay bedrock that made for comparatively easy walking. In another fifteen minutes they were at the road.

Here, the three of them squatted down to wait. The logging road was little more than a wider gouge in the earth, graded and leveled a bit, with deep ruts where the truck tires fitted. It looked like the inverse of an extra-wide railroad bed. Here, of course, there was no sheltering, leafy canopy. It had all been chopped down and dragged away, and so the sun fell down on them like physical blows to the top of the head.

It was nearly high noon when they arrived. The logging road was almost literally on the equatorial line. The whole sky seemed to be sun. The guides dragged some broken branches from the embankment, used their parangs to chop four posts and notched them for crossbars. They laid more sticks and leaves across the top of this open box to create a miserable bit of shade, and the three of them squatted beneath it, sipping water from Kip's canteen, too stunned by the heat to even speak.

After an interminable, changeless time, they had to get up and move a few feet to stay in the shade. The two guides squatted back down again. Kip dragged his pack over and used it for a stool. More time passed, and the two Iban guides agreed that it was taking longer than usual for another truck to roar by. On the return journey to the longhouse, Kip wouldn't be with them, and they could make much better time, but it was still at least a four-hour hike for them, and it wouldn't do to be caught out on the trail at nightfall. Antu roamed the jungle after dark. If Kip decided to come back with them, then they would all have to start back even sooner. What did Tuan want to do?

Kip thought of the little boy back in the longhouse, the inexplicable, disorienting power of his presence, his casual, contemptuous rifling of Kip's innermost thoughts and secrets, and he decided he would rather stay by the road. People said the logging trucks ran all day and all night. They were relentless. Surely one would be along soon. The guides shrugged. More time passed. They all got up and moved sideways to stay in their little patch of shade. His watch was reading ten after two, and the Ibans were glancing nervously at each other when off in the distance, they heard again the howling roar.

It was the biggest truck Kip had ever seen. A filthy, mud-spattered beast, its windshield reflecting the sun like a baleful Cyclopean eye and hurtling down the rutted road at sixty miles an hour. The engine block alone seemed as big as a house, and behind it, fishtailing crazily over the bumps and ruts, were forty tons of timber. Three enormous tree trunks, sixty to eighty feet long, were chained to the flatbed. The whole roaring, shrieking, terror bore down on them like an avalanche.

Like an idiot, Kip stood up and stuck his thumb out. Well, what else was he supposed to do? He stood there, six foot two inches of white man in straw hat, tan shorts and white "Minnesota University" T-shirt, his blond beard and hair sticking out in all directions, his thick, wire-rimmed glasses goggling at the truck as it hurtled towards him, the very incarnation of hell on wheels.

"Tuan! Tuan!" The guides pushed him back from the edge of the road as the hideous vehicle, without slowing even a fraction, seemed to veer towards them. Kip caught a slip-stream glimpse of a pockmarked face in black sunglasses and red bandana headband, peering down at him as the truck howled past. The flatbed streaked by, jumping wildly out of the ruts, the gust from its passage whipping their pitiful little shelter back into indistinguishable roadside trash. All three of them ducked. The Ibans jumped back up immediately and ran out to the center of the road, waving their arms frantically after the departing banshee.

And to Kip's surprise, the truck seemed to slow. And then he heard it downshift. And downshift again. And one of the Ibans ran to snatch up his pack, and the other Iban urged Kip into motion, and together the three of them ran, scrambling and tripping, down the rutted, red clay road beneath the terrible sun after the savage metal that was rolling to a halt more than a quarter mile away.

The mighty engine was lumbering in neutral when Kip finally staggered up to the side of the truck. He could hear tinny music with a frantic rock beat coming from inside the cab, a shrill counterpoint to the continuous thunder of internal combustion. He was dizzy and reeling from the heat as he gazed up at the pockmarked face in black sunglasses and red bandana that stared down at him. The face seemed to twitch and jerk from side to side in time to the music.

"You English?" the face asked.

"American," Kip replied.

"Ah! Fuck you! Fuck you!" The face broke into a yellow-toothed grin. "I speak fucking American. I speak fucking English. Japanese, too. I speak six fucking languages. Know how I learn? Learn dirty words first. Best fucking way. You want ride, asshole?"

"Yes."

"Hop in, you cunt."

And moments later, Kip was up in the filthy cab that was rank with the smell of diesel oil and rotted shrimp paste. The cacophonous rock music yammered Asian language lyrics at him from a cassette machine that swung on a strap from the dashboard. The maniacal driver twitched and jerked, different parts of his body keeping double and triple time to the music as he threw the gearshift into first. The engine bellowed like a bull, and they began to inch forward.

"Hit the road, Jack!" the driver shouted, grinning madly and beating a frantic tattoo on the steering wheel with his free hand. Kip tried to smile and looked out the window at his two Iban guides who stood, barefoot and solemn by the side of the road. He waved out the window, and they slowly raised their hands and waved back.

"Wait!" Kip shouted. "Stop! I haven't paid them. I forgot!"

"Fuck 'em!" the driver shouted and laughed and threw the gearshift into second.

"No! Stop! Wait!" Kip looked from the driver back out the window, started to reach for his pack on the floor, then suddenly reached behind himself and fumbled in his hip pocket for his wallet. The truck was starting to roll now. The driver hit the next gear and the next. Kip pulled out mildewed Malaysian money from his wallet, oversized red, green and blue notes. He leaned out his window, the hot air whipping past him, and looked back at the two Ibans watching him disappear down the road. "Thank you!" he cried, and flung the colored scraps back at them. The paper whirled and twisted crazily in the hot wind and was sucked down beneath the wheels of the flatbed.

Kip leaned back in his seat. "Jesus, what a shit I am," he said.

"Shit! I know shit!" the driver shouted gleefully. "What other dirty words you know?"

"I'm a prick!" Kip shouted.

"Prick!" shouted the driver.

"Oh, shit," Kip said.

"I know shit already!"

"No, I mean . . . oh shit, never mind."

"I know shit!"

"Good!"

The truck had eighteen gears, and in a few minutes, the driver had worked his way up through all of them. They tore through the smashed jungle like a jet bomber at ground level.

"Lucky fuck they with you!" the driver shouted over the howl of the wind, the roar of the engine, and the frantic yammer of Asian rock. "I think you fucking antu. Ghost! Try run you down. What you do out here, prick?"

"Research!" Kip shouted back, deciding not to mention that he was, indeed, researching ghosts.

"You search for AIDS tree?"

"What?"

"AIDS tree. Tree cures AIDS. Medicine tree Americans find. They come back, try find more. No can. We cut 'em all down. All fucking gone." The driver laughed at this great joke, nodding graciously out the window as if the forest appreciated it, too. He twitched and jerked in time to the music and briefly took both hands off the wheel to light a cigarette "I'm Tiger," he shouted, grabbing the wheel in the nick of time to avoid disaster.

"You're what?"

"My American name. Tiger. Chinese name, Tong. Iban name Tak. You American. Call me Tiger."

"OK, Tiger."

"What your name?"

"Kip."

"OK, Kip. You know any more dirty words, Kip?"

Kip thought a moment. "Sucks!" he shouted.

"What 'Sucks?'"

"This 'sucks!'"

"This sucks?"

"Yeah, this sucks!"

"This sucks!" Tiger shouted with glee and beat a double tattoo on the steering wheel. "You want durian, Kip?" He pointed at the floor of the cab where two ripe durian about the size of footballs were rolling wildly back and forth, bumping into Kip's pack. A green-colored fruit with a thick, knobby skin, the flesh of durian was so indescribably rich and potent, it couldn't be consumed along with alcohol or it would ferment in the gut and the eater could die from bloat. It was notorious both as an aphrodisiac and as the most rotten scent in Southeast Asia.

"No thanks!" Kip shouted.

"Good time, durian. When durian come down, skirts go up. Go fuck, fuck!" Tiger laughed wildly and jiggled in his seat as the truck careened around a bend.

"Ular!" he shouted and pointed ahead. A strip of black something lay across the road. It flashed below, out of sight.

"What?"

"Ular! Snake! Big fucking cobra! I run him down yesterday. Fucking snake like lie in sun. I run him down. Everyday run him down. You like pill, Kip?"

"What?"

"Like pill?" Tiger reached into a plastic sack beside his seat and pulled out a handful of little red and white pills. He sorted out one of each and popped them in his mouth like breath mints. "Take fucking pill, no need fucking sleep. Just drive fucking drive."

"Why don't you fucking sleep?"

"No fucking can. Company wants us fucking work. All time work. Drive day. Drive night. Sleep little bit. Drive day. Drive night. You want pill?"

"No thanks."

Tiger started beating an even faster tattoo with one hand on the steering wheel while he flicked cigarette ash out the window with the other. "This sucks!" he shouted happily.

Kip wondered what happened when Tiger encountered another half-breed, hophead driver, coming like a bat out of hell in the opposite direction. He looked around for a seat belt but saw none.

"You no like durian, Kip. Try this." Tiger fumbled in his plastic sack and pulled out a little white paper envelope. He handed it across, and Kip tried to decipher the label as he jounced up and down on the cracked vinyl seat. There was a filigreed logo stamped in red ink, some Chinese characters, and the English words "Paris Emotion Pill."

"Take before you fuck. Go fuck, fuck, all night. Four, five fuck, fuck. Wake up morning. Dick all gone. Used up. Small, small."

Tiger laughed and held up his thumb and forefinger a fraction of an inch apart. Then he suddenly pointed at the road in front of them.

"Ular!" he shouted, and swung the wheel.

Kip caught a glimpse of a black snake, six to eight feet long, slithering across the red clay road. The truck leaped for it, heading for the ditch. The snake flashed out of sight over the edge of the embankment. Tiger cursed and swung the wheel back in the opposite direction too hard and too fast. The front tires jammed in the ruts. For an instant, the cab froze in time and space, one side tilted towards the sky, and then forty tons of severed, revengeful, jungle hardwood rammed into it from behind.

The cab exploded like a clapped paper bag. Kip flew out the sprung door like a pilot on an ejection seat. Jungle, road and sky revolved around him, beneath him, above him. He saw the truck flatbed jackknifing up over the crushed cab and the three enormous tree trunks burst free from their chains. They rose, vertical once again, triumphantly towering, free again to reach for the sky, free even from their roots that had bound them to the earth, free at last to soar for heaven, and then it all went black.

———

In London, Lady Gloria revolved in her sleep, slippery as a fish in pink satin. Across town, Mislov Rapolovitch lay still as death in black silk pajamas. In Florida, Beth Phillips thumbed the remote on her television set, and the flickering screen crackled down into a fading blue spark. In Honolulu, Gordon Coburn stared through tinted slabs of office glass at the setting sun, which transformed the surrounding ocean into a vast plane of beaten gold.

And in Borneo, Kip Stallybrass opened his eyes and saw the image of the strange little boy from the longhouse, sitting cross-legged in the air and floating in front of him. Kip was lying, half on the ground and half on the exploded seat cushion from the truck cab. He moved his head from side to side, trying to shake the image of the little boy from his eyes. His blue pack was lying just a couple of yards away to his left. Off to his right, he could see the crumpled remains of the truck cab. One of the massive tree trunks had fallen across it, mashing it into grotesque junk. The other tree trunks and the flatbed were splayed out across the road like a giant's game of pick-up-sticks. Kip looked back directly in front of him, and the little boy was still there. Floating in the air. Considering. The two of them stared at each other, and after a certain pause, the little boy made a small gesture with his hand and pointed up in the sky. Kip looked up and saw a diminutive, single-engine plane passing overhead. It wheeled, turned, and circled back, swooping down along the length of the road, its mosquito buzz becoming a droning, thrumming roar, and then everything went black again.

————

He woke up in the hospital in Kuching. A brisk English doctor with tuffs of black hair sprouting from his nostrils was peering into his eye with a tiny flashlight.

"Ah! Here we are then, are we?" the Englishman said.

Kip promptly went back to sleep.

He had several more transitory encounters like this with the doctor and also with a Chinese nurse who came in at various odd hours to change his intravenous feeding bottle. Then one morning he actually woke up feeling hungry. He said this to the nurse, and shortly thereafter, the doctor reappeared.

"Feeling hungry, are we?" the doctor said, and peered into his eyes once again with the little flashlight.

"Yes."

"That's a good sign. I'm Doctor Smythe. Know who you are?

"I'm Kip. Kip Stallybrass."

"Are you now? That's good you know. We didn't, you see."

"Where am I?"

"In hospital. Kuching. Capital of Sarawak. State of Malaysia on the island of Borneo. Damn lucky to be here, too."

"Yes," Kip agreed and floated off again. When he woke up, Doctor Smythe was again bending over, peering into his eyes with the flashlight.

"We have to stop meeting like this," Kip said.

"Fine with me, Mr. Stallybrass. We've got others could use this bed."

"How did I get here?"

"MAF."

"MAF?"

"Missionary Air Force. American chaps fly about up in the ulu and Kalimantan converting the Ibans and Kayans. This fellow happened to fly over as you were lying there in the ditch. Made a rather chancy landing. Picked you up and ferried you down here. Are you a Baptist?"

"No."

"Well, you should be. After that."

"I should thank him."

"You can't, I'm afraid. Government booted him out. Shouldn't have been where he was, and definitely shouldn't have flown all the way down here. If he hadn't, of course, you'd be dead."

"Yes," Kip agreed, quite certain of this.

"Government wants you out of here, too. But you've had a severe concussion, and you're not going anywhere for a while. Once you're out of hospital, I strongly recommend you don't do any traveling for two or three weeks. Give time for the internal swelling to go down. Make sure there's no clots. Otherwise, you're all right. Nothing broken."

"What happened to Tiger?"

"Tiger?" Smythe's eyes narrowed suspiciously. "What tiger? You're not raving, are you?"

"Tiger was the driver. Of the truck."

"Oh. No idea. You're all we got. I have the address of the MAF chap if you'd like to write to him sometime. One Charles Brown. From Texas."

Kip went to sleep again and dreamed he was in a cartoon panel along with Tiger. He was staring straight out of it and couldn't see what was drawn in the panels on either side, but Tiger was looking over into the next panel and shouting, "You're a good fucking man, Charlie Brown." The little boy from the longhouse was sitting cross-legged in the air outside the panels, looking down at them and reading the comics.

He was in the hospital for five days. On his release, he rented a room in the rear of a small hotel that overlooked the narrow alleys and courtyards along the back of a row of Chinese shophouses. He couldn't afford the Kuching Holiday Inn. Indeed, he was very nearly penniless, although he didn't inform the Malaysian government of this fact. They were irritated enough at him for having become involved in a logging accident. The Sarawak authorities had received so much international bad press over their rapacious logging companies, they were suspicious of any Westerner who came close to them. They feared Kip was really a muckraking environmental journalist in disguise, and they would have deported him at once were it not for his medical condition. If they had, they might at least have paid for his return trip ticket, Kip reflected. His sojourn in the hospital and the recuperation afterwards caused him to miss his return flight date, and the airline he had booked it on had given up being Mr. Nice Guy about things like that. Charles Brown, the air-borne missionary and Good Samaritan, had apparently picked up Kip's pack along with Kip and brought it down with him to the Kuching hospital. The pack still contained his precious research, but his passport, his traveler's checks, his wallet and credit cards were all missing. The American counsel would replace the passport. And the credit cards didn't matter much as they were nearly tapped out anyway, but money was a definite problem. His only resource was the small account he had opened in a Kuching bank with the rent deposit refund check that Barbara had sent him. He had six hundred US dollars there. He calculated that after two weeks of hotel and meal expenses, he would have maybe four hundred dollars left, about an eighth of the cost of a one-way ticket from Kuching to Minneapolis. He supposed he could throw himself on the mercy of the American counsel, but that would be certain to go on his record and seemed a poor start to the beginning of a career in international anthropological research. Money was definitely a problem.

He didn't let it bother him, however. He had a more serious problem to address, which was the existence of that strange little boy back in the longhouse. He moved his mind in a cautious, circuitous fashion around this issue, gingerly approaching the memory of what had occurred with the little boy and then quickly backing away from it. He knew that if he really accepted his memory as fact, really believed that what had happened actually had happened, then he would have to change a great many other things in his belief system. The little boy seemed to suspend the rules of time and space, of cause and effect. There was no rational explanation for him. And if the supposedly universal rules of rationality were not really universal after all, then there was really no rational explanation for anything. All rational explanations were just delusions. Kip had always thought that the deluded ones were the people he studied. He had never really credited shamanic journeys as being anything more than delusions, for example. His theory to explain the surprising parallels between the stories of shamans in isolated and widely separated parts of the globe was that they were all recounting a common sense memory of the universal experience of birth. Their shamanic journeys were all illusory returns to the womb.

But believing in the possibility of actual shamanic journeys was small beer compared to believing in that little boy. As a practical matter, if he talked about his experience or wrote about it, at least in the near future, his chances for a university post would become even more problematic. University departments wanted to hire sober, rational researchers and teachers. You were allowed revelatory, apocalyptic experiences only after you had tenure. Kip didn't want to be relegated to the margins of his profession, classified as a spacey, parapsychology buff. Besides, what had occurred was not only wholly unprovable and without a scrap of physical evidence, it was also in some respects rather embarrassing. If he had any sense, he would dismiss the memory of what had happened as a hallucination brought on by his concussion. That probably was exactly what it was. Given time, he might even convince himself of this. As long as, and this was his real fear, the omnipotent little mind reader didn't reappear in front of him sometime, floating cross-legged in the air.

He worked this out over a period of several days while waiting for the swelling inside his head to go down. He also spent a day composing a careful letter of thanks to Charles Brown in Texas. It was difficult to thank the man for saving his life while at the same time discreetly inquiring if he had also lifted his wallet. The rest of the time he sat by the window in his little room, watching the leisurely life of the knob-tailed Kuching cats who patrolled the alleys behind the Chinese shophouses. After a week, he washed up in the hotel's communal shower, dressed in his most presentable shirt and shorts, which were still pretty scruffy, and paid for an hour's internet access at the business center of the Grand Margherita Hotel so he could check his email. Amidst the sea of spam and outdated trivia, he discovered the news that the Seventh Annual Conference on Shamanistic Practice had been moved to Honolulu. He took to visiting the docks, and two days before his visa ran out, he managed to book passage on the Tunglin Maru, a tramp steamer that was in port on its way up to Kota Kinabalu in Sabah, the northern Malaysian state of Borneo. In addition to various tons of obscure cargo, the Tunglin Maru had steerage accommodations for three hundred people. Two hundred and ninety seven of these triple-tiered bunks were occupied by indentured laborers from southern India on their way to work in the Sabah rubber tree plantations. After dropping them off in Kota Kinabalu, the Tunglin Maru would continue on through the Sulu and Celebes Seas to Zamboanga in the Philippines. From there it would travel to Tinian and Saipan, sail back down to Kwajalein in the Marshall Islands and then back up to Hawaii. After six weeks at sea, Kip would arrive in Honolulu utterly broke and more than a month early for the conference. Nonetheless, the pack that Charles Brown had rescued still contained his recordings and notebooks. He could use the time on board ship to write a first draft of his talk for the conference. And as for that extra month, Honolulu seemed a better place to be indigent than most.

He went back online at the hotel and emailed an abstract of his proposed talk, confirming his attendance at the conference but declining the discounted accommodations at the Earl Court Waikiki. He would, he claimed, be staying with friends. The Tunglin Maru sailed in the evening on a falling tide that sped the rusting old hulk down the Kuching River like a racing yacht. The glimmering lights of Borneo fell behind him into immemorial dusk.

CHAPTER SEVEN

God, he wanted to gag! That stale, musky scent was suffocating him. It was like something curling out from beneath a mildewed pile of unwashed laundry. A wad of old towels and sweaty socks and twice-worn underwear stuffed in a corner of a closet and left to rot, that's what she smelled like. And this was supposed to be his Public Relations Director! Worse, she was his lover. Carol Nickle sat in the guest chair on the other side of his desk, swiveling back and forth with a commandingly casual attitude as if this were her office instead of his and sending off periodic drafts of scent like an oscillating fan. The speakerphone beeped.

"Cynthia from reservations on two."

He couldn't risk talking to Cynthia on the speakerphone in front of Carol. When Cynthia thought he was alone, she called him "Gordie." He smiled at Carol and cautiously picked up the receiver.

"Gordon Coburn speaking."

"Hi, Gordie," said the little voice in his ear.

Carol swiveled around in the guest chair in front of him and surveyed his office furnishings and mementos with a proprietary air. She was dressed in another one of her broad-shouldered silk jackets, this one a bright crimson set off with a creamy ivory scarf. Gordon imagined he could actually see her sending off invisible waves of effluvium. Christ, she stank.

"Hello, Cynthia, how are you this morning?"

"Is somebody with you, Gordie?"

"Yes."

"Oh," said the little voice, disappointed. "Well, guess what?"

"What?"

"I just reserved the Presidential Suite for two weeks in September."

"That's wonderful! Who to?" Gordon glanced over at Carol who looked at him quizzically.

"To a Lady Hortense Crawley-Smith from England. She's a Viscountess. Like a Queen or something."

"Well that's great. When is she arriving?"

"September third. She wants to attend that conference we're having. The shaman thing. And Gordie? Room 2202 is open tonight."

Gordon looked at the red-jacketed Carol, swiveling impatiently back and forth in front of him. He sniffed and exhaled quickly. "Good idea," he said.

"You can come?"

"Yes."

"All right! Room 2202, tonight. What time?"

"You tell me."

"Eight o'clock?"

"I'll write it in. Good work. Thank you, Cynthia."

He hung up the phone and leaned back in his leather executive chair. He leaned back as far as he could. Every inch further away he could get from Carol the better.

"We've rented the Presidential Suite for when Earl and Suzuki-san are here in September."

Carol shrugged her broad shoulders, unimpressed. Gordon imagined even that little movement sending another zephyr of body odor wafting across his desk. What in God's name did she do? Or didn't do, that could create a smell like that? He really should talk to her about it just on the basis of sound management. She did, after all, represent the hotel.

But his relationship with Carol was delicate, to say the least. It was two weeks since the embarrassing incident with the travel agents, and it was a subject they still hadn't discussed despite having slept together six times now in the anonymous bedrooms of the Earl Court. The affair was Carol's idea. Gordon was shocked that first night in Room 1410 when she walked in and casually started to strip. Shocked and then appalled when the powerful B.O. which had first assaulted him in the gym came on as strong as she did. With inspiration born of desperation, he had hit upon the idea of their showering together, and this had become their standard mode of foreplay. If not for that, Gordon doubted he could have risen to the occasions. But once Carol was bathed and fragrant with the Earl Court's bath gel, she was an attractive and surprisingly inventive lover, albeit more demanding than he liked. There remained, however, an uncomfortable, unspoken edge to their relationship. Gordon needed to clear the air in more ways than one.

"Carol," he said. "Melanie is coming back to work today."

Carol touched the floor with her toe and slowly rotated around in her chair to face him. "So?" she said.

"I'm going to speak with her. I won't tell her about us, of course."

"You ought to fire her."

"Fire her? What for?"

"For being in the way."

"In the way of what? I mean, I can't . . . fire her."

"Sure you can. You're General Manager."

"But she hasn't done anything. That is, nothing I can fire her for. She doesn't deserve . . . she's good at her job."

"Is she better than me?" Carol eyed him with a cold ferocity, like a bird readying to gobble a bug.

"No, of course not. Not, not at that. But, look! She's a very nice person. And besides, it only makes sense to treat her well. After all, she was there that morning, too. Obviously. She could say something, too."

"Are you going to keep sleeping with her, then?"

"No. I don't want to."

"But you'd sacrifice."

"I'm just going to talk with her. Find out what her feelings are. It makes sense, and it's the decent thing to do."

Carol stood up and leaned over his desk to stare him in the eye. Her smell was a physical force, like being embraced by a bear. "If you sleep with her again, your ass is grass."

Gordon let his jaw hang open. If he breathed through his mouth, he couldn't smell as much. "Carol, let's be clear about something. If I'm seeing you, it's because I want to, not because I have to."

"Good."

He decided to forge ahead. It was time to take control of this situation. "There's really nothing you can do, anyway," he said. "Those travel agents would never believe it was me they saw. They wouldn't even recognize me. They saw some naked guy, and I don't think they looked at his face. Besides, they've all left. Gone back to California."

Carol stayed leaning over the desk, staring at him as Gordon gulped air through his mouth.

"I want to see you tonight," she said.

"I can't tonight."

"You're sleeping with Melanie?"

This was getting complicated. "I swear to you, I am not sleeping with Melanie."

"Then cancel whatever you've got." Carol stood back up and squared her crimson shoulders. "I want to see you tonight. Find us a room. You can leave the number on my voice mail." And with that, she turned and swept out.

Gordon stared after her, his emotions veering between relief and trepidation. He had gotten some things out in the open with Carol, but he wouldn't say he had exactly cleared the air. He had been successful in the most important thing, though. He had cast doubt on her ability to blackmail him. At least he hoped so. Still, he had better see her tonight. It was vital to reestablish his authority. Once that was back in place, he could begin to miss these assignations and slowly, gently, disengage himself. For now, he better cancel with Cynthia instead.

He poked at his speakerphone. The black box winked at him and spoke in a shy, sweet voice, "Reservations, this is Joy."

Gordon cut the line off without saying anything. He didn't want to ask for Cynthia by name. He didn't want the whole reservations staff knowing that he wanted to speak with Cynthia in particular. They'd immediately start asking each other why he wanted to speak with Cynthia in particular. He poked at the speakerphone again. This time it sounded as if it smoked two packs a day.

"Reservations, this is Karen."

Damn. He cut the line off, waited a moment, and poked again.

"Reservations, this is Frank."

Hell and damn. This was taking too long. He had a hotel to run. But wait! He had a perfectly legitimate reason to call Cynthia back. He poked at the black box again.

"Reservations, this is Cynthia."

"Cynthia! Ah, good. This is Gordon. Listen, when is that Lady, that Englishwoman arriving in the Presidential Suite?"

"September third."

"OK, good." Gordon leafed through pages of his desk calendar towards September. "And what was her name? Crawling?"

"Lady Hortense Crawley-Smith."

"OK. I want to make sure to welcome her myself. And Cynthia, I'm sorry, I'm going to have to take a rain check on tonight."

"Gordie! Why do you say you can if you can't?"

"I'm sorry, I–" Gordon stopped in mid-sentence and stared down at the first week of the month of September in his desk calendar. There across the top of the page, someone had written in fierce black capitals, "You will die this month."

"How about tomorrow night?"

"What? OK. Sure." Gordon answered without thinking.

"OK then, tomorrow night at eight. Room . . . " The speakerphone went silent. "Room 1218 is open."

"See you there," Gordon said hurriedly, and cut the line.

He quickly punched in another extension. The speaker-phone blinked and spoke in a deep, gravely voice. "Security," it said.

———

Meanwhile three miles up in Manoa Valley, the Earl Court's Director of Group Sales, Howie Berg, tickled the sole of his client, Janet Sorenson's foot. She giggled and curled her toes. Howie kept on tickling. Janet kicked and paddled her feet, thrusting them back down beneath the covers.

"Stop it," she said. "This is supposed to be a breakfast meeting. Go get breakfast."

"OK," Howie agreed. He turned and padded across Janet's one-room cottage from the bed to the refrigerator. He was wearing nothing but a pair of faded blue boxer shorts, and his belly and butt bulged out comfortably fore and aft. Janet admired his profile and once again mentally thanked Gordon Coburn for preempting their business lunch two weeks before. The lavish dinner Howie had bought her instead had allowed them both to drink a little wine, take a walk on the beach underneath the stars, and before she knew it, this big, tickling, teddy bear in blue boxer shorts had shambled into her life. Now he made everything in her familiar little cottage seem tiny and new, like a dollhouse for munchkins. She giggled again.

"What?" Howie asked from the sink.

"Nothing." Janet returned to her stack of letters and emails. "Here's one from Borneo."

Howie sang, "Way down south, down south in Borneo."

"He wants to give a paper on 'Iban Shamans versus Iban Ghosts: Theatricality and Spectacularity in a Borneo Longhouse.' This looks good."

"Oh Borneo, Oh Borneo Babe," Howie sang and padded back across the room with two glasses of orange juice.

"It's a post-doc study, though." Janet said, frowning. "He's not with any university. He goes in the maybe pile for now."

And Janet put the letter from Kip Stallybrass on the larger of two stacks of abstracts and proposals regarding shamanism. They were arriving from every corner of the earth. In Janet's little Hawaii cottage there were letters, express paks and emails from a Bulgarian studying dervishes in Turkey, from a Frenchmen investigating initiation ceremonies in Korea, and from an Australian documenting the Tantras of Tibet. There was a Hungarian "Ethno-semiotic Approach," a description of the Kumano female shamans of Japan, an examination of the Kootenai Indian shamans of western Montana, and an account of the New Moon Sacrifice as practiced by the Amur Nanai in northern Russia. Actual shamans were coming in person from the Wintu Indian tribe in Northern California, from the Yakut in Siberia, the Mapuches in Chile, the Padhar tribe near Gujarat in India, and the Galibi Caribs of French Guyana in South America. And all this was just one day's mail.

"Maybe what?" Howie asked. "Maybe you won't let him come?"

"Oh, he can come," Janet said, accepting her glass of orange juice. "Anybody can attend. But we're already up to nine hundred attendees, so everybody can't give a paper. There aren't enough meeting rooms. A committee decides who gets to talk and who gets to listen. I have to read his abstract and decide if we can recruit a good respondent."

"Nine hundred attendees," Howie mused.

"We'll have more before we're through," Janet said. I bet we go over twelve hundred."

"Well," said Howie, "as Director of Group Sales, I'd say an impressive figure like that . . . " He pinched her bottom underneath the sheet.

"Don't, you'll make me spill," Janet giggled and gulped her orange juice.

"An impressive figure like that requires that we have another business meeting. How about a business dinner tonight?"

"Have we finished with business this morning?"

"Hum. Maybe not," Howie said, and carefully set his glass of orange juice down on the nightstand.

―――――

And three miles east in Kahala, a Honolulu neighborhood of extravagant beach front homes, Christine Larren wafted out onto her lanai in a peignoir, fed a few seeds to her pair of green cockatoos, reclined on a chaise lounge with coffee and oranges at her side, and prepared to update herself on the recent acquisitions for the Earl Court Waikiki's art collection. Using a silver filigreed letter opener that had once belonged to the Medici, she slit open a mud-spattered aerogram from her son, George, writing her from somewhere on the Sepik River in New Guinea. "I hate you, Mother," it began.

> I hate you! You knew what this would be like, and you sent me to this godforsaken hellhole anyway. Bugs! Cannibals! I hate it! I hate you! We're stopping again to rub clay into the cracks of the dugout or we'll sink. And this river is nothing but snakes and crocodiles and man-eating bugs. No wonder the art here is "primitive." What

would you expect from the evil, benighted people who choose to live here rather than commit suicide immediately? If I survive to Port Moresby, I will ship you three dugout loads of witch doctor masks and ugly carvings of demon gods. They're as authentic as they need to be, and I hope they curse you to a hell as dreadful as this one.

Your Son,
George

—————

"Looks like somebody's got it in for you, all right," said Dick Brukowski. He stared gloomily at the September page of Gordon's desk calendar and its fiercely scribbled note, "You will die this month."

In an earlier age, Dick Brukowski would have been known as the House Detective or "House Dick," but a prestigious chain like the Earl Court did not employ "House Dicks," so Dick Brukowski was spared that eponymous title. He was known as "Chief of Security." But lots of people at the hotel, even Gordon, liked to call him their "House Dick" when he wasn't around. Brukowski just sort of looked and acted like a "House Dick." He was a beefy, lugubrious man who had been an M.P. in the navy for twenty years before mustering out at Pearl Harbor and finding work in the civilian sector. After twenty years in uniform, Brukowski could now come to work in Aloha shirts, and he seemed to select them in a deliberate attempt to enliven his personality. Gordon regarded the pink ukuleles and green sharks that were frolicking over his Chief of Security's abdomen with distaste.

"When are you going to get a handle on this?" Gordon asked. "If this guy's for real, I've only got four months to live."

Brukowski extracted his wallet from his hip pocket, and from it, he dug out the note from the Tylenol box and the tiny ribbon of paper from the fortune cookie. He set the two scraps of paper alongside the desk calendar and stared at all three of them gloomily. "Why don't you take September off," he said.

Gordon snorted. "That's not possible. There's too much going on in September."

"I thought September was supposed to be slow?"

"It's never *supposed* to be slow."

"Well," Brukowski sighed, "this is tough. There's no similarity between these three. The first two were done on different machines. And the handwriting on this one looks disguised. I talked to the waiters. I talked to the maids. They're not talking. You got anything else for me to go on?"

"If you flip back through that calendar, you'll see pretty much every appointment I've had since the first of the year. That's most of the people who've been in this office and could have written that."

"When you weren't looking?"

"Maybe," Gordon said doubtfully.

Brukowski sighed.

"Did you track down the place that made these?" Gordon asked and pulled a plastic bag of fortune cookies from out of a drawer in his desk.

"Yeah. It's a Chinese bakery in Mapunapuna. Course they say they didn't do it. Had to be somebody here at the hotel. They showed me how easy it is to pull one of those little fortunes out of a cookie and put another one in. Hey," Brukowski brightened momentarily. "Are those the same cookies from that night?"

"Yeah. I think so."

"Why don't you open some more? See if they're the same."

Gordon looked uncomfortably at the bag in his hand. This idea had occurred to him, but he just hadn't felt like doing it. He reluctantly pulled a cookie out of the plastic sack. It looked like a bleached, bent oyster. He snapped it in half and crumbs fell on his polished koa-wood desk. He studied the little ribbon of paper inside.

"What's it say?" Brukowski asked.

"Keep romance in perspective," Gordon said in a flat tone of voice. He didn't like this latest fortune much more than his first one. The advice seemed just a little too relevant.

"Let me try," Brukowski said and fished out a cookie. He snapped it open and peered at the prediction. "Your dreams can come true if you believe in yourself," he read aloud and smiled vaguely.

Gordon wondered sourly what dull dreams populated Brukowski's imagination as Brukowski snapped open another cookie and read, "A 'no' means 'later'." The Security Chief scratched his chin. "Hum," he pondered. "A 'no' means 'later.' I wonder if this is talking about the bakery or the waiters. Or maybe the maids."

"Look, Brukowski!" Gordon said irritably. "This isn't—"

"Earl Pressler on one," his speakerphone announced importantly.

Gordon looked wide-eyed over at Brukowski, took a deep breath, and picked up the receiver. "Hello, Earl, how are you?" he said.

Pressler had a rich, authoritative voice with a distinguished East Coast accent. "Fine, Gordon. How are you this morning?"

"Very well."

"I expect you're busier than hell with that renovation."

Gordon looked at the cookie crumbs spread over his desk. He hadn't done a thing all morning except arrange illicit assignations and worry about these ridiculous predictions. "It is a busy time," he said. "Where are you calling from, Earl?"

"I'm back in Connecticut. I'm on my way to Saudi Arabia tomorrow. Wish I was heading out your way."

"We'd love to have you."

"Thank you. Well, listen, Gordon, the reason I'm calling is I think this renovation is an excellent opportunity to incorporate some of those civil defense guidelines we received out there after hurricane Iniki. Now you weren't there, then, were you."

"No I missed it."

"Damn lucky for you. It was a mess. And it didn't even really hit Oahu. Took out Kauai instead."

"I heard."

"Well, we're spending forty million, so let's make sure the meeting rooms can handle it if we have to do a vertical evacuation."

"I think that's been taken care of, Earl, but I'll double-check."

"Good, thanks, I knew you'd be on top of it. How's the weather?"

"Great."

"Great. Good. Keep up the good work. Well, Aloha."

"Bye, Earl."

Gordon hung up the phone and pursed his lips.

"Was that Earl Pressler?" Brukowski asked in awe-struck tones.

Gordon nodded.

"What's wrong?"

"Nothing. Nothing's wrong. It's just one of Earl's one-minute roundup calls."

Earl Pressler called twenty different hotels every day and talked to the General Manager at each property for one minute. That meant Gordon heard from him about once a month. The routine was meant to let the Earl Court's General Managers know that Earl cared and was "on top of things." And it was surprisingly effective.

"OK Brukowski," Gordon said suddenly. "You know what I know. Get out there and solve this thing. I've got work to do."

A few minutes later, Gordon was striding through his lobby on his way to the second floor meeting rooms. He looked like he felt. Important. Dedicated. A man charged with serious responsibilities, but nonetheless a charming man and a gracious host. As usual, he was wearing a coat and tie. The Earl Court chain expected this of all their General Managers, even the one in Hawaii. This was fine with Gordon because otherwise he could easily be mistaken for a towel boy, given his youth and customarily eager and cheerful manner. On this expedition, his imposing image was reinforced by a white plastic hard hat he carried underneath his arm. The dome above the visor was screened with the hotel's Earl Court logo, and because it was Gordon's hardhat, it was coded #1.

The forty million dollar renovation was already underway in parts of the hotel. In addition to the new, puke-colored paint and wallpaper Gordon had agreed to, they were also installing new lighting fixtures in the meeting rooms. The hotel had begun construction in the late 1980s, and so the meeting room light fixtures were either on track lighting or, in the case of the chandeliers, hung from cables in such a way that they could be moved. It made them look a little tacky, but because of a tax bill Congress had passed in 1982, it also meant that these lighting fixtures could be, and had been, depreciated in only four years. If they had been wired into the building, they would have been considered part of the building, and then they would have to have been written off over a period of ten years or more. The 1982 tax bill had a number of such generous wrinkles for real estate investors, and it had caused a terrific hotel building boom in the eighties. This was followed by a predictable hotel bust in the early nineties. Nationwide, more than five hundred hotels went bankrupt and had wound up in the hands of various savings and loans, which had funded the mortgages. When the savings and loans went bankrupt, the hotels wound up being owned by the federal government.

The Earl Court Waikiki had avoided this fate because of Hawaii's invincible popularity. But in Waikiki, the cable-hung chandeliers had another disadvantage besides looking tacky. They posed a danger in a hurricane.

Hurricane Iniki was a force four hurricane that had swept up the Molokai channel in the fall of 1992, heading straight for the island of Oahu and Waikiki. At the last minute, it had veered off and struck Kauai instead. Packing 160 mile an hour winds, it had devastated that island. Miraculously, only three lives were lost, but there was more than a billion dollars worth of damage, and Kauai's tourism industry was wiped out for nearly two years. Bad as that disaster was, it was minor to what would have occurred if Iniki had kept on course and struck Waikiki instead. As it was, the storm surge had left the Waikiki hotels with hundreds of fish flopping in their lobbies and tons of sand that had to be vacuumed out of their swimming pools. A quarter million people had evacuated Honolulu's vulnerable, low-lying shore areas when Iniki threatened, but that still left many thousands of tourists stranded in Waikiki. For their safety, the hotels relied on "vertical evacuation," which meant gathering everyone in bunker-like ballrooms and meeting rooms well above sea level. This was assumed to be safe enough providing the meeting rooms weren't hung with chandeliers that a force four hurricane like Iniki could suck off the ceiling and turn into a thousand pieces of flying shrapnel.

"How's it going?" Gordon called up at an electrician on a moveable catwalk in the Ilima Room. It was one of the smaller meeting rooms, about sixty feet wide by one hundred feet long and twenty feet high.

"OK, boss! Howzit?" the electrician called back to him. "Number One, eh!" he said, smiling down at Gordon's hat. He was a local guy, dressed in Levi's and a T-shirt, with a halo of frizzy black hair curling out from beneath his own hard hat.

Gordon smiled back up at him. He liked being called "Boss" by working guys. Especially after dealing with the likes of Carol Nickle and Earl Pressler. "How are you hanging the new chandeliers?" he asked. "Are they screwed in there good?"

"Real good."

"Can I see?"

"Sure. Come on up."

Gordon clambered up the metal pipes that supported the moveable catwalk. Its platform was set about four feet below the ceiling, so when he stood up, his head and shoulders poked up over the acoustic ceiling tiles and into the crawl space above. Although this crawl space was located above the meeting rooms, at first sight it appeared as a vast netherworld. Gordon looked off into a seemingly infinite darkness that extended far beyond the boundaries of the Ilima Room. While this hidden world undoubtedly related to the space below, it appeared to be organized on wholly different principles. Cables and wires snaked off in random directions, pausing occasionally to coil themselves into little piles before snaking off somewhere else. Big, faintly rumbling air conditioning ducts divided and redivided themselves and sent spurs angling off to distant destinations. Instead of resting on the acoustic ceiling tiles below, everything was suspended by steel rods fastened into a dark, overarching, concrete canopy reticulate with I-beams and buttresses and stretching off into dim infinity.

"We bolt 'em in real good," the electrician said, and tugged on a newly installed steel rod dangling from the concrete overhead.

"Hey, Russell!" cried a voice from below.

"What?" the Electrician called back and ducked down beneath the ceiling tiles. Gordon turned slowly, surveying this mysterious over-underworld which seemed so unfamiliar but which was also part of his domain. He heard a sudden rumbling and then a thumping, eructing boom as if one of the big air-conditioning ducts was commenting on his presence. He turned and caught a brief glimpse of a steel cable uncoiling and whipping towards him. He started to duck, but it struck him a vicious blow, knocking him backwards, down below the ceiling tiles onto the catwalk and then off the catwalk. The Ilima Room cartwheeled.

"Hey, Boss!" the Electrician shouted.

"Help!" Gordon cried and felt a fierce constriction in his chest.

"Got you!" the Electrician shouted from above his head as the floor swayed far below, "Grab the pipe!" The man was flat on his stomach on the catwalk, hanging over the edge and clenching the back of Gordon's suit coat, rucking it up into a wad across his shoulder blades and choking the breath out of him.

"I . . . Can't breathe!" Gordon choked out. He flailed his arms. "Can't reach!" He could hear his suit and shirt ripping. He was going to fall. But it wasn't September yet!

"Grab 'em!" the Electrician cried. Gordon flailed wildly, pinwheeling, dog-paddling the air. The stitches on one shoulder of his suit coat ripped away like a zipper flying open. He twisted, half fell, and grabbed one of the catwalk pipes. "All right!" The Electrician grinned down at him in relief. "Close, yeah?"

The General Manager of the Earl Court did not cut as impressive a figure on his way back to his suite as he had on the way out. His suit coat was in rags over his arm, and most of the buttons had ripped off his shirt. He kept his hard hat underneath his suit coat so the #1 couldn't be seen, but he knew that if he hadn't donned that particular vanity when he left his office, he might be dead. The steel cable had caught him across the crown of his head as he ducked, and the hard hat had done its job. All that had really suffered was his wardrobe and his dignity.

And his confidence. Hanging literally by a thread off the edge of the catwalk made the prediction "You <u>will</u> die in September" come home to him in a visceral way. Death was going to happen. Maybe in September. Maybe tomorrow. Maybe right now. Gordon knew it. Felt it in his bones.

Should he have Brukowski investigate those electricians? Could they be part of the plot against him? What could their motive be? He had been surrounded by six of them by the time he climbed down off the catwalk. The foreman was profuse in his apologies and had begun to abuse Russell and the other workmen, but they pointed out, fairly enough, that they had called Russell down, and how were they supposed to know anybody else was up there? No, it was just an accident. It couldn't be part of the plot against him. It wasn't September yet.

He had forgotten about Melanie. He stepped off the elevator at the Earl Court Club on the thirty-fifth floor, looking like an earthquake victim, and there she was behind the Concierge Desk. "Gordon?" she asked in surprise. "I mean," she looked from side to side, "Mr. Coburn?"

"Melanie!" Gordon said in shock. He looked quickly over his shoulder. "Welcome back!" He looked from side to side. There was no one else around. "I mean, Hi."

"Hi."

"Good to see you."

"What happened to you?"

"Oh, little accident with the renovation. It's nothing. How was your . . . ah . . . vacation."

"Good." She gave him a roguish glance. "But it's going to be good to get back to work."

Melanie was wearing a bright, floral print muumuu, the uniform for the Concierge staff. The high-necked, missionary-styled dress, recreated in bold tropical colors, was a wonderful foil for roguish glances. She came from a large Hawaiian family that was forever having parties and weddings and baby luaus, and Melanie always acted as if she were at a party herself, even when she was at work. The guests loved her for this, of course, and that's why she had a "front of the house" job at the Concierge Desk.

"Right. Good." Gordon said.

"Want to go on another "fam tour" tonight?" she giggled.

"No! I mean, I can't tonight."

"How about tomorrow night?"

Tonight was Carol. Tomorrow night was Cynthia. Earl Pressler had called. Somebody was trying to kill him. He was going to die in September. He looked like a rag picker. He had to change and get back to work. "I can't then either, Melanie, but we need to talk. How about—"

"Night after tomorrow?"

"Yeah. Yeah, that would be good. I'll let you know what room. Melanie, I'm sorry, I've got to change and get back down to the office." And smiling weakly, Gordon beat a retreat to his suite.

"Coo! Coo!" thundered the fat white pigeon from his lanai as he entered. Over the last few months, the bird had made Gordon's thirty-fifth floor railing its home base. It strutted up and down there several times a day, cooing loudly whether there were any impressionable female pigeons around or not. Gordon had become rather fond of it. From time to time, he even broke up some of the specialty Hawaiian lavosh from his in-room snack bar and tossed the crumbs out onto the lanai for it. But not this time. He tossed the hard hat and his torn jacket onto a chair and flopped onto his bed. "Coo! Coo!" roared the pigeon. "Oh shut up," said Gordon.

But the General Manager of the Earl Court Waikiki was a resilient fellow, and by the time he inserted his universal passkey into the lock of room 2202 that evening, he was resolved to take control of the Carol Nickle situation at least. What with Melanie and Cynthia and the renovation and being stalked by some anonymous employee scattering predictions of death, he had enough to deal with. He didn't need a third illicit liaison with a woman that smelled like toe jam. Besides, what he had told Carol that morning was perfectly true. Those travel agents were long gone, and they would never believe he was the nude guy with a hard-on anyway. Carol had nothing on him. It would be her word against his as long as Melanie didn't say anything. Melanie was the one he had to keep happy, and she didn't smell. This relationship with Carol, Gordon decided, was history.

He entered quickly. He was dressed in linen trousers and a polo shirt which was effectively camouflage for him, but he still didn't want to linger out in the corridor and chance being seen. He kicked off his shoes and sat down on the bed to wait. Room 2202, he observed idly, was exactly like room 1410 where Carol and the travel agents had discovered him with Melanie. Both rooms enjoyed the romantic mauka view and both had yet to be redecorated in shades of puke. They were done in the "Classical Tempo" color palette. Gordon gazed down at the subtle taupe carpet, over at the Etruscan brown drapes, back at the dusty mauve bedspread. He remembered again that unconsummated morning with Melanie. His rampant profile. His frontal display. That "Wow!" from the women crowding the doorway. He felt again a surge of sexual power and aggression. There was a light knock on the door.

"Hi," Carol whispered as he let her in. She was wearing a filmy little black dress, almost a negligee. She slipped inside the room, hung her purse on the doorknob, wrapped her arms around his neck and gave him a long French kiss.

"Gordon," she giggled girlishly when she pulled away, "you're panting."

"Yeah," Gordon smiled, breathing through his mouth. "Carol, we need to talk."

"Want to shower, first?" Carol slipped the spaghetti straps of her filmy black dress off her shoulders and gave a little shimmy. The dress slithered off and fell down around her ankles. She stepped elegantly out of it wearing nothing but a lacy black triangle held up by a thread that ran round her hips.

Gordon clung to his resolve. His relationship with Carol was going to be history. He was firm on that. But tonight was tonight, after all, and she seemed in a very different mood from this morning. Besides, he had at least two good reasons to shower with her. One reason was that then he could stop breathing through his mouth, and the other reason was getting bigger. "Sure," he said. "Let's get wet."

But once they were actually under the shower with the nozzle set on mist, slippery as seals with bath gel and with its scents of mink and lemon rising up about them, he felt a qualm. "Carol," he said, "this may not be fair."

"So? What is? Would you like me to wash you?"

"I don't want to take advantage of you."

"You can take advantage of me, Gordon. I like it. Can I wash you here?"

"Yes, but, you should know, ah! You should know that I've decided this is our last night together."

"But it's going to be a great night!"

"Yes. You see what with, what with the renovation and, and other things, I'm just under too much . . . pressure . . . right now."

"I understand."

"You do?"

"You're an important man. A very *big* man."

"Well, thank you."

"A *very* big man."

"Getting bigger."

"Oh, yes!"

"Yes!"

"These nights with you have been very special for me, Gordon. I will treasure this one most of all."

"That's really wonderful. Wonderful! Wonderful!!"

"Maybe we better—"

"Yes. We better."

As Carol emerged from the shower, she unhooked the two Earl Court, terrycloth bathrobes and shrugged into one. "Follow me, Gordon," she said, "and I'll dry you."

"You seem different, tonight," Gordon said as he followed her out into the bedroom.

"It's a special night. Now stand right there while I dry you here." She kneeled. "And here. And here. And . . . oh, I forgot. Stay right there. Don't move."

Carol rose from her kneeling position and walked back to the door where her purse was hanging from the doorknob. Along the way, she reached down and swept up her filmy black dress.

"Forgot what?"

"In my purse. It's something for you."

She turned, holding something small and black up to her face. POW! The camera's strobe flash caught Gordon open-mouthed, in rampant, full, frontal display. Carol swiftly turned, opened the door and, wrapping her robe tightly around her, disappeared out into the corridor. Blinded by the flash, Gordon didn't even know she was gone until he heard the door slam and her distant laugh. Not a girlish giggle any longer, but a harsh laugh that faded down the length of the corridor. "They'll recognize you now!"

CHAPTER EIGHT

Black hatred. Contempt. Disgust. A writing scream of rage was clenched inside his throat. He wanted to release it. Scorch the earth with it. Turn the universe to a cinder with it. He wanted to turn, fling, fly, rip down walls, level the city. He was Dresden, Hiroshima, Nagasaki. The imploding, exploding, all-destroying life hate of the nihilistic everything!

Mislov Rapolovitch had been scooped by *The London Times*.

And to salt the wound, the *Times* was using their photos to celebrate the sickening goody-goodness of Lady Gloria Ryder. The nauseating nobility of her Lancelot, Tom Leary. The anaphylactic fatuousness of that librarian in Hackney and her noxious banality, "Story Hour!" Photos just like Mislov's were being used to inform and motivate good deeds! For children! Even orphans! Mislov wanted to throw up! He stood rigid, black, and still in his hotel room as galaxies of rage and fury collided within him. Spread out on the bed were the ghastly pages from the *Times* that featured Gloria and the Junior Minister at Education, Tom Leary, as part of an in-depth article on the growing problem of illiteracy in Great Britain. There the two of them were with the Program Director of Story Hour and a gaggle of Dickensian children in front of that Victorian library in the East End. The *Times* photographer had even gone inside the library and shot Lady Gloria reading to a wan little blond girl off in a corner. How despicable!

Mislov snatched up the contact sheet with his own shots of what had transpired there in the East End. He noted with sour satisfaction that his talent hadn't deserted him, even if his luck had. The nanoseconds of time he had chosen to capture on film created a far different impression from what appeared in the *Times*. An energetic smile on Lady Gloria's face had in the next moment become a brief look of wide-eyed shock. That was the moment Mislov had recorded. And the Junior Minister's expression of beaming satisfaction had been stopped in such a way as to produce a salacious, eyelid-drooping leer. But Mislov's shots were useless now. The relationship between Lady Gloria and Tom Leary had already been exposed in the most flattering of lights. Any tabloid editor would laugh in his face if he tried to submit these photographs. They weren't scandalous. They were just bad photos. Decency and goodness had won out. He shivered, feeling a gust of . . . What? Longing? It rolled through him like a wave. These two were falling in love. That was obvious. It was also obvious that he never would. Or could. Love would never come to him. He had never wanted it before. Hate was all the passion he needed. His hate was enough. Wasn't it?

"No! Yes! No!"

In a convulsive fit of rage, Mislov snatched up the newspaper and ripped both it and the contact sheet in half. He stuffed them violently down into the wastebasket, saw Lady Gloria's happy, energetic smile crumple beneath his fingers. And paused. He knew better than this.

He pulled the papers back out of the wastebasket and smoothed them out on the bed. His subjects were celebrated now, yes. They were renowned as good, decent, admirable citizens. And who knew better than Mislov Rapolovitch that good, decent, admirable citizens were ideal subjects to put in the crosshairs of a lens. The higher they rose, the harder they fell. He set the ripped half of the contact sheet with Tom Leary's salacious leer down on the newspaper, positioning it next to Lady Gloria's energetic smile and right above all those darling little children. Surely something could be made of this. He mustn't lose heart.

A half hour later, Mislov was in position outside Tom Leary's flat. It was still quite early on a Saturday morning, and traffic was light. Not that it mattered. Traffic was no longer a problem for Mislov, because he had purchased a large, black, BMW motorcycle for his London expeditions. It was equipped with high-impact plastic saddlebags for stowing away his various camera bodies, lenses, and flash equipment, and while the engine was extremely powerful, it was muffled to the point of being whisper quiet. The motorcycle was like his own, personal Batmobile, and Mislov treated it like a lover. Pulling up across the street a half block away from the flat, he switched off the engine and took off his black helmet with its Darth Vader windscreen mask. Despite the early hour, it was already unusually warm. He wiped his brow and glared resentfully up at the cheerful blue sky and golden rays of sunshine beaming down into the city. He stood up, straddling his motorcycle in black leather pants that had begun to feel rather sticky. With his legs splayed out on either side of the bike, he looked like a huge, black insect waiting for prey.

And sure enough, before long the Minister's gray Rover purred down the quiet street and stopped in front of the flat.

A discreet beep from the horn, and a moment later Tom Leary himself bounded out the front door and down the steps. He was wearing a light khaki suit and a bold blue tie, and he carried a case in one hand. He slung it in the back seat of the Rover, jumped in after it, and the car purred off. A half block down the street, the black BMW whispered away from the curb and accelerated smoothly along behind.

It was child's play for Mislov to tail the Rover. The motorcycle's lightning quick acceleration and ability to thread through traffic allowed him to stay several car lengths back, zooming up only when the Rover made a turn and then falling back again when he was sure he wouldn't lose it. He hardly even needed to stay that close because it was clear from the route the Rover was taking that the Minister was on his way to Parliament. But to Mislov's surprise as they neared that destination, the Rover rolled right on down Birdcage Walk and Great George Street, past the Houses of Parliament and on over Westminster Bridge. Could he be going to Waterloo Station? Cursing, Mislov pulled up to one car length behind the Rover as they swept around the big roundabout. Just as he feared, his quarry took the second exit. Mislov peeled off directly behind, and they hurtled together down into the short tunnel and then up the long alley past the queue of taxis toward the drop off point. What was he going to do? There was no place to park. Once Leary had disappeared inside the train station, Mislov would never find him. There was no way of knowing what train he was taking, where he was going. He was going to lose him!

Biting out curses in an obscure Balkan dialect behind his Darth Vader mask, Mislov pulled out and zoomed past the Rover to the drop off point. Swinging in around the red cones and the perpetual construction, he jumped the curb and butted the bike up against the wall as the Rover pulled up behind him. Leary leaped out with his travel case as Mislov bent over the cycle's saddle bags, furiously pulling out cameras and lenses. Leary strode blithely on towards the station. He was whistling! Mislov could hear him whistling! The Rover purred away down the alley. A camera strap caught on Mislov's Darth Vader helmet. He tore the helmet off and finished hanging his various black and glittering cameras and lenses around his neck and off his shoulders till he was bandoleered like a bandit chief. Regret and sadness were foreign, contemptible emotions for Mislov, but he cast an almost wistful last look at his BMW motorcycle, beautiful, black, and abandoned there on the sidewalk. The police would confiscate it within five minutes, he knew. Turning his back on it, he ran towards the train station and disappeared inside, a black block of fury in pursuit of a whistling man in a light khaki suit and a bold blue tie.

Tom Leary thought it was all lovely. Lovely day. Lovely countryside. Even a lovely little set of briefing papers regarding proposed improvements to the national curriculum, which he had brought along to read on the train. Progress seemed possible. He smiled optimistically and glanced out the window at the lovely checkerboard of meadows and hedgerows flashing by. It was a rare, beautiful, sunny day and unseasonably warm. He set down the briefing papers and shrugged out of his khaki suitcoat. Light material though it was, it was still too hot. He glanced down the aisle at a peculiar bearded man who sat facing him at the end of the car. The fellow was wearing a black turtleneck and leather pants and was sweating profusely. He also had a variety of straps wrapped uncomfortably about his neck and shoulders with various cameras and lenses dangling down his torso.

Tom smiled at him in comradely fashion, acknowledging the heat. The man made no response other than to glare stonily at him, a look cold enough to make one shiver despite the temperature. The man then proceeded to take out a pack of cigarettes from a pouch on his belt and light up beneath a no smoking sign.

Tom decided to let it go and returned to his happy contemplations of the British countryside and the many opportunities for improving its education system. For him, time flitted by, and before he knew it, the train was stopping in the quaint village of Tupington where Lady Gloria was waiting for him in a sporty little two-seater.

"Tom!" she called out and tooted the horn. Tom spotted her and loped down the short flight of stairs from the station platform to the car park. He hopped into the open car, and the two sped off, leaving Mislov back up on the platform, smiling ferociously and clicking off bursts of shots with a telephoto lens. His instincts hadn't failed him. His two honest, admirable citizens had reunited for a dirty weekend. This was going to be worth a dozen BMW motorcycles.

"See the *Times*?" Tom asked as they rolled out of Tupington and down a narrow country road lined with sheep meadows.

"Yes," Gloria said. "Hated that profile of me. My nose looked enormous. You looked good, though."

"Bloody marvelous! Not how I looked, I mean, but the whole thing. The article. How did Glynis do it? How did she get them to print all that?"

"Positioning."

"Positioning?"

"That's what she said. You'll have to ask her what it means. I just live in awe and wonder and accept whatever gifts she bestows."

"Well, it's damn amazing, and I'm sure it's done my career a world of good. I must thank her. And by the way, I think you have a very handsome profile and a nose that's perfectly charming from any angle."

Gloria smiled and tilted her chin up, very aware that her profile was on display. Tom took a deep breath and gazed admiringly up at the azure sky overhead. It was a flawless blue with just a small squadron of puffy white clouds tacking along low on the horizon. "You didn't have to lay this weather on just for me," he said

"It's the least we could do," Gloria replied. "After you gave up your constituency garden party for us."

"Only someone who has never been to a constituency garden party could think that a sacrifice." Tom held the flat edge of his hand just beyond the windshield of the car so it could ride the stream of air whooshing by. His palm flipped and soared in the wind like a swallow. The little two-seater was now whizzing alongside a low stone wall beyond which lay a deep green meadow and a small brook lined with trailing willows.

"Well, you're right," Gloria said. "I haven't ever been to a constituency anything, I'm afraid. The truth is I've never been much involved in politics."

"No need to apologize for that."

"What can your ministry do for Sadie?"

"Excuse me?" Tom looked back over at her. Gloria was clenching the wheel tightly and had a deep frown of concentration on her face.

"Sadie. Sadie Connor. The little girl you gave a ride to the other week in Hackney. The orphan in the newspaper."

"Right. Sadie. Well what would you want us to do for her?"

"Everything! She doesn't have a proper home. No mother and father. Her uncle's never there. Her wretched aunt watches telly all day and sends her out for beer and chips with the dole money. The local school is a joke. Shakespeare couldn't learn to read there. And despite it all, she is a sweet, considerate little thing. And bright as a new penny even if she can't read."

"How do you know all this?"

"I've been back there four times. And I'd like to know just what your ministry plans to do about her."

Tom withdrew his soaring hand from the flying wind. He laced his fingers in his lap, studied them for a time, then gazed up, straight ahead down the road. "Well, nothing, I'm afraid. The ministry can't just bash in and take her away from her legal guardians."

"They're not guardians. They're indifferent slobs."

"Do they beat her?"

"God, I hope not. Why?"

"If they were abusive, really abusive, government might be able to intervene. But if her guardians are just . . . bad at it." Tom sighed. "Ministries only deal in millions. Millions of pounds. Millions of people. If you want to do something about an individual, if you want to do something about Sadie, you have to do it yourself."

Up ahead, a fluffy, white barricade appeared on the narrow road. Gloria slowed and then stopped a few feet away from a flock of sheep that were ambling across the macadam from one gorgeous green meadow to another. She and Tom stared at them in silence for a moment, and then Tom sat up and leaned forward to stare.

"Those sheep have four horns!"

"They're Jacob Sheep. One of my father's enthusiasms a few years ago. He's forever getting wildly excited over some new thing or other. For the estate."

"Four-horned sheep?"

"They're rather rare."

"I should think." Tom watched the last of the fluffy little creatures ambling off into green grass as high as sheep's heaven. "Plump little hedonists, aren't they."

"You know," Gloria said, "I bet Sadie has never even seen a sheep. A sheep in a meadow." Looking over, Tom saw a single tear running down her cheek. And for all her plots and subterfuges, it was in that unplanned moment that Gloria won his heart.

Her father, the Marquess, was out front to greet them as they rolled up the curving gravel drive in front of a vast, rambling, red brick mansion. Like Tom, he too had doffed his jacket because of the weather, revealing in his case a pair of red braces that matched a jaunty bow tie.

"Recognize you from the *Times*," he cried, shaking Tom's hand warmly. "Capital article! Wonderful influence on my daughter! Deeply grateful! She used to be photographed with these pimply layabouts who—"

"Daddy," Gloria said quickly, "the sheep are wandering all over the road."

"Ah! Saw the sheep, did you!" the Marquess exclaimed. He grasped each of them by the elbow and escorted them through carved oak doors and into the front hall while burbling away behind a gnawed gray moustache. "That's good. That's good. They're Spanish, you know, the sheep. Came over with the Armada. Or their forebears did. Swam ashore from the wrecked galleons. But see here, sheep are really nothing. What you must see is our Druid Circle."

"Oh, Daddy," Gloria said. "That depressing old pile of rocks."

"Depressing? No, no! Not any more. Had it all cleaned up, you see. Dug out the weeds and stumps, laid down turf and shrubs. Splendid little garden now. And we've had studies done. Archaeologist practically wept when he saw it. At least 2,000 years old, he says. And listen, here's the best part." The Marquess lowered his voice confidentially. "You can predict the equinox with it. By the sunrise. It's a proper little Stonehenge!"

"I look forward to seeing it," said Tom.

"Well," Gloria sniffed, "I shall use a calendar to predict the equinox and not have to get up so early. But I do want to show you the grounds, Tom. After you wash up, let's go for a ramble."

"Good! Good! Excellent! Yes!" said the Marquess. "Go for a ramble. Lovely day. Excellent. Tea's at four. Dinner at eight. Enjoy yourselves!"

Back in the village of Tupington, the emotions of Mislov Rapolovitch plunged to the opposite pole from Lord Ryder's sunny effusions. He had established himself in a revoltingly twee little room above the public bar at Tupington's Whistle and Toad pub. Looking at the tatty, photocopied tourist brochure left out on the dresser, he had discovered that this township was the country seat of Gloria's father. The estate was a short ways outside of town and portions of it, the brochure informed him, were open for public tours on the third Sunday of every month. It was obvious that rather than running off for a "dirty weekend" as Mislov had supposed, the Junior Minister at Education and Lady Gloria Ryder were in fact visiting her father, which was an eminently civilized and decent thing to do. Mislov had sacrificed his beautiful BMW for nothing. He might as well send his photos of the two gratis to *Town & Country Magazine.*

Mislov made a noise somewhere between a cough and a snarl, like a jungle cat somehow cheated of a tethered goat. As soon as he had entered the room, he had stripped off his turtleneck and leather pants, and he was now nude except for black silk bikini briefs. He glared around at the dreadful coziness of his quarters, and his eyes fastened on the curtains which were, of all things, pink chintz. Pink chintz with a specially rosy glow from the sunny day outside.

"No!" he cried again, and began to struggle back into the sweaty embrace of leather trousers and wool turtleneck. Once again, he strapped on his cameras, lenses, and a belt of film canisters that looked like massive silver bullets. Mislov Rapolovitch refused to believe that in this awful world of pink chintz and sunshine there wasn't something exceptionally nasty going on. If there was, he was the man to find it.

In her own room in her father's mansion, Gloria was venting her own irritations with life. "I do wish Daddy didn't blither on so," she confided to Glynis Mortimer. "He's such an embarrassment at times."

"Quite like you," Glynis said absently. The formidable executive secretary was seated in a wing chair with a book in her lap and gazing at the view through French windows that opened onto a second floor balcony. In the distance, the idyllic lawns and meadows of Lord Ryder's estate fell away toward a far off glade through whose leafy green arches could be glimpsed the occasional silver flash of a meandering brook.

"Glynis?" Gloria said sharply. "Quite like me?"

"Yes, M'Lady," Glynis said, turning from the view. "There's a marked family resemblance."

"I blither?"

"You enjoy company, M'Lady," Glynis said carefully. "And you share your feelings with your companions in an open, generous fashion, which is usually quite welcome because of your cheerful, warmhearted nature."

"I blither."

"You have your father's nose."

Gloria held up her hand. "Enough, Glynis, you're only digging yourself deeper." She snapped open her suitcase and began to unpack. "What are you reading?"

"Jane Austen. *Pride and Prejudice.*"

"Haven't you read that before? Even I've read *Pride and Prejudice.*"

"I've read it three times, actually. This is my fourth."

"What's there that brings you back?"

"Consolation. I find Austen consoling."

"Hum." Gloria held up a pair of tan slacks from her suitcase and studied them critically.

"I think," Glynis continued staring out at the view, "it's her voice. The voice of the omniscient narrator. The traditional novel is very consoling in that regard. It gives us the best illusion we have of the mind of God. I think it's no accident that the novel kept rising in popularity during the time when God was losing His."

"Here, tell me what I should wear," Gloria said. She took out a pair of white shorts from her suitcase and held them up next to the tan slacks.

"This is for your walk about the grounds with Mr. Leary?"

"Yes."

"The shorts, of course."

"I knew you'd say that. You're always suggesting I reveal more skin when he's around."

"What you should do is discover a way to reveal all of it. Why don't you take him skinny-dipping?"

"Glynis!" Gloria exclaimed, genuinely shocked.

"There's a little stream, isn't there? I think I can see one out there. Is there a pond?"

"Skinny-dipping? You mean, nude? Without bathing suits?"

"Yes. It worked wonderfully well with Clyde and me. Got him over his shyness. There's something about being naked together in water. Inhibitions just peel off with the clothes."

"You and Clyde went skinny dipping?" Gloria giggled.

"On our first date. In a small tributary of the Roanoke River in West Virginia. It was a day rather like this one. Beautiful, but excessively warm."

"Well, I'm not sure I can manage Tom as well as you did Clyde."

"Nothing to it. Take off your clothes and the man will take off his, I guarantee you. You can do it behind separate trees, if you like."

"Hum." Gloria giggled again. "Where has Clyde got to, by the way? We barely met him and he disappeared."

"He said he was going to walk into town. I'm going to follow on and meet him in the pub."

"I do like your Clyde, you know." Gloria said. "He's just . . . huggable. Like a big teddy bear."

"Yes." Glynis allowed herself a small smile. "He is."

In the Whistle and Toad Pub, the big teddy-bear himself was lowering a pint of bitter and enjoying a fascinating conversation with the woman behind the bar regarding the local clay when Mislov Rapolovitch sat down next to him and ordered ouzo. Clyde looked over at this unusual request and saw an even more unusual sight, a bearded man dressed all in black, sweating profusely, and virtually bristling with camera equipment.

Mislov looked back at Clyde and saw a big bear of a man, balding a bit on top, with wide, innocent blue eyes. Mislov took an instant dislike to him. He did that with everyone, of course, but he felt an especially virulent distaste for this – yes, it had to be one – this American. It was probably that congenital smile, that friendly aura. Here was a comfortable, comforting man. Mislov indulged a brief fantasy of sweeping the bar stool out from under him with an *osoto gari* kick and then dropping down to crush his larynx with a brutal, straight-arm chop.

"No ouzo," said the woman behind the bar curtly. "We don't stock that." A middle-aged housewife type, no doubt responsible for the pink chintz curtains upstairs, she seemed to regard Mislov with much the same attitude Mislov felt towards Clyde.

"Vodka, then," said Mislov. "No ice."

The American regarded the baker's dozen of camera bodies and lenses hanging round Mislov's torso. "I bet you're a photographer," he said.

Mislov's eyes narrowed. Was the man mocking him? The karate scene went off in his head again like a strobe flash. But with those wide, innocent, American eyes staring at him, he couldn't be sure if he was confronted with irony or idiocy. He turned away without a word and waited for his vodka. It appeared in a quarter-full water glass without a cocktail napkin.

"So, the clay, then," said the woman behind the bar, turning immediately back to Clyde. "People have been making pots around here since before the Romans. I read Druids used to paint themselves with our clay. It's blue, you know. Blue-gray."

"You know where I could find some?" Clyde asked eagerly. "I didn't bring my wheel, but I could bring a few pounds back to London with me, wrapped up in plastic. If I can throw a decent pot with it, I'll send you one."

"Well, no need of that. But if you want clay, down by the brook is probably the easiest place–"

"This vodka is warm!" Mislov cried.

Both Clyde and the woman behind the bar looked over at him as he stood up, sucking his tongue, trying to scrape the taste off with his teeth. "It's disgusting. Who makes it?"

"It's British," the woman said coldly.

"British?" Mislov stared down at his water glass in horror.

There was a brief pause, and then Clyde spoke in awe-struck tones. "Warm, British vodka," he said. "Want a taste of my bitter? As a chaser?"

"No!" Mislov said harshly. "I want to rent a motorcycle. Where can I do that?"

"In London," said the woman.

Mislov stared at her stonily. "Then I wish to obtain some tourist information from my gracious host. How can I get to the Ryder Estate?"

"That's easy," said Clyde. "You can walk. I just came from there. There's a public footpath that comes out a block down the street. By the post office."

"You can't stray off the footpath, though," the woman said tartly. "The Ryder grounds are private property." She nodded at Clyde. "He's a guest, there. So he's all right."

Mislov gave Clyde a cold, calculating look, threw a five-pound note on the bar and left without a word.

Back at Lord Ryder's stately home, Gloria and Tom emerged from the cool, oak-paneled front hall into balmy afternoon air that seemed almost tropical. Gloria was glad she'd worn her shorts. "This way," she said and headed off across the gravel drive towards a crumbling, gray stone wall covered with climbing roses. "First I'll show you where the moat and portcullis used to be. Then where the four towers used to be. Then where they used to—"

"Aren't you going to show me where anything is?" Tom asked. "At present? This little garden, for example. It looks quite nice."

"Yes, it does, doesn't it. But you can see that for yourself. Daddy will upbraid me frightfully at dinner if I don't point out to you the things you can't see. He's very proud of them. This is one of the oldest castles in England. It's just not here any more." Gloria giggled. "Cromwell tore it all down in 1648."

"Well, when was all of that built?" Tom asked, turning and waving his arm back at the rambling, red brick pile behind them.

"Just a century or two ago, I'm afraid. They call the architecture fifteenth century perpendicular. Part of the Gothic revival of the period."

Tom pointed up at a three-story clock tower that rose up behind the main entrance to the mansion. "Is that the right time? It says we're nearly late for tea."

"No, you mustn't believe the south face clock. It's always dashing ahead. Besides attendance at tea isn't compulsory. It's dinner we mustn't be late for."

"Well, if at dinner your father asks me about any of the things I can't see, I shall tell him you showed them to me and I found them fascinating."

"Thank you."

"So what would you like me to actually see?"

Gloria hesitated. "Let's walk down to the brook. I'll show you the weir."

And the two stepped off a path lined with primroses and onto a vast green sward that rolled in graceful, undulating curves dotted with leafy green copses down toward the distant glade where the meandering stream winked and beckoned in the sun.

In another corner of the estate up by the Druid Circle, Mislov petted his Nikon and began to take pictures. He couldn't believe his good luck. It had returned to him again at last. He had been right about this appalling world of chintz and sunshine. There was indeed something nasty, something unsettling, something downright gruesome going on in it. He clicked off a single frame and then squatted down to try a different angle.

The Druid Circle was situated on a small knoll and consisted of twelve, rough-hewn, granite slabs of rock each six to seven feet tall and four feet across. Some two thousand years before, they had been upended and set in a circle about twenty-five yards in diameter. Even in the bright sunshine of a balmy afternoon, the ancient stones created a brooding, somber zone. In their ranging shadows crouched a time when all England was a single wilderness of northern rainforest and the few strange men who dwelt within it worshipped oaks and yews and painted themselves blue with woad and clay. Mislov clicked off another shot from the low angle and decided to try a wider angle lens. That would allow him to heighten the impact of the foreground image and still capture the surrounding ring of stone megaliths that blotted out the sky. He took another light reading on his subject, a rectangular block of stone in the exact center of the circle. Sprawled across it was the dead body of a four-horned, Jacob sheep. The little head lolled at an impossible angle and its fluffy white fleece was matted and bloody. The creature's throat had been cut, its stomach slit open, and the internal organs removed. Through the viewfinder, the scene leapt toward his eye. The glistening heart and liver were set on either side of the carcass. It appeared that someone had sacrificed the animal in order to read its entrails. He could see this image on a million tabloids already, and the headline, "LORD RYDER'S CRUEL RITES."

"Click." He squeezed off another frame.

As Mislov pursued his vocation, Vicki, the woman behind the bar at the Whistle and Toad pub, was discussing his unique qualities with Glynis Mortimer.

"So as soon as your husband left to look for his clay, I went upstairs to, well, to tidy up, you might say. This rude man with the cameras, he paid cash, you know, in advance, otherwise we never should have accepted him, well this man has absolutely no luggage or clothes or any possessions at all besides what he carries around on his back! So there's no clue in his room what his intentions are, except!" Vicki held up her forefinger dramatically. "Except for a sheet of little pictures I saw that he left out on the dresser." She leaned forward and whispered. "They're pictures of Lady Gloria! Lady Gloria and some man!"

"A man? Do you know who?" Glynis asked.

"No. Had a nasty grin on his face, though. And his nose was all crooked like he'd been in a fight." Vicki leaned back and sniffed. "The pictures of Lady Gloria weren't very flattering, I must say. She looked scared to death. Now I ask you, what do you think this fellow is up to with his cameras and his leather pants, asking about Lord Ryder's estate?"

"He was going to walk the public footpath?"

"Yes." Vicki sniffed again. "Your husband told him all about that. I wish he hadn't."

"Well I just walked here that way, and I didn't see anyone."

"Then I wager he's slipped off the path despite I told him he shouldn't. He's probably lurking about the grounds right now taking more pictures."

Lady Gloria and Tom Leary had by now come upon the brook at the further reach of Lord Ryder's estate. They had pursued an erratic, ambling course down the vast green sward, wandering from one leafy copse to another, each little stand of trees occasioning the memory of some picnic or game of hide-and-seek or other scene from Gloria's childhood. Centuries of cultivation had left no meadow or tree in Lord Ryder's domain without its place in the productive scheme of things, but the grounds on either side of the brook had intentionally been allowed to grow wild. Here was where rabbit and mole and fox and badger and the other small, wild creatures so dear to the English heart could find a home. As Gloria and Tom neared the brook, they passed wild orchards of crab apple, wild cherry, and sloe trees. The odors of blossoming fruit mingled with the scents of dog rose and meadow sweet. Soon they were on a narrow path, closed round by green undergrowth and thickets of silver birch and alder with only occasional glimpses of the distant estate on the hillside to remind them of confining customs like afternoon tea. Ahead, they could hear the brook chuckling at them, and with a turn in the path, it seemed to leap up like a friendly water spaniel, shaking itself, spraying glinting droplets through shafts of sunlight, sniffing and panting round rocks, dashing ahead and then back and then ahead again, inviting them on down the path, deeper into the glade and its safe little island of wildness.

Back up on the public footpath, strolling towards town with three rolls of slaughtered lamb tucked safely into a pouch on his film belt, Mislov felt a warm inner glow that could almost be interpreted as satisfaction. Even happiness. He pretended to whistle like Tom Leary and then laughed a laugh that silenced birds for yards around. It was still dreadfully hot, of course. Under his black wool turtleneck, a heat rash had formed a red ring around his neck, and as he walked, his leather pants squished with sweat. The camera straps chaffed. The lenses poked and jabbed. But he had got the shot. Even though he had paid dearly for these photos, soon others would pay and more dearly than he. He smiled a ferocious smile and then blinked, stared, reached automatically for a camera.

Staggering towards him on the public footpath was a figure as bizarre and intimidating as himself. A huge man, dripping wet, clothes clinging to his knotted and straining muscles, he was streaked and daubed from his bald head to his American shoes with blue-gray clay, and he was carrying something in front of him as if for sacrifice, something wrapped in plastic and heavy enough to make even a man of his size tip forward and stagger. "Hi!" he shouted. "Get any good pictures?"

It was that idiot from the pub! Mislov dropped down on one knee. The low angle would make the fool appear even more enormous and threatening. He used the zoom lens, racked it out to medium telephoto, and the American came staggering into frame with his burden held out in front of him as if in offering. "Zick! Zick! Zick!" The motor drive clicked and whirred. The American's face, streaked with blue-gray clay and contorted with effort, was captured on film as a rictus of dumb, zombie anguish. "Zick! Zick! Zick!" The man was nearly on top of him. Mislov jumped aside.

"Look up there," the American said as he staggered past. "That's what you should photograph."

Mislov turned and looked. "You're right!" he cried. He racked the telephoto again to stack the image and brought it all into one frame, the staggering American, lurching Quasimodo-like up the hillside and in the background, the vista of Lord Ryder's rambling, red brick mansion with its distinctive three-story clock tower. The whole scene was washed with lovely, golden, late afternoon light, but with the swift addition of a graduated filter, Mislov was able to color it all apocalyptic orange. "Zick! Zick! Zick!"

"Have a look down by the stream, too," the American called out over his shoulder. "There's some beautiful spots down there."

Down by the stream, Gloria and Tom had reached the most beautiful spot of all. The murmuring weir only dropped two feet, but it held back the impetuous brook long enough to create a small pond that was fringed with purple loosestrife and shielded by trailing willows. Here the water was smooth, clear and deeply green, and it seemed quite still until it approached the weir when little ridges appeared in its surface and it made a sudden dash for the drop, curving over in a smooth, shimmering shoulder of liquid diamond and pearl. Gloria and Tom sat side by side on the bank and breathed it all in – the moist air, the golden sunlight, the glinting water lights. All around, the sheltering willows and scented herbage created a delicate chiaroscuro of greens and purples and pinks to screen them off from the world. The gentle cascade of water over the weir made a little wall of sound as well. It seemed the most private, intimate Eden in all outdoors.

Gloria gazed down into the clear, green water and saw the slim shadow of a trout sleeping near the bottom. "This reminds me of when I first saw you in the House of Commons," she said. "Looking down from the Distinguished Strangers Gallery."

"It doesn't remind me of the House," Tom said. He breathed in deeply and let out a long sigh. "The peace!" He looked longingly at the cool water. "We should have brought our bathing suits."

Gloria felt a calming sense of inevitability. "We don't really need them," she said. "I won't look if you won't. There's no one else to see except some sheep way up there on the hill."

"Really?"

"Of course. Here," Gloria stood up. "This is Ladies behind this tree. That's Men's over there. I'll meet you in the center of the pond."

And moments later from up on the hill, Mislov saw the barest glimmer of white as Gloria draped her shorts over a tree branch. He had just shot off another roll of film on the Modern American Druid staggering with ominous burden up toward the Ryder mansion. Now he was idly taking the idiot's second suggestion by sweeping the length of the brook with his medium telephoto zoom. It was the merest flutter, a tiny patch of white in the mazy green. He studied it a moment longer, and he could swear he saw a slim, auburn-haired figure slipping through the willows towards the water. "Zick! Zick! Zick!" He hit the motor drive automatically, but there was no film left in the camera.

Mislov cursed. Should he try and get closer? Or look for a better angle? It was too far in either case. Even with the medium telephoto, she had only been a tiny dot. And if he tried to go down into the glade, he could get lost, or they might hear him thrashing around in the undergrowth.

He quickly unbolted the zoom lens from its camera body, stowed it in a belt pouch, and pulled out the heaviest weapon in his arsenal, his fixed focus, twelve hundred millimeter telephoto. He had been lugging it along in its own case since Waterloo Station, and its strap had chaffed his shoulder raw. A little over a foot long and with a huge spherical outer element, the lens looked like a glass bowl set inside a mortar. He bolted it into the camera body and hefted the weight. It was difficult to hold steady. He really should have a tripod. Looking around, he spotted a picturesque stand of fruit trees a few yards up the hill. They looked climbable. He needed more elevation anyway.

In three minutes, Mislov was fourteen feet up in the air, stretched precariously along the denuded limb of a half-dead, half-flowering crab apple tree. He nestled his heavy telephoto lens into a forking branch, trained it down on the distant glimmer of water in the glade below, and the intimate scene there slammed into his face like a cream pie. There they were, Lady Gloria Ryder and Junior Minister at Education Tom Leary, bobbing about in the center of the pond. "Zick! Zick! Zick!" Shimmering heat waves and intervening, out-of-focus tree branches gave the whole image a watery, impressionistic quality, but it was definitely them. The good, decent, admirable citizens who were supposed to be setting an example for children. "Zick! Zick! Zick! Zick!"

But he had to restrain himself. All he could see was their heads, and there was nothing special about two people swimming. He would wait until they came out, and then if he was right about the glimpse he had caught earlier, he would be able to bag the most highly prized trophy in the tabloid photographer's pantheon. Celebrity nudes. A naked Lady and an MP in the buff. Even better, when their nude frolics were published along with his gruesome shots of the sacrificed lamb in the Druid Circle and the ominous clay-blue figure stumbling with mysterious burden towards the Ryder mansion, the headline writers would froth at the mouth with prurient fantasy and hypocritical rebuke. "NAKED REVELS OF LEARY AND THE LADY." "THE MP MAKES A SACRIFICE." "NUDE LAMB KILLERS READ TO CHILDREN." "RIDE-HER, LEARY!" "FRANKENSTEIN LOOKS FOR PARTS." "TAKE A DRUID TO LUNCH."

Gloria's reputation and Tom's career would be damaged beyond repair. Whatever else they did in life, this was all they would ever be known for. Mislov chuckled, looked up from the viewfinder to rub the sweat out of his eyes and saw Glynis Mortimer striding towards the foot of his tree.

To Mislov, she looked exactly the sort of woman who typically inhabits public footpaths, a middle-aged busybody wearing steel-framed glasses, blue top, brown shorts, and sensible shoes. She strode up to where he had shed all his extraneous equipment, looked down at the pile of cameras and film belts, back up at him with his massive telephoto roosting in the branches and called out cheerily.

"Hallo. Taking pictures?"

Another master of the obvious. Mislov glowered down at her and peered back into his viewfinder. "Yes. Go away."

"What of?"

"Birds."

"Wager you can see them a long way away with that. Can you make out the pond? Down in the glade?"

"Yes. Go away." Mislov kept his eye glued to the viewfinder, ignoring her, and there was a long interval of silence. He hoped she had taken the hint and left. Wait! There! Now! They were coming out of the water! Yes! Yes! "Zick! Zick! Zick! Zick! Zick!"

"What are you photographing, now?" Came the woman's voice from below.

Mislov laughed his bird-silencing laugh. "A rosy breasted thrush." Zick! Zick! Zick! "And a long-beaked wobbler." Zick! Zick! Zick!"

"Never heard of those birds before. I say, have you noticed that your tree's on fire?"

"What?" Mislov looked down and saw to his utter astonishment that the woman was right. There was a ring of fire around the trunk of the tree. It was licking up into a fierce little blaze along the dead, decaying half which was the part supporting him. "It's on fire? It's on fire! How is it on fire?"

"It's a hot day. You better get down from there before that branch breaks. Here, hand me your camera." Glynis held up her hands for it, and Mislov, baffled to the point of befuddlement by the flames licking up towards him, obediently dangled the camera with its massive telephoto lens down to her on its strap. "Got it!" Glynis cried. She took a couple of steps away from the tree and snapped open the back of the camera.

"What are you doing?" Mislov shouted.

"Exposing this film."

"Stop!" Mislov made an awkward, flailing leap for her. The tree branch broke from the force of his spring. Glynis stepped aside, and Mislov crashed into the earth amidst pieces of decaying crab apple. There was a sharp crack as if another branch had broken. Mislov cried out in pain. "My leg!"

"What's the matter with it?" Glynis was holding his film up to the sunlight and unspooling it from its little metal can.

"My film! Stop!" Mislov lunged up, but his leg buckled beneath him. "Ah! My leg! What are you doing? Stop! I think I've broken it!"

"That's too bad." Glynis plucked the end from another little can. A swift, arms length pull and more film spiraled to the ground. She tossed the empty can aside and plucked the end from a third.

"Arrgggg!" Mislov crawled toward her, dragging his useless leg behind him. Glynis calmly took a few steps back and plucked the end from a fourth can.

"If that leg really is broken," she said, "you're only doing yourself more damage. Stay put, and I'll call for an ambulance."

"Leave my film alone!" Mislov cried in agony as she plucked the end from a fifth can. "Why are you doing this? It's theft! I'll have you arrested!"

"I'm not stealing your film. I'm leaving it here with you."

"My pictures!" Mislov clawed at the rustling, useless strips of celluloid on the ground.

"Those were what was stolen. Now they're back in simple sunlight and fresh air where they belong. There, I think that's all of it." Glynis dropped the last empty can of film into a tangle of black and brown spirals.

"Ahhhhh!" Mislov cried. He rolled in torment on the ground, and the film wrapped its coils around him. "Let me— Just— You— Come— Come over here and help me back into the shade."

Glynis looked down at his writhing black form glaring up malevolently at her from the grass. His hands flexed.

"I think not," she said carefully. "I will call the ambulance, though."

"You bitch!" Mislov screamed. "How did you set my tree on fire?"

"With lighter fluid. From your cigarette lighter. It was in that pouch with your film. Nasty habit. You should give it up." And with that, Glynis turned and strode off, back towards the footpath and the Ryder mansion.

Later that evening, Gloria met up with her formidable Executive Secretary and her husband Clyde at the head of the stairs on their way down to dinner.

"Glynis!" she cried. "I have so much to tell you!"

"And I you, M'Lady," Glynis said dryly.

"Your plan worked perfectly." Gloria cast a quick glance at Clyde and blushed

"Not entirely."

"No, really, it did. You're quite right about men you know," she said as they entered the drawing room and were met at the doorway by a very stiff and uncomfortable looking Tom Leary who nodded meaningfully across the room.

"Ah! There you are!" Gloria's father cried. Holding his arm with a proprietary air was a familiar, tall, horsey, hungry-faced woman. "Now we're all here," said the Marquess. "We can go in. Gloria, you know Hortense, of course. And Glynis, you've met. Hortense, this is Glynis' husband, Clyde Mortimer. Clyde, this is my very good friend, Lady Hortense Crawley-Smith. She helped advise me on our Druid Circle."

The witch on Lord Ryder's arm smiled her ravenous smile and gave his hand a loving pat.

CHAPTER NINE

Kip woke up on a ghost ship floating on the Christ Child. His fever was gone. The seasickness had left him. He didn't even feel hung over. Hours or days before he had vomited out every half-digested scrap of food in his stomach, and he felt curiously light now, an airy husk that, if there were even a breath of wind, could lift off its bunk and waft through the deserted hold, alighting on any of the hundreds of empty bunks, stacked four high in row after row of thin, hard, seersucker-striped mattresses. He could float like a leaf and settle here or there with no worry of offending any occupant, any dark, grim rival. He was alone. Alone. All, all alone. Alone on a wine dark sea. And, he realized now, the engines had stopped.

Had they reached Zamboanga already? Or had the old ship just expired, given up the ghost somewhere out on the Sulu Sea. Perhaps he had slept right through Zamboanga and they were already at Tinian or Saipan. How long would that have been? Ten days? Unlikely.

The emptiness of the hold was intensified by his memory of it filled with two hundred and ninety seven Tamil laborers from southern India. Gloomy, dour men with much to be gloomy about, they owned nothing, not even their own lives. They were indentured to the Sabah rubber tree plantations in

Northern Borneo, and each of them had sold three or more years of himself in advance. When Kip had joined them in Kuching for the last leg of their journey to Kota Kinabalu, they had stared at him, as expressionless as the shadows of trees, as he made his way through the windowless hold to the two hundred ninety-eighth, two hundred ninety-ninth, and three-hundredth bunks which they had left unclaimed. All three of these bunks were located at the furthest end of the hold, up against the engine room bulkhead and a foot below a rusting metal ceiling that dripped oily water and flaked lead-based paint with every throb of the old ship's diesels. It was forty-four hours to Kota Kinabalu.

The first night wasn't too bad. After ten minutes of staring at the dripping, flaking ceiling, he got up, shouldered his pack, and made his way back through the hold, back past the thickets of staring, expressionless Tamils, and up the metal stairway to the deck. From there, he had watched the lights of Kuching fall away below the horizon, and he had spent his first night out there in the open, curled up against a lifeboat, using his pack for a pillow. Unfortunately the Captain, a choleric Chinese man, had literally tripped over him while inspecting the lifeboats shortly before sunrise the next morning.

"Ha! What you?" the Captain had cried, stumbling past his ear. Kip had no idea who was shouting down at him in the early morning darkness. "What me? What you!?" he had grumbled back, sleep drugged and sore from his cramped, huddled night.

"What me? What *me*? "What *you*?" The Captain screamed. Kip blinked open sticky eyelids and saw a round, hard face beet red with anger beneath a white captain's hat emblazoned with gold filigree. "You laugh? You laugh at me!?" The Captain's spittle sprayed his cheeks.

"No. No! Sorry. Not laughing. No."

"Get below! Sleep in bunk!"

The Captain stomped off to inspect the next lifeboat, and Kip gathered up his pack and stumbled back down into the hold. He had barely made his way to the three miserable empty bunks at the back when one of the Chinese crew shouted down into the hold and the Tamils all rose up to queue for breakfast. Breakfast was fish heads and rice, and Kip was two hundred and ninety-eighth in line.

The next night he had spent partially in the two hundred and ninety eighth bunk and partially in the two hundred and ninety ninth. There was little to choose between them, and little sleep to be had in either. Living with the Ibans, he had become accustomed to bathing three or four times a day in the clear jungle streams. After one night in the sweltering hold, he was sticky with sweat and oil, covered with little flecks of paint and rust, and he feared another attack of crippling crotch rot. By the time they arrived in Kota Kinabalu, he was desperate for a bath.

The Tunglin Maru tied up at the Kota Kinabalu docks at five in the afternoon. The Tamils, after journeying 7,000 miles in the rusty old hulk, had become both progressively more agitated and progressively more glum as the ship entered the harbor. By the time it was being warped into the pier, a dozen different fierce arguments were raging in the hold, and men raced up and down the metal staircase to the deck, clutching their meager possessions to their chests and crowding the ship's rail for a glimpse of their place of servitude. Kip decided to take advantage of the one benefit of his grimy bunk in the back and stayed out of their way. Only when the hold was completely empty and he could hear the men clambering down the gangplank and shouting to one another from the shore did he shoulder his pack again and head for the deck. He never left his pack, even for a moment. It contained his notes and recordings along with the rough outline of his paper, "Iban Shamans versus Iban Ghosts," for the Honolulu Conference.

"Ha! What you?" came the Captain's salutation as he emerged up onto the deck. Kip nodded at him respectfully and said nothing, not wanting to risk another exchange.

"You go ashore, now," the Captain said, cheerfully, nodding and smiling. His aggravation of the previous morning seemed entirely dissipated.

"No," said Kip, "I just came up to see."

"Go ashore. Go ashore. See better."

"But I'm going on to Honolulu."

"We here twenty-four hour. All night. Leave tomorrow. Plenty time see KK." The Captain waved his arm at the city as if he were laying it at Kip's feet. In the distance, beyond the warehouses and the crowd of Tamils on the wharf, a tall, mirrored spire of a building dominated the city. A city with a building like that, Kip thought, was sure to have a shower in it somewhere.

"Is there a cheap, a really cheap hotel?" he asked. "With a shower? Or a bath? I want to mundi."

The Captain exchanged a brief series of remarks in Chinese with one of the crew. The crewmember, a bandy-legged man with a face flat as an iron, laughed, nodded and jogged off down the gangplank. "Follow him," the Captain said, pointing. "He lead you good hotel. Plenty cheap."

Two days at sea cleaned and freshened the sense of smell, so as Kip followed the crewman into one of Kota Kinabalu's old shopping districts, he was ravished once again by the overpowering odors of a Borneo seacoast town. The smoke from burning joss sticks mingled with the aroma of skewered meats barbecuing at curbside satay stands. Acrid, smothering fumes from slabs of raw rubber were laced with the sinus firecrackers of scalded chili peppers. Baskets of fragrant bananas, mangos, and pineapples in one shophouse competed with the cloying scents of obscure mushrooms and powdered deer horn from a next-door herbalist. The bandy-legged crewman led him down a street lined with two-story, open-front shophouses. Their signs were mostly red or yellow and hung like a series of banners, all reading vertically downwards irrespective of their being written in English, Malay, or Chinese. After a few blocks, the crewman stopped by an open-front coffee shop furnished with small, round, marble tables and bentwood chairs. A few middle-aged Chinese towkays in the typical uniform of white singlets and baggy black shorts sat there silently sipping their *ayer lemau* or *kopi susu*, iced lemonade and a sludge-like coffee sweetened with condensed milk. Next to the coffee shop were an open doorway and a flight of stairs. The crewmember looked at Kip, smiled, and pointed vigorously. Kip took a few steps up the stairs and looked back at him. The man smiled, laughed, and waved him on by stretching out his arm and flicking the back of his hand at him as if he were brushing away flies. Kip shrugged his pack higher up on his shoulders, turned, and climbed the rest of the way.

He emerged onto a tiny landing barely big enough for himself and his pack. Cut into the wall opposite him was a door and next to that a window with a counter like a little tollbooth. There was a bell on the counter. Kip slapped it with his palm, and after a moment, a middle-aged Chinese woman who looked like a barrel clothed in a floral print tunic pushed aside a curtain in the back of the tollbooth and stared at him impassively.

"I'd like a room," Kip said. "Ada bilik?"

"How long?" she asked.

"Just one night. Satu malum."

The woman's eyes widened slightly. "All night?"

"Yes," Kip said. "But more important, I want a bath. Mundi? Ada?"

The woman nodded contemptuously.

"Can I see?" he asked.

She disappeared behind the curtain, and a moment later, the door opened and she waved him into a long narrow hall lined with doors. "Li, li, li!" she said peremptorily and led him halfway down the hallway to an open lounge where a dozen young Malay and Filipino women were sitting on folding chairs. They all looked up at him expectantly.

It was like a seventh grade dance back in Minnesota. Darleen and Cindy and Monica and all the other thirteen year old girls lined up against the wall in the school gym, looking at him with a mixture of hope and resentment and himself pacing along in front of them and finally, ineptly, rudely, pointing, and then remembering to mutter "would you like to dance?" Several of these girls didn't look much older than Cindy or Monica did then, but they wore more makeup and had tighter clothes. Two had on figure-hugging batik sheaths. Others were wearing gauzy, transparent tops through which he could see their heavily embroidered red or black bras. As his eyes roved past one girl, she dimpled an inviting smile and cocked her head inquiringly.

"A bath. What I want is a bath," Kip said suddenly, turning away from the expectant gallery. His pack slammed against the doorjamb, making him stagger. The seventh grade class tittered. "Mundi?" he asked, and there was a louder chorus of giggles behind him. The Chinese Mamasan looked at him in puzzled irritation. "Li, li, li!" she said again, and gesturing him to follow, she led him down the hallway. There was an explosion of titters and giggles back in the room.

Behind a door at the end of the hallway was a typical Malaysian bath consisting of a sloping concrete floor with a drain and a concrete cistern with a bucket. It looked clean. Kip stared at it for a few moments as he contemplated his sudden wealth of options. "How much," he asked finally, "for a bath. Just a bath, nothing else."

The Mamasan looked puzzled. "Girl in bath?" she asked.

"No. No girl. Just the bath. Mundi saja."

"Mundi saja?"

"Yea."

The Mamasan snorted contemptuously. "Sepuloh ringit," she said.

Kip did a quick calculation and agreed. Ten Malaysian dollars were worth about three and a half U.S. That was not an insignificant amount for him, but if it would help to stave off another monstrous rash, it was worth it. He set his pack up on the edge of the cistern where it wouldn't get wet and asked for soap and towels. The Mamasan held out her hand, and Kip dealt out a bright red, Malaysian ten-dollar bill from his pitifully thin wallet.

A few minutes later he was sluicing cold water from the cistern over his head and shivering with delight. "So I got a bath in a whorehouse in Kota Kinabalu," he said to himself cheerfully, totting up another experience that most guys from his seventh grade class in Minnesota had likely missed.

He sluiced another bucket of cold water over his shoulders and wondered whatever became of Monica. She was hot. He began to soap himself and heard a chorus of giggles. He looked around, and there was sudden silence. He began to soap himself again. More giggles. He looked up. The walls of the bathroom stopped a foot short of the ceiling, and three girls from the room down the hall were up there peering down at him. One of them even looked a little like Monica with red pouty lips and a knowing smile of approval. They stared at him. He stared at them. And then they exploded in shrieks and giggles. A distant shout from the Mamasan caused all three of them to vanish, but not before Kip became intensely aware that after . . . what? Nine months? He was hornier than hell. It was only through persistent sluicing with cold water from the cistern that he was able to bring himself back down to a condition where he could comfortably put on his pants.

Toweled dry and clothed in his one change of clean clothes, he shouldered his pack, took a deep breath, and opened the bathroom door. He was going to walk down the hall past the open lounge of smiling, knowing, giggling, dimpling, inviting girls, and this time he would smile back at them. He would smile a knowledgeable, manly, appreciative smile. He might even pause to chat with the Mamasan standing there by the open door. He might even ask her in a casual way how much it would be to spend an hour or two with one of her girls. Or even all night. How much could it be after all? Perhaps he could indeed afford it. He had plenty of time. The Tunglin Maru didn't sail till tomorrow afternoon, and what was he going to spend money on back on board the rusting old hulk anyway? He might as well spend it here. He owed it to himself.

The Mamasan was indeed waiting for him halfway down the hall. As he neared her and the open lounge, he constructed his manly, ironic, appreciative smile, the sort of James Bond expression that might be worn by a man in a tuxedo strolling through a Monte Carlo casino. "Trimah kasi. Thank you," he said suavely to her and wheeled to survey the beauties in the lounge. His smile froze.

They were all there, the Monica and the Cindy and the Darleen in their batik sheaths and their embroidered bras, all looking up at him, roguish and expectant. But sitting there among them, cross-legged on one of the folding chairs, was the little ten-year old Iban boy from back in the longhouse. The same omniscient, omnipotent little mind reader that he had last seen floating over the road by the wrecked logging truck. And the smile the little boy was wearing was truly ironic, appreciative, all knowing, and tinged at this moment with a certain salacious glee.

Kip's image of himself collapsed. He was not a tuxedoed James Bond in Monte Carlo. He was a backpacking vagrant. A marginal academic in camper shorts and T-shirt with frizzy hair and wire-rimmed glasses standing in the hallway of a fifth-rate Borneo whorehouse and chickening out.

"You want girl now?" the Mamasan asked.

"No. Not now." Kip said, staring at the little boy. It was obvious that no one else in the room could see the half-naked little voyeur. He was invisible to everyone but Kip. Kip could imagine the nasty imp floating cross-legged over the bed if he should attempt sex with any of the girls in the lounge, floating over the bed and peering down at them with that same jaded, prurient curiosity. Kip's incipient tumescence shriveled. "No. No girl," he said again. He turned and trudged down the bleak hallway to the stairs.

He wandered aimlessly through the streets and eventually found himself in a shophouse restaurant near the open market with a quart bottle of beer in front of him. He stared at it numbly. Was this how it was going to be for the rest of his life? Every time he got a hard on, it would be like rubbing a lamp? His little genie would appear, and then the lamp would go out. He decided to order dinner, too. There were at least some appetites he could satisfy without calling up his nosy little nemesis. He supposed he did owe the boy something. The kid had saved his life, after all, by summoning the plane back there on the logging road. At least it had seemed that way. But maybe the little boy hadn't saved him. Maybe he was only observing. Observing Kip's life as if it were a microbe on a slide.

He finished off five quart bottles of Anchor beer along with a glass of Hennessey brandy and a plate of fried rice with prawns, egg, and char siu pork, and around eight in the evening, he reeled out of the shophouse restaurant like a top at the end of its spin. Stumbling back and forth beneath his backpack as if someone was yanking his shoulders left, right or backwards every time he took a step, he staggered down the street towards the docks, past the spitting fires of curbside satay and noodle vendors and out onto the gloom of the concrete wharf where, in the distance, he could see a tug starting to push the old *Tunglin Maru* away from the pier.

"Hey!" he shouted. "Hey! Wait for me!" He lurched into a run, weaving drunkenly across the concrete. In front of him, the two ships continued their absurd, slow motion ballet. It hadn't been twenty-four hours. It wasn't even the next morning. "Wait!" The captain had said plenty time. "I paid for Honolulu!" The gangplank was up. "Not Kota Kinabalu!" They were leaving him behind. "Wait!"

The side of the ship was five yards from the concrete wharf by the time Kip charged up to the edge and leaped, flailing over the gap like an airborne crab. He grabbed the lower bar of the guardrail, and his solar plexus slammed into the metal edge of the deck, his backpack driving the last breath of air out of him from behind. With a desperate, convulsive jerk, he threw one leg up and hauled himself up under the guardrail onto the deck. He lay there gasping for five minutes, then he rolled back to the edge and was sick.

He never saw anyone. It didn't take that many men to work the old freighter, and they must all have been busy getting the ship underway. After lying flat on the deck for half an hour, he managed to get up on his hands and knees, crawled over to the metal staircase and half climbed, half fell down into the hold. There was a toilet down there with one miserable little sink. He didn't trust the water, but he was in no condition to go through the process of filling his canteen, dropping in the purification tablets and waiting a half hour. He just put his head down under the faucet and gulped. Then he was sick again in the toilet. Then he gulped some more water, staggered out into the hold, and collapsed onto the first bunk he found.

How long he lay there, he didn't know. At least a day and another night. Perhaps two days and two nights. Perhaps three. He lay there for hours, hugging his pack, immobilized by sickness and profound depression. It might have been the beer and brandy, or a suspect prawn in the fried rice, or the blow to his stomach, or the dubious water he gulped from the sink, or the pitching and yawing of the Tunglin Maru as it entered onto the open sea. It was probably all of those things, but he was desperately ill. He lay in the hold for days, all alone, a ghost on a ghost ship.

And now the engines had stopped. But if he concentrated, he could still hear a very slow, steady throb, as if the ship were just barely making headway. And in the silence, he could also hear shouted orders from up on deck, the first voices he had heard in days. There was a sudden, resounding boom and the whole hold reverberated. Then there was a high-pitched, whirring noise and more booming thumps against the side of the hold. Curiosity overcame him. He rose up from the bunk, and it was a measure of his ethereal, disembodied state that he left his pack there as he climbed, pausing frequently because of dizziness, up the metal staircase into the sunlight.

The crew was abandoning ship, at least that's what he thought at first. The lifeboats had been winched up from the deck and lowered down the side. He could see three of them about fifty yards away motoring across a sea that was a startlingly deep shade of blue. There were only two men to a boat, however, and all three boats were heading toward another freighter just a quarter mile away. Puzzled and weak, he clung to the metal guardrail and studied the distant scene. The sunlight and fresh breeze made him feel better, and he realized suddenly that he was ravenously hungry. Off in the distance, the three lifeboats neared the other freighter, and he could see tiny figures climbing over the railings, somehow clambering down the side of the ship, and dropping into the lifeboats. Occasionally someone missed a lifeboat and splashed into the sea. Kip glanced down and saw that heavy rope netting was hanging down the side of the Tunglin Maru. He looked up again at the tiny figures swarming down the side of the distant freighter. It went on for about five minutes until the lifeboats were crammed full, and then even though there were still people lining the rail and clinging to the side of the ship, the boats turned away and started motoring back. As they neared, Kip counted about thirty people to a boat. There were three boats. There were more people still back on board the other ship. He glanced back down at the heavy rope netting. At least ninety people were coming on board the Tunglin Maru in a few minutes, and no matter who they were or why they were coming, he knew where they were going to sleep. If he wanted a decent bunk for the rest of his journey, he had better go claim it now. He turned and headed back down the metal staircase into the hold.

He staked out a lower bunk for himself where there seemed to be at least a hint of cross ventilation, not too far from the metal staircase. He sat there and waited, and after a time, he heard scrabbling, rattling sounds through the side of the ship. Then there was the thump and patter of many feet on deck and shouts of encouragement and alarm, and finally after what seemed an interminable time, the first wave of ninety began to climb down the metal staircase into the hold.

They were all Chinese, mostly young men, but there were also a number of young women and a scattering of middle aged couples as well. The men were all dressed in cheap white shirts and ill-fitting pants, the women in high-necked, dark blue tunics and trousers. They seemed to have even fewer possessions than Kip. A small bag was all most were carrying, and many had nothing at all. A few were soaking wet. Arriving down in the hold, they looked around blankly at the tiers of bunks, ran off a little way down one or another of the aisles, then back to the staircase to call up to a descending friend. Once assembled, small groups started to fan out to investigate. About twenty-five people had climbed down into the hold before one of them discovered Kip.

The man stared at him in shock. Kip smiled and nodded and ventured one of his two phrases of mandarin. *"Nee how ma?"* he said which he believed meant, "How are you?" The man shouted in alarm, and within a few seconds, Kip was surrounded by a staring crowd of Chinese, a crowd that grew steadily larger as more and more of them climbed down into the hold. Kip nodded and smiled politely at the newcomers. *"Nee how ma?"* There was a murmur of amazement. He decided to try his remaining phrase of mandarin, *"Nee chee na lee?"* which was supposed to mean, "Where are you going?"

A sudden storm of comment and discussion rose up around him. A single man stepped forward, and silence fell again. It was totally quiet except for the faint, slow throb of the diesels. The man addressing Kip looked to be in his mid or late twenties and had the compassionate, intelligent face of a scholar. He spoke in painful, halting English, even slower and more deliberate than the throbbing engines.

"I . . . Zhou Chen," he said, holding his hand to his chest.

"I . . . Kip Stallybrass," Kip said holding his own hand to his heart.

"We . . . " The man waved at all the others surrounding them. "We . . . go . . . America."

"I . . . go . . . America." Kip said, and there was a soft murmur from the crowd.

"America . . . *meiguo* . . . beautiful country."

"Yes," Kip agreed.

"You . . . *toudu*?" The man asked.

Kip smiled and shrugged and shook his head. The man tried again. "You . . . ride snake?"

Kip could only offer a pained look of bafflement. The man turned to confer and there was a sudden babble of advice. He turned back and silence fell again. By now all ninety or more of the first wave were down in the hold and clustered around Kip, staring at him from the surrounding tiers of bunks like opera goers in the balconies.

"We . . . " The man waved his arms at his fellows once more. "We . . . China . . . *Fuzhou*. We . . . *toudu* . . . America. Ride snake. America . . . *meiguo*."

Kip held his hand to his heart again. "I . . . American," he said. "I . . . go . . . home . . . America."

The man's eyes widened in surprise. "You . . . America?"

Kip nodded. "Yes."

The man turned to discuss this startling news and there was a prolonged exchange of opinions. Kip continued to nod and smile at various members of the participating audience. After a few more minutes, the next wave of ninety from the lifeboats started to descend into the hold, and the first group began to break up in order to claim their bunks. As they ran off, they shouted at the newcomers coming down the staircase and pointed back at Kip.

The news of his existence rose up the file of descending newcomers like a wave, demonstrating another interesting property of waves. Two or more of them can move through the same material at the same time in opposite directions. So like two opposing waves passing through each other in the water or like a line of traffic slowing while still moving forward, the news about Kip passed up through the descending line of Chinese, producing a brief, still moment of amazement as the startling fact of him intersected with a particular individual, and then each wave continued on, one down, the other up.

The news reached the deck, and there was a brief interruption in the descending stream of Chinese down the staircase. Then two crewmembers came clattering down. One of them Kip recognized as the bandy-legged, flat-faced, smiling man who had led him to the whorehouse in Kota Kinabalu. Only now he wasn't smiling. He and the other crewman grabbed Kip roughly off the bunk, shoved him over to the metal staircase and pushed him up.

"Ha! What you!?" the Captain screamed as Kip's head emerged above deck. "What you!?" What you!?" He grabbed Kip's shirt by the shoulders and yanked him the rest of the way up. Once he was standing on deck, Kip was a foot taller than the Captain, which seemed to make him even madder. "What you!?" he shouted. "What you doing? Not belong!"

"I'm going to Honolulu." Kip said.

"You suppose stay KK!"

"I paid for passage to Honolulu. In advance."

"You fool!" The Captain shoved him into the arms of the two crewmen who had followed him up out of the hold. They grabbed his arms from either side. The Captain turned and shouted at the second wave of Chinese who were crowding the deck and staring wonderingly at Kip. They began to once again file down into the hold, and the Captain stormed back to the guardrail to watch the lifeboats which were already back at the other freighter and picking up another load. The boats made three more trips back and forth between the two ships until nearly five hundred people had clambered up the rope nets and filed down into the hold of the old Tunglin Maru where there were bunks for only three hundred. All the while, the Captain paced up and down the guardrail, alternately shouting at his fearful, wondering passengers and fuming and glaring at Kip.

When the last of the new arrivals had climbed aboard, the two crewmen released him in order to help winch the lifeboats back up on deck and then haul up the nets in preparation for getting underway. It was a complicated task that took about half an hour, during which time the other freighter steamed off and several of the newly arrived Chinese men reemerged from the hold to watch. One of them was Chen, the young man with the refined, compassionate face who had held Kip in halting conversation about *meiguo*, the beautiful country. When everything was tied down, the Captain finally stopped pacing and turned. He barked out an order to the crew. The flat-faced crewmen and one other man grabbed Kip from either side. Chen, standing to one side with the small group from the hold said something, but the Captain shouted him silent and once more rounded on Kip.

"You suppose stay KK. You stupid!"

"But I paid—"

The Captain barked another order at the two crewmen. They half lifted Kip up and ran him towards the guardrail.

"But I—"

They reached the rail and without even breaking stride, the two men grabbed him by his legs and arms and threw him overboard. He soared out, spread-eagled, half tumbled over on his back, and fell into the warm, enclosing waters of the Christ Child.

———

Peruvian fisherman had named it centuries ago. It was the warm current of water, which occasionally flowed between the ports of Paita and Pacasmayo on the western coast of South America. The warm water drove away the sardine catch, and so the fishermen had to sail home with empty nets. But if the warm current came, it came in December, so at least the men were home for Christmas. For that reason, they called the phenomenon "El Nino," The Christ Child.

By the time Kip fell into its warm embrace, "El Nino" had come to refer to a complex interweaving of global climatic changes which contributed to hurricanes in Hawaii, droughts in India, floods in Ecuador, and forest fires in West Africa. As Kip plunged beneath its waves off the eastern coast of the Philippines, El Nino was causing an unusually dry, sunny summer for Gordon Coburn's guests in Waikiki and a particularly wet and rainy one for Lord Ryder's sheep in England. In its simplest incarnation, El Nino was a stupendous pool of warm water, larger than the United States, larger than Antarctica, more than three thousand miles east to west and a thousand miles north to south. One or two degrees warmer than the rest of the ocean, the pool expanded every few years in the Western Pacific and made a slow progress eastward around the equator over a period of twelve to eighteen months, arriving at Peru in time for Christmas.

Kip was a speck in El Nino's westernmost tip which was located directly over the Philippine Trench and a few hundred miles south of the Cape Johnson Depth. The thermocline which marked the dividing layer of warm surface water from the deeper cold water was about a hundred yards below him, but the Philippine Trench itself continued on down into a staggeringly deep cleft in the earth's crust. He had forty-three hundred fathoms or eight thousand meters or nearly five miles of ever colder, stiller water below him. It would have been small solace to know that among its other mysterious manifestations, El Nino had tilted the water levels in the

Pacific, and the part of ocean where he choked and struggled and foundered was a foot shallower than normal.

"Why?" he shouted as he returned to the surface. "What did I do?" Water streaked and beaded his glasses, but because he wore an athletic strap to keep them from slipping down his nose, at least he hadn't lost them. He could see the crewmen and the Captain leaning over the rail of the ship above him. A swell lifted him towards them and then dropped him away. "Why? Please!" Another wave slapped him in the face as he shouted, making him choke and cough. He heard the Captain's barking laughter and saw him turn away. Then he caught a brief glimpse of Chen's face at the rail and saw something sailing through the sky. A ring. A life preserver! He saw it splash into the water twenty yards away, and he thrashed through the rising and falling seas towards it. Above, he could hear the Captain shouting and cursing in Chinese. The seas hid the life preserver. Had he gone past it? Which way? Was he swimming the right way? He stopped and looked frantically from side to side, trying to stand up on a swell, trying to stand on four thousand fathoms of water. There! A flash of disappearing orange. He churned towards it, grabbed it and clutched it to his chest.

He looked back up. Only one crewman was still visible at the rail. He heard the Captain shout, and even that man disappeared. No doubt the Captain was ordering the crew to get the ship underway. They were going to leave him. Soon the Tunglin Maru would drop below the horizon, and he would be altogether alone, adrift in a watery vastness so immense, just trying to conceive of it drowned the mind. He gripped the life preserver and broke into an involuntary sob. The name alone made him weep. "Life preserver." It wasn't much to ward off eternity, just a little ring of plastic wood with a rope strung round the rim so several pairs of hands could cling to it. But there were no other hands. There was no one else but him for a thousand thousand leagues.

"OK, where are you?" Kip shouted. For now was the time for the little Iban boy to appear. Now was when his nemesis and savior should materialize once again, floating cross-legged over the waves and pointing up at a helicopter or over at an approaching aircraft carrier. Kip wanted to see him now. "Come on!" he cried. "Do your stuff! It's show-time!" But the little boy was nowhere to be seen. Perhaps he had lost interest. Perhaps he didn't work his magic off the island of Borneo. Or perhaps he was irritated at Kip for turning his back on the roomful of willing women back in Kota Kinabalu. Whatever it was, the little boy never did appear, and after a time, the sun abandoned him as well. It set quickly over the equator, falling and turning into a red ball that was quickly gobbled up by a black-toothed sea. The sun fell as if it were plummeting down into the ocean trench far below, down into stygian blackness so deep and vast it would never rise again.

But while his little miracle worker did not appear, a small wonder did occur. The Tunglin Maru did not sail away. It stayed there, wallowing broadside in the seas and making no headway whatever. Occasionally, one or another of the crew would lean over the side to see if he was still there. One man waved at him, and he waved back, which made the man laugh. He thought he saw Chen once more, waving, and once the Captain leaned over the rail to look at him. Kip gave him the finger. While sometimes he drifted apart from the ship, just as often they would drift back together, and he was seldom more than a hundred yards away. But there was a time after the sun had set that the ship did disappear in utter darkness, and during those infinite moments, a black terror gripped him, a fear so intense he thought he might die from it alone, and in unreasoning, blind opposition, he hoisted himself up on the life preserver and shouted at the sea and the dark. It was a blind, inarticulate yawp, but the sound of his own voice made him feel better, so he began to sing. He sang "Glory, Glory Hallelujah" and "When Johnny comes marchin' home again, Hurrah! Hurrah!" and "Oh Lord, won't you buy me a Mercedes Benz," and with his singing, the stars came out and the moon rose, and he could see that the old Tunglin Maru was still with him, still wallowing in the sea about a hundred yards away. She stayed with him all night.

Morning came in washes of gray and blue, and far, far up in the sky, the thin cross of an albatross became visible. It was an elegant, elongated silhouette that circled with never a wingbeat until it decided to drop down to investigate Kip's edibility. As it swooped down towards him, the distant, beautiful bird became surprisingly large and decidedly ugly with a fierce, hooked beak, greasy feathers and voracious, glaring eyes. He splashed water at it, and it shrieked and flapped away. Shortly after that, the Captain began shooting at him.

There was a little splash as if a fish had broken water followed almost instantly by a distant clap. He didn't know what it was. Then there was another splash and another clap. Then another, quite close. The ship was about two hundred yards away by this time, and with his water streaked glasses, it was hard to make anything out clearly, but he was fairly certain he could see the Captain's white cap and that the man was leaning over the rail and pointing something at him. The little figure jerked slightly, and there was another splash and a clap. Two other tiny figures appeared at the rail alongside the first, and then all three disappeared.

And ominous or wonderful, shortly after that, he could see them winching up one of the lifeboats from the deck and lowering it down the side of the ship to the sea. Two crewmen motored across the waves towards him, and he wondered if they were just getting closer in order to shoot him properly. But no, they motored right up alongside and pulled him into the boat.

When Kip clambered over the guardrail back on board the Tunglin Maru, the Captain was indeed standing there on deck holding a rifle. Several of the crew stood beside him, also holding guns. An opposing group of men consisting of Chen and thirty or more of the new passengers stood clustered around the entrance to the hold. They were unarmed but looked determined. Kip was too weak to stand and nearly collapsed on the deck between the two groups. He clung to the rail for support, dripping water and waiting for whatever was going to happen next. The Captain glared at him wordlessly while fingering the rifle, then barked out an order to his men. Three of the crew broke away, ran towards the stern of the ship and disappeared down a hatch. Then everyone waited.

After a time, Kip was sure he was going to faint, so he just sat down on the deck. The sun rose slowly in the sky. The Captain stood glaring at him and fingering the rifle. Kip's clothes dried.

And then the engines started.

A great cheer broke out, both from the men on deck and from the five hundred people down in the hold. The Captain looked surprised. He turned back toward the stern of the ship, then looked back down at Kip sitting on the deck, hesitated, and started to put his rifle to his shoulder. But by then Kip was surrounded by the cheering passengers from the hold. They slapped him on his back, stood him up and shook his hand. Some of the men were weeping with joy. More people poured up the metal stairs and spread out around him on the deck, cheering and weeping until he was engulfed by the joyful crowd. He saw Chen's happy face in front of him. The man was laughing, pumping his hand up and down in a furious handshake, and grinning from ear to ear.

"You . . . good . . . luck!" Chen shouted.

———

Kip had more than a month on board the Tunglin Maru to figure out why a penniless, academic castaway who couldn't get laid in a whorehouse was considered a good luck charm. Zhou Chen, who had studied English and held a degree from Fuzhou University, explained it to him in infinitely slow and deliberate conversations aided by frequent reference to a Chinese/English dictionary. The five hundred people sharing the three hundred bunks down in the sweltering hold were all illegal immigrants to the United States, or at least they hoped to be. Each had paid twenty-five to thirty thousand dollars to a "snakehead," a man who arranged passage to *meiguo,* the "beautiful country," with the assistance of a shadowy, interlocking association of triads, tongs and gangs stretching from China to New York. The journey could take months or even years and often wound around and doubled back through a dozen or more countries. That's why they called it "riding the snake." The smuggling ring had arranged the mid-ocean transfer between the two freighters in order to disarm any suspicions of the Tunglin Maru when it docked in Honolulu.

The old ship had never put into Hong Kong or Shanghai or any of the other likely jumping off places for illegal immigrants, so how could it be carrying any?

Actually, none of the Tunglin Maru's passengers had paid the twenty-five thousand dollars yet because *toudu*, "stealing passage," was a C.O.D. business. A tenth of that sum was still a dozen years' salary back in rural China. For each person down in the hold, twenty or more relatives clear across Fujian province had contributed to the downpayment. Once the passengers arrived at the ultimate destination in *meiguo* – which was down around East Broadway in lower Manhattan – other relatives already established in the United States would pay the balance owed. If those relatives didn't pay, members of the New York Chinatown's Fuk Ching gang would drag the newly arrived immigrant off to some private spot in *meiguo* and beat him to death with hammers. The default rate was very low.

So the Chinese down in the hold and bound for America were like the Tamils who had previously occupied their bunks and gotten off in Borneo. It was just that instead of indentured work in Sabah rubber tree plantations, the Chinese would labor in American take-out restaurants. They would fry rice and scrub woks and work hundred-hour weeks. It was illegal and exploitative, but they wouldn't complain. They could make seven hundred or even a thousand dollars a month for those hundred-hour-weeks, and they would sleep and eat where they worked and save virtually every penny they earned. In two or three years, they could pay off their relatives. A few more years, and they could start their own restaurants or even make a visit back to Fujian province and brag about their success. That's what others had done before them, and with the stories they would tell about *meiguo*, the cycle would begin again.

"Why . . . leave?" Kip asked Zhou Chen one day up on deck as they sailed across a sparkling sea with a spanking tradewind tossing their hair. "Is . . . home . . . China . . . so . . . bad?"

Chen's scholarly face looked pained and angry. "I . . . wife . . . one . . . child." He said. "Second . . . child . . . must . . ." He leafed through his little Chinese/English dictionary, its flimsy pages flapping in the wind. He found the entry he was seeking and pointed.

"Abortion." Kip read aloud.

Chen flipped through his little dictionary again and pointed.

"Hysterectomy," Kip said.

"China . . . cannot . . . live . . . China," Chen said. "I . . . leave . . . now. Wife . . . baby . . . five . . . years . . . maybe." Tears dripped from Chen's eyes, and the gusting tradewinds whipped them away to join the sea. Chen said that many on board were like him, driven from home by China's draconian population policies. Forced abortions and mandatory hysterectomies were common. Some villages even had quotas for abortions and set up roadblocks to check for pregnant women. The passengers' fear of having to go back to China was what had rescued Kip from the sea. In the hold of the Tunglin Maru there were men and women trying for a second time to reach *meiguo*. Their first attempt had occurred several years before on board a Hawaii-bound smuggling boat named the Eastwood. The Eastwood's engines had also failed in the middle of the Pacific, and they had radioed a distress signal. The rescue wound up involving half a dozen

American and international agencies including the Navy, the Immigration Service, and the U.N. High Commission for Refugees. The ultimate result was that all 524 passengers on board the Eastwood were repatriated to China. The government there imposed heavy fines on them and required forced labor from those who couldn't pay. To make matters worse, the snakeheads refused to return their deposits or to cancel their smuggling contracts. Many on board the Tunglin Maru simply had to try for America again. It was the only way they could pay off their debt.

There was a terrible sense of déjà vu among those passengers when the Tunglin Maru's engines had failed like the Eastwood's. Down in the hold, it was thought to be more than just coincidence that the ship should die just when the Captain tossed overboard the first American most of them had ever seen. The engineers had worked throughout the night to restart the engines without success. When morning came, they were still wallowing broadside in the sea, and the Captain's only option was a distress signal that would probably bring the U.S. Navy. He was facing loss of a thirteen million dollar cargo and many, many years in prison. That was when he had started shooting at Kip out of pure rage and frustration. Some members of the crew managed to convince him that murdering an American in front of five hundred witnesses would only make their situation worse, so he had agreed to Kip's rescue. The crew had then tried to restart the engines one more time, and after a good night's rest, or just out of sheer crankiness, they worked. With this, Kip's reputation as a good luck charm was assured. The Captain didn't dare harm him. If he had, the five hundred desperate immigrants in the hold might have mutinied and tossed the Captain himself overboard.

So maybe he was a good luck charm, Kip concluded, at least for others. And he felt lucky as he sailed for a month through the South Seas, enjoying the best bunk in the hold and all the time he wanted on deck. He spent long, dreamy hours up there, working on a longhand draft of his paper for the conference, watching dolphins play tag in the ship's bow wave during the day, and seeing the southern cross drop steadily down towards a phosphorescent sea at night.

He started giving English lessons to Chen. It was the least he could do in return for the life preserver. After a few days, others asked if they could listen, and before long he was teaching a daily class of twenty. They met up near the bow of the ship where the fresh wind blew the new words from one mouth to the next and the whole group of them rose and fell ten feet or more with each passing swell.

One day Chen asked him about the songs they had heard him singing through the night after he had been thrown overboard.

"What is 'Benz?'" Chen asked.

"A . . . car. The song . . . asks God . . . for . . . a . . . car."

Chen grinned at him suddenly. "I . . . want . . . car."

"I . . . want . . . car," said another of his students. The others grinned and laughed and nodded. They all wanted cars.

Kip smiled back and shrugged. "Well . . . I can't . . . give you . . . a car. But . . . I'll . . . teach you . . . the song."

And so he taught Chen and the others the old Janis Joplin tune, and it became a kind of anthem for five hundred illegal Chinese immigrants. They thought it was a wonderful song. He often heard them singing it up on deck and down in the hold. He heard them humming it in their bunks as they drifted off to sleep. "Oh Lord, won't you buy me a Mercedes

Benz. My friends all drive Porches, I must make amends.
Worked hard all my lifetime, no help from my friends. So
Lord, won't you buy me a Mercedes Benz."

The ship stopped for a day each at Tinian, Saipan and
Kwajalein where they loaded and unloaded dry cargo. This
was part of the subterfuge that the Tunglin Maru was an ordinary tramp steamer, and all 500 people "riding the snake"
had to stay out of sight down in the forward hold. Kip was
permitted up on deck, but remembering Kota Kinabalu, he
didn't venture ashore. All in all, it was a happy time. He
was getting his work done. He had new friends like Chen
who liked and admired him. He seemed to have the run of
the ship, and the Captain largely ignored him throughout the
rest of the voyage.

The shock came around midnight, just a few hours out
of Honolulu. He felt someone shaking him awake and heard
Chen's voice whispering in his ear.

"Kip . . . Kip . . . I . . . Zhou Chen. I . . . try . . . help.
Captain . . . Fuk Ching . . . want . . . kill . . . you. No . . . talk.
Trust . . . me." And then Kip heard the sound of scissors next
to his ear and felt Chin snipping off his hair. "Trust . . . me!"
Chen whispered fiercely, gripping Kip's head and forcing it
down on the pillow. Kip's reddish blond hair had grown to
almost shoulder length, and he felt his tresses being gathered
up and sheared away, almost at the roots. His head felt naked
and cold without them. In a minute he was virtually bald.
"Follow . . . me!" Chen whispered. "Quiet!"

Kip slipped out of the bunk to follow, and as soon as he
stepped away, one of his other English students began stuffing
rope and canvas under the blanket on his bunk and arranging his shorn blond locks on the pillow so that it looked as
if he were still there asleep. Another one of his students was

standing watch in the dim light by the metal stairs. The rest of the hold was shadowy and dark. Chen started to climb when Kip grabbed him from behind.

"Wait! My pack!" He whispered.

"Leave!" said Chen.

"I can't! My paper! I–"

"Leave . . . here! Think . . . you . . . here!"

"But!"

"Trust . . . me! I . . . get! Later!"

Chen began to climb. Kip cast an anguished look back at his pack, lying on the bunk against the wall where he always kept it when he slept. He felt like he was ripping apart inside, but he turned and followed Chen up the stairs to the deck.

Another one of his students was standing watch at the top of the stairs. Chen ran Kip over to one of the inverted lifeboats lashed to the deck and motioned him to crawl underneath it. There was a ten-inch gap up by the bow of the boat, and by turning his head sideways and wriggling like a snake, he was able to slide through it into the little cavern.

"Stay!" Chen said, lying on his belly and whispering through the gap. "When . . . we . . . go . . . plane . . . you . . . run . . . swim. Captain . . . think . . . you . . . tell . . . police. He see . . . Fuk Ching . . . kill."

"Chen," Kip whispered. "Thank you. You . . . save . . . my . . . life . . . twice."

Chen grinned and stuck his hand under the boat. Kip gripped it, and they shook hands sideways.

"You . . . good . . . luck!" Chen said and disappeared.

Kip huddled under the boat and calculated how far his luck might take him. The dummy with the new wig back in his bunk might buy him a couple of hours, but it wouldn't fool anyone for long. The Captain must have decided that once the ship was in port, Kip's value as a good luck charm was outweighed by the danger that he might talk. Kip had no intention of talking, not after Chen and the others had saved his life. He wasn't going to get them arrested and sent back to forced labor and mandatory hysterectomies. But the Captain couldn't be sure of that, and no doubt he didn't want to take chances with his thirteen million dollar cargo. Kip just hoped that when it came time to "run . . . swim" he could at least see some land to "run . . . swim" to.

The little gap by the bow of the lifeboat gave him a narrow view out over the side of the ship, but only dark ocean and moonless sky in varying shades of black were to be seen there. After an hour or more of peering at darkness made even thicker by passing rain showers, he thought he could see tiny twinkles of light bobbing up and down on the horizon. Another hour passed, and through the little window of his seaborne cave, he saw the dark edge of the world transform itself into spangled towers banked by mountains of jewels. Honolulu and Waikiki rose up out of the night, rose up out of the black sea like the cliffs of a fairy kingdom. The grand hotels, thirty and forty stories high and built so close to the ocean they seemed to float on it, were aglow with yellow incandescent, red neon, green florescent and white halogen light. Behind them, the flickering lights from homes and the sulfurous yellow from streetlights wound along the ridgelines of the island and spilled down into its darkened valleys like rivers of electricity flowing towards those fantastical, glittering palaces on the beach. The night air, washed by rain showers and purified by thousands of miles of tradewinds, made the vision of this Polynesian city seem unnaturally crisp and clean and bright, like some imagined future. It was a dream afloat. Afloat here in the most remote place on earth.

Kip was so fascinated by this glowing, twinkling, sea-riding metropolis, he nearly forgot his danger of being murdered before he ever set foot in it. The ship was still several miles offshore when he heard a shout from down in the hold, and a few moments later, someone came clattering up the stairs and ran forward. A few moments more, and he heard the Captain shouting, and then two crewmen came running back along the deck and clattered back down into the hold. There were more shouts down below, and dozens of people began streaming up the stairs. Kip wormed his way back toward the stern of the lifeboat and huddled there in the darkest part of his cave. Through the gap by the bow, he could see feet crowding up against the rail, and he heard the wondering gasps of the passengers at their first sight of *meiguo*.

The Captain began shouting again. The crew barked out orders, and one by one, the pairs of feet disappeared from the rail. He heard them clattering back down into the hold. Off the starboard bow, a tiny yellow pilot boat was showing them the way into the harbor. The ship seemed to be turning. A dark, low-lying island rotated through his view. Lining its edge were huge, illuminated gantries that looked like the battle creatures in *Star Wars*. The ship seemed to be entering quieter water. And then in the distance directly in front of the bow, he saw a beautiful golden spire, a square clock tower, illuminated by spotlights, with a clock face on each side reading three a.m., and below each clock face in large green lettering was a single word, "Aloha."

"Ha! What you?!" He heard the Captain growl. "What you?! What you?!" He was stalking past the lifeboat, and as he passed, he gave its hull a rap. Kip heard him rapping the hull of the next lifeboat in line further along the deck. Then the Captain shouted, and again there was the sound of running feet on deck. It was time, Kip decided, to "run . . . swim."

He slid forward on his belly, turned his head sideways and wriggled through the gap. He didn't even pause but continued to wriggle across the little portion of deck to the guardrail, pulled himself under it, and for the second time on his voyage, plunged overboard into the warm waters of the Pacific.

He stayed submerged as long as he could, swimming underwater away from the ship. When he finally broke water, gasping for breath, he was nearly parallel with the ship's stern, and he saw a tug on the opposite side, preparing to nose the ship up against the pier. He had planned to swim for the beautiful, golden Aloha Tower, but now he could see that the huge pier that the Tunglin Maru was angling into was much closer, only a hundred yards or so away. He struck out swimming directly for it and reached it only a little after the ship did. There were enormous tires along its edge, ship bumpers. He climbed up around one, using its tread for hand and footholds, and after a year of traveling through jungle and ocean, a year of holding fast to his purpose among headhunters, smugglers, and dirty-minded little mind-readers, he set foot once more onto America, *meiguo*.

But there was no thrill, no satisfaction in it. He felt nothing but a terrible, angry, empty pain. The whole reason for his journey, the single cause and reward for all his trials had been snatched from him at the very last moment. His pack with all his notes, his recordings, his outlines and drafts was still back on board the Tunglin Maru. He would never see it again. His year of travel and trouble had all been for nothing. He would never give his paper at the conference. He would never be hired by a university. His Ph.D.

was worthless. His education was worthless. His life was worthless.

He couldn't let it go. Even the murderous Fuk Ching gang didn't scare him. What did he care if they killed him? He climbed up onto the pier and started moving in a running crouch, making his way along the wharf toward where the Tunglin Maru had docked.

The wharf was a vast, gloomy, concrete plain dotted at various points with stacks of roll-off, roll-on containers. He ran up to within thirty yards of the ship and hid in the shadows behind one of the semi-trailer sized metal boxes. From there he saw what struck him as the strangest sight of all the strange sights he had seen in his entire yearlong odyssey. Crouching there in the darkness, he saw five hundred desperate Chinese from Fujian province run off the Tunglin Maru and get on board a row of waiting tourist buses. And every one of these illegal immigrants was wearing a loud Hawaiian Aloha shirt and carrying a plastic souvenir shopping bag.

Chen had told him after one of their English lessons that the smuggling ring had chartered two planes to fly their human cargo on from Honolulu. Once they were on American soil and past customs and immigration, the passengers were nearly home free. Only a few relatively modest bribes were necessary to see them through airport security and on to their ultimate destination of Chinatown in New York. The snakeheads must have decided that some cover was needed for this large, peculiar group of people as they made their way through American airports, and what better cover could there be for acting strange than being a tourist from Hawaii? They could all hide in plain sight.

He watched all five hundred run down the gangplank and onto the buses, and he was thinking desperately all the while that once they were gone, he might try to slip back on board the ship and hunt for his pack. Once each bus filled up, it rolled away without waiting for the others, and the whole procedure took place in frantic, intense silence and was over in a few minutes. Soon, the last man came hurrying down the gangplank carrying an extra large souvenir bag in his arms. He looked familiar, even in his Aloha shirt, and as he trotted towards the last bus, Kip realized the man was singing. "Oh Lord . . . won't you buy me . . . a Mercedes Benz."

Kip picked up the second line, whistling it from his hiding place behind the container. "My friends all . . . have Porches . . . I must make . . . amends."

"Oh Lord . . . won't you buy me . . . a Mercedes Benz," The man sang. He got in line to board the bus, but just before getting on, he set the big plastic souvenir bag down on the ground and got on the bus without it. The doors closed. The bus rolled away. And a few minutes later, Kip ran up across the shadowy, deserted wharf and retrieved his pack, which was resting inside the plastic bag.

He sprinted away, across the concrete plain and out an access road leading to the city. In a few minutes he found himself emerging onto a sidewalk that ran alongside a wide, empty, six-lane highway called Ala Moana Boulevard. He was directly in front of a handsome, old, stucco and tile building that was surrounded by big trees and a wide, grassy lawn. It looked like a restful haven after his months of metal and ocean and concrete. He walked back beneath one of the trees, lay down flat on the grass and rested. He lay there for quite some time. When he finally felt his breathing calm and heard a few birds chirping in the tree above him, he sat up and looked around at Hawaii. Pairs of headlights from early morning commuters were rolling down Ala Moana

Boulevard. Directly across the highway were two gigantic condominiums that looked like upended Norelco shavers. He glanced back at the old, stucco and tile building behind him, saw a sign on it and laughed out loud. He was lying in front of the Department of Immigration.

He stood up. He was broke, but he was all in one piece. He had his pack. He had his research, his notes, the draft of his paper, and he had nearly a month to prepare for his talk. The sky was just beginning to lighten in the east. He shouldered his pack and began to hike in the direction of the pink and gold clouds, up the boulevard towards Waikiki.

CHAPTER TEN

"One Club Sandwich, one Chicken Salad, one Papaya Boat!"

Evelyn Fujii shrieked out the order and slapped Benjamin on the butt. "You make 'em good, Benjamin!" She cried above the clattering and banging. "This could be Coburn's last meal!" Everyone in the kitchen roared with laughter. It was the first of September.

Out in the Surfside Coffeeshop, the General Manager of the Earl Court Waikiki tried to steady his hand as he set his coffee cup back down onto his saucer. He was unsuccessful, and the china made a nervous, trembly little sound. He slumped back against the banquette, stared dully out past pink sprays of bougainvillea at the golden sands and sparkling blue water and thought about death.

Death. The Grim Reaper. The Dark Angel. Was it coming for him? And if so, what difference would it make? What had he done with his life that was worth a damn? What had he contributed? A tan? Not even that. He had given tourists a sunburn, but he had charged them a couple of grand for it. He hadn't contributed. He had just consumed. He was a tube for expensive, meaningless experiences that traveled from his eyes and his mouth to his anus and left him as hollow as when he began.

Immersed in these reflections, Gordon stared blindly off at a bright yellow catamaran floating on a turquoise and aquamarine sea. Two more anonymous predictions of death had arrived that morning which made a total of thirteen altogether. Actually, these last two were more commands than predictions. A note had been stuffed into the pocket of one of his dress shirts when it came back from the hotel laundry. "September is coming," it had read, "say your prayers." Most shocking of all, however, was the huge injunction that had been trampled into the freshly raked sand of Waikiki Beach itself. The letters were so large, they were illegible to anyone on the ground, but Gordon, awakened at five thirty that morning by the raucous cooing of the fat, white pigeon, had walked out onto his lanai to shoo it away, looked down from the thirty-fifth floor in the gray half light, and saw "TIME TO DIE" emblazoned across the otherwise empty expanse of sand.

"Muggy today," Howie said. "Wish this Kona weather would let up." And after a pause that Gordon didn't bother to fill, he added, "El Nino. That's what's doing it."

Gordon still said nothing. Death, he was thinking, should hold no terrors for him. He was already in hell. Besides, he knew how he was going to die. He was going to fuck himself to death. He had arrived at this lunch after a "nooner" encounter with Carol Nickle in 1303. The previous evening he had disported himself with Cynthia in 2611. And in a few hours he was scheduled for another night's romp with Melanie in 814. He was nothing but a gerbil with a hard on. There was no way off this treadmill, either. He would stagger about the hotel from one joyless assignation to the next until he dropped, a shriveled husk.

A fat, white pigeon flapped across the beach, wheeled, and flew straight at him. Its broad, beating wings and sharp yellow beak grew larger and larger until at the last second, it threw its wings up, fanned its pinfeathers to break against the air, and settled heavily onto the edge of the planter. Smoothing itself and bobbing slightly, it fixed Gordon with a beady red eye. Gordon thought it looked like the same damn pigeon that woke him up that morning. The horny one that was always bellowing its "Coo! Coo!" out on his lanai. There couldn't be too many pigeons that big. Had it started following him? He looked around on the table for the breadbasket, but the busboy hadn't brought it yet. The pigeon also surveyed their table and, finding it barren, flapped heavily away.

"See the weather report this morning?" Howie asked. "There's a big tropical depression a couple of thousand miles east. El Nino always docs it. This is how Iniki got started. You missed that."

Deep in his own tropical depression, Gordon still said nothing. With trembling hand, he extracted a small bottle from his suitcoat pocket and shook out two Vitamin E gel caps and a "Male Toner" ginseng tablet. He had Viagra with him at all times, of course, and walked around with a continual headache, seeing the world through a blue haze because of it. But Viagra did nothing for his libido, which was in desperate need of supplements. Clutching the Vitamin E and ginseng in his palm, he realized they hadn't been served their ice water yet either and looked about in vague irritation for the busboy.

"Why am I here, Howie?" he asked.

This question, along with Gordon's haggard look and wandering gaze, made Howie unsure of how profound a response was expected. Another long pause unspooled between them. Eventually, Gordon continued in an aggrieved tone. "I've got a few other things going on, you know. Meeting negotiations are your job."

"But you're the one who—" Howie stopped himself and took a breath. "I'm sorry," he said and looked over his shoulder to make sure Janet wasn't approaching. "I couldn't get anywhere with her."

"Well you can tell that to Earl Pressler and Suzuki-san. They'll be here in less than a week."

"She's got us dead to rights. The number of meeting rooms are specified in the contract."

"So why don't we just cut the fee?"

"She says they don't care about money at this point. They're academics. They want the rooms."

Gordon sighed and slumped against the banquette again, husbanding his strength. Just what he needed, another iron-willed woman who knew what she wanted from him. The previous hour with Carol had been grim. His Director of Public Relations no longer cared to indulge him with foreplay in the shower, preferring instead to lie on the bed in some stage of undress and watch him strip in front of her. When it came time for their lovemaking, the depth and force of her body odor was undiminished, a claustrophobic vise of a smell that left him limp as linguini. Carol had wrung her pleasure from him nonetheless, and as a fillip, she had given him another copy of his picture, the full frontal nude displaying the kind of rampant energy she expected from him. She hoped it would serve as a reminder. She was certain it would serve as a reminder to the Orange County travel agents. She had dozens of those pictures along with appropriate letters all ready to be mailed out, copies to Earl Pressler.

He was doomed. He couldn't break it off with Melanie or Cynthia either. They naturally would want to know why he was breaking it off, and no matter what he said, they would begin to suspect. They'd probably talk to their friends. In a few days it would be all over the hotel, and Carol would be certain to learn. He was doomed. Doomed.

The Vitamin E and ginseng in his palm were turning slippery with sweat. He looked around again for the damn busboy who was supposed to bring them ice water and saw Janet Sorenson returning from the ladies room.

"Here she comes," he said quietly to Howie, and summoning the last of his strength, he rose valiantly from the banquette with a gracious smile.

"How did you select these new colors you're putting everywhere?" Janet asked as she slid in behind the table.

Gordon's gracious smile took on a rigid quality. "A designer in California," he said.

"What do you think of them?" Howie asked.

"Very unusual. Different."

"Yes, they are," Gordon agreed, hoping to move on. The full ghastliness of Timmy's "Tamarind Summer" collage was now apparent to all and on a massive scale. After the expenditure of nearly forty million dollars, the Earl Court Waikiki looked like puke throughout its exterior and atrium spaces. But hundreds of men and women were still working furiously to finish and install all the trim, fixtures, carpeting, wallpaper, towels, napkins, china, bedspreads and a thousand other appointments in varying vomit-complementary shades. Gordon was driving them to complete the work before the arrival of Earl Pressler and Kenji Suzuki. The orangish barf browns and regurgitated pear tones that he had recommended in a moment of weakness were now coating everything.

To the hotel staff, it was an even bigger joke than Gordon's imminent demise.

"How is your conference shaping up?" Gordon asked, not wishing to dwell on this other subject. "Any shamans coming?"

"Two or three dozen, actually. We're very pleased. There's a huge resurgence in shamanism worldwide, of course, especially in the United States."

"Why is that?" he asked politely.

"I think it's a result of the age of science we're living in. Science accustoms people to want hard evidence for everything, even spirituality. They don't trust ecclesiastical authority or religious texts anymore. But anyone can take a shamanic journey and discover the truth of other realities, the realms of the spirit, for themselves."

"Ah ha," said Gordon.

"You could also say," said the busboy who was finally filling their water glasses, "that shamanism is an individual, democratic religion dating from Paleolithic times which the Neolithic, agricultural societies tried to expunge because they needed hierarchical religious structures to support the state, and now that so many of us in modern civilization have returned to the hunter-gatherer mode, shamanism is making a comeback. Butter?"

Gordon stared up dumbfounded at the busboy, a tall man with reddish-blond hair and wire-rimmed glasses who set the water pitcher on his cart and turned stiffly back to them with a lopsided smile and proffered butter tongs.

Janet and Howie also stared up at him, agog. "Yes," said Janet after a moment. "I mean, thank you. Butter." The busboy carefully set large pats of butter pearled with dew and embossed with the Earl Court logo on each of their bread plates. "It's also part of the whole ecology movement, of course," Janet added.

"And experiments with drugs like LSD in the sixties and seventies," said the busboy. "They gave people the idea but not the methodology."

"Right," said Janet. "And there's holistic medicine."

"And NDE's," said the busboy.

"Yes," said Janet.

"They're all contributing," the busboy concluded, "but if you trace them back, I think you're right. It's all a result of the age of science after the age of faith. I'll get you some bread."

The busboy wheeled his cart away, leaving a dead silent banquette behind him.

"My God," said Gordon after a time.

"Exactly," said Janet.

"At least he finally brought the water." Gordon regarded the sticky mess of Vitamin E and ginseng in his palm.

"What are NDE's?" asked Howie.

"Near Death Experiences," Janet said. "People who've been declared clinically dead and then have come back to life. They say the experience is like the shamanic journey."

"Well, I hope you're not having any of those," said Gordon and shielding his lips with his napkin, surreptitiously tried to lick his palm.

"Of course we are."

"Deaths?" Gordon lowered the napkin and looked across at her, appalled.

"Shamanic journeys. They'll be dozens. Hundreds. We have master shamans from all over the world giving classes."

"Well what goes on? How do they teach this? With drugs? He was talking about LSD." Gordon openly licked his palm, made a face and reached for his ice water.

"Oh no. Hardly any shamans use drugs. Oh, there are some Amazon tribes like the Conibo that do. But nearly everywhere else, a shaman uses a drum. A steady, monotonous drumbeat is all it takes to initiate and sustain a shamanic journey. They probably use drugs down in the Amazon because of the humidity. A skin drumhead won't stay taut in that climate."

"It's pretty humid right here," said Howie. "El Nino."

"Oh, can it with El Nino, Howie," said Gordon and focused again on Janet. "Do you mean to tell me that in two days I'm going to have hundreds of juju men running around here beating drums and dropping dead? Or pretending to? I thought you were giving talks?"

"We are giving talks. We're also giving Master Classes in shamanism."

"Howie? Why didn't you tell me this? You know who's coming in Friday."

"How do I know what a Master Class in shamanism is? Sounds academic to me."

"You know what they are," Janet said irritably. "I told you."

"You told me about Alice in Wonderland."

"Alice in Wonderland?" Gordon cried.

"Some bread for you," said the busboy smoothly, using his tongs to place a hard roll on each of their bread plates.

"Alice in Wonderland," said Janet, throwing Howie a look and assuming the rhetorical lectern for Gordon's benefit, "is a story that recounts most of the elements of the shamanic journey. There's an animal familiar, the White Rabbit, an entrance into the earth through the rabbit hole, a long tunnel that Alice falls through, and then an emergence into a lower world that is populated with power animals like the Caterpillar and the Cheshire Cat, and which operates by its own rules of logic, a logic that seems quite illogical to people in ordinary reality."

"That's very good," said the busboy enthusiastically. "I've never heard that comparison before."

"Thank you," said Janet. "I use it in my undergraduate classes. It makes the whole thing more accessible and less threatening."

"Yes," said the busboy. "Of course, Alice doesn't go through the purification and suffering that's required of most initiates before a master shaman allows them to begin."

"Yes, well she has a little, but you're right. And there's no rushing water as she makes the transition through the tunnel, but there are enough similarities to make me think that Lewis Carol might have had a drum somewhere in his closet."

"Yes, when you think about it, that wide sea where the Walrus and the Carpenter–"

"You seem to know a hell of a lot about this," Gordon interrupted.

"I've made a study of it," the busboy replied.

"Well, why don't you go make a study of where our order is."

The busboy squinted at him, nodded shortly, turned on his heel and walked off.

"Try to run a hotel in Hawaii," Gordon said, "and the only people you can hire are hippies from California."

"Is he from California?" Janet asked.

"Damned if I know where he came from. Listen, we all know why we're here, let's get down to–"

"One Club Sandwich, one Chicken Salad, one Papaya Boat!" Evelyn Fujii announced cheerily and began serving their lunch.

Gordon clamed up and tried to recover a degree of equanimity. He rubbed his palm with his napkin under the table and noted that the splotched, vomity pattern Timmy had designed for the table linen at least had the advantage of concealing Vitamin E stains and other debris. Someone could be sick all over it, and you'd never know.

"We'll never have to wash this," he said sourly.

"Excuse me?" Janet asked.

"Nothing. Sorry. Look. We're sorry about the meeting rooms, but they just won't all be ready in time."

"Howie told me they're all ready now."

"You did?" Gordon glared at Howie.

"Well, not exactly, Janet," Howie said. "Yes, they're technically ready, but—"

"Why'd you tell her that?"

"Well, because they are."

"No, they aren't, not if they're full of—"

"Actually," said Janet, "it doesn't matter to us if they're ready or not. All we require is a room, a podium, and some chairs. Believe me, compared to most university lecture halls—"

"Well, that's not the issue," Gordon said. "Some of the rooms are being used."

"But we've reserved them. It's in the contract."

"Yes, but—"

Gordon was interrupted by a warbling sound from his cell phone that was lying like a pet turtle on the table next to his Papaya Boat. "Excuse me," he said curtly reaching for it. Janet and Howie exchanged silent, recriminatory glances and addressed their Chicken Salad and Club Sandwich.

"Gordon Coburn speaking," Gordon said into the phone.

"Gordon, Christine Larren," enthused the overblown, high-society voice in his ear. "We're just getting out of customs, and they're fabulous!"

"That's great, Christine," Gordon said. "What are these again?"

"The Tantric sculptures George sent me from Nepal. He's such a Dear! There's this incredibly fierce, scowly bronze with about two dozen arms that he decorated with little offerings. And he found some erotic temple carvings that are just delightful! They're actually lightning rods even though they're made out of wood. What's supposed to happen is when the goddess of lightning is streaking down out of the sky about to strike one of the Nepalese temples, she'll see these sexy shenanigans carved on the outside walls and get so distracted, she'll miss! Isn't that a stitch?"

"How sexy are they, Christine? This is a family hotel."

"Oh, don't be a prude, Gordon. Besides, what about those in-room movies you show? The question is, where do I put them?"

"Put them in with the New Guinea stuff."

"The Ilima Room?"

"Right." Gordon's eyes met Howie's across the table."

"When am I going to be able to actually install all this artwork, Gordon?"

"After the carpeting goes down. They tell me that's happening day after tomorrow."

"Ah, yes, that lovely carpeting. Gordon, have you seen the Color Association's new forecast for the next five years?"

"Yes. Christine, I'm—"

"It's not what Timmy's giving you."

"I know. I'm going to have to—"

"The Earl Court is marching to the beat of a very different drummer."

"Christine, I'm in a luncheon meeting. I'm going to have to ring off. Congratulations on your . . . things."

Gordon set the phone back down beside his Papaya Boat, crossed his arms and looked seriously across the table. "The conference rooms—" he began, but the phone warbled at him again. "Damn! Excuse me." He snatched it up. "Christine, I'm in a—"

"This is Cynthia, Gordie."

"Oh. Hello. I'm sorry, I'm in a—"

"Who's Christine?"

"She's our art buyer. I'm really busy right now."

"I just called to say I love you, Gordie."

"Well, that's . . . nice." Gordon rolled his eyes and saw Dick Brukowski, his Chief of Security, lumbering across the Coffeeshop.

"You know the Stevie Wonder song," Cynthia said in his ear and then began to sing in her little girl voice. "I just called . . . to say . . . I love you."

Brukowski pulled up at their banquette, breathing heavily, and announced, "We've got a lead on the death threats."

"I just called . . . to let . . . you know . . . I care," Cynthia sang.

"What?" Gordon asked.

"I just called—"

"I'll call you back," Gordon said clicking off the call.

"Death threats?" Janet asked.

"Gordon's been receiving death threats, written in the sand," said Howie.

Janet burst out laughing. "Like love letters?"

Gordon glared at Howie. "Not all of them," he said to Janet. "Just the one this morning. And it's not funny. Who is it Brukowski?"

"It's someone working at the hotel."

Gordon stared up at him for a long moment as he processed his response to this news. "We knew this," he said finally.

"Right, but now I've got a witness, a local kid, a surfer. He was out before sunrise, 'cause the surf was up this morning, and he saw them running up and down the beach." Brukowski looked from side to side and dropped his voice. "There were three of them."

"Three?" Gordon asked.

"Three," Brukowski nodded significantly. My plan is to walk the property with this kid until he spots one."

"We've got eighteen hundred employees, Brukowski."

"Yeah, it may take awhile. Have I got your permission?"

Gordon reflected a moment. The man heading this investigation, he noted hopelessly, had on an Aloha shirt that featured yellow submarines and smiling baby octopuses.

"Yeah, go ahead," he said at last. "But don't go telling everyone what you're doing. We're trying to keep this quiet, remember?"

"Well, we're not doing a very good job of that. I can't question everybody and keep it a secret at the same time."

"Just get on with it. Keep me informed."

Brukowski nodded and lumbered off. Gordon shook his head and dabbed sweat from his face with his napkin, leaving a smear of Vitamin E and ginseng across his forehead. "About the meeting rooms," he said, turning once again to Janet. "You can see we're really in a frenzy here. We're finishing a forty million dollar renovation, and we've got the owner of the hotel from Japan and Earl Pressler who runs Earl Court International both arriving here on Friday for the blessing on Saturday. There's a huge amount of work we need to finish before they get here. Several of the meeting rooms are being used right now to store a very valuable collection of Asian and Pacific art that's scheduled to be installed on Thursday, God willing. So, here's what I'm prepared to do."

Gordon raised his water glass for a sip and saw that he had at last secured Janet and Howie's attention. Both of them were staring fixedly at his forehead. He took another sip of water and another and finally drained the glass. Howie was right. It was damned muggy today. "As soon as the rooms are cleared," Gordon said, setting down the glass, "your people can of course use them. Up until that time, because we are obligated, the Earl Court will provide, at our expense, other meeting rooms in other hotels. Hopefully, we can find them within walking distance here in Waikiki. If buses are required, we will provide those too, also at our expense. Now in return, I hope you can do us this favor. As much as possible, can you schedule these shaman classes, the drumming and the . . . what did you call them? Trips? As much as possible, can you schedule those in the other hotels? If you can try and do that, and because I realize that this is an inconvenience, The Earl Court will refund twenty percent of your deposit money. That's twenty thousand dollars. I hope you'll agree that's more than generous."

"Won't work," said the busboy, refilling Gordon's water glass.

"What?" Gordon nearly shrieked at him. "What do you mean, it won't work?"

"I certainly wouldn't want to give my paper in a hotel across town. Nobody would come. The whole conference is too tightly scheduled. People will only go to the talks in this hotel."

"Your paper? What–? Who asked you, anyway?"

"I'm–" The busboy flashed an embarrassed glance at Janet. "I'm giving a paper on Saturday."

"Hell if you are!" Gordon said.

"Hell if I'm not!" The busboy snapped.

"You're fired!"

"So what?"

"What's your paper on?" Janet asked.

"Iban Shamans versus Iban Ghosts. Based on field research I've been doing in Borneo."

"Oh! You're Mr. Stallybrass!"

"That's right. And you must be Janet Sorenson."

"Yes. Oh, it's so good to meet you."

"Good to meet you."

Janet and Kip shook hands across the table while Gordon and Howie stared at them as if the two had suddenly revealed themselves to be Gargolians from the planet Tutu.

"I apologize for meeting like this, though," Kip said. "Kind of embarrassing."

"Perfectly all right," Janet replied. "I'm going to try and make your session. I expect there's going to be a very lively discussion."

"Well, I really appreciate all you've done. It means an enormous amount to me."

"Have you met your respondent?"

"Carl Brodkins? No, not yet. I'm a little intimidated, frankly. Is he still at Stanford? I don't even know."

"Emeritus. Don't be scared of Carl. He's a teddy-bear."

"Ah, Janet," said Howie, interrupting the collegial flow, "I think we can accept Gordon's offer, don't you think. It is very generous."

"It may be generous from his point of view," Janet said. "But Mr. Stallybrass is right. It won't work."

"Why the hell not?" Gordon exploded.

"Don't swear at me." Janet said sharply.

"Yeah, don't swear at her," said Howie.

"Stay out of this, Howie," Janet snapped. "I can take care of myself."

"Yeah, stay out of it, Howie!" said Gordon. "What do you mean by 'We' anyway? Whose side are you on?"

"Damned if I know," said Howie mulishly.

"As Mr. Stallybrass just pointed out," Janet said coldly, "our conference is very tightly scheduled. And we sent the meeting room assignments out a month ago. People plan which sessions they're going to attend very carefully. Minute by minute, in fact. There'd be mass confusion if we tried to bus them back and forth to other hotels at this point." She looked up at Kip. "I think you're right, they'd just mill around here."

"It'd be a disaster," Kip agreed.

"Will you shut up!" Gordon cried. "You're fired!"

"Who cares."

"I'm going to have you escorted off the premises," said Gordon, reaching for his cell phone.

"By who? That ex-navy bozo?" Kip sneered. "I thought you had him out rounding up your assassins. By the way, what's that crap on your forehead?"

"Security," said Gordon into his phone. "This is Gordon Coburn. Get some people over to the Surfside Coffeeshop

immediately. We've got a crank employee causing a disturbance. In fact, get Brukowski back here, and tell him to bring
along his witness."

Gordon closed the call, and there was an awkward silence
as the four of them waited.

"I wish you would clean your face," Janet said at last.
"It's very distracting."

"What? Where?"

"Up here," said Howie, gesturing to his own forehead.
"It looks like baby poop."

Gordon wiped his face with his napkin.

"Now you got some on your nose."

"It's Vitamin E," Gordon said, scrubbing with the other
side of the napkin. "Can't see it on here."

Kip snorted in contempt. "Look, you don't have to escort
me anywhere, I'm just going to leave."

"No, you stay here," Gordon said. "I'm going to find out
if you're the one."

"If I'm the one what?"

"You'll find out."

"Ms. Sorenson," Kip said. "I do apologize."

"It's quite all right Mister– Doctor Stallybrass."

"I had no intention of disturbing your lunch. It's just
that what you were saying was so interesting–"

"Well, so were you, very interesting. And since you're
one of the conference participants, I'm very grateful for your
support in turning away this last minute attempt by the hotel
to renege on the terms of our contract. I'm sorry if you've lost
your job over it."

Kip laughed. "This job didn't really figure in my career
plans."

"Well, I hope our conference helps with those. I will make certain to attend your session. Which will," Janet gave Gordon and Howie each a cold glance, "be held in the assigned meeting room as scheduled. If there's any artwork in there, just push it out of the way."

"Right," said Kip.

"Honey, I think you're being a little unreasonable," said Howie.

Janet stiffened and flushed red.

"If any of that artwork is damaged, Ms. Sorenson," Gordon said, "I'm holding your organization responsible. And as for you," he said to Kip, "you better not set foot on this property again, session or no session. I don't care if you've giving a paper or not."

A wild, steely glint appeared behind Kip's wire-rimmed glasses. He leaned down, shoulders hunched, fists jammed against the table and thrust his face into Gordon's. "Try and stop me," he said. "If you think I'm going to let some self-important, paranoid twit of a hotel manager keep me from giving my paper, you're crazy. Not after what I've been through."

Gordon shrank against the back of the banquette. This busboy reminded him of stories he'd read about disgruntled post office employees with assault weapons. He was relieved to hear Brukowski's gravelly growl.

"What's the problem?" Brukowski and two burly security guards grabbed Kip's arms from either side and pulled him back upright.

"Oh, look, it's Captain Kangaroo," Kip said.

"Brukowski," said Gordon, sitting forward once again. "Good. Where's your witness?"

"Right here," Brukowski nodded over his shoulder at a wide-shouldered sixteen-year old tanned to the color of milk chocolate and naked except for a droopy pair of surfer shorts and a spackling of sand on his stomach.

"Do you recognize this man?" Gordon asked the boy sternly, nodding at Kip.

"Yeah," said the boy.

"You do?"

"Yeah. Howzit, brah," the boy said.

"Hi, Nathan," said Kip.

"You know him? Was he one of the ones on the beach?"

"Yeah."

"Ha!" Gordon exulted. "We got him!"

"Not this beach. Queen's Surf. He showering there sometimes. He's one of the homeless. Lives in Kapiolani Park." Nathan looked at Kip's busboy uniform. "I never think you got a job, man."

"I don't any more," said Kip. "But what they pay you here isn't enough to cover rent, anyway."

"Yeah, these jobs suck."

"OK, enough of that!" said Gordon in near terminal exasperation. "Get him out of here, Brukowski, and make sure he doesn't come back."

"I will be here on Saturday to give my paper!" Kip shouted to the astonished guests of the Surfside Coffeeshop as the two guards marched him out past the rows of banquettes.

Brukowski and Nathan started to follow but then Brukowski turned back. "You about through here, Mr. Coburn?" he asked.

"Why? What now?"

"We got a call from Civil Defense. They want us to run hurricane disaster drills for the next couple of days. Just in case. There are some bad storms out there."

"I knew it," said Howie. "El Nino."

CHAPTER ELEVEN

At about the same time that Kip was being ejected from the Earl Court Waikiki, Gloria's father, Lord Ryder, boarded a plane at Heathrow with a witch. He and Lady Hortense Crawley-Smith were also on their way to the Seventh Annual Conference on Shamanistic Practice. They were flying British Airways over the pole to San Francisco, spending the night there, and continuing on the next day to Honolulu. Lady Hortense was elated. She had been employing a dozen or more different charms, amulets, chants, and potions on Lord Ryder for weeks, and this was the first time that any of them had appeared to have any effect. Lord Ryder was irritatingly impervious to most spells, it seemed. Indeed, Lady Hortense was unsure which one of hers had suddenly enticed him to join her. Henry – for their intimacy had at least progressed to the use of first names if nothing else – Henry still had a number of appalling habits that had yet to succumb to witchcraft. Like gnawing at his moustache as a rabbit might at a carrot. Also a stubborn resistance to eating anything more adventuresome than meat, potatoes, and puddings. And he had the infuriating practice of wandering off on inexplicable errands without any warning beforehand and nothing but opaque comments like "Oh, taking a turn about the grounds" when he returned. This happened at Heathrow just prior to the call for first class boarding. Lady Hortense returned from the lavatory to find their carry-on bags abandoned and about to be whisked off by blue-coated, purse-lipped security personnel. Lord Ryder was nowhere to be seen. He was off at a pay phone leaving a message on his daughter's voicemail.

"Hullo, Gloria. Your father here. Are you there? Pick up! You're not there. Well, this is the message, then. I'm popping off to Hawaii for a few days with Lady Hortense. I want to pick up some tropicals. For the greenhouse I'm putting up at the estate. Hortense has business there. Don't know what, exactly. Some conference. But she's booked a posh suite at the Earl Court. This is the Earl Court in Hawaii, mind, not the tube stop. Anyway, her suite has three bedrooms and she offered me the use of one. Seemed economic. And it's been raining bloody hell for weeks. Wanted a bit of sun. Love you. Cheers."

Lord Ryder had to use a pay phone because he refused to be tied to what he called the "electronic leash" of a cell. This was another source of irritation to Lady Hortense who had no option but to wait by the gate and hope he would turn up. The boarding crew had called for first class, the handicapped, small children, frequent flyers, and rows thirty-two through eighteen before he finally meandered back.

"Where were you?" she asked sweetly, powerful jaw muscles bunching behind a tight smile.

"Oh, just taking a turn," Lord Ryder replied.

Lady Hortense silently ground her teeth and groped for a blackened, foul-smelling root deep in the recesses of her purse. She resolved to somehow shave pieces of it into Lord Ryder's in-flight meal.

They were not the only ones flying to the conference that night. On board their same BA flight over the pole were five professors from various British universities, one from Hungary, and two from Germany. There was also a dervish from Turkey and a medicine man from Kenya. All over the world, men and women were packing, reviewing notes, forgetting toothbrushes. Many were making several days' journey through sweltering jungle or over freezing tundra just to get to an airport. Planes were lifting off from Zagreb, Denpasar, Katmandu, Quito, and Nome. From Tokyo to Santa Fe, security scanners were x-raying luggage and picking up the ghostly outlines of drums and rattles, feathers and masks, strips of bark and books of chants. The images glimmered briefly on the screens and passed on by, unremarked and unremembered.

But on other screens, different phosphorescent blobs glowed and swirled, and these were very carefully noted. The National Weather Service was tracking half a dozen storms across the Pacific during this, the height of the hurricane season. While Lord Ryder and Lady Hortense were sleeping fitfully high over the North pole, technicians watching satellite video transmissions marked the increasing strength of a tropical depression about fifteen hundred miles southeast of Hawaii and upgraded it to the level of a tropical storm. Formerly designated by the code "E2," it now merited a name. Since it was being tracked by the team in Honolulu, they christened it with a Hawaiian name, "Makini."

And in Waikiki, the sultry kona weather that Howie had complained of during lunch continued unabated. It was, as he had pointed out, one of the effects of El Nino, the global climatic phenomenon that was also contributing to the storms out in the Pacific as well as the rainy weather on Lord Ryder's estate. El Nino was perhaps also partly responsible for the General Manager of the Earl Court retiring to his air-conditioned suite at five in the afternoon and taking to his bed. Numb with work and stress, Gordon was staring dully at his TV only to be treated to another disquisition on El Nino by a local news anchor who seconded all of Howie's observations.

"El Nino was with us when we had hurricane Iwa in 1982 and hurricane Iniki in 1992," the anchorman said in voiceover as the screen showed shots of "Kauai, Sept. 11, 1992." Gordon watched the entire roof of a house peel away and then shatter into a thousand pieces of blown kindling. The debris flew by wildly over otherwise remarkably banal scenes captured on home video. It was interesting, he thought, that you couldn't actually see the wind. You could only see what was in it. This observation seemed deeply meaningful to him somehow, but then the announcer intruded on his reverie, "Residents are urged to have several days' supply of canned food, bottled water, a battery-powered radio—"

Gordon flipped off the remote. Hurricane drills. Now on top of everything else, he was supposed to do hurricane drills. It was too much. He rolled over and stared sideways out his lanai windows. The sky looked clear and calm. "You will die in September." The sentence had become a mantra for him. It had rolled through his mind a thousand times a day, and now it actually was September. This had always been a red-letter day, he reflected. When he was growing up, September first was like New Year's Eve because while September marked the death of summer, it was also the beginning of the school year, and that was the birth of the New Year as far as a kid was concerned. Outside on the lanai, the familiar, fat, white, self-important pigeon fluttered down through his upended sightline to its accustomed position on the lanai railing. It puffed up its neck feathers and cocked its red, accusatory eye as if trying to meet his sideways look. A booming "Coo! Coo!" penetrated the sliding glass doors and rode above the quiet hum of the air-conditioning. Gordon groaned and rolled up to sit on the edge of the bed. He still had to inspect the progress of the renovation on a dozen floors, which would take him at least two hours. Then he had a working dinner with the heads of housekeeping and food and beverage service to go over a multitude of issues ranging from the blessing ceremony on Saturday to the in-room flower arrangements for Earl Pressler and Kenji Suzuki. After that, Melanie was waiting for him to frolic gaily in room 814 all night. And now thanks to El Nino, he was going to have to get up before six to review hurricane drills at a breakfast meeting with Brukowski. He gritted his teeth. One more thing. All he needed was one more thing.

And a few hundred yards up the beach, Kip Stallybrass was seething beneath the slopes of Diamond Head. He was enraged over how he had been treated. It was embarrassing enough to be revealed as a busboy in front of one of the leaders of the conference, but then to be fired and summarily ejected by that overweening "twit of a hotel manager." It was too much. To think that he had persevered through jungle and ocean, headhunters and tongs only to have his one reward, his only chance to present himself to his peers and possible employers blocked. Thwarted! Banned!

"Ha!" He shouted aloud.

The late afternoon sunbathers looked up curiously from the sand and saw a gangly homeless person with a backpack shouting angrily at no one. Kip was seated on a park bench overlooking Kaimana Beach. The bench served as both his living room and bedroom. The cold shower on the beach was his bath. When he wanted company, he walked across

Kapiolani Park to the Honolulu Zoo and listened to the gibbons and howler monkeys.

"As if anyone could stop me!" He muttered and clamped his jaw shut again. If an omnipotent Borneo mind reader and a speed-crazed rainforest logger and a raging Chinese flesh smuggler couldn't prevent him from giving his paper, neither could Gordon Coburn!

"No wonder he's getting death threats!" Janet Sorenson exclaimed bitterly. She was sprawled in her reading chair beneath the ceiling fan of her little Manoa cottage with a stack of abstracts beside her. But she wasn't reading. She was glaring up at the fan plowing through the humid air and replaying the lunch with Howie and Gordon again. And again. And again. Howie, of course, had been the worst. His "Honey, I think you're being a little unreasonable" had been the last straw. "Honey!" "Unreasonable!" "Honey!" Yeech! Howie's razor and the odd bits of clothing that he had left around her cottage were now stuffed into a plastic bag from Manoa Safeway and set out by her mailbox.

Howie himself was getting methodically drunk and replaying their lunch in a Korean bar on Keeaumoku Street. "Can it, Howie," was what he remembered. "Stay out of it, Howie." "Shut up, Howie." "Yeah, shut up, Howie." He ordered another scotch and glared like a terrorist at the TV up over the bar. A weatherman whose body had been electronically cut and pasted over a map of the Pacific was waving foolishly at swirling, phosphorescent blobs.

———

Gordon, Janet, Kip, and Howie were still dealing with the rag ends of their Monday evening in Honolulu when, ten time zones away, Tuesday morning arrived in England. Glynis Mortimer entered Gloria's London flat punctually at nine a.m. to find her employer nearly berserk and pacing back and forth, telephone to her ear like a Doberman at the end of a short leash.

"Glynis!" she cried. "Father's run off with that witch!"

"Excuse me, M'Lady?"

"They've— Wait! . . . No, it's just another bloody apology for keeping me on bloody hold. 'Your call is important to us.'" she parroted. "If it's so bloody important, answer it! '. . .will be with you shortly.' I'll be short with you, if you ever get on. God in heaven!"

"Something has happened to Lord Ryder, M'Lady?"

"He's run off! With Lady Hortense! To Hawaii!"

"Oh dear."

"They're sharing a suite!"

"Worse and worse."

"Do you suppose they've eloped? No! How could he? But he said they're sharing a suite! Enough bloody musak, all right!" She shouted into the phone and then began whining in a singsong. "' . . . It's a long and winding road . . .' I hate it! Is she going to marry him? Put him under some Polynesian spell? Sunset, rum, moonlight, and then a little chapel by the beach? . . . No it's not *my* honeymoon, you idiot!" Gloria pounced on the receiver in her hand like a Doberman attacking a bone. "I want to go to Hawaii! Next available flight! . . . First class. Any class. Just so it's as soon as possible. Today! . . . One person traveling."

"Two, M'Lady," said Glynis Mortimer, taking a deep breath and drawing herself up.

"Two, Glynis?"

"Two. I'm quite fond of Lord Ryder. I would like to be of assistance."

"Thank you, Glynis. You're a brick."

"Happy to be of service, M'Lady."

British Airways flights were full, so Glynis got on the line with a travel agent she had used during her days as a corporate executive secretary. He booked them on Virgin, departing that afternoon to Los Angeles with a connection to a Hawaiian Airlines flight that would put them into Honolulu at 4:00 p.m. Wednesday afternoon. Glynis then left immediately to inform Clyde, get her passport, and pack a bag.

"Zick! Zick! Zick!" As Glynis walked down the steps of Gloria's flat and along the sidewalk to her car, Mislov Rapolovitch's motor drive whirred quietly across the street. He was hidden in the back seat of a taxi with his telephoto zoom, capturing on film every awkward moment, every casual, unconscious grimace Glynis Mortimer might make. He had been at it for ten days. His broken leg, encased in a walking cast, was stretched out across the seat. It ached and itched, but that only served to intensify, if possible, his purpose. "Zick! Zick! Zick!" Scandal. Shame. Ruin. "Zick! Zick! Zick!" The modern furies would visit Glynis Mortimer. "Zick! Zick! Zick!" And Lady Gloria Ryder. "Zick! Zick! Zick!" Mislov would lead them to their prey. "Zick! Zick! Zick!" He had the skill, the talent, the patience, and above all, the desire. "Zick! Zick! Zick!"

Unfortunately, all he had so far were a thousand shots of two women walking up and down the stairs in different outfits. He also had photos of a dozen fashionably dressed members of the Greater Anglia Literacy Committee. Not the sort of thing to put a gleam in the eye of a tabloid editor. He did have shots of Tom Leary walking up the stairs at seven one evening and walking down the stairs at seven the next morning. Damning as these facts might be to the tabloid readership, Mislov had to confess that the photographs themselves were rather dull.

But he was confident that something nasty would turn up, just as it had with that sacrificed lamb on the Ryder estate. By now, he was familiar with the morning routine at Gloria's flat, and it was unusual for the Mortimer woman to leave so soon. Mislov debated having the taxi follow her car but decided to stay put, and he was rewarded within the hour by the sight of Glynis Mortimer arriving once again, this time along with Clyde whom Mislov remembered as that cretinous potter he had met in the Whistle and Toad Pub. "Zick! Zick! Zick!" The man escorted her up the stairs, and Mislov recorded that scandalous moment. "Zick! Zick! Zick!" Glynis withdrew a key from her purse. "Zick! Zick!" Wait! Was that a Fodor's? Mislov zoomed in with the telephoto. "Hawaii!" She was carrying a Fodor's Guide to Hawaii! "Zick! Zick! Zick! Zick! Zick!"

An hour later, Mislov was paying off the cab at Heathrow airport a few car lengths behind where Clyde had pulled in to unload Glynis and Gloria's luggage. It was useless, he decided, to try and keep out of sight any longer. He could hardly blend in with the crowd. He turned and limped slowly along the sidewalk. His walking cast, a big black fiberglass boot, gave him a rolling gate rather like a sailor with a peg leg. What with his black tee shirt, black jeans, and his shiny black and chrome bandoleers of camera equipment, he could have passed for a pirate or even Blackbeard himself. He limped along, smiling malevolently, to where the three were saying their farewells, raised his camera and took a picture of Glynis and Clyde kissing goodbye. "Zick! Zick! Zick!"

"What?" Glynis said sharply, jerking around at the sound. "You?"

"Yes." Mislov replied. "Me." He laughed his bone-chilling laugh. "Aloha," he added and limped on in towards the ticket counter.

"Glynis?" Gloria asked. "Is that . . . him?"

"I'm afraid so, M'Lady."

"That's him all right," Clyde agreed.

"'Aloha?'" Gloria looked from Clyde back to Glynis. "He said 'Aloha.' He must know where we're going. How does he know that?"

"I have no idea, M'Lady."

"Is he following us?"

"It would appear so, but," Glynis glanced at her watch, "there may be something we can do about that. If you'll see about the tickets Lady Gloria, I'll just make a phone call. Good bye Clyde, dear," she said, turning to her husband, "Take care."

Gloria's eyes widened as Glynis and Clyde exchanged a surprisingly passionate kiss. Fifteen minutes later, they widened once again as she and Glynis approached the security gate, and six blue-jacketed security personnel surrounded them, one of them leading a beagle on a leash. In another moment, however, it was clear that the blue jackets were actually closing in on the black-bearded man bristling with camera equipment, smiling a malevolent smile, and rolling along immediately behind them with his peg-legged gate.

"If you'll come with us, Sir," said one of the security men.

"Why?" asked Mislov.

"If you'll just come along, Sir."

"What's that dog doing?" Mislov cried, looking down at the beagle who was sniffing suspiciously at his cast.

"Just a standard security check, Sir."

The beagle half-turned and started to cock its leg.

"Get that mutt away from me!" Mislov shouted, trying to kick the beagle with his cast.

"Here, Fred, none o' that," cried the man with the leash, tugging the beagle back out of harm's way. Four of the men closed around Mislov and half-lifted him off the ground.

"Now, Sir," said the head man, "we don't want to make a scene, do we. Let's just come along."

"I have a plane! You'll make me miss my plane!" Mislov shouted as the four men hustled him through an unmarked metal door that the head man was holding open. The beagle and the sixth man followed along behind, the beagle straining at the leash. "You idiots don't—" The metal door slammed and Mislov's cries were abruptly cut off.

"They probably suspected plastic explosives," Glynis remarked later to Gloria as the two settled into their first-class seats aboard Virgin.

"I wonder why?" Gloria asked with quiet irony.

"Well, he's a very suspicious looking fellow," Glynis sniffed. "Besides, I've read how plastic explosives can be molded like the plaster in a cast."

"Indeed."

"Yes. And the batteries in a camera can be adapted to serve as a firing mechanism."

"That's useful to know."

"Yes. It was."

———

Also on board that Tuesday afternoon Virgin flight were scholars of shamanism from England, France, Yugoslavia, Russia, and the Ukraine. And traveling with the Russian professor was an actual Yukutia shaman from Northern Siberia. Conference attendees were taking off around the globe like a scattered flock of birds starting up from a field. They rose up from Korea and Okinawa, from Peru and Mexico, from South Africa, Mongolia, Thailand and Tibet. At thirty thousand feet, they wheeled and gathered in the sky and made final presentation notes on papers such as "The Shamanic Power of Oracles in Ladakh," "The Acceptance of Tang-Ki Shamanic Healers in Taiwan," "Vedda Dances and Healing Rites in Sri Lanka," "The Diagnosis of Disease among Hmong Shamans of Laos," and "The Religious Traditions of the Kootenai Indians of Northern Montana." A few of their flights were slightly delayed or rerouted because of the storms across the Pacific. The winds of tropical storm Makini had begun to reach 85 miles per hour with gusts up to 105, and the National Weather Service upgraded it to hurricane status. Moving west-northwest at about sixteen miles an hour, it was expected to pass harmlessly by five hundred miles to the south of the Hawaiian Islands. Of more concern was another storm, Hurricane Orlinda, which was packing winds of 100 miles per hour with gusts up to 120. Far to the east, it was moving west on a direct course for Hawaii. But the paths of hurricanes were notoriously erratic, and the usual pattern for such storms was to break up and drift to the north or south long before reaching the islands.

So as Tuesday reached the international dateline, transformed itself into Wednesday and began to roll on around the Pacific towards China, a scattering of shamans and scholars began to float down into Honolulu. And by the time Wednesday had circled the earth and reached Hawaii, the scattered arrivals had become a descending flood. Between two and three p.m. alone, a dozen shamans and a hundred academics disembarked from taxis and buses beneath the Earl Court Waikiki's porte-cochere. Arriving along with them were Lord Ryder and Lady Hortense.

Because of the crush at the airport and because Lady Hortense found him rather fascinating, the two wound up sharing a cab with John Ogongo, the witch doctor from Kenya who had flown with them in the first class cabin aboard British Airways from London and had turned up again on the next day's flight from San Francisco. Mr. Ogongo, a vigorous looking man of about fifty, wore a grizzled white beard, Savile Row suits, and a wily expression. He was traveling alone, although back in Kenya he possessed nine wives. He had become the richest witch doctor in Central Africa through the prescription of powerful love potions and the reputed ability to curse distant heads of state with painful, debilitating diseases. When traveling abroad, however, he usually dropped the "witch" from his professional title.

"Nine wives, Doctor Ogongo? Nine?" Lady Hortense simpered as the cab rolled along Kalakaua Avenue. She was scrunched between Lord Ryder and Doctor Ogongo, and after the long flight and the sudden heat of Honolulu, the masculine stench from the two men was deliciously rank. Nostrils flaring, her ravenous eyes swept voraciously from one man to the other. "Isn't that rather exhausting?" she asked.

"No. No. Quite invigorating," Doctor Ogongo smiled a sly smile. "But I use medicine to keep up my strength."

"Should think you'd have to keep it up with a stick and string," grumped Lord Ryder, and a moment later, their cab swept underneath the Earl Court's porte-cochere.

"Welcome to the Earl Court, Lady Hortense," said a harassed-looking young man who approached them as they were registering at the front desk.

"Thank you," said Lady Hortense, handing him a dollar bill. "You can take our luggage to the Presidential Suite."

The young man winced slightly, turned and called out, "Front!" A bellboy leaped forward. The young man handed him the dollar and turning back, said, "I'm Gordon Coburn, General Manager of the resort. If there's anything I can personally do to make your stay more pleasant, don't hesitate to call me."

"It would be more pleasant if there weren't so many workmen about." Lady Hortense said, casting an imperious eye around the lobby. "Looks scruffy."

"I apologize for that," Gordon said. "We're laying new carpeting, but by tomorrow—"

"Well that's a good idea," Lady Hortense interrupted, pointing down at a swath of the newly laid carpeting beneath her feet. "This old stuff is disgusting. By the way, Lord Ryder, Marquess of Sudbury will be sharing my suite. He's— Now where—? Doctor Ogongo? Did you see—? Where in blazes did he go?"

And as Lady Hortense gazed around the Earl Court lobby in frustration, Lord Ryder's daughter looked down on the Earl Court from a mile overhead with much the same attitude. Having flown directly from London with no layover, only a change of planes, she and Glynis were now just an hour behind her elusive father. "They must be in one of those buildings down on the beach," she said.

Glynis Mortimer, who was in the aisle seat, had to stretch over to look out the window. "Very pretty," she said and returned to her murder mystery.

"Glynis, you amaze me."

"Indeed, M'Lady?"

"After flinging ourselves halfway around the world, we are about to land in Hawaii to free my father from the clutches of a witch, and you sit there calmly reading a book."

"Well, reading is a worthwhile activity, Lady Gloria. Why else have we been promoting it through your committees for the past nine months?"

"Of course, but—" Gloria sighed. "Looks like you've got a ways to go. Have you figured out whodunit, yet?"

"Not yet."

"Better flip to the end, then. We'll be landing soon."

"Impossible, M'Lady. For a reader that's the equivalent of committing suicide."

————

On Thursday morning, hurricane Makini's sustained winds intensified to 120 miles per hour with gusts of up to 150. It also shifted course and began moving north-northwest. The National Weather Service put out high surf advisories for the south shores of all islands, but held off any more serious warnings as the storm's diagonal course was still expected to take it well southeast of Kauai. Meanwhile, hurricane Orlinda was weakening as it intersected with a large low-pressure system, which created high elevation winds that began to sheer the storm's top off. With the low elevation steering winds blowing it one way and high elevation contrary winds blowing it another, Orlinda started to break up and drift north.

"Hurricane Makini could be another story, though," announced a morning disk jockey as Howie Berg was driving into work. Howie was stuck in a traffic jam on Kalanianaole Highway and listening impatiently to the top-rated drive-time show on the radio. It featured two disk jockeys, one with a smooth, professionally slippery delivery and the other with a blunt, flat-footed style as if he were using words he had only recently learned. "Makini," said the smooth one, "is behaving the way Iniki did a couple of days before it decided to take out Kauai."

"Right," said the blunt one, "and for those of you who need to brush up on your Hawaiian, here's the definition of Makini, which is pronounced Maaah-kini with a little line over the 'a.' First definition from our Hawaiian dictionary, 'A group of spears tied together, used as a battering ram in war.' Second definition, 'Many deaths, death-inflicting, deathly.'"

"Isn't that swell," said Howie aloud.

"So don't take any chances, folks," said the smooth DJ "Be prepared to fill up the bathtub and roll out the duct tape."

"And stay tuned . . . " said his partner.

" . . . for the news you *need* to know," the smooth one finished up as they segued to a golden oldie, Elvis Presley singing "Heartbreak Hotel."

But at the Earl Court Waikiki, the DJs' warnings and Elvis' lament went unheard by Gordon Coburn, since he commuted in an elevator. From his thirty-fifth floor suite, he emerged down at lobby level to check on the installation of the three million dollars worth of Asian and Pacific art that Christine Larren and her son George had collected for the hotel. The vast lobby, now newly carpeted and appointed in shades of puke, was roughly the size and shape of a football field. As he walked across from the elevators, he passed by several clusters of pale academics already deep in animated discussions, noticed a number of odd looking people he assumed were shamans including a man dressed in Levi's with a feather in his hair who was watching him solemnly, and finally came upon Christine Larren, outfitted for the day in a khaki designer pants suit. She was supervising four burly workmen who were positioning a huge stone head on a pedestal just to one side of the registration desk. The head had a fierce, gap-toothed grin and looked like a gigantic, semi-squashed Halloween pumpkin.

"What's that?" he asked.

"A balu," Ms. Larren replied. "It's a Burmese ogre."

"An ogre? Why are you putting an ogre in the lobby?"

"Well, I'm trying the best I can to match your color scheme, Gordon. Besides, this is an exceptional piece. It was part of a wall frieze of a battle scene from the Ramayana."

"But an ogre?"

"Well, don't worry. See, here come your guardian lions." She nodded across the lobby. Outside beneath the porte-cochere, another team of four men was walking alongside a forklift truck on which was borne a huge bronze lion inlaid with tiny bits of colored glass and mirrors. "You men better go help them," she said, releasing the four by the stone head.

"Guardian lions?" Gordon asked.

"You've got a pair of them to protect you from evil spirits," Ms. Larren said proudly. "They're going just outside on either side of the entrance. Those little bits of inlaid glass reflect, you see, and evil spirits can't stand the sight of themselves, so they stay outside."

"Who believes that?"

"The Thais. But you can too, if you like. Now across from our balu, I'm putting a Kwan Yin, Chinese goddess of mercy, and over there, one of your Buddhas, actually it's a Bodhisattva, is going next to Hanuman, the monkey god–"

"Young man! Young man!" Lady Hortense Crawley-Smith blared in a foghorn voice from across the lobby and came sailing towards them beneath a broad sun hat and behind a three-foot rope of pearls. She flashed a brief, evaluating glance at Christine Larren, who flashed a similar one back at her. Two neutral but powerful dreadnoughts passing each other on the high seas.

"Young man!" Lady Hortense said, pulling up to Gordon and looking down her long nose at him. "You introduced yourself to me as the manager of this hotel. Is that correct?"

"Yes, I'm the General–"

"Well, the Marquess is missing."

"Marquess? We . . . we don't have a Marquess," Gordon stuttered. "Unless . . . Christine? Are you–?"

"Exactly! Quite!" Lady Hortense interrupted in her stentorian blare. "You don't! Lord Ryder, Marquess of Sudbury is nowhere to be found! We arrived together. He was supposed to share my suite–"

"Ghastly thought!" snapped Lady Gloria Ryder, who strode up to face Lady Hortense from the other side of Christine Larren. "What have you done with my father, you witch!"

"You? What are you doing here?" Lady Hortense cried. "And you!" she added on an even higher note as Glynis Mortimer appeared next to her employer.

"We're here to rescue my father," said Gloria, flushed with anger. "Where is he?"

"I have no idea. That's my—"

"He said he was staying with you."

"He was supposed to, but he disappeared."

"A likely story. He's not registered under his own name. Why doesn't he ever answer your phone?"

"My— my phone? *You're* the one who kept ringing last night! And hanging up! What an impossible intrusion! I thought it might be him!"

"This woman is a thief!" Gloria said, turning to the general group. "A thief and a witch and she's kidnapped my father."

"Ridiculous! Ludicrous charge!" said Lady Hortense.

"I second it," said Glynis Mortimer.

"You? You're—"

"Mr. Coburn! Mr. Coburn!" cried Janet Sorenson in a voice of furious panic as she joined the circle around Gordon. "Where are our registration packets?"

"Registration packets?" Gordon asked blankly.

"Our registration packets! Our registration packets! Our registration packets for fifteen hundred people! They're queuing for them right now, upstairs in front of the conference rooms! Where are they?"

"I don't know. That's Howie's job."

"Where's Howie?"

"Gordie!"

"Where is the Marquess?"

"Gordie!"

"Where is my father?"

"Gordie!" shrieked a small, little voice. And the entire group turned to see Cynthia, Gordon's darling reservationist lover, her cute little girl's face streaked with tears. She stood there like a lost child in a department store, choking and gulping as Gordon and the five formidable women stared down at her.

"I know why you hung up on me Gordie," she said finally. "I just called to say I love you. And you hung up on me! You said you'd call me back. But you didn't! And I know why! You're sleeping with someone else! A friend of mine saw you and her go into 814 the other night. We're through, Gordie! And I quit!" And bursting into tears, Cynthia turned and ran away.

Gordon and the now silent group of women watched her run, sobbing, out through the lobby entrance past the guardian lions. And then Ms. Christine Larren, Lady Hortense Crawley-Smith, Lady Gloria Ryder, Mrs. Glynis Mortimer, and Professor Janet Sorenson all turned to look at Gordon. "Withering" could only begin to describe their combined glare. The Burmese ogre was by far the friendliest face in the group.

Thursday went downhill from there. Lady Gloria demanded that someone search Lady Hortense's room. Lady Hortense threatened to call the British counsel if anyone did. Janet Sorenson threatened to sue if the registration packets were not produced. Christine Larren pointed out that she was already an hour behind schedule with the lobby art and that everyone was in her way. Brukowski appeared in his capacity as Chief of Security with Nathan, his surfer witness, in tow. Glynis Mortimer took one look at them and at Brukowski's pink and yellow aloha shirt featuring hula girls in coconut bras and proposed that the police be called instead. Lady Gloria and Lady Hortense agreed, at which point Howie dashed in, forty-five minutes late because of the traffic jam on Kalanianaole, and was chewed out by Gordon in front of Janet and the others.

"Where the hell have you been, Berg?"

"Traffic jam. There was an accident—"

"Never mind the excuses, just find—"

"Our registration packets!" Janet interrupted with icy ferocity. "If that's not being too 'unreasonable.'"

Howie said that the registration packets were stored right where they were supposed to be in a closet behind the registration tables, and he and Janet headed off to find them. But before she left, Janet turned and addressed the only comment that any of the women had made directly to Gordon since the weeping Cynthia had run away from him.

"Pig!" she said.

"Quite," seconded Lady Gloria.

"Indeed," affirmed Glynis Mortimer.

"Disgusting," even Lady Hortense agreed.

"So if you don't mind, Gordon, I'll just get on with decorating your sty," said Ms. Larren, finishing him off. All five women strode off in various directions, leaving Gordon standing in the center of the lobby as fixed and rigid as if he were tied to a stake.

"Hey, Mr. Coburn," Brukowski said after a moment. "Isn't that the busboy we kicked out of here?"

Gordon looked around dazedly, but made no response.

"Is that him?" Brukowski asked Nathan, pointing across the lobby.

"Yeah," said Nathan. "He's all dressed up."

Brukowski lumbered over to the front desk and had them call for backup, and in a few minutes Kip Stallybrass was pulled out of the queue of academics waiting for their registration packets and ejected from the Earl Court Waikiki a second time.

"I'll get you!" Kip shouted at Gordon as Brukowski and the security guards walked him across the lobby. "You can't stop me! I'll get you!"

CHAPTER TWELVE

On Friday morning, hurricane Makini's sustained winds reached 125 miles per hour with gusts up to 160 as it moved along parallel to the island chain about 385 miles south of the Big Island of Hawaii. But even though it was gaining in ferocity, the storm was happily once again on a westerly course that would take it harmlessly past the islands. The skies over the Earl Court Waikiki remained a balmy blue, and while it was still muggy, the only effect of Makini was some especially high surf rolling in toward the golden sands. Nathan Kahaanao decided to skip his appointment with Brukowski to look for suspect employees at the Earl Court and headed out instead to catch some waves.

Inside the hotel, however, the balmy airs of Paradise had little effect on the frenzied staff. Earl Pressler and Kenji Suzuki were both due to arrive within hours, and the renovation, while ninety-five percent complete, was still not quite finished. The art installation in particular was way behind schedule. The Alii Conference Room was still occupied by an eighteenth century Thai bronze of the seated Buddha subduing Mara, the evil spirit, as well as three marble Chinese Star Gods representing Happiness, Affluence, and Longevity, and a mural of Balinese water nymphs bathing in celestial streams. The Ilima Room hadn't even been touched. It was chock-a-block with fearsome masks from New Guinea, lewd temple carvings from Nepal, and sculptures of various minor and major deities from throughout Southeast Asia. The delay was due partly to the overly ambitious renovation schedule but also because Christine Larren, her son George, and Timmy, the interior designer from Los Angeles, kept getting into screaming fights.

"You don't know a thing about these, Mother!" George Larren shrieked, standing in front of two huge New Guinea war shields that were painted white, black, and ochre red with faces designed to terrify the enemy. "Not a fucking thing! Just let Timmy and I get on with it!"

"You're not putting those in the loggia!"

"Yes I am!"

"Speaking as the one who *designed* the loggia–" Timmy began.

"I *wouldn't* speak about it, if I were you," Ms. Larren interrupted. "It's ghastly! At any rate, this is meaningless. I've already put Buddha's apostles in the loggia."

"You what?" George cried.

"Your Sepik River stuff can go up on the third floor by the toilets."

"You–! You–!" George burst into tears, turned, and ran from the Ilima Room. Timmy threw George's mother a furious glare and ran after him. On his way out, he passed Howie Berg and Janet Sorenson, who were on their way in.

"See!" Janet said, snapping at Howie and waving at the room with a sweeping gesture. "Get your loot out of here!"

"Christine," Howie asked, grim-faced. "How long?"

"I can't even start on this room until tomorrow," said Ms. Larren.

"We have this room reserved!" Janet exclaimed. "For our conference!"

"I'm sorry. Blame the people who gave me this impossible schedule."

Janet turned to Howie. "You incompetent–"

"Lay off!" shouted Howie suddenly. "I didn't make the damn schedule! I just work for the guy!"

"So? What does that make you . . . 'Honey?'"

Howie's furious scowl darkened till it was almost a match for the New Guinea war shields. "You're not the only one who has to deal with shit in their life," he said.

"You can choose the shit you work for."

"You're asking me to give up my job? For you?"

"No. For yourself."

Howie stared for a moment. "Yeah. Sure," he growled finally. "Look, you've got this room reserved, so go ahead and use it. Use it the way it is. There's nothing in our contract that says how we're supposed to decorate it."

Outside in the sparkling, splashing, blue and white surf, Nathan Kahaanao, flat on his tummy and sleek as a seal, paddled joyfully out toward the big waves. On his way, he passed by Kip Stallybrass who, in order to evade hotel security, was paddling grimly in toward the beach. Nathan was aboard his bright yellow, handcrafted "North Shore Underground" surfboard. Kip was using the lid of a broken Styrofoam cooler he had found in the trash. On this, he had set his notebook and his new dress slacks, shoes, and aloha shirt which he had purchased with his severance check from the Earl Court. They were protected from the spray by a double-sealed, plastic shopping bag. When he was close enough to the beach to stand up, he abandoned the cooler lid and waded in the rest of the way holding the shopping bag over his head. He used the beach shower, changed in the men's room, and a half hour later, sauntered into the Earl Court's main conference room along with fifteen hundred others for the first plenary session of the Seventh Annual Conference on Shamanistic Practice.

"Hell with them," said Gordon later that morning when Howie mentioned the confrontation with Janet Sorenson in the Ilima Room. "If she's unhappy, good. We don't want this bunch of witch doctors coming back. They just better not damage anything in there."

Gordon and Howie were standing out beneath the porte-cochere. The hotel limousine had phoned in. Earl Pressler had been met at his private jet at Honolulu airport and the limousine was just now turning onto Kalakaua Avenue. Estimated time of arrival was three minutes away. Howie and several other members of the hotel's senior staff were on Gordon's left. Carol Nickle was on his right. Due either to the heat of the day or else perhaps the tension of the moment, his Public Relations Director was particularly ripe that morning, and it was obvious to Gordon that no one else wanted to stand next to her. Gordon, however, was keeping her close. Thursday's slide downhill had ended with Carol demanding that he engage in certain peculiar practices in room 1016, and despite his revulsion and his staggering fatigue, Gordon had made a date with her for the following night as well. After Cynthia's catastrophic revelations and her weeping dash through the lobby in front of dozens of guests and employees, Gordon knew it would only be days or even hours before Carol and Melanie heard about her. Operating on the principle of triage, he was concentrating on keeping the news from Carol, and he figured the best way to do that was to keep her close no matter what she smelled like. It was unlikely anyone would gossip to her in front of him. If he could keep her in the dark, at least she wouldn't present her nude photos of him to Earl Pressler and Kenji Suzuki in person. After those two left, well, maybe he could think of something by then. He stood desperate, pale, swaying slightly, beside his reeking lover, before his vomit-painted hotel, with his guest list of witch doctors, and waited for the arrival of his boss.

The hotel limousine was a ridiculously long white stretch used primarily for honeymooners from Japan. The front doors glided by and were followed by nearly five yards of creamy white siding and black tinted glass windows framed with little sparkling lights before the rear doors coasted to a halt in front of them. The Bell Captain swept open the door and Earl Pressler — tall, silver-haired, distinguished — leapt out like a politician on the campaign trail.

"Gordon!" Great to see you! How are you?" he cried, grasping Gordon's hand and pumping it warmly.

"Great, Earl. How was your trip?"

"Great! Great! Great to be here!"

"Great! Let me introduce you to some of the staff."

"Great!"

Gordon took him down the line, beginning with Carol Nickle who presented him with a fortuitously fragrant ginger and pikake lei.

"Aloha," she said, and kissed him on both cheeks.

"Aloha," Earl Pressler replied. He smiled and inhaled the fragrance appreciatively. "Thank you," he said. "Lovely."

Gordon himself held his breath during this delicate moment, but the sweetness of the ginger and pikake apparently rose above the odor of public relations, and Earl Pressler continued graciously on down the line. He shook every hand warmly and told everyone they were doing a great job.

"Well, this is great, just great," he said once he had met everyone. He looked about eagerly. "Take me on the tour Gordon. Let's see how the place looks."

"Love to, Earl, right this way."

"What the hell are those?"

"Guardian lions, Earl. They protect us from Evil Spirits."

"Evil Spirits, Gordon? You worried about Evil Spirits?" Earl Pressler laughed heartily.

"Not really, Earl," Gordon said, laughing heartily too. "They're part of Suzuki-san's new art collection. Some of it's still being installed."

"So!" Earl Pressler paused twenty yards inside the lobby trailing a gaggle of senior hotel staff and an entourage of personal assistants behind him. "This is what forty million dollars can do." He threw his head back, put his hands on his hips, and revolved slowly with a big grin on his face, taking in the new decor. When he had completed the revolution, the grin was gone. He blinked, head still thrown back, and started another turn. A quarter way through, he stopped. "This looks like puke," he said.

Titters and smothered snorts of laughter rippled through the staff grouped behind Gordon.

"Gordon? What the hell is this?"

"It's . . . it's Tamarind Summer," Gordon stammered.

"It's what?"

"Tam– It's Suzuki-san's design. That is, his designer's design."

"He wanted this?"

"Yes."

"Couldn't you counsel him against it? My God! Forty million? Makes me want to stick my head in a bucket."

Howie attempted an ironically sympathetic chuckle. Earl Pressler looked at him with an expression of angry bafflement, and Howie bit it off abruptly.

"What's that ugly thing?" Earl Pressler asked, pointing at the stone head on its pedestal by the registration desk.

"A balu," said Gordon.

"A what?"

"A balu. It's a Burmese– a Burmese– a Burmese sculpture."

"Well, why'd you put it there?

"It's part of Suzuki-san's–"

"So you can make a face at everybody who checks in? They're making faces at us, I'll bet. When does Kenji get here?"

"Less than an hour. His plane was right behind yours."

At this moment, an Oglala Sioux Indian, a shaman in full regalia including eagle feather headdress, buckskin fringed jacket and carrying a tom tom under his arm, walked silently by them. Earl Pressler looked at him. Blinked. Looked at Gordon. Looked again at the Sioux. Looked at the balu. Looked back at Gordon. "Where am I staying?" he asked finally in a terse, executive tone.

"Here?" Gordon asked weakly.

"What *room* am I staying in?"

"Ocean Suite Two."

"Kenji's in the Presidential Suite?"

"No, he's in Ocean Suite One."

"Why didn't you put him in the Presidential Suite?"

"It was booked."

"Couldn't you reserve it for him? Jesus, Gordon, he only owns the fucking hotel. I'll be out front to meet him in an hour." Earl Pressler jerked his head at his assistants, and he and his entourage swept on towards the elevators, leaving Gordon and his staff silent beside the stone balu.

For Kenji Suzuki's arrival, Christine Larren and Timmy the interior designer also joined the welcoming party out front beneath the porte-cochere. However, Timmy and Christine Larren weren't speaking to each other, and when introduced, Earl Pressler didn't have much to say to them either. He shook hands coldly and turned his back. Everyone stood there, silent and grim, until the long, stretch limousine slid past them once again with its black tinted glass and little sparkly lights. The rear doors coasted to their exact position. The Bell Captain swept open the door, and Kenji Suzuki – short, balding, humble – emerged bowing and smiling.

"Welcome, Kenji! Great to see you!" Earl Pressler cried and stepped forward to shake his hand.

"Thank you. Thank you. You are kind of coming, Earl."

"I am? Yes! No! Wouldn't miss it. Delighted! Great! Delighted to see you! Great!"

Carol presented Mr. Suzuki with another ginger and pikake lei, and Gordon started taking him down the line for introductions. The formalities beneath the porte-cochere took longer because Kenji Suzuki was even more punctilious than Earl Pressler, and he exchanged bows with everyone as well as shaking their hand. Several members of Mr. Suzuki's staff also emerged from the limousine, and they also began introducing themselves to the line of staff members, which occasioned more bows, more handshakes, and also the exchange of business cards. This caused Earl Pressler to feel he had been remiss, and he introduced three of the assistants traveling with him. A second round of handshakes and bows began, and soon it became a sort of feeding frenzy of politeness with about twenty men in suits smiling, trading cards, shaking hands, and bowing and bobbing like the pigeons on Gordon's lanai.

At last, it was time once again for The Grand Tour. With the wisdom born of cowardice, Gordon asked Timmy and Christine Larren to walk ahead with Mr. Suzuki in order to point out the finer aspects of their design. He and Earl Pressler followed, and they were followed in turn by the hotel staff and the combined squads of personal assistants from Osaka and Connecticut. Mr. Suzuki proceeded as far as the Guardian Lions at the lobby entrance and paused there for a brief lecture from Christine Larren on reflections and Evil Spirits. Mr. Suzuki bent close to see himself reflected in the little embedded mirrors and then jumped back in pretended shock and fear. Twenty men in suits laughed heartily. The group proceeded a few steps further on, and then Timmy called a halt in order to provide Mr. Suzuki with a few illuminating words on how best to experience the overall concept.

Mr. Suzuki continued to nod and smile throughout this progress. "Ah so," he murmured to Timmy's comments. And, "Yes." And, "I see." And, "Yes, I see," all the while smiling and nodding. Even once he had entered the hideous lobby and was surrounded by the swirling barf browns streaked with tones of regurgitated pear, he continued to nod and smile. It had its effect. A subtle easing traveled through the group of staff and assistants. The smiles and laughter, now tinged with relief, began to ring with a genuine quality. Even Earl Pressler's ramrod stiff posture became more flexible, looser. After all, Gordon thought, Japanese tastes in color *were* different. Suzuki-san had hired Timmy, after all. He probably liked Timmy's work. And maybe it wasn't so bad, really. If you looked at it with an open mind. Mr. Suzuki did pause, a little nonplussed, at the sight of the Burmese ogre ogling at him from beside the registration desk, but Christine Larren stepped in smoothly with the story of what a coup they had scored in securing this piece for a mere sixty thousand dollars, and how if it weren't for the recent troubles in the Myanmar Republic, they couldn't even have gotten it out of the country as it had been part of what was considered a national treasure. Mr. Suzuki nodded and smiled once more, and the group passed on towards Kwan Yin, the Goddess of Mercy.

Yes. Mercy, Gordon thought as they approached her. Mercy. Perhaps this shapely, smooth-skinned, white marble goddess would prevail over the Burmese ogre across from her. And Hanuman, the trickster Monkey God next to her. And the New Guinea warrior demons up in the Ilima Room. And the Tantric devils and the spirit elephants closeted there with them. And the Vishnus and the Sivas and the Garudas and the dragons and the hundreds of other confused and confusing spirits walled up inside this hotel, who were now probably prevented from leaving by the reflecting mirrors on the Guardian Lions out front. Here, before Kwan Yin, all would be well. The renovation would be approved. The smiles would be real. Cynthia and Melanie and even Carol would forgive him. Yes, he thought, perhaps he could get through this whole business scot-free. And then, the drumming started.

"TUM, tum, tum. TUM, tum, tum." And periodically, a shrill chant. "Ai, yi, yi, yi, yi, yi, yi. Ai, yi, yi, yi, yi, yi, yi."

"What's that, Gordon?" Earl Pressler asked. "Little early for the Polynesian show, isn't it?"

"Probably coming from one of the conference rooms," Gordon said.

"What conference is that?"

"Seventh Annual Conference on Shamanistic Practice. We've got fifteen hundred attendees. Filled the hotel up. Even in September."

"TUM, tum, tum. TUM, tum, tum." "Ai, yi, yi, yi, yi, yi, yi. Ai, yi, yi, yi, yi, yi, yi."

"Sounds like the injuns are coming."

"Well, could be," Gordon laughed weakly.

"What's 'Shaman. . . Shamanistic Practice?'"

"They're . . . ah . . . they're kind of like doctors."

"Hum. Doctors," Earl Pressler nodded approvingly. "Doctors are good spenders."

Suddenly, Gordon saw Melanie. Dressed in her bold, tropical print hotel muumuu, she emerged from the elevators at the far end of the lobby, looked around, spotted their group, and began striding towards them. Even at this distance, there was something about that stride. She knew. Gordon knew she knew. Melanie had heard about Cynthia, and now she was coming for him. Coming for another confrontation, another public revelation of another one of his illicit affairs, only this revelation would occur right in front of Earl Pressler, Kenji Suzuki, and Carol Nickle.

"Tum, TUM, tum, tum. TUM, tum, tum." "Ai, yi, yi, yi, yi, yi, yi. Ai, yi, yi, yi, yi, yi, yi."

"How long do they keep that up?" Earl Pressler asked.

"I'm not sure. Tell you what, Earl. I'll just go check on that. You and Suzuki-san keep on with the tour. Suzuki-san?"

"Yes, Gordon?"

"Excuse me. I'll be back soon."

"Yes, Gordon. You mine the store."

Trotting over to a pair of moving escalators, Gordon leapt onto the up side and bounded up it two stairs at a time, rocketing up to the second floor lobby concourse which was a sort of vast balcony or foyer for the conference rooms. Also about the size and shape of a football field, the concourse was open on one side and overlooked the gardens and the beach.

"TUM, tum, tum. TUM, tum, tum." "Ai, yi, yi, yi, yi, yi, yi. Ai, yi, yi, yi, yi, yi, yi."

The drumming and chanting sounded louder, but the area was largely deserted. Gordon trotted across to the Orchid Conference Room directly opposite him, opened one of its double doors and stepped inside. A sparse scattering of academics sprawled about on rows of conference chairs looked over indifferently and then turned their attention back to a pale man at the front who was bent over a podium reading something in a thick accent.

"In Okinawa," the man read, "the power of the Sho King had to be constantly renewed through court ceremonies which involved female shamans singing traditional *omoro* and rubbing their palms while in trance."

Gordon turned and peered back out through the crack between the double doors. He could see a narrow slice of the lobby across to the escalators.

"Among the Nanai," the man droned on behind him, "who are one of the twenty-six Northern peoples of Russia and belong to the Tungus Mandshurian branch of the Tungus linguistic group, it is said that female shamans are more powerful than men because they have plenty of fog or clouds around them when they are flying in the air to their ancestors."

There she was! Peering through the crack in the doors, Gordon saw Melanie rising up on the escalator towards him. She stepped off onto the lobby floor, looked from side to side, hesitated, and then strode directly for the Orchid Room. Gordon turned and ran up the aisle between the rows of chairs and past the man at the podium.

"So clearly, female shamans are just as–" The man paused, frowning, as Gordon dashed past him and through the service entrance behind the podium. He emerged from the semi-darkened conference room into a suddenly white, antiseptic, hospital-like corridor. He paused, leaning against the wall and breathing heavily. Even here in this remote tunnel in the bowels of the building, he could hear the faint sounds of distant drumming and shrill cries.

"TUM, tum, tum. TUM, tum, tum." "Ai, yi, yi, yi, yi, yi, yi. Ai, yi, yi, yi, yi, yi, yi."

He walked about twenty yards down the corridor past some stainless steel gurneys used for transporting food from the kitchens. Stopping at another service entrance, he cautiously opened it a crack and heard another lecture in progress.

"Claude Levi-Strauss provided us with the parable of a great shaman, a compelling performer of healing rituals, but this shaman is famous not because he cures. He cures because he is a great shaman. This kind of wholeness, wherein healing is as natural as breathing, is what many feel has been lost in western medicine. But while we may cry crocodile tears over this loss, who in this room, if they were infected with tetanus, would trade penicillin and a booster shot for the shaman's drum and mask? And yet–"

Gordon quietly closed the door and walked another twenty yards to the next service entrance and opened it a crack.

" . . . actually very appropriate for this topic," a lilting voice with an Anglo-Indian accent was saying.

"CLANG!" The sound of steel gurneys bumping together came echoing down the corridor. Without thinking, Gordon quickly opened the door and slipped inside the conference room, finding himself behind the speaker at the podium and looking out at a small knot of about twenty listeners. They were clustered in the center of the room while off against the walls were jumbled ranks of scowling war shields, awe-struck spirit masks, and stacks of other grinning and leering carvings and statuary. A pot-bellied, twenty-armed Tantric demon smiled at him from the opposite end of the room.

"Welcome."

Gordon realized the speaker, a man with jet-black hair and wearing a long, loose, embroidered vest, had turned and was looking back curiously at him. "Excuse me," Gordon said. He nodded at the man and stepped past him to slide into a seat in the second row.

"Professor Welles," the speaker continued, "who has done extensive work in the Blackwater River region and also with the Biwat people of New Guinea, told me before we began that sacred masks such as the one over there on your left are hung in spirit houses, and their power is considered so great, only the village chiefs are allowed to touch them and only initiated males are allowed to even see them. As the feel-good groupies of the New Age rush to embrace shamanism – or perhaps 'acquire' shamanism is a better description, in the same way they suddenly feel the need to acquire sports util-ity vehicles – they would do well to remember that in many indigenous cultures, shamans are asked to inflict disease as often as they are asked to cure it. Here lies the power to do ill as well as to do good."

Gordon looked cautiously around him and noticed that intimidating woman with the foghorn voice, the English aris-tocrat who had berated him the day before about some miss-ing traveling companion. She was sitting in the front row next to the man who had arrived with her, a silver-bearded African in an expensively tailored English suit.

"This alarm," the speaker continued in his precise, ironically inflected lilt, "has been sounded in a number of recent books and articles aimed at the mass market. What is interesting is that these alarms come not from traditional religious forums where we expect them, but from advocates of the dominant ideology, Science.

"Leading the charge, as one might expect, was Science's most ardent contemporary spokesman and popularizer, the late Carl Sagan. In his final book, *The Demon-Haunted World*, we are treated to the rather astonishing posturing of the dominant, one might say triumphant ideology, which has obliterated or eviscerated a thousand cultures and spiritualities attempting to recuperate for itself the role of set-upon and desperate victim. While Mr. Sagan's book has a few perfunctory, respectful pages about 'traditional religions' – for this read 'big, safe, and irrelevant' – the bulk of the time is spent debunking anything Science deems 'irrational,' ranging from flying saucers to parapsychology. It reminds one of a Roman general patrolling the borders of the empire with a few legions and putting down all the pesky insurrections and guerrilla wars that always seem to be cropping up. Crucifying them, you might say."

The speaker paused to sip at a glass of water, and Gordon took the moment to stand up and walk as unobtrusively as he could to the back of the room.

"For this reader," the speaker continued behind him, "the no doubt unintended message of *The Demon-Haunted World* is that Science, for all its power and undoubted value, cannot be a substitute for religion or spirituality, much as Mr. Sagan might have wished that it could be. Nor, unfortunately, can Science seem to coexist with religion. For a direct and eloquent exposition of this view, I urge you to read Brian

Appleyard's excellent volume *Understanding the Present*. Mr. Appleyard points to a way out of this box of Science versus Religion. Perhaps it can serve. At the 'Present,' however, many people in western societies are grabbing at any straw that comes along. Shamanism is one, and this straw has two ends."

Beneath the twenty-armed embrace of the Tantric demon, Gordon cautiously opened one of the double doors to the lobby, stuck his head out, and looked from side to side.

"TUM, tum, tum. TUM, tum, tum." "Ai, yi, yi, yi, yi, yi, yi. Ai, yi, yi, yi, yi, yi, yi."

Melanie was nowhere in sight. Gordon stepped outside and sprinted fifty yards to the end of the concourse where a walkway led out to the "Starlight Lanai," a huge outdoor terrace that was ordinarily used for Sunday evening tea dances overlooking the beach and gatherings too large to fit inside. He looked down from the walkway, and his jaw dropped.

"TUM **TUM**, TUM TUM. **TUM**, TUM, TUM." "AI, YI, YI, YI, YI, YI, YI. AI, YI, YI, YI, YI, YI, YI."

At least a thousand academics and shamans were gathered in an enormous ring on the terrace around twenty Native American Indians, men and women from various nations, who were performing a traditional shamanic dance. He saw a young woman dancing in a floating shuffle, one foot forward, then back, carrying a fan of eagle feathers and dressed in beautiful white buckskin with foot-long fringe swaying from her cape. The men were prancing, also floating, feet hardly seeming to touch the ground, heads jerking from side to side in animal postures, a bird or a horse, their faces fiercely colored. One man had a six-inch black stripe across his nose and eyes, the rest of his face a deep red ground. Another's face was an orange mask to match an orange shirt. One man was wearing a spiked sunburst of feathers suspended out from his back. Another dancer in simple brown buckskin somehow seemed the most commanding of all despite black-framed glasses and a comfortable, suburban face. They danced and floated, and in the center of the ring, five or six men were gathered around a large tom tom, beating it in unison and crying "Ai, yi, yi" in just the rhythm Gordon remembered from old movies. Periodically, one of the men beat the drum louder, "TUM **TUM** TUM TUM," raising the tension. Suddenly that man looked up, straight up at Gordon. It was the same solemn man with the single white feather in his hair who had been watching him in the downstairs lobby the day before.

"Mr. Coburn? Mr. Coburn?"

Gordon turned and saw a stern woman with steel-rimmed glasses striding up the walkway towards him. Against the kaleidoscopic background of beach, palm trees, bikinis and Indians, she stood out because of her soberly sensible attire. She wore a blue top, brown walking shorts, and sturdy Birkenstocks.

"I'm Glynis Mortimer," she announced. "We met yesterday, but we weren't introduced."

"Yes. Of course," Gordon said, distracted to the point of idiocy. "I hope you're enjoying your stay."

"Not really." Glynis looked at him sharply. "I'm accompanying Lady Gloria Ryder, whose father is missing."

"Oh, yes. Sorry. Is he still?"

"Yes, and I want to inform you that Lady Gloria is at the police station now filling out the necessary forms for a search warrant. We want them to search Lady Hortense's room."

"Lady Hortense?"

"Lady Hortense Crawley-Smith! Whom you also met yesterday. She and Lord Ryder were to occupy the Presidential suite. Really, I must say you seem remarkably unconcerned considering that—"

Gordon suddenly staggered forward, nearly bumping into Glynis. He half turned, and Melanie Kalanikoa clipped him on the chin with a right cross.

"Fucker!" she shouted.

Gordon fell on his ass on the walkway.

"Motherfucker!" Melanie shouted down at him. "You think you can fuck around on me? Just cause you're the boss? Fuck you!"

She turned on her heel and stomped back up the walkway into the lobby. Gordon sat dazedly on the concrete, one arm stiff behind him holding himself up and rubbing his chin with his other hand.

"Are you all right?" Glynis asked from above as, from below, the sounds of drumming and the shrill cries picked up volume and tempo.

"TUM **TUM**, TUM TUM. "AI, YI, YI. AI, YI, YI."

"Yeah. Yeah, I'm OK," Gordon said, shaking his head.

"TUM **TUM**, TUM TUM. TUM **TUM**, TUM TUM."

"But I wish they'd shut up down there. What are they doing, anyway?"

"I believe it's a rain dance," Glynis said.

"A what?" Gordon looked up at her, aghast.

"I saw the morning's list of conference activities posted inside. It said there would be a demonstration of traditional North American rain dances on the lanai at eleven. This conference is quite—"

"They're doing a *rain* dance? A *rain* dance? In my hotel? On Waikiki Beach? A *rain* dance?"

"TUM **TUM**, TUM TUM. "AI, YI, YI. AI, YI, YI."

"I'm afraid so."

Gordon rose to one knee and hauled himself up. "I'm . . . I'm not having a good day," he said.

"Well, perhaps you deserve it."

"That's supposed to make me feel better?"

"No. More informed."

"Oh." Gordon reached his feet and reeled dizzily. Glynis held his arm to steady him.

"TUM **TUM**, TUM TUM. TUM **TUM**, TUM TUM."

"I admire her gumption," Glynis said, nodding back up the walkway after Melanie. "The one yesterday, too. I've worked at companies where the bosses slept around. Usually the women just suffer in silence."

"I don't think Cynthia and Melanie were suffering."

"Of course you don't think so. You're the boss."

"I'm also their– Or I was– They didn't act like they were suffering."

"'Act' is the word, isn't it? So, maybe they were acting. To themselves as well as to you. You're their boss. You can hire and fire. You can double their salary or take away their livelihood on a whim. If you've never been flattered by the sexual attentions of someone in that position of power over you, you've never been horrified by them either. Or terrified. They might have found you revolting. How do you know what they were really feeling? Were they ever anything more than pretty ciphers to you?"

"TUM, **TUM**, **TUM**, **TUM**, TUM, **TUM**, **TUM**, **TUM**, TUM, **TUM**, **TUM**, **TUM**, **TUM**, **TUM**!"

At last, the drumming stopped. Glynis dropped her steadying arm. She and Gordon stared at each other in the silence. And then, there was a round of applause.

But while the drumming had stopped on the lanai, it continued on in his head. It was with him throughout the rest of the day and into the night. It stayed with him through the remainder of Earl Pressler and Mr. Suzuki's tour of the grounds. It was with him all during an interview with the police and afterwards when they made a futile search of the Presidential Suite for traces of Lord Ryder. It got louder throughout a seven-course dinner in the Zebra Room with Kenji Suzuki sitting next to him and Earl Pressler and Carol Nickle seated directly across. It reached a thunderous pitch in the underground nightclub, Cuffs, where first Earl Pressler and then Kenji Suzuki each paid to have one of their assistants "arrested" by the waitresses in black fishnet stockings and held for "ransom" in the chrome jail cell behind the bar. And as midnight approached and he staggered down one of the endless, curving corridors he had carpeted in shades of vomit, staggering towards his assignation with Carol Nickle in room 2323, the drumming in his head seemed to fill the world.

"Come in, Gordon," Carol said as he stood in the doorway with his General Manager's universal pass key in his hand. Gordon stared at her in shock. Carol had borrowed one of the waitresses' uniforms from Cuffs, and she was dressed in a tight, low-cut, shiny-black swimsuit with black fishnet stockings riding over her thighs and fake white cuffs with ebony cuff links ornamenting her wrists. She was standing, standing on the bed, and she was dangling a pair of chrome handcuffs in one hand.

"How do you know what they were really feeling?" Glynis Mortimer's question about Cynthia and Melanie thundered in his head. "Had they felt like he did now?" he wondered, staring at the handcuffs. "If they did, I am really, really sorry."

CHAPTER THIRTEEN

The sirens went off at five a.m. Sometime between three and four in the morning, Hurricane Makini had made a dog-leg right. It was now heading due north at fourteen miles an hour on a direct line for the Hawaiian Islands. Sustained winds were reaching nearly 180 miles an hour with gusts up to 230. Makini was now rated "Category Five," the highest, or "Catastrophic" level of hurricane. Iniki, for all the destruction it had wrought, had only been a Category Four.

The sirens wailed across the entire length of the state. The center of the storm was still more than three hundred miles from any of the islands, and no one could predict where it might make a landfall. Up in her tiny cottage in Manoa Valley, the soaring whoop of the sirens shocked Janet Sorenson from nervous anxiety dreams about the conference into even more anxious wakefulness. Out in Hawaii Kai, the hard, insistent blare dragged Howie Berg from drunken, dreamless slumber into a splitting, hangover headache. Beneath a street light near Kaimana Beach, Kip Stallybrass looked up from practicing his talk, listened to the metallic wailing for a moment, and then grimly returned to reading his paper aloud to the ocean. In the Earl Court Waikiki, a few VIPs like Earl Pressler and Kenji Suzuki received discreet telephone calls warning them fifteen minutes in advance of the general alarm. The rest of the guests awoke to the wailing sirens and a blinking message light on their phones. Gordon Coburn received a call a half hour in advance, but his phone rang uselessly in his empty suite.

"The most important thing now is not to panic," said the smooth disk jockey on the radio.

"Right, keep cool," said the blunt one.

"Hear that, everybody?" said Janet, sitting in a traffic jam near Manoa Shopping Center. It was only fifteen minutes since the sirens had jerked her out of bed, but hundreds of her neighbors were already driving to Safeway in the morning darkness in order to buy the batteries, flashlights, duct tape, canned goods, bottled water, and other emergency supplies that the DJs had been telling them to stock up on all summer. Janet herself was just trying to get to the Earl Court.

"We've got plenty of time to get ready," said the smooth one in the same cheerful yet cautionary tones he used for bank commercials. "Right now all we've got is high surf, and if you look up, it's actually a beautiful clear sunrise."

"But that," said the blunt one, "is because Makini is sucking up all the bad weather in front of it, and it's still three hundred miles away. The weather service says we can expect clouding and then heavy showers starting early to mid afternoon."

"Winds up to thirty-nine miles an hour will extend 160 miles from Makini's center."

"And where that center will hit is anybody's guess."

"Right now, Makini is playing eeny, meeny, miney—"

"Moe!" said Janet. And fed up with being patronized, she punched at her radio to flip over to NPR. Howie, who was once again on Kalanianiole Highway heading in from Hawaii Kai, did the same at the same moment.

And at the Earl Court Waikiki, Earl Pressler, Carol Nickle, and Kenji Suzuki were in private conference around the coffee table in Gordon's office when Gordon himself appeared in the doorway sans coat or tie, his suit slacks rolled up to his knees, and his bare feet covered with sand. All three looked up and stared at him, Earl Pressler baffled and angry, Carol Nickle contemptuous and triumphant, Kenji Suzuki disdainful and aloof.

Earl Pressler was the one who finally spoke. "You're fired, Coburn," he said. "Pack up and get out."

Gordon, dead still in the doorway, looked across the room and saw himself reflected in the tinted slabs of glass that were still glossy black from the darkness outside. He saw his broad, koa wood desk reflected there, his leather executive chair, his trophies, mementos, his crystal dolphin from the sheik, the plaque from the Boy Scouts, the bronze golf ball from his birdie, and then his gaze fell down to the three sitting by the coffee table in real life. He nodded and walked in. "OK," he said flatly, heading around behind his desk.

"Kenji and I are leaving for the airport in ten minutes, so that's how long you've got."

"I've got a little work to do first."

"Forget it. You're out."

"There's a—"

"You're through!"

Gordon looked over for a moment, then started rummaging through one of his desk drawers. "You're going to miss the blessing," he said ironically.

"The blessing's been canceled. There's a hurricane coming, in case you haven't heard. What did you do, spend the night on the beach?"

"As a matter of fact, I did," Gordon said, pulling a ring binder out from the drawer. He looked up at Carol. "I just turned around, walked out on the beach and spent the night there. I was feeling sort of trapped."

"Ha!" Carol Nickle exclaimed.

Earl Pressler snorted. "You're cracked, Coburn. Get some help."

Gordon sat down in his leather executive chair. "I did," he said and began flipping through the pages of the ring binder. "Spending a night on the beach by yourself is a good idea. I recommend it."

Earl Pressler snorted again. "Kenji told me you recommended this puke-awful color scheme that's all over everything."

"Yeah, I guess so." Gordon looked up. "Sorry, Suzuki-san. I thought it was what you wanted."

Mr. Suzuki stared at him coldly. "It makes me want to toss cookies," he said.

"You seemed to like it yesterday."

"He hates it!" Earl Pressler exploded. "He only went along because you said it's what the market wants. Now he's hoping the hurricane takes it all out so he can start over! So do I!"

The phone on the desk began ringing. Gordon ignored it. "Well, I sympathize–" he began.

"Sympathize!"

"–But there are a lot of people who happen to be staying inside this color scheme at the moment, so I can't really hope that a hurricane–"

"This is a forty million dollar fuck up, Coburn! And speaking of fuck ups!" Earl Pressler snatched a photograph from off the coffee table. "Take a look at this! Look at yourself!" Pinching one corner of the picture with his thumb and forefinger as if it might soil his hands, he thrust it out at arm's length at Gordon. "One of the travel agents you flashed a few months ago had a camera with her. She sent this back to Carol."

The phone stopped ringing. In the silence, Gordon looked across the room at the nude photo of himself rampant upon a field of Gulfstream Beige and Caribbean Blue, the "Classical Tempo" color scheme of the old Earl Court. He smiled wryly. "Hum," he said. "Another Kodak moment." He glanced over at Carol. "One of them sent it to you? Is that the story?"

"Yes," said Carol, sneering. "I'm glad. It's been hell keeping this a secret all these months."

"I'll say."

The phone started ringing again.

"Now the truth's out," Carol said.

"Some of it," Gordon agreed.

"If you're talking about that other girl you've been screwing," Earl Pressler said, "Carol told us about her, too. The whole hotel knows after that incident in the lobby the other day. You've opened us up to God knows what kind of sexual harassment suits. If they come down, you're going down with them."

"And I deserve it," said Gordon crisply. "Look Earl, if you and Kenji are flying out of here, you better get going. Traffic out of Waikiki is going to be hell. Carol, I may not work here any longer, but you do, and I believe your post at this moment is down by the concierge desk in the main lobby. You're supposed to be assisting with crowd control. Earl, truth is I think I'm grateful to be fired, and when the hurricane's gone, I'm out of here. But right now, this hotel is supposed to start executing a vertical evacuation for nearly two thousand people."

Gordon held up the ring binder. The cover was titled *Emergency Procedures*.

"Now I've been doing the drills," he continued, "and there are at least two dozen things I'm supposed to see to within the next forty-five minutes. If you've got somebody else you think can handle it, get them in here now. Otherwise, I need to get on with it."

The phone stopped ringing and then started again almost immediately. Earl Pressler glanced at it, looked back at the *Emergency Procedures* binder, took a deep breath, and stood up.

"Do it," he said. "You do it. Kenji? All right with you?"

Mr. Suzuki nodded disdainfully and also stood up.

"Don't fuck up this one, Coburn," Earl Pressler said. "Do something right for a change."

And with that, he and Kenji Suzuki walked out.

"Carol?" Gordon said. "Concierge desk? Main lobby?"

Carol flushed and stood up quickly. "You look like shit," she said.

"Yeah, but I feel great," Gordon replied to her departing back.

And he did. For the next twelve hours, he lived up to his reputation as the youngest, sharpest General Manager in the entire, worldwide, Earl Court chain. Knowledgeable, decisive, firm, yet calm, he got a thousand people, half the guest list, evacuated from the beachfront Earl Court to inland civil defense shelters. Two hundred rental cars were moved from the basement garage to save them from flooding. Extra security staff and lifeguards were put to patrolling the beach to shoo away thrill seekers, and they saved two people from drowning in the ever-wilder surf. Water storage tanks on the roof of the hotel were topped off. Kitchen staff, those who reported to work, prepared great vats of food and served it free, cafeteria style, to anyone who turned up. By noon when it began to cloud over, the remaining guests and employees had started to meld into one grimly cheerful, all-in-the-fox-hole-together group.

"You never have plate lunch?" Benjamin asked Lady Gloria as he spooned gravy over rice for her. "If you gotta have last meal, this is the one."

"Where did you get that Aloha Shirt?" a professor from Berkeley asked Brukowski as they stood in line for seconds.

"I figure anything as ugly as this hotel is sure to keep standing," Howie declared as he stood Kip Stallybrass to a beer at the Beachboy Bar.

"I know it's safer here than in that rickety cottage where I live," Janet Sorenson reassured Glynis Mortimer as they sat down with their plate lunches at a banquet table.

"Doctor Ogongo has nine wives back in Kenya," Lady Hortense confided to Carol Nickle as they rode the elevator together down from her suite.

"Yeah, but your boss will probably kick me out again," Kip said glumly and set his half empty beer down on the bar next to the final draft of his paper.

"God, what if father's lost his wits and is wandering around outside somewhere?" Lady Gloria said as she joined Glynis, Janet, and several other women at the banquet table. Unable to eat her plate lunch, she stared out at the darkening sky.

"At this point, I think it's illegal to deny you shelter," Howie told Kip.

"Nine wives!" Lady Hortense emphasized as Carol escorted her through the cafeteria line. "He is renowned in

Africa for extremely powerful love charms." She lowered her voice a notch. "Other kinds of charms as well. He's given me one of each. With instructions."

"Professor Sorenson! Professor Sorenson!" Kip saw Janet walking by with several other women who were clearing their plates and stood up from the bar. "There's no reason to cancel the sessions!" he said, jogging up to her. "The hurricane's not here yet!"

"I'm sorry, Doctor Stallybrass, but we have to get ready for it," Janet said. We can't endanger—"

"But I won't be able to give my paper!" Kip wailed.

By three in the afternoon, the wind started to pick up even though the center of the storm was still two hundred miles away. Makini's course hadn't wavered. It was still on a direct line for the island of Oahu and Waikiki Beach. This was the same pattern that hurricane Iniki had followed, but at the last moment, that storm had veered off to clobber Kauai. Hurricane Makini showed no signs of changing course, but it had slowed and was now moving towards the guests of the Earl Court at only ten miles an hour. Several hundred were still in the hotel, and by now the civil defense shelters were full. The barometric pressure had plummeted, and people lay about in their rooms with the air-conditioning on, mopish and lethargic, staring out at the dirty sky and the frothing, mountainous surf.

"It's going to get a lot worse," Gordon said, his voice booming out over the speakers in the main conference room to the assembled employees. "Hurricanes create what they call a storm surge. It's a huge dome of water maybe sixty to seventy miles wide, and we're going to have twenty, maybe thirty or forty foot waves crashing in here. They'll probably carry clear across Waikiki and over the Ala Wai Canal. So any of you who aren't absolutely necessary, it's high time you headed home to your families."

Gordon paused, and several dozen people got up and began to file out. "Thank you for coming in today," Gordon said. "And good luck." He waited a few more moments. "For all of you who are staying on to help . . . again, my heartfelt thanks. We are going to begin a vertical evacuation of this hotel in just a few minutes. No one, not a single guest can be allowed to remain in their room during this storm. Winds as strong as the ones we've got coming can rip the glass right out of the windows and suck people out behind them. They can even rip out non load-bearing walls. It isn't safe for anyone to be down in the lobby areas, either. Remember those thirty-foot waves. The safest place to be is right here, in these conference rooms, and we have to make absolutely sure that nobody's left out. Housekeeping has lists of all the occupied rooms. We're going to knock on every door, and then we're going inside every room to make sure that everyone gets the message. People are allowed to bring one bag. We encourage them to bring at least one change of clothes and any valuables. We also would like them to bring along a couple of pillows and a blanket as they are going to have to bed down in here for the night."

While Gordon was speaking, the winds outside began gusting up to thirty miles an hour, and as the employees emerged clutching the room lists, they could see the tops of the coconut palms bending and tossing, anguished silhouettes against the cloud wrack. Gordon took up a semi-protected position on the second floor concourse between the elevators and the top of the escalators. From this point, he was able to guide both the guests coming down from the rooms above as well as the ones coming up from the ground floor. Since the concourse was open on one side, he was also able to monitor the weather. The white beach pigeons, he noticed, seconded his choice of location. A row of them were huddled on the floor in the lee of the thick concrete balustrade, sheltering from the wind and rain that were lashing the gardens below.

The vertical evacuation took three and a half hours, and Gordon never left his post the entire time. He kept in touch with civil defense and key personnel throughout the hotel by using his cell phone. People spilled out towards him in waves whenever the elevator doors opened, and when he judged that the main conference room had reached capacity, he began directing the later arrivals to the smaller rooms on either side, the Alii, Hibiscus, and finally, the Ilima. By that time, it was after six in the evening and utterly black outside. The hotel lights had come on at five and had already, ominously, flickered twice. The wind had quartered and was now whistling in from the open end of the lobby carrying almost horizontal bands of rain from where the walkway led to the Starlight Lanai outside. It howled with Venturi-like acceleration down the big tunnel created by the concourse. Gordon, soaked to the skin, was simultaneously trying to communicate on his cell with civil defense and to cope with an irate guest who was plucking at his sleeve as the last wave of guests from the elevators flowed past them.

"I've got a count of eight hundred and thirty . . . thirty-three guests and a hundred and—"

"Hey, I'm gettin' wet out here!" the man shouted.

"—thirteen employees," Gordon shouted into the phone. "No, thirteen! A hundred and thirteen! That's so far! There may be more!"

"You gotta get me a mattress! I can't sleep on the floor. My sacroiliac—"

"We can't–"

"Look, you already broke my arm here!"

"What? What are you talking about? No, sorry, not you–"

"Are those the authorities?" The man leaned in and shouted at the receiver in Gordon's hand. "I'm registerin' a complaint with the management of this hotel! My name's Sidney Kramer–"

"Who are you?"

"I'm Sidney Kramer, and–"

"You're the sorehead from New Jersey! Who's suing us! What are you doing here?"

"I'm seein' my lawyer, and you ain't seen–"

"Excuse me!" an older man with a ragged moustache and an English accent stepped off the escalator and trotted up to Gordon. "Are you in charge here?" he shouted over the wind. "I'm looking for my daughter!"

"Eight hundred and thirty-four! No, thirty-five!" Gordon shouted into the phone as he saw another man in a black T-shirt rising up towards them on the escalator.

"You don't give me a mattress, I'll sue your ass off!"

"My daughter! She's staying at this hotel!"

"Is she English?" Gordon shouted back. "Somebody English just went into the Ilima Room! Kramer! Get inside and take cover! You can get hurt out here!"

"What's the Ilima Room? Where?"

"I get hurt, and you're really in for it!"

"It's over there!" Gordon turned and pointed.

And saw it coming. He recognized it. It was the same one that used to wake him with its thunderous cooing out on lanai. The one that glared at him from the planters in the coffee shop. The big one with the heavy flapping wings, bright yellow beak, and red accusatory eye. Flying now with a tail wind. Faster than it had ever flown. Zooming up from a white speck in the darkness. He tried to duck, but the wind gusted, and the bird veered. It had no control either. It was huge. White, yellow, red. He was sorry about Cynthia. And Melanie. Carol, too. But he had done a good job. Finally. At least for a few hours. And then five pounds of pigeon flying at fifty miles an hour drove its beak into his skull.

———

"It is bloody dark in here. I can't— Can you?"

"I can't see a thing."

"Hand's in front of my face, and I can't see it."

"Is it better outside?"

"Doubt it. Lights off throughout the hotel, I'll wager. Besides how do you find the door?"

"What's that noise?"

"Which noise?"

"That thumping. Hear it? Dum, dum, dum, dum."

"Don't know. Something loose in the wind?"

"It's drumming."

"Drumming?"

"Sounds like it's coming from the main conference room next door. Shamanic drumming, probably."

"Shamanic what? What for?"

"Making an appeal."

"To who?"

"Take your pick. Enough examples in here. Never saw such a rogue's gallery. That thing with twenty arms? Half glad the lights went out. By the way, my name's Henry."

"Carl."

"That's my daughter over there. Gloria, this is Carl. Carl . . . ?"

"Brodkins."

"Carl Brodkins. That's our friend Glynis Mortimer next to her. Don't know what the name of the poor bugger on the floor is. How is he, Glynis?"

"Can't tell. He may be dead."

"God."

"If it wasn't so dark."

"Done in by a pigeon. Broke the bird's neck, if it's any consolation."

"Was that the only flashlight? I think the idiots took our only flashlight."

"Hey! Anyone have a torch? Flashlight?"

"No."

"Not me."

"Don't think so."

"Why would the emergency lights go out?"

"Cause it's an emergency."

"I'm gonna sue this hotel for every cent it's got."

"Daddy?"

"Yes?"

"Since we're all probably going to die soon anyway—"

"Don't talk like that. Perfectly safe—"

"Can you tell me what in heavens name you had in mind running off to Hawaii? And where have you been the last two days?"

"Told you on the phone. Left a message on that bloody machine of yours. Didn't you get it? Wanted to pick up some tropicals for the estate. New greenhouse."

"So you ran off with a witch?"

"Didn't believe she was a witch at the time. Don't believe in that nonsense, I told you. But she is potty, I'll grant you that."

"Listen! That drumming is louder."

"Someone else is doing it. Another drum, same rhythm."

"What's the word on the storm?"

"Radio said it's stalled."

"Just waiting out there, deciding what to do."

"Hell of a thing. Hell of a name. 'Makini.' Why couldn't they give it a decent English name?"

"Because we're in Hawaii, Daddy. Don't be a Neanderthal."

"Not a Neanderthal. I'm an Englishman, I prefer to be sent to my Maker by an English storm."

"Who is your Maker, out of curiosity?"

"Well, that's bloody rude. Who're you?"

"Not an Englishman."

"Right."

"Interesting question, though."

"We'll all find out soon enough. This poor devil's leading the way."

"I feel bad. I hope we didn't make it come true."

"What? Ya made a pigeon fly into his head? I don't think so."

"We told him it was time to die."

"It was a joke, Benjamin."

"But look what happened."

"I've told people to go fuck themselves. Lot of 'em did. I don't feel bad."

"But we—"

"Hell, if I hadn't been out there tryin' to get a mattress from the guy, the dumb bird might of missed him. But I ain't gonna beat myself up over it."

"Three of us wrote 'time to die' in the sand, and look what happened."

"We weren't the only ones."

"I put a note in his Tylenol."

"Who's that? Concepcion?"

"Yes."

"What did you do?"

"I told him he should feel bad and he was going to die. I was angry because he let Carla go."

"That was months ago."

"That's when I did it."

"I wrote in his calendar months ago."

"Howie? Is that you?"

"Yes."

"What did you do?"

"I wrote 'You will die this month' across September in his desk calendar. I did it sometime back in the spring."

"Why?"

"I was pissed off cause of how he was screwing up our negotiations. For your conference."

"So these death threats he was getting? You made them?"

"Only one."

"I made two."

"What did you do?"

"Sent him letters."

"I steamed open his mail and put a note in with his VISA statement."

"Wow, bet that got him going. Death with interest."

"You people must have really hated him."

"I didn't hate him."

"He wasn't so bad."

"I made his papaya boats."

"We've had lots worse."

"Why'd you do it, then?"

"It was just kind of fun. He was such a big deal."

"Scary."

"And silly."

"I was just pissed off."

"And Brukowski keep coming around asking about that fortune cookie. That's what give me the idea."

"Right."

"Right. And then he asking about the Tylenol bottle. Concepcion, you must've been scared."

"I was. I thought I gonna lose my job. This first time I tell anybody."

"Who did do the fortune cookie?"

"Not me."

"Not me."

"Nobody did the fortune cookie?"

"Maybe they next door, beating the drum."

"Brukowski. Isn't he one of the ones who went off to find a doctor?"

"With our only flashlight. Yeah."

"Well, if he doesn't find one soon, I think your predictions will come true."

"If this guy's life depends on that idiot, he's a goner."

"Carol went, too. Carol Nickle, maybe she find one."

"I shouldn't have written that thing. I feel rotten."

"Me too."

"Amazing that you were all doing it. How many of you?"

"Well, we've got five . . . no six in here. I bet there were ten or twelve of us."

"It's like that mail fraud scheme in reverse."

"What's that?"

"It's a way to convince people you can predict the future. You start with a list of a thousand people and mail them all a letter predicting the outcome of some event like a boxing match or a soccer game. Only to half the people, you predict one side's going to win, and to the other half, you predict the other side's going to win. Then afterwards, you take the list of five hundred that got the right prediction, divide them in half and predict some other event, fifty percent one way, fifty percent the other. After seven times, you're left with seven people who are convinced you can predict the future. For them, you've been right seven times in a row."

"Then you hit them up, I bet."

"I think that's usually what happens, yes. You ask the seven that are left for money to bet on your next prediction."

"Statistical scam artist."

"That'd work, I bet. If ya didn't know about the others, you'd never think seven in a row was just luck."

"Be a remarkable coincidence."

"Yes, but you could say all coincidence is just a result of limited historical knowledge. If you don't know anything about what's happened before, nothing seems remarkable. It's all just a series of random accidents. If you know all the history, there's nothing remarkable either. It all seems quite logical."

"You talk like you know everything."

"Glynis is an omniscient narrator."

"Hardly, M'Lady. There is no Omniscient Narrator in life, I'm afraid. The listeners have to tell the story."

"God is dead?"

"Maybe he's an actuary."

"Maybe he's just on vacation."

"Shame! Shame on all of you! A man is dying. Or dead. You mocked him in life. And now you're mocking God."

"I'm sorry if we offended you."

"You should pray! Pray for his soul, and pray for your own. Pray for forgiveness."

"Not a bad idea. Who to?"

"Ach! Terrible!"

"No, I mean it. Which one of the– What'd he call it? Rogues gallery in here did you have in mind?"

"There is only one God."

"Think so? Wait till the lights come on."

"And he's going to send you to hell."

"Look, Mr.– What's your name?"

"Charles Brown."

"Charles– Charles Brown? Your name is Charles Brown?"

"Yes."

"You ever used to fly a plane in Borneo?"

"Yes. How do you know that?"

"I'm Kip Stallybrass. You saved my life."

"What?"

"I'm the guy you picked up alongside the wrecked truck and flew down to Kuching."

"This man saved your life?"

"Now that is bloody remarkable."

"You're that one? Kip Stallybrass?"

"It's me. You ever get my letter?"

"Yes. I thought the Lord would bring us together again."

"Amazing coincidence."

"Just limited historical knowledge according to Glynis."

"I had to give up my mission because of you, Mr. Stallybrass."

"And you don't believe in God?"

"I'm sorry."

"They wouldn't allow me to stay in Kalimantan after I violated Malaysian airspace. Even though I did it to save your life."

"I'm sorry. But . . . I don't think it was just me. I think there was some . . . higher power that brought you there."

"Thank God, you do believe."

"In something. Sometimes."

"'Sometimes at night.' Ernest Hemingway said that, right Glynis?"

"Correct, M'Lady."

"I'm not sure you'd approve of what I believe, Mr. Brown."

"You have hope of salvation."

"Lemmie get this straight. You were out in Borneo, and this guy saved your life? What were you doing out there?"

"Researching my paper . . . that I never got to give!"

"And you?"

"MAF."

"MAF?"

"Missionary Air Force."

"I've got to ask this. Mr. Brown, did you take my wallet?"

"Well . . . yes. The cash. Since I had to leave the country . . . and that was because of you . . . I prayed, and . . . I may have sinned, but in a good cause. I used it for the mission."

"Well . . . fine. I just wondered."

"If anything can make you believe in God, Mr. Stallybrass, I should think this would."

"'Fraid not. Just makes me believe in coincidence."

"Try, Mr. Stallybrass. Or you're lost."

"Who are you, Ma'am?"

"Beth Phillips. My husband and I are with you, Mr. Brown. There is one God."

"Praise Him."

"Praise Him."

"Let us hold hands, Mrs. Phillips. Are you there?"

"Yes."

"Let us hold hands and pray for Mr. Stallybrass. Pray for his soul."

"Please don't."

"Yes, we shall."

"Yes, we shall."

"Really, you don't—"

"Dear God, we—"

POW!

"What the hell was that?"

"I saw a flash."

"Something electrical?"

"Lights coming back on?"

"Where'd it come from?"

"Don't know."

"God, did you see those masks?"

"I was looking at that thing with twenty arms. Swear it moved."

"Those masks were awful."

"I saw the dirty ones. The sex acts."

"Benjamin, I scared."

"Everyone scared."

"Bloody good reason to be."

"So much for your soul, Stallybrass."

"Yeah, don't pray for him no more."

"I never asked you to."

"Well, if it's any consolation, Mr. Stallybrass, you wrote a damn fine paper."

"Mr. Brodkins?"

"Yes."

"You read it?"

"Yes, I was going to be your respondent."

"I know, but– Well, thank you."

"Are you planning to publish it?"

"I'd like to, but I haven't any plans."

"Well, write me. If we get out of here alive, I may be able to place it. In fact, since you haven't read it here, you could read it at Stanford next month."

"At Stanford?"

"I'm running an interdisciplinary colloquium. Your paper would fit in beautifully."

"Thank you! Thank you, yes! That would be– I'll– I'll be happy to."

"That's wonderful, Carl. It is a good paper."

"Janet? You've read it?"

"Yes. I thought it was excellent."

"So, Stallybrass, maybe this is your lucky day. Even if you are goin' to hell."

"Mrs. Phillips"

"Yes, Mr. Brown?"

"Mr. Phillips?"

"Yes Sir?"

"Let us pray for all these sinners. In the privacy of our thoughts."

"Yes."

"Yes."

"And Mr. Stallybrass, since you are incapable of prayer, I will only ask of you that you pass on my gift of life."

"Pass on your gift of life?"

"Go and save the life of another. The act may prove your own redemption. Now, let us pray."

"Excuse me. Sorry. Don't want to interrupt. Just keep praying. But . . . Daddy?"

"Yes?"

"Where have you been the last two days? We were worried sick!"

"Right. Well, when I came back from the lav on board the plane out of Heathrow, I spied Hortense shaving little bits of something into my food. Didn't eat it of course. Didn't say anything. She went to the lav, and I examined the contents of her bag. Grotesque. Remembered what you said about the witch business. Don't believe in it myself, of course, but I'm afraid Hortense does. I should have turned back in San Francisco. Final straw was in the taxi coming to this hotel. She started fawning over this African fellow—"

"I was not fawning!"

"Hortense? You here?"

"Yes! Over here! I've heard every word you've said! And I was not fawning!"

"Bloody were too!"

"Bloody was not! Do not believe him, Doctor Ogongo! I was not fawning!"

"Most flattering, though, Lady Hortense."

"Bloody hell! He's here, too!"

"I am very glad that none of my spells did work. I am most uninterested in you, Lord Ryder."

"Mutual, I'm sure. What I did, Gloria, soon as we arrived, I jumped back into the taxi and had the driver take me to another hotel. No intention of sharing a suite with a woman who thinks she's a witch."

"I *am* a witch!"

"See, told you she believes that rubbish."

"Your disbelief is what is rubbish. Can't you feel the power that surrounds us here?"

"Yes. It's called a hurricane."

"I thought you were too bullheaded to be bewitched, Daddy."

"Humph. Levelheaded is the word. Can you cite one instance, Hortense, just one, of your hocus-pocus nonsense ever having any effect whatsoever?"

"I am here to learn. There are others more powerful than I."

"No doubt."

"Lord Ryder? How did you know Lady Gloria and I had followed you? How'd you know we were here?"

"When I learned this blow was coming, I called Gloria. Wanted to let her know I'd be all right. Couldn't get hold of her. You either. Nothing but these bloody answering machines. Eventually called the House of Commons and got hold of Tom. He told me."

"Actually the real reason you're all here is cause of that guy lying on the floor."

"How's that?"

"He's the one who lowered the rates and made it the bargain of the century. Right, Janet?"

"Yes, that's probably true."

"So he is our 'Primum Mobile.'"

"Our what?"

"Prime mover."

"Oh he was the prime mover around this hotel, that's for sure. But if I get out of this, he's not going to be moving me around any more. I'm going to quit."

"You're going to quit?"

"Yeah, I'm going to take your advice, Janet. I can choose who I work for. So I'm going to work for myself."

"Howie, I'm sorry."

"No, you were right. I'm grateful. I've got an idea for a little tour company I want to set up. Eco-tourism, cultural tourism. It's the hot new thing."

"Howie?"

"Yes."

"I really respect you for that."

"Gloria?"

"Yes, Daddy?"

"You're close to that poor sod on the floor?"

"Yes?"

"Can you tell if he's alive? Is he breathing?"

"I can . . . maybe. I think so."

"We should loosen his clothing and find something to keep him warm."

"I can do that. Can someone find a blanket?"

POW! POW!

"Benjamin!"

"What is that?"

"Electrical disturbance."

"It's coming from somewhere over there."

"OW! Stuck your bloody finger in my eye."

"Sorry."

"Where are those people who went for the doctor?"

"With our flashlight."

"Right."

"Here's a blanket."

"Where?"

"Here. Oh, sorry!"

"He needs a doctor, and not one of your potty witches either."

"You ought to be careful, you know, Henry. If a woman at this conference says she's a witch, well . . . she has resources."

"Don't tell me you believe that rubbish?"

"Well, I don't disbelieve it. How about you, Janet?"

"What?"

"Do you believe in them?"

"In what?"

"Witches."

"Oh. In the field, Carl, yes I believe. When I'm back home, writing up my notes, generally not."

"Well, I'd call this the field. Wouldn't you, Kip?"

"Feels like it."

"Think Henry should call it all rubbish?"

"Hell, no."

"Wait, I thought you didn't want us praying for your soul."

"Well, that was just embarrassing."

"You'd sooner believe in witches and benighted devils than in the one true God?"

"No, but– Tell me something, Mr. Brown, what are you doing at this conference?"

"Actually, Mr. Stallybrass, I heard about it from you."

"From me?"

"In your letter. You mentioned that your purpose was to attend this gathering of atheists, heathen and idolaters."

"I don't think I called it that. Actually, I think a majority of us are agnostics."

"Little difference."

"No, it's a rather large difference, at least in my opinion."

"Just another mask of Satan."

"Well putting the mask aside for a second, you mean just because I mentioned this conference in my letter, you came out for it?"

"I'm on my way to a new mission in New Guinea. I paused on my way to spread the word of God."

"Ah, you're here to convert people."

"There is no soul so black that it cannot be saved."

"You are very arrogant, Mr. Brown."

"I agree."

"So are you, Mr. Stallybrass."

"Oh? Who are you?"

"Vimal Vickramagai. I am a colleague of Professor Brodkins. Mr. Brown believes his one true God is better than any other. So do you."

"I'm not sure I believe in any God."

"Listen, there's a hurricane comin'. I'm gonna go with Charley Brown here. Can't hurt."

"Your God is Science."

"I think he's got you, Kip."

"Your church is the scientific method. Your catechism is questioning. Never-ending questions."

"Well, OK. Yes, you're probably right. But I've had my faith shaken lately."

"Field work can do that."

"Mr. Brown, why isn't there a crucifix or a Madonna and Child somewhere in this hotel? A Christ set out between a Buddha and a mask for the entertainment and edification of the vacationer?"

"Because that would be blasphemous."

"To you, Mr. Brown. To the believers in these spirit masks, this arrangement is blasphemous."

"They are sunk in darkness."

"So, I might point out, are you."

"Mockery is a tool of Satan."

"The dictatorship of relativism, that's what the Pope called it."

"You're speaking ex-cathedra now, Mrs. Phillips. But as Mr. Stallybrass pointed out, most of us here are agnostics, and most agnostics would love to free themselves from that dictatorship of relativism. It seems 'unchristian' to blame them for trying. In their own way, they are seeking God."

"No point in arguing with the Devil, Mrs. Phillips."

"I'm not the Devil. I'm sure he could make a much better argument than I can."

"I thought your paper was excellent, though, Professor Vickramagai."

"Thank you, Professor Sorenson."

"Sorry I missed it, Vimal, but I'd like a copy. You coming next month?"

"I'm going to try, Carl. From what you and Professor Sorenson say, I should come to hear Mr. Stallybrass."

"My paper isn't that—"

POW! POW!

"What the hell?"

"Again?"

"Benjamin! I scared!"

"You see 'em? That one with the eyes?"

"I saw Lady Hortense. She looked as if she were doing some kind of dance."

"Hortense? What are you up to?"

"I'm cursing all of you."

"Benjamin!"

"Oh, give it a rest, Hortense."

"These flashes. It's like a strobe. Is someone taking pictures?"

"Is anyone in here with a camera?"

"Hey, is someone taking pictures?"

"Where the hell is that Nickle woman? And Brukowski, the idiot, with our flashlight?"

"And a doctor."

"Yes."

"So what shook your faith in science, Kip?"

"I . . . met someone."

"Someone unscientific?"

"You could say that."

"Did he do magic? Like Hortense, dancing the rumba over there?"

"He had godlike powers."

"That doesn't make him God."

"Now on that point, I agree with you, Mr. Brown. We all have godlike powers."

"Then let's turn the hurricane around."

"I don't feel so godlike."

"Why not? You can fly through the air. Make your thoughts appear instantaneously in someone's head on the other side of the earth."

"I can?"

"The airplane and the telephone."

"Oh, that."

"Yes, they're banal. But a hundred years ago, to do such things would be godlike. It still is in some corners of the world. Mr. Brown's point . . . godlike powers don't make you God."

"But they do deplete your ability to believe."

"Or your credulity, to put it another way."

"In another hundred years, people may be able to visit other planets, do telekinesis and travel through time. That won't make them God either."

"We travel through time now."

"Exactly."

"So what do you believe in, Carl?"

"In essence, probably nothing very different from what Mr. Brown believes."

"I doubt that."

"Well, either faith is available to you or it isn't. Not much you can do about it."

"Faith is like a poster for illiterates, right Glynis? 'Illiterate, can't read? Call this number.'"

"And if you do call, you get a bloody answering machine."

"And the answer goes, 'You have reached the number you have dialed.'"

"Not true. Evidence for faith is all around us. It's largely just a matter of paying attention."

"The banquet is laid, but nobody comes."

"I agree, Mrs. Phillips."

"It's from the Bible."

"Really? I'll have to look it up."

"I don't know, Charley, maybe Brodkins here does believe in what you do."

"He has hope of salvation."

"Well, my view is that all religions — as opposed to faith — all religions are a pastiche. All we have in this postmodern age is pastiche. We have to peel away layer after layer of myth, story, symbol, parallel anecdotes accreting over time from within and without, each religion cross-fertilizing, commenting on the others, usually asking for total allegiance – like Mr. Brown – but with our historical perspective, less and less likely to get it."

"So what do we do about that?"

"Listen to the drums. The shaman's journey is a way to blast down through all those layers of meaning and interpretation. Get through the historical granite, and you get to something singular, real, believable . . . the act of faith. Howie, you say either faith is available to you or it isn't, but the shaman's journey is a way of making it available."

"So that's why you organize this conference, Janet. You're out after converts like Mr. Brown."

"Not exactly. I'm not saying people have to do it or go to hell. I'm just saying it's available."

"I hold a different view."

"Of course you do, Vimal."

"Yes. You were talking about mysteries. There is a saying that there are only three great mysteries, air to the birds, water to the fish, and humanity to itself."

"You're saying we are God?"

"Not exactly. I am saying that what makes us human is language. Talk. It is our joint creation that in turn creates us. Language gives us identity. It is what empowers us to think, and that empowers everything else. We live in, by, and through language. It surrounds us, and we all, together, create it. This hurricane 'Makini.' What does that word mean to you?"

"Sounds like something tiny."

"Wish it were."

"It's a Hawaiian word. Means 'battering ram. Death-dealing battering ram.'"

"Oh, God."

"Benjamin!"

"Howie, don't scare people."

"Sorry, but . . . it does."

"Yes, but now it also means 'something tiny' as Miss Gloria just said."

"Makini-weine."

"I like that meaning better."

"There, see? The language grows. They say a picture is worth a thousand words, but a word is worth a million pictures. A billion. As many as there are people who know the word. Each has their own picture, their own meaning of it, in their heads. It's theirs. It's unique. And yet they share it with everyone else. And every time they use a word, a single word, they contribute to the creation of the soul of us all."

"If you haven't suffered a great loss. Lost someone you loved. Or are about to . . . it may be easier not to believe in something."

"Don't cry, honey."

"I'm sorry Mrs. Phillips. We didn't mean . . . It's just . . . Just academics talking. It's how we comfort ourselves."

"Go ahead and talk. It's all right."

"'A dog might as well speculate on the mind of Newton, let each man believe what he can.' That was Charles Darwin, M'Lady. If any of you want to pray, to whomever or whatever, I think Mr. Coburn here on the floor would be grateful and probably not too particular."

"Indeed."

"Yes."

"Then let's all of us hold hands."

"Yes, let's."

"And pray."

"OK by me."

"And me. Join with us Mr. Brown. You too, Kip, won't hurt. Vimal?"

"Happy to."

"Benjamin?"

"Here."

"Janet?"

"Howie?"

"Daddy?"

"Glynis?"

"Yes."

"All together, then–"

POW! POW! POW! POW! POW!

"Eh! Ha! HA! HA! HA!"

"God Damn!"

"What?"

"I know that laugh!"

"Who?"

"It's that photographer! The one who followed us to Heathrow."

"The one who was spying on Tom and me? At Daddy's?"

"Yes."

"Eh! Ha! HA! HA! HA!"

"You bloody pervert! Stop– Ow! Ah!"

"Don't, Daddy!"

"Can't sneak about–"

"Ow!"

"What're you doing?"

"Sidddown!"

"OW!"

"Daddy! Sit down, and stop surging about! You'll trip over somebody and break a leg!"

POW!

"Eh! Ha! HA! HA! HA!"

"He's over there!"

"Where's there?"

"Hortense? Ogongo? He's close to you! Hortense, he was taking pictures of you doing the rumba."

"What?"

"Grab him! Bust his camera over his head!"

"He's a tabloid photographer, Hortense. He wants to put you on every newsstand in the U.K."

"And the U.S."

"You'll be seen by everyone dancing about in front of these bloody masks."

"No!"

"Yes! You'll be in supermarkets next to the cabbage along with snaps of the living Elvis."

"How vile! Do something, Doctor Ogongo."

"You have the charms, Lady Hortense."

"The charms? Yes! Ha! Um baga um ga! Um baga um—"

"No! That's the love charm!"

"Why are you people all sitting in the dark?"

"Cause the bloody lights are out!"

"Not if you turn them on. Brukowski?"

"Switch is over there, Carol, by the door. I was trying it before I left."

"And you left it switched off? Idiot!"

CHAPTER FOURTEEN

As Carol Nickle flipped on the lights in the Ilima Room, the eye of Hurricane Makini came to a dead stop a hundred miles away. Wild as the night seemed immediately outside the Earl Court, it was nothing compared to the seething chaos that extended in ever more violent, primordial confusion over that hundred-mile distance towards the eye. At the inner vortex, winds were reaching 210 miles per hour, and seas were towering nearly the height of the Earl Court itself. Within the eye, an eerie zone of still air and absolute darkness prevailed, and the ocean tossed itself back and forth in a nervous chop. But for every mile closer the eye traveled, the winds howling through Waikiki would increase another mile or two per hour. And the eye hovered, poised a little south and roughly halfway between the islands of Oahu and Kauai, an utterly negative space deciding what to do next.

Back in the suddenly illuminated Ilima Room, the brief, frozen tableaux resembled the still passing of the hurricane's eye. Then all hell broke loose.

"What's—?"

"What are you—?"

"Give me that camera, you cur!"

Lady Hortense leaped, panther-like, over several hotel staff lying on the floor and fastened herself upon Mislov, who was standing like a black exclamation mark near the door. Janet and Howie looked up like guilty teenagers from a passionate clinch on the carpet. Lord Ryder, running to assist Lady Hortense, tripped over the prone Gordon Coburn and piled headlong into Doctor Ogongo, who also was rushing to her aid. The two men careened into Carol Nickle and fell to wrestling on the floor. Conception discovered herself to be leaning against the belly of the Tantric demon and went into screaming hysterics within its twenty-armed embrace. Brukowski pointed in surprise and anger down at Kip.

"What are you doing here?"

"I've injured my back," announced Sidney Kramer, rising to his feet.

"Release it! Give it to me!" Lady Hortense shrieked at Mislov. "You despicable voyeur!" Mislov looked up into her raging eyes and, astonishingly, let go of his camera. Lady Hortense yanked it away, but because the camera hung from a strap around Mislov's neck, her fierce tug tipped him forward on the unsteady foundation of his cast, and unbalanced, he fell forward with his legs crossed. There was a sickening crack.

"Daddy! Stop fighting!" cried Gloria, hopscotching across various startled guests and staff sprawled about on the floor. Glynis Mortimer took a more circuitous but faster route by the New Guinea war masks and got to Lord Ryder and Doctor Ogongo first. "Now stop it!" she said sharply, and reaching down, she pinched each man by an ear and pulled them apart.

"Ow!" cried Lord Ryder.

"Eh!" shouted Doctor Ogongo.

"I've injured my back," Sidney Kramer said again loudly. "And I want everybody's name here in case—"

"I've broken my leg," interrupted Mislov, one-upping him from the carpet in which his nose was now buried.

"We know that," said an irritated Glynis Mortimer.

"My other leg."

"Now behave!" said Glynis, releasing Lord Ryder and Doctor Ogongo, who stood on either side of her, huffing, snorting and glaring at each other as they adjusted their clothing.

"She broke your leg?" Sidney Kramer asked enviously.

"No more than he deserves," said Lady Hortense. "Come, Doctor Ogongo, we shall not quarter with this rabble." And grasping the good doctor's elbow with one hand and Mislov's camera with the other, she swept out between Carol Nickle and Dick Brukowski onto the lobby concourse. The wind, whistling by at about fifty miles per hour, caused her to shriek and stagger, but Doctor Ogongo held her upright. The two turned, and lacking only broomsticks to complete an image of airborne witchery, disappeared in a blink down the concourse.

"You can sue her for a bundle, I bet," Sidney Kramer said to the prostrate Mislov.

"What's her name?" cried Mislov into the carpet.

"Yeah!" Kramer glared over at a startled and confused Brukowski. "You let her get away."

"Her name is Lady Hortense Crawley-Smith," said Gloria. "She's a witch."

"Well, better not let her fly the coop," said Kramer to Brukowski, "or you're gonna be liable for this one too."

Brukowski, clutching a still-lit flashlight, turned questioningly to Carol Nickle, but Carol had the wind knocked out of her from the collision with Lord Ryder and Doctor Ogongo and could only shrug. Brukowski heard a grunt of pain and looked down at Mislov as that black nemesis rolled over, levered himself up on one elbow, fixed Brukowski with a glittering, midnight glare and snarled, "Get me her name and address!"

The house detective nodded dumbly and disappeared out onto the concourse with the flashlight. "And phone number!" Mislov shouted after him.

"Is the ambulance here?" Glynis asked Carol Nickle and nodded back at the still figure of Gordon Coburn on the floor. "That man is gravely injured."

"And I've got a broken leg! Legs!"

Glynis ignored the snarling photographer at her feet. "Is it here?" she repeated.

"No," Carol coughed and took a deep breath. "The phone lines are down or something. We can't get through."

"Well is there a doctor? I mean a real doctor?"

"Yes, but he's busy, too. He'll be here as soon as he can."

"See here," said Lord Ryder. "The fellow's going to expire there on your wretched carpet if you don't do something."

"And I've got two broken legs!"

"Oh shut up, or I'll kick them!" said Gloria.

"Drive him to the hospital yourself, then," Carol snapped, finally getting her wind back. "We've got to take care of guests first."

"I bloody well will. Where's a car?"

"There aren't any. We moved them all out of the garage because of flooding."

"What's the bloody use of that suggestion, then?"

"Daddy, stop swearing."

"There's the hotel limo," said Howie. "It was still parked down under the porte-cochere last I saw. Don't know who can drive it, though. You've got to have a chauffeur's license."

There was a brief pause, and then Kip spoke up from a cross-legged position on the floor. "I've got one," he said. He unfolded his long legs and rose slowly to his feet. "I drove a taxi when I was in grad school."

"Bully! That's the lad," enthused Lord Ryder. "Get started, then, shall we? Gloria, Glynis, gather up those blankets. We'll improvise a stretcher."

"Stretchers!" snarled Mislov from the floor. "If you're driving him to the hospital, you can drive me."

"You?"

"Me."

"Ballocks! Will not!" thumped Lord Ryder.

Mislov turned his obsidian glare on Carol Nickle. "My leg has been broken by one of your guests, and you refuse me transport to a hospital?"

"That's worth millions!" Sidney Kramer said in awe-struck tones.

"No, we'll take you too," said Carol, buckling quickly. "Or they'll have to if they're using the hotel limousine."

"It's the bad penny, isn't it," said Glynis. "Well, can't be helped. Let's do these stretchers."

And a few minutes later, an odd procession emerged from the Ilima Room onto the second floor lobby concourse. First came Gloria Ryder and Janet Sorenson, staggering a little as the wind hit them and holding on to each other for support. Then came the two stretcher crews with Howie and Lord Ryder in the lead, each man clutching the corner of a blanket. Kip and Charles Brown held the rear two corners of the first blanket, and between his four bearers, Gordon Coburn swayed like a dozing vacationer in a hammock. The second stretcher crew was led by Benjamin from food service and Professor Vimal Vickramagai. Mislov swayed between them, glaring malevolently back at a brawny young pool attendant and Professor Carl Brodkins, who had also volunteered to be a bearer. Carol Nickle and Glynis Mortimer brought up the rear, and Sidney Kramer, feeling slighted and left out, bid them all farewell in an aggrieved tone. "Ya slip and drop 'em, you're toast," he said by way of encouragement.

No one replied as the shocking torrent of wind ripping through the concourse made everyone speechless, and the "tinkling prayer wheels" that the Larrens had brought back from Nepal were clattering away at express train volume along the further wall. Leaning into the wind, the little group made their way to the escalators, and since these had been turned off, awkwardly began to descend the uneven stairs. A row of Lohan, blue and white porcelain figures of Buddha's disciples, watched them stagger down the steps, listening impassively as Mislov cursed his bearers and the swaying blanket that bumped his broken legs – the second one now in a jury-rigged splint – against the metal walls. At the foot of the escalator, the group was met by a white stone sculpture of Kinnari, a celestial being that was half woman and half bird. They moved on past a Thai bronze of Hanuman, the Monkey God, catching and making love to the Queen of the Ocean, Supanna Matcha, and they traversed the vast, deserted space of the ground floor lobby under the gaze of four carved wooden Lokapala, Chinese Guardian Kings, set at the four cardinal points of the compass. Blankets swaying, they paraded past the Burmese stone Balu and the Chinese Kwan Yin, and another, black-painted incarnation of Hanuman who was known in Thailand to also be the Son of the Wind and able to fly.

No one said much, even though the ground floor lobby was somewhat protected from the wind and therefore quieter.

Kip gazed at the childlike face swaying in front of him and thought that Gordon Coburn seemed as peaceful and as cryptically happy as a nearby marble Buddha smiling down at him from a pedestal. Except that Gordon had a trickle of blood running down his forehead. Kip glanced over at Charles Brown lugging the other rear corner of Gordon's blanket. "You wouldn't guess it to look at him," Kip said, "but this guy was a real prick."

Charles Brown, who had turned out to be a balding, red-faced man as short and round as Kip was tall and gangly, looked up sternly. "God will judge him, Mr. Stallybrass, not you."

"Yeah, probably tonight," Kip said. They trudged on a few more steps past the smiling Buddha. "So, since I'm driving this prick to the hospital, does it qualify?"

"Qualify for what?"

"Saving a life. Payback. Will you let me off the hook?"

"It's not me who has you on a hook. Ask God."

"Which . . .? Hey, wait a second! I just thought of something," Kip called out. "Has anybody got the key?"

"The key?" Lord Ryder queried.

"To the limousine."

The procession stopped.

"Of course somebody . . ." Lord Ryder turned to Howie. "You've got the key, haven't you?"

"The key? No, I don't have the key," Howie said. "Carol, have you got it?"

"The key to the limousine?" Carol called from in back. "Yeah."

"Of course not. Why would I have it?"

"Well, what the bloody hell . . .?" Lord Ryder began.

"What am I supposed to do?" asked Kip "Jump it?"

"You idiots!" Mislov shouted from the depths of the second blanket. "Idiots! Idiots! Idiots!"

"That will be enough out of you," said Glynis Mortimer. Bending down, she tugged sharply on Professor Brodkins' corner of Mislov's blanket. The photographer yelped and was quiet.

"Maybe the driver left it in the ignition," Howie said.

"Would he do that?" Kip asked.

"We've come this far, we might as well see."

Just then, the lobby lights flickered and went out, and the group was once again plunged into utter darkness.

"Bloody hell," said Lord Ryder from in front.

"Oh shit," said Carol from behind.

"Futu-ti mama ta." Mislov contributed in Romanian from the depths of his blanket.

There was a period of silence except for the wind howling outside.

"Now what?" Kip asked.

"A miracle?" Gloria proposed.

"It's what we need." Carl Brodkins said.

At that point, the lights came back on again. Everyone cheered.

"Thank God," said Charles Brown.

"Which one?" Kip laughed.

"Don't get started on that again!" Lord Ryder admonished.

"Yes, we better get a move on," said Janet.

"Yeah," Howie agreed. "Unless we want to get stuck in the dark with the 'Prime Mover' again." He started forward hurriedly, and the rest of the procession followed on behind.

"Bet this is how most of this statuary got created, though," Kip said glancing back at the sculpture of Hanuman dancing on air. "Minor miracles make believers of people."

"Or wishing for them does," Vimal Vickramagai added. "And maybe we made our little miracle happen by wishing for it."

"I don't think—"

"Oh do shut up!" Gloria said.

"Sorry." said Kip, chastened.

Dozens of tiny processions glimmered in the reflecting mirrors of the guardian lions as the little group shuffled outside between the two silently roaring beasts. But while those lions were silent, the storm roared like a thousand lions at once out beneath the open porte-cochere. The wind ripped and howled through the exposed space, carrying a horizontal hailstorm of twigs, leaves, and miscellaneous trash along with a driving rain. Even so, the bearers were rewarded with the sight of the huge, white limousine still parked at the curb.

"My God, it's like Moby Dick!" Janet shouted back at Howie over the wind.

"See if it's open!" Howie shouted back to her.

Clutching each other and bent nearly double against the wind, Janet and Gloria struggled to the front of the limousine's whale-like length. Janet tried the passenger door.

"It's open!" Gloria shouted back needlessly.

"There's no key!" cried Janet who was leaning inside to look.

"There's no key," Gloria shouted back.

"Idiots!" shouted Mislov from his blanket. "Ignoramuses! Buffoons!"

"Quiet!" said Glynis sharply, giving his blanket another tug.

"Carol!" Howie turned and shouted back over the stretchers. "Maybe it's at the valet stand. Where they keep the keys locked up."

"But they're locked up!" Carol shouted back. "I haven't got the key to that either!"

"Fools! Dummkopf! Stupido!"

"Well try!" Howie shouted.

Head down, Carol pushed her way through the wind over to the valet stand and tried the handle of a wooden cupboard hung on the wall. It swung open to reveal three sets of keys hanging on little hooks. Carol scooped up all three, and with the wind behind her, whipped back across the porte-cochere to Kip. "Any of these work?" she asked.

"Don't know. I can try. Here." Kip took the keys with one hand and handed her his corner of the blanket. Carol clutched it and glowered down at Gordon who swayed before her, cradled comfortably in his blanket like a sleeping child and smiling up at her with a cryptic smile.

"You son of a bitch!" Carol said.

"What?" Charles Brown looked over at her.

"Sorry."

"What did you say?"

"I wasn't talking to you."

"Who then?"

"No one."

"God hears you."

"He's a son-of-a-bitch!" Carol exploded, shaking her corner of the blanket and glaring down at Gordon. The rain spattered the General Manager's tranquil, sleeping face, and he smiled beatifically back up at her.

"This is it! Hey! It started!" Kip had to shout at them from over the top of the limousine as the ferocious roar of the wind made it impossible for anyone to hear the engine. "Get them in back!"

The soaked bearers, wet clothes flapping, wind howling past their ears, flying bits of grit stinging their faces, carried the smiling Gordon and the cursing Mislov back along the length of the limousine which now had its little sparkly lights all aglow. Lord Ryder yanked open the rear door, and taking Howie's corner of the blanket as well as his own, backed into the velvet plush and leather-lined cabin, laying Gordon out on one of the long, leather sofas that ran along either side.

"Where's that idiot with the flashlight?" Mislov snarled up at Carol Nickle as his bearers brought his swaying blanket into position. Where's that woman with my camera?"

"I'm sure it's fine," said Carol in her soothing, hotel administrator's voice, "just—"

"Why? Why are you sure of that, you bedraggled little trick? You look like a wet albino rat! If he ever does find it, it's the film that's important. Bring it to me!"

"No!" Cried Janet, Glynis, and Gloria all at once. All three were clustered around the rear door as Benjamin and Professor Vickramagai maneuvered to hand the two corners of Mislov's blanket to Lord Ryder inside.

"It's not just that woman, that Lady Whatsis, he photographed," Janet said to Carol. "Howie and I . . . " She turned to Howie, and even in the teeth of the hurricane, they both blushed.

"Eh! Ha! Ha! Ha!" Mislov chuckled from deep in his blanket. "They were pawing each other in front of that handsome statue with all the arms. Hard to tell where your hands left off and that one's began. But don't worry, you're only background."

"Oh!" Gloria gasped. You!" She turned to Glynis. "He took a picture when I was loosening . . . I was bending over to see if that other man was alive."

"Oh, that's what you were doing," Mislov laughed. "Of course."

Gloria looked at Janet and Howie. "And you two were kissing in front of that godawful demon thing at the same time? Glynis! What if Hortense develops that film? She could destroy the ones of her and just send him back those others. Or send them in herself to one of his nasty papers."

"Would she do that?" Janet asked.

"I'm afraid so," said Glynis.

"What a marvelous creature," Mislov chortled.

"All right, hand him to me," Lord Ryder said to Benjamin and Professor Vickramagai.

"'Witches' Orgy in Hawaii!'" Mislov laughed up into Lord Ryder's face as the Marquess grasped his blanket and backed him into the limousine. "'Ryder Rapes Dying Man!' Eh! Ha! HA! HA! HA!"

"Shut your trap," the Marquess told him and dropped him rather heavily on the second leather sofa across from Gordon. Mislov cried out in pain and cursed.

"I'm going to ride along with 'em, Gloria," Lord Ryder said, sticking his head back out the door.

"Daddy! Why?"

"Someone should. Make sure he doesn't roll about. Feel responsible for the chap."

"Well, I'm coming with you then," Gloria said, and climbed in past him.

"Nonsense! What are you doing?"

"I'm not leaving you alone with that evil man."

"I'm not alone. And he's got two broken legs."

"I'm coming with you, and that's that. Glynis!" Gloria turned to call out to her Executive Secretary. "See what you can do about that film."

"Of course, M'Lady." Glynis looked over at Janet and Howie. "I could use some assistance."

"You bet," said Howie.

"Safe journey," Janet said to Gloria and Lord Ryder and slammed the door.

The vast white limousine pulled away from the curb, rounded the circular drive under the porte-cochere and proceeded out the hotel driveway. Just before it reached the first speed bump, the power went out throughout Waikiki and much of Honolulu's urban core. The four passengers inside the limousine cabin were not immediately aware of this, because the car's dark tinted glass made it hard to see out anyway. What they did notice was the springboard like bounce as the luxury vehicle – which had only two axles and four wheels despite its absurd length – rose and dived as its front end passed over the speed bump at twenty miles an hour. Mislov shrieked a Balkan imprecation, and Gordon nearly bounced off his leather sofa onto the floor. Gloria and Lord Ryder caught him and were trying to put him back in place when the rear two wheels of the limousine trampolined over the speed bump.

"Dracului!" Mislov screamed as his broken legs jounced against each other.

"Steady!" cried Gloria, cradling Gordon's head and chest.

"Bloody hell!" enunciated Lord Ryder. He hammered on the black plate glass that divided the passenger cabin from the driver, and being rather familiar with limousines, managed to find the button that powered the glass down so he could shout in Kip's ear.

"Watch how you bloody drive! We've got an injured man back here!"

"Futu-ti mama ta!" Mislov cursed.

"Moby Dick!" Gordon shouted, although no one but Gloria realized it was him.

"Sorry," Kip called back. "The lights went out."

"No they haven't. I can see 'em straight ahead of you."

"The city lights. It's a power outage. The whole city's out."

"Bloody hell and damn! Can you find your way?"

"It's going to make it harder. That woman in the hotel gave me directions, but I don't know the city that well."

In unknowing confirmation of this, Kip slowly nosed the limousine out the hotel drive, and since there were no traffic lights operating and no street signs visible outside his headlight beams, he carefully nudged the huge car illegally across the six lanes of Kalakaua Avenue and proceeded the wrong way down a one-way street toward the Ala Wai canal.

But there was no one around to complain. The streets were deserted and totally dark. In the seething night, the ghostly white limousine with its sparkly little lights crept through the canyons of the city like some odd submersible craft investigating a wreck in the depths of the ocean. If Kip had sunk to the bottom of the Marianas Trench out in the Pacific, those immeasurable deeps might have been like this. Except down there, the waters were still, and here they roiled and seethed and rushed. The limousine tires swished through hubcap-deep puddles. The windshield wipers seemed to push aside an inch of water with every frantic sweep. The rain drummed furiously on the metal roof, and the wind howled and roared around them, carrying random pieces of alternately whimsical and deadly debris. A potted croton thumped into the limousine's side. A plastic ribbon reading "Wet Paint" plastered itself briefly against a window. Kip saw a metal road sign tumble through his headlight beams and sail, Frisbee-like, into the trunk of a coconut palm, nearly decapitating it. The great white car moved slowly but steadily through the watery torrent, an unchallenged leviathan.

Inside the cabin, one of the Jonahs burst into a wild peal of happy laughter. It was Gordon. "Eight fourteen!" he shouted, eyes still closed and smiling his cryptic smile. "Twenty-one twenty-three! A gerbil with a hard-on!" He laughed again like an infant with a fresh bottle and lapsed back into smiling silence.

"God," said Lord Ryder after a moment.

"He was shouting about Moby Dick a minute ago," said Gloria.

"He's bonkers."

"There's an elephant," said Kip from in front.

"What?" The two Ryders, father and daughter, spoke as one.

"Du-te dracului," Mislov snarled in guttural contempt.

"What d'ye say? Lord Ryder repeated.

"There's an elephant out there."

"God, Gloria, he's gone potty, too."

"I tell you, there's an elephant! Come up and look."

Gloria and Lord Ryder leaned forward and back as the limousine braked and came to a halt. Lord Ryder got up and, crouching so he wouldn't bump his head, scrambled to the front of the cabin and stuck his head through the open divider into the driver's compartment. "God! It is a bloody elephant!" he shouted.

"What?" This time Gloria and Mislov spoke as one. Gloria scrambled up to the front.

"An elephant?" Mislov shouted. "How can there be an elephant, you boobies!"

"It's an elephant," Gloria said in amazement.

"Arggggh!" Mislov karate-chopped the leather sofa with the edge of his hand.

"What's it doing?" Gloria asked. "How did an elephant get here?"

"There's a zoo," Kip said. "The Honolulu Zoo is just a quarter mile up the road. It must have escaped. Probably the storm blew something down."

The three stared through the windshield past the sweeping wipers at the watery vision in the headlight beams. A full-grown bull elephant stood there square in the middle of the road. Head down, its trunk switched nervously back and forth in time with the windshield wipers, and its tusks gleamed brilliantly in the halogen headlights. The elephant raised one foot and splashed it down again on the pavement as behind it, three zebras galloped briefly through the headlight beams and disappeared.

"See that?" Kip asked.

"Whole bloody zoo's out."

"Do you think it's going to charge?" Gloria asked.

"Better not!" Lord Ryder said. "Hit the horn. Damn thing's hogging the road."

Kip hit the horn a one, two, three blast. The elephant raised its head and trumpeted back at them. It was at least three times taller than the limousine.

"Shit," said Kip. He flicked on his high beams and hit the horn again.

"What are you doing?" Gloria cried.

The elephant trumpeted back angrily.

"Charge him!" Lord Ryder shouted. "Charge him first!"

"No!" Gloria grabbed Kip's shoulder. "Back up!"

"I can't back up!" Kip flicked his high beams on and off frantically. "I can't see a damn thing behind me." He leaned on the horn.

"Do it!" Lord Ryder shouted. "Charge! Charge!"

The elephant trumpeted and lowered its head.

"Shit!" Kip spun the wheel and goosed the gas. The limousine slewed sideways, bumped violently over a curb, cut across the lawn of a condominium and sped down a watery cross street.

"OW! AH!" Mislov shrieked from in back. "My leg! What are you doing?"

"We're escaping from the elephant!" Gloria shouted as she scrambled past him to try and peer out the tiny window in back.

"Elephant? Elephant?!"

Gordon emitted another happy, gurgling laugh from the opposite sofa.

"Argggh!" Mislov karate-chopped randomly in the air.

"Where are you headed?" Lord Ryder shouted in Kip's ear. "Where are we?"

"I'm not sure. I was supposed to go up to the Ala Wai, go left and then right over a bridge."

"Go right now, then. Wait! No! This is a bridge. You're on it. We're crossing."

"It may not be the right bridge."

"I don't think the elephant's chasing us," Gloria said, scrambling back up between Mislov and Gordon. "And I couldn't see any more zebras."

"Zebras!" Mislov shrieked. "Zebras?"

"Where are we?" Gloria asked, sticking her head into the driver's compartment beside her father.

"We're crossing the bridge."

"Some bridge," said Kip. "I don't know which bridge."

"What road are you supposed to be on?"

"McCully. Actually Beretania."

"Well which is it?"

"We're supposed to go up to Beretania, take a left and stay on it all the way down to the Capitol Building and take a right. Queens Hospital is on Punchbowl Street."

"So what street are we on? Slow down."

"Idiots!" Mislov shouted from in back. "You don't know where you are!"

"Oh, put a sock in it," Gloria said over her shoulder. "Maybe we should stop and ask," she said turning back.

"Ask who?" Kip braked, slowing the limousine to a crawl. "There's nobody out."

"Except the bloody elephants."

"Knock on a door, then!" Gloria said briskly, sounding rather like her Executive Secretary. Go knock on a door and ask!"

The limousine came to a stop. Kip and Lord Ryder were rebelliously silent.

"Ask?" Lord Ryder said finally. "Knock on doors?"

"Well, what else are we going to do? Just drive about in the dark hoping to stumble upon a hospital? I'll ask." Gloria turned and started back for the rear door.

"No you won't." Lord Ryder turned and followed her. "Woman walking around strange streets on a night like this. Knocking on doors. I'll ask."

"I can ask."

"I'll ask!" Lord Ryder thundered. He opened the rear door to the howling night, looked out, and closed it again. "Black as pitch out there. Couldn't find a door to knock on."

"Is there a torch?" Gloria called up to Kip.

"A flashlight?" Kip fumbled in the glove compartment. "No. Yeah! Wait a second, here's one under the seat." He passed it back to Gloria who started to hand it on to her father but then hesitated, biting her lip.

"Now you'll be careful, Daddy?"

"Not to worry. Perfectly fine," Lord Ryder said reaching for the flashlight.

"Well . . . watch out for elephants," said Gloria handing him the flashlight.

"Futu-ti dumnezaii tai! Du-te dracului!" Mislov snarled.

Gordon burst into another happy peal of laughter.

"God. What a potty night," said Lord Ryder. He opened the rear door and disappeared into the storm.

— —

Out in the Pacific, the eye of the hurricane began to move. The fearsome stillness, the absence, the near vacuum that was the eye edged northward, and so the chaos of obliterating seas and death-dealing winds that swirled around the eye also moved north. In Waikiki, the gusts rocking the long, white limousine increased another mile or two per hour. Inside the limousine, Gordon, Kip, Gloria, and Mislov fell silent, just the four of them now, all together and all alone, listening to the howling, whistling, slapping sounds hurtling around them. The dim little cabin, illuminated by a few low-wattage bulbs set in crystal sconces, rocked back and forth in the tumult like a lonely yacht far out at sea. A particularly heavy gust of wind thumped against the side of the limousine, and Gordon spoke. "You can't see the wind, only what's in it," he said. This time he didn't laugh. Eyes closed, he looked pensive, even solemn behind his smile.

Time passed. Five minutes. Ten? An hour? "What a rotten idea," Gloria said aloud as she tried to peer through the dark-tinted glass of one of the windows. "How could I have . . . He's always wandering off. Do you think he's all right?"

"With any good fortune, he's dead," said Mislov.

"You will die in September!" Gordon cried out and laughed a gleeful laugh.

"Oh!" Gloria choked back a sob and stared at Mislov and Gordon in horror.

"Good God," said Kip.

"Eh! Ha! Ha! Ha! Ha! Ha!" Mislov's evil chuckle joined Gordon's happy laughter like night following too soon upon the sunrise. "I like this one," he said.

"You stink!" The General Manager responded happily, his eyes still closed, his face a map of peaceful bliss.

Kip and Gloria burst into laughter.

"He has his moments," Kip said.

"There's something to like, yes," Gloria agreed.

"Fools!" Mislov snarled. "You laugh? This storm will kill us all."

"Think so?" said Kip. "No point taking you to the hospital, then. Maybe we should let you out here."

"Good idea," said Gloria.

"You can't," Mislov sneered. "You're too 'nice.' You're too grotesquely, sickeningly 'good.'"

"Why are you so bad?" Gloria asked. "Why are you so nasty, evil, and awful?"

"Because it pleasures me." Mislov fixed her with his black and baleful gaze. "Because I hate you. Because I am what I am."

"I'm Popeye the Sailor Man." Gordon caroled.

"Arrrrgh!" Mislov snarled as the laughter and giggles from Gordon, Kip and Gloria all together filled the cabin. He sat half upright on the sofa, grabbed a slim crystal vase with a single rose that was set into the wall and hurled it across the cabin at Gordon. The vase bounced harmlessly off the leather sofa, and the rose floated gracefully down around Gordon's feet.

"Arrrrrgh!" Mislov snarled again and flopped back down on his sofa. He lay there rigidly staring at the ceiling.

"OK, cool it," said Kip. "Or I'll come back there and tie you down."

Mislov said nothing. His fingers flexed. Silence fell again except for the howling wind and drumming rain.

At this point, the lights came back on in half the city. There was a blue white flash of light and a loud report rocked the limousine.

"What's that?" Gloria exclaimed.

"Power line. A transformer blew up," Kip said peering ahead through the windshield. "Shit! It's live!"

Gloria stuck her head through the divider to look. Between them and the Ala Wai Canal, an electrical cable was writhing and jumping around on the street like a huge snake spitting sparks from its head.

"Streetlights are back on. We should get out of here," Kip said. "That thing could fry us."

"We can't leave Daddy!" Gloria said and shrieked as the sparking cable leapt for them and danced back.

"It doesn't look like it can reach, but . . . "

"Maybe you should have let them pray for your soul back there in the hotel," Gloria said staring through the windshield.

"Too embarrassing. I didn't deserve it."

"Who does? I think that's the point."

"Do you believe in that? God and angels and all that?" Kip asked, watching the spitting power line nervously.

"I think so. I think I read a letter from an angel once," Gloria said.

"I've been followed around by one. A dark angel."

"So, you believe?"

"I'm agnostic. Like that Vimal said, I'd like to believe. I try sometimes."

"Me too. I think that's the best we can do."

"Other times, "Kip smiled wryly. "I think God is just . . . other people."

"Is that a quote?"

"Hell!" Mislov barked loudly from behind. "The quote is 'Hell is just other people.'"

"You're fired!" The General Manager said sternly from the opposite sofa, and he laughed a deep, resonant belly laugh which swept Kip and Gloria up with it, and suddenly volleys of laughter were ricocheting around the cabin. Shrieks and giggles and sidesplitting guffaws that reduced all three of them to the same happy, helpless, innocent state.

"You bastards!" Mislov screamed. He sat up, hands at chest level, fingers rigid and extended, head jerking from side to side, eyes wide, black, and mad. "You are God! When you laugh, I hear Him laughing. Laughing at me! That's what He does. That's all He does. Laugh! That's all there is. Me and God, laughing! There's nothing else! You don't exist! You're Him! And this raving fool!" Mislov rolled off the leather sofa onto the floor. Useless legs dragging behind him, he crawled towards Gordon who continued to chortle and shout. "Twelve nineteen! Six oh one! Eleven twenty three!"

"OK, I'm coming back there!" Kip shouted and started to climb back through the divider window. His own legs, kicking up and down behind him like a swimmer's, knocked the automatic gearshift stalk on the steering wheel from "Park" into "Drive," and the limousine began rolling forward toward the sparking power line and the swollen waters of the Ala Wai Canal. The passengers inside were too engaged with one another to notice.

"Stop!" Gloria cried. She grabbed Mislov's cast, halting his grotesque, terrible crawl.

"Arrrrrgh!" Mislov turned and sitting bolt upright, thrust the heel of his hand at Gloria, aiming to shatter her nose and drive the splinters of bone into her brain but instead hitting the top of her head a jolting blow. She reeled to the back of the cabin, stunned. Mislov crawled after her.

"Hey! Stop! You—!" Dangling halfway through the divider, Kip reached down and grabbed both of Mislov's broken legs by the ankles.

"Arrrrrgh!" Mislov turned again, jackknifed up and threw the heel of his hand at Kip's face. The blow fell short.

"Eight twenty-four! "Six nineteen!" Gordon laughed.

"Arrrgh!" Mislov reached for Gordon's throat.

But stopped. And sighed. And sank to the floor. Gloria had konked him over the head with the crystal vase.

"Twenty-two, twenty-two!" Gordon chortled. "Nine, one, one!"

"Nine, one, one," Kip said, gasping. "Nine, one, one. That's a good idea."

"What?" Gloria gulped.

"The lines may be down, but this limousine must have a cell phone. I'll call for help." He dropped Mislov's legs and slid back into the driver's compartment.

"Hope you don't get an answering machine," Gloria said.

"Oh shit!" Kip shouted.

"What?" Gloria asked and then shrieked as the limousine, missing the sparking power line by inches, tipped forward and slid over the embankment into the rushing waters of the Ala Wai.

Ordinarily a placid flow, the canal was now a seething rush of water filled with debris washed down from the valley streams. The limousine, being fairly watertight, sank slowly, nose first.

"Get out! Hurry, or we'll drown!" Kip shouted. He started to open the driver's door to escape, then looked over his shoulder at Gloria struggling with the inert bodies of Gordon and Mislov piled up in back against the divider. He hesitated, looked down at the water swirling up around his ankles, and swore, "God damn it!" Turning, he crawled up at a forty-five degree angle, pushing his way back through the divider window into the passenger cabin. "Get out the downstream side!" he shouted, struggling up the incline to the rear passenger door.

"What about them?" Gloria cried, pointing at Gordon and Mislov.

"Hell and damn!" Kip grabbed Gordon by the shoulders and hauled him up towards the rear door. Gloria attempted to do the same with Mislov. Reaching the door, Kip twisted the handle and shoved. The current helped snap the door open and water gushed in at the bottom. "Quick!" he shouted as the cabin started to fill.

The water cascading in splashed the unconscious Mislov in the face, causing him to open his unfocused eyes and stare deliriously up at Gloria as she struggled to haul him to the door.

"I love you, Hortense!" he cried.

"Bloody Hell!" Gloria said.

"I love you!"

"Well crawl up on your own then! Swim for your bloody life!"

Fiercely obeying her command, Mislov hauled himself, hand over hand, up the side of the leather sofa against the rushing tide. Kip, one arm wrapped around Gordon's chest, pushed himself up, halfway out the door and stared hopelessly at the rushing torrent sweeping past him.

"Over here! Look!" he heard Lord Ryder shout. Kip looked over and saw the Marquess on the bank of the canal surrounded by police and ambulance workers. Blue and red lights of patrol cars strobed in the background and a yellow utility truck was raising a crane up to the transformer box. The snaking, sparking power line danced dangerously by, making everyone duck.

"Hand him up! Quick!" shouted a policeman, reaching down for Gordon.

Kip pushed Gordon towards the outstretched hands, but Mislov shouldered his way past him out the door and grabbed the hands instead.

"Bloody hell!" Lord Ryder shouted. "Him again? Where's my daughter?"

"I can get him!" Shouted another policeman. He reached down and grabbed Gordon's shoulder.

"Watch out!" shouted an ambulance worker as the spitting power line arced over their heads.

"Where's my daughter?" Lord Ryder cried.

"She's here!" Kip shouted. Holding onto the doorjamb with one hand, he turned and held his arm out to Gloria, who was struggling desperately up against the cascading water. Holding on to him with one hand, she reached the doorjamb and clung there until other policemen could reach out and pull her and then Kip to the relative safety of the bank.

"Watch it!" A policeman shouted. Everyone ducked as the power line leaped from the wet street and whipped past them.

"Anybody else?" the policeman shouted.

"No!" cried Kip.

"Get the hell out of here!" Lord Ryder bellowed, hugging his daughter and running for the police cars. The ambulance workers lifted Mislov onto an aluminum stretcher, piled Gordon on top of him, and hoisted the two up as one. Crouching to avoid the lashing power line, the entire group ran stumbling back to the police cars and ambulance.

"Here it comes again!" shouted a utility worker from up on the crane. The power cable danced past, sparking across the street, blown by the fierce wind, flipping up then arcing down, straightening out like a spear spitting sparks, diving for the rear end of the limousine that was still sticking up whitely out of the canal. The limousine's gas tank was in the back.

———

The massive explosion that lit up the street created a thunderball of flame and a gigantic, cracking, resonating shock wave of sound that was heard even above the wind for blocks around. In all basic respects, this shock wave was like the rogue wave that rolled up on the beach outside Gordon's office nine months before and like the waves of cascading dominos in the Mechanical Cabaret Theater that tripped a small lever to make a large weight fall. This wave was somewhat different because it traveled through the air at the speed of sound, wild though the air was and filled though the air was with an infinite number of other waves traveling in an infinite number of other directions. Even though the energy from the explosion had to travel against the wind, because it sped along at the speed of sound it still reached the eye of the hurricane a hundred miles away in seconds. Of course the energy was enormously attenuated by then. While it was deafening to Kip, Gloria, Lord Ryder and the others sheltering behind the police cars, by the time it reached the eye of the storm, the wave of sound was barely more than one molecule of air bumping against another. Nonetheless, later reports would show it was just about at that time when hurricane Makini started to shift course once again. Moving in a northeasterly direction now, the storm swirled through the middle of the two hundred mile wide stretch of ocean between the islands of Oahu and Kauai and proceeded steadily on into the remote north Pacific, where it dissipated in the arctic seas. Its passage through the Hawaiian isles caused considerable property damage, but miraculously occasioned no loss of life.

Some indeed did call that comparatively harmless passage a miracle, an act of God. Others said it was merely chance. Gordon, Kip, Gloria, and Mislov didn't say the storm shifted direction because of their own innumerable decisions, large and small, that brought them to Waikiki. Or that in the process of alternately endangering and saving one another's lives, they all together caused a Big Bang. But if chaos theory is right and a butterfly's fluttering wing can cause a hurricane, then surely an exploding limousine can cause one to change course. Perhaps even people can. No one can be sure of the explanation, but as Gordon said sweetly to Mislov as he lay on top of him on the stretcher, unconscious, his own eyes closed, smiling beatifically down into Mislov's maddened, questioning stare, "We have to keep looking."

Epilogue

By the time September came again the following year, dozens of other hurricanes, typhoons, earthquakes, epidemics, eruptions, coups, revolutions, explosions, crashes, plagues, political crises, scandals, and minor wars had also come and gone. For most people, hurricane Makini was a dim memory. But the anniversary of its passing also marked an anniversary of another kind, and Doctor Ogongo and Lady Hortense Crawly-Smith celebrated it with a bottle of Dom Pérignon on the terrace of the Savannah Lounge at the Earl Court Hotel in Nairobi, Kenya. Later, they would retire to Lady Hortense's suite where Doctor Ogongo could once again cheat on his nine wives while simultaneously picking up a substantial fee for continuing Lady Hortense's studies in witchcraft. But first, a toast. Lady Hortense raised her crystal flute of bubbly and looked coyly over its rim into Doctor Ogongo's eyes.

"Zick! Zick! Zick!" Operating with a 400-millimeter telephoto from across the street, Mislov captured three more images of his beloved. He hated her, of course, but he also loved her, and it was excruciating for him to see her with Ogongo. He hitched his way a few yards down the street – for he walked now with a permanent limp – and turned to rattle off another ten or twelve shots of her alone without Ogongo in the frame. Those shots would be useless for tabloid purposes, but that didn't matter. The photographs were for him. They were all for him. He had hundreds, thousands, but he wanted more. More shots of those eyes. Those incredible, raging eyes that had ravished him when he first looked into them back in Hawaii a year ago. They enslaved him. He had tried to escape, but he couldn't. He couldn't stay away. It was as if he were under some kind of spell. Why? Why? He didn't know, but "Zick! Zick! Zick! Zick! Zick!" In an agony of unfulfilled desire, he finished the roll and hurried on down the street before her bodyguards could spot him and administer another beating.

———

In Palo Alto, California, Kip Stallybrass and his girlfriend May Ling also had something to celebrate, Kip's appointment as an instructor in anthropology at the University of Santa Cruz. May Ling, an American Chinese whose grandparents had emigrated from China back in 1949, was still finishing her Ph.D. in computer science at Stanford, but since they both would be in the Bay Area and able to see each other, and since Kip even had a shot at a tenure-track position at Santa Cruz the following semester, they considered his new job an enormous stroke of good fortune. They celebrated the way Kip liked best by going to a Chinese restaurant he had never been to before.

"OK, this is a test," May Ling said as they waited for the garlic eggplant and Kung Pau shrimp. She took a piece of paper out of her purse and unfolded it. "I got this e-mail forwarded to me this morning. It's called 'Religious Truths.' Here's the first one. 'Shit happens.' What's that?"

"The truth?"

"That's Taoism. What's Confucianism?"

"Don't know."

"Confucius say, 'Shit happens.' How about Buddhism?"

"Buddhism?" Kip took a moment. "I don't know, what?"

"'If shit happens, it isn't really shit.' Now you ought to get this next one, 'Zen.'"

"What is the sound of one shit—" Kip began.

"'What is the sound of shit happening,' right. That's Zen. What's Hinduism?"

"Don't know that."

"'This shit happened before.' OK, here are the rest, 'Islam: If shit happens, it is the will of Allah. Protestantism: Let shit happen to someone else. Catholicism: If shit happens, you deserve it. Agnosticism: What *is* this shit?'"

Kip burst out laughing. Smiling, May Ling continued.

"'Atheism: I don't *believe* this shit! Judaism: Why does this shit always happen to *us*?' And, . . . 'Jehovah's Witness?'"

Kip shook his head.

"'Let me in your house, and I'll tell you why shit happens.'"

They were laughing so hard, it even made the hard-faced waitress smile a little as she served them their rice. Kip took the opportunity.

"Excuse me," he said, "but do you have a Zhou Chen working here?"

"Zhou Chen?" The waitress looked suspicious.

"Zhou Chen. He's a friend of mine. I thought he might be working here. I owe him something. I'd like to pay him back."

"No. No Zhou Chen." The waitress turned away abruptly and strode off to another table. Kip and May Ling exchanged a look. Kip shrugged. There were lots more Chinese restaurants. He would keep trying.

———

At the Geneva airport in Switzerland, Lady Gloria Ryder and her executive secretary, Glynis Mortimer, boarded an afternoon flight to London, and Gloria used the air phone to call Sadie and Tom at her flat to let them know she'd be home in time for dinner that evening and church the next morning. The UNESCO conference on literacy had been worth attending, but she had no intention of jeopardizing her guardian status regarding Sadie. Being home for dinner was rarely missed. Neither was attendance at church. Tom and Gloria had both been raised in the Anglican faith, and Gloria had returned to it, claiming she thought it would be good for Sadie. Tom tagged along and usually, despite their mutual doubts about the doctrine and the misogyny and the strife-filled history of the church, they had to privately admit the service often resulted in their thinking about things they ordinarily never thought about and that was probably a good thing. In any case, all three of them turned up in a front pew every Sunday morning to the great delight of the local pastor. Most of his other parishioners were at least seventy years old.

Gloria hung up the air phone and taking out a newspaper, glanced over at Glynis Mortimer, who had settled back in her seat with a book.

"Tom says Daddy has a new enthusiasm."

"What's that?"

"Alternate energy. He was asking Tom about government subsidies for windmills and solar panels. He says he wants to make the entire estate energy self-sufficient."

"Well, more power to him," Glynis said, and allowed herself a small smile.

"Right," Gloria agreed wryly. "He says he doesn't want to be at the mercy of the power companies the way we were in Waikiki last year. If the electricity hadn't come back on when it did, they never would have found us." She extracted a newspaper from the seat pocket in front of her and glanced down at Glynis' book. "What's that you're reading? I haven't seen it before, and you're nearly finished."

"Actually you did see it. I was reading this exactly one year ago when we landed in Hawaii."

"You never finished it?"

"No, I lost my copy in all the kerfuffle. But I spotted this one in a bookshop at the bottom of a stack all covered with dust. What I've got left to read is just enough to take me to London."

"After all this time, is it turning out the way you hoped?"

"Oh, I suppose. Ending a book is tricky."

"Like an affair, I suppose."

"Rather, yes. And with a book, there's a strong implication that the writer has nothing further interesting to say. Novelists used to treat their endings like birthday parties with presents for all the characters, all neatly wrapped up and handed round. Now, it's trendy to leave the reader hanging. They end in *medias res* rather than begin there."

"I prefer the other kind of ending. We get enough in *medias res* in here," said Gloria, opening her newspaper.

They both settled back and began to read.

Gordon Coburn marked the one-year anniversary of hurricane Makini by undertaking his third shamanic journey in ordinary reality. Over the previous year, thanks to the guidance and mentoring of Ben Whitefeather in Arizona, he had successfully made a dozen, other-reality shamanic journeys. Although still a novice shaman, he was now proficient enough to recognize when ordinary reality was taking on transforming, shamanic character. Unlike his other-reality shamanic journeys – which he and Ben always carefully planned beforehand – ordinary or this-reality shamanic experiences seemed to just happen. They surprised you by casually evolving out of daily life, and often it wasn't until several months or years after one of these journeys had taken place that you realized their true nature. Gordon now knew that his first intimation or flash of shamanic awareness as an adult had happened more than a year ago when he was inspecting the chandeliers in the Earl Court conference rooms and was struck on the head while peering into the over-nether world of the space above the ceiling. Of course, his second, truly transforming journey had taken place on the night hurricane Makini had passed between the islands. He had recognized that experience for what it was as soon as he had regained consciousness in the hospital. Now, a year later, he was knowledgeable enough to realize he was taking an ordinary-reality shamanic journey while it was still going on.

He had returned to Hawaii to clean up some lingering legal affairs, and a year and a night after hurricane Makini, he got up early in the morning in his little Waikiki condo rental and made the short drive into Diamond Head crater. When he drove through the mauka tunnel in the side of the crater, he was reminded of Janet Sorenson comparing the beginning of shamanic journeys to Alice in Wonderland falling through a hole in the earth. The tunnel walls, carved and blasted from the lava rock, had a smooth, pebbly surface and undulated with soft lumps and curves like water. A row of bright lights led down the center of the rounded top.

That was the first of three tunnels. As he walked across the cool, dusky floor of the old volcano, the clouds above were a pastel mauve, just edged with brightness from the sun that was beginning to rise out of the Pacific on the other side of the crater walls. The trail up from the crater floor began as a paved sidewalk but rapidly gave way to a rocky, dusty defile that switchbacked up the inside of the crater, past tangled thickets of black kiawe scrub and tuffs of golden pampas grass. Halfway up, there was a lookout point with a view towards Koko Head. The sun was just above the horizon, and the ocean was a bright plate of silver. The trail then dove into the second tunnel, which was narrow, unlit and barely high enough inside for him to stand upright. It was utterly black, and if it weren't for a metal handrail he surely would have tripped and fallen. He couldn't even see a light at the end, because the tunnel curved, blocking any glimpse of the exit. Still, an odd kind of light did accompany him. The bright silver glare off the surface of the ocean outside had left its burning imprint on his retinas. A glowing, white, amoebae-shaped mandala rimmed with red receded before him as he moved towards it through the darkness. It was remarkably like his memories of the mandalas in his other-reality journeys.

Emerging from the second tunnel, the trail immediately became a steep flight of ninety-nine concrete steps cut into a notch in the crater wall. The outward-facing, vertical sides of the stairway were painted a bright yellow, and even though the paint was old and flaking badly, it made his climb seem a bright and heavenly Ascension.

The last tunnel was equipped with an ancient, spiral metal staircase and rose vertically, straight up through the rock. It was as black as nothingness at the bottom, but a faint half-light appeared as he wound up the spiral stairs, revolving through the darkness towards a glimmering that eventually became a shaft of light. A final duck of the head and a crouching crawl underneath a lip of concrete and at last he was able to stand. Stand in bright sunlight and a cool, morning breeze. Stand atop the peak of Diamond Head with the whole world before him.

As with most shamanic journeys, he had come to water. The ocean was a vast plain of silver and blue, a geography with drifting continents of cloud shadow, and the horizon line was well over a hundred miles off. He imagined he could see as far as to where the eye of hurricane Makini had been when it stalled, blowing down telephone poles and sending high surf rolling up into the hotel lobbies. He looked down at the hotels from his eyrie in the clouds. Of all the resorts in Waikiki, the Earl Court had reported the most severe damage. Even though the property was newly renovated, Kenji Suzuki had decided to make what insurance claims he could and have the entire resort repainted and refurbished once again. Gordon hadn't seen the inside, but the new exterior was now complete. He could see it far below him, gleaming white like all the other hotels. They looked like a row of upended sugar cubes except for the pink splash of the old Royal Hawaiian. The tiny buildings marched along the shore flanked by pencil-thin lines of surf while, forty miles off, the misty peaks of the shadowy Waianae mountain range flared in the morning sun.

Hardly anyone else made the climb at that early hour, and the few who did were all quiet in the expansive silence. All except for a blond infant ensconced in an aluminum-framed backpack who occasionally gave forth with a gurgling laugh. A young, fit-looking couple outfitted with hiking boots and canteens had carried the child up on their backs. Gordon found a spot a few yards away from them where he could sit on a crumbling wall and gaze out at the morning world. A nearby historical marker informed him that his view was possible because of an abandoned First World War Fire Control Station that had been built atop the peak back in 1910. From this vantage point, the defending forces could triangulate range and direct mortar fire at enemy ships. But the expected enemies had never arrived, and now Gordon sat where the Fire Control Station had been, smiling at the broad ocean.

The blond baby in the backpack spied something wonderful off in the distance and gurgled and laughed. Gordon laughed too and wondered why. Why were things funny? Was God laughing at us? Or was laughter the dispensation of God? Maybe laughter itself was Godlike. When we laugh, we rise above pain. We rise above indignity. We even rise above incredulity. We "get it." Maybe in the way God "gets it."

A laugh was really the best thing, he concluded. It meant that somebody, somehow, was apprehending some piece of how the world works. There were no pigeons or elephants or other spirit animals to show him the way on this particular journey. The infant was his teacher. "Oh, I get it!" the baby was saying. "That's funny."

ACKNOWLEDGEMENTS

My parents encouraged my writing and even the *idea* of my writing since before I could spell, so first thanks go to them. Deep thanks also for the hospitality extended me in the homes of my sisters, Janice Manning and Sheila Moore. In addition to love, food, and a warm bed, my stays with them and their families provided the knowledge – or at least the temerity – to write the scenes set in New York and London. I also am deeply grateful for the hospitality of the many Iban families who shared their homes with me during my two years in Sarawak. I've been very lucky with my teachers and mentors beginning with the English Professors at Grinnell College and the University of Washington and continuing with my Creative Directors and cubicle mates at Fawcett McDermott Cavanagh, Ogilvy & Mather, and MVNP advertising agencies. Roger Jellinek was the first publishing industry professional to support this novel, and he continued to support it long past the time any industry professional should have given up. Thank you, Roger! Linda Connor directed me to sources of information on anthropological studies of shamans and shamanistic practice, but she must be absolved from any of the errors that may have resulted. The keen and ecumenical minds in the Crossroads writing group provided warmhearted support, for which I am very grateful. This book would still be a manuscript without the recognition provided through the Amazon Breakthrough Novel Award, and it is a much better book than it might have been thanks to the professionalism of the Amazon CreateSpace "Team Fusion" of Emily, Kimberley, Maria, Kristen, Molly and Abdur-Rahim and designers Kristin, Lindi, Michael, Danielle, and Tiffani. So many friends contributed support and encouragement that I can't name them all, but a particular shout-out to those who went online and posted reviews of the first chapter during the ABNA competition. Finally, to Sarah Wayne Callies, who managed to grow from ages twelve to sixteen in the same house where the first draft of this novel was written, and to Valerie Wayne, who managed to stay in love with the writer while that was going on, who was the first to read every chapter as it came out of the printer, and who still wanted to marry the guy when it was finally finished . . . Thank you!

Made in the USA
San Bernardino, CA
27 March 2019